THE CHILDREN OF SPARTA

JOURNAY UNKNOWN

THE RELAUNCH OF VOLUME ONE

TRAVIS G. CAMPBELL

Library of Congress Control Number: 2021902986

ISBN

978-1-7364054-0-6 (Paperback)
978-1-7364054-1-3 (eBook)

1. Fiction, Fantasy, Historical, Adventure,

4 3 2 1

TABLE OF CONTENTS

PART I

THE DIVINE COUNCIL

CHAPTER 1

THE ASSEMBLY

[Parthenon / Mount Olympus, 180 Light-Years after the Great War of Gods]

From white to blue, lightning flashed across the open skies of Mount Olympus, ending its crusade at the marble entrance of the Parthenon. It didn't take long for the roar of thunder to come trailing confidently behind. In that moment, under the din of the storm, a familiar clapping of footsteps electrified the Olympian halls with life.

Suddenly, the footsteps stopped. A being stood in the middle of the council hall. Only a glassy reflection moved like ripples of water in the wind. The being stretched out his hands and a blue aura emitted from his body while patterns of rich gold dispersed from the tips of his outstretched arms. Then, his body disintegrated into a mist.

The aura filled the place with a breathtaking glow of blue lights and a cool sensation. So bright was the aura surrounding the being in the mist that he was almost invisible. The golden patterns that traced his body flowed outward and surged throughout the council hall creating exquisite designs—designs that displayed a story from a past life.

"It's beautiful," said an unknown voice from within the hall.

Suddenly in the mist, two eyes of silver lightning sparkling with rage appeared and searched for the one who spoke. "Show yourself," he commanded as the exquisite, golden designs ascended like shimmering stars in the cold, night sky.

"No, no! Why did you stop? Why?" In came the messenger god and her golden footwear gracefully flapping their wings as she drew nigh to the one in the blue mist.

All of the sudden, the mist slowly dissipated and the figure inside sprouted wings. His eyes grew wider until they were as full as the moon at the start of every new month. Then there stood an onyx-colored owl who had feathers that glistened with a metallic, turquoise sheen just like the male blue peafowl.

"How dare you think you can hide from me?" asked the onyx-colored owl. "I sensed your presence the moment my feet touched the doorway."

The one with the wings on her footwear approached, gliding upward, and the onyx-feathered owl set his eyes downward. "So, I guess you were putting on a show for me," she replied while electric currents surged through the body of the onyx owl.

"No show."

"It's fine, Zeus," she quipped with a gleam in her eyes. "I always appreciate your true form—it's undoubtedly beautiful," she continued again before shaking her head in disdain. "It's a shame you and the other Olympians have to hide it from the other gods."

Those words vexed the onyx bird. "Hermes," Zeus replied, questioning the maiden god, "why are you here?"

"Forgive me, Zeus. I tend to get too excited and comfortable when you're comfortable," Hermes replied, bowing her head to show her respect to the head deity.

"What brings you here at this time? Do you have news of something of importance?"

The wings on Hermes's footwear lifted her while a mischievous smile crossed her face. "You know I do, Zeus," she replied with a playful unwillingness to reveal her secret so easily. "It's a message from your brother."

Zeus centered all his focus toward Hermes. "Brother?" he replied with a sense of uncertainty on how to reply. "Which brother do you speak of … Hermes?" he questioned the fair maiden.

"You know, Zeus," Hermes said, turning around to give him her back. "That 'brother' of brothers." She spun back around suddenly, revealing a ruby red apple in the palm of right her hand. The apple floated away from her hand and floated closer toward the onyx-colored owl, on whose face a troubling expression appeared.

"Impossible," was Zeus's disbelieving response. "Why would he reach out to you? He is exceptionally careful about his comings and goings."

Hermes reached for the tip of her garment's collar and pulled it downward, revealing an image of a star pointing northward on her chest.

The eyes of the onyx owl lost their light and grew fearfully grim, then suddenly his head rotated all the way around without turning his torso. "Hera," Zeus said, aghast, before he flared his massive wings above his head and burst into a shower of blue feathers and shimmering blue lights.

In came a sagacious, silver-white-haired woman, power walking her way toward Zeus in a silky, coral-colored toga with a ten-foot train that flowed with her every movement toward Zeus. Her distinctive, tricolored eyes of Mediterranean blues and greens were fixed on the olive-skinned deity, with all his hoary hair fluffy as the white clouds, standing with his hands held behind him while the blue shimmering lights floated downward. "Take me for a fool," said Hera with a slight hint of indignation. "I felt it. You promised, Zeus. We '*ALL*' made an oath not to change back! It would be wise to follow the very oath you firmly advocated."

A brief smile appeared on the man's olive face, but Hera could not see it as Zeus kept his back turned. Hera waited a minute, but still got no response. She knew he was ignoring her, which was more wood to the fire. Hera also knew that Zeus was always the first to arrive at the council hall; this was typical of him to do when there was an assembly of the Olympians for council. Zeus, still ignoring Hera, allowed his thoughts to consider the agenda for today's council assembly, as well as all the questions that would require answers—answers he failed to have himself. *But Athena will have them*, he thought to himself.

"Yeah," he said aloud as he pushed his lips upward and nodded to himself while admiring the grandeur of the assembly hall. Athena always knew best when her knowledge was needed—after all, she was the god of genuine wisdom and fairness. This was just one of the reasons why Athena not only had the most faithful followers among the Greek empire, but she had an admirable city-state named after her as well.

Zeus smiled from the inside, but outwardly his face remained uneasy. Athena was inevitably Zeus's favorite offspring and deity. She was also the most respected among her fellow gods—even Hera had to acknowledge her respect for Zeus's daughter. Zeus knew this was hard for Hera to do, but it became possible when Athena ferociously chastised her own father for deceiving married women into bed with him and Hera. Zeus laughed to himself; he recalled the moment of this encounter so vividly, as if it had occurred yesterday.

"You continue to ignore your hypocrisy, but I will not," Hera said sternly while moving toward Zeus. Suddenly, her fury shifted when she sensed someone else's presence. "Who else is here?" Her voice was frantic as she tenderly touched him on the back of his left shoulder where his long strands of white locks brush against the back of her hand.

Hera's touch and voice pulled Zeus out of his trance while a nervous thought entered his mind: he was worried that Hera would sense the presence of the messenger god. Zeus looked into Hera's distinctive, tricolored eyes and said, "No one—just us."

Hera, of course, did not believe him; but Zeus turned away from her and settled his gaze on the center of the council hall. His eyes glowed silver and white, and suddenly four marble trumpeters stood in the center of the council hall. He closed his eyes, and then, reopened them with a flash of blue lightning. The eyes of the four sculptures ignited— just like his own—before they sprinted off to the four corners of the council hall and changed into lightning bolts that vanished and reappeared as trumpeters atop the four corners of the Parthenon. With the power of the sun above their heads, they lifted their massive, bronze trumpets—which shone a bright, yellow gold onto their marbled faces— and blew, producing an illustrious sound that was loud enough for every Greek god and demigod to hear. No matter where these Greek gods were on the ground below, or in the skies above, they always heard the trumpets' call from Mount Olympus.

With every new stanza from the trumpet cries, the four sculptures took the images of gods on the Mount, both old and new alike. Five minutes passed on Apollo's sundial before the inhabitants of Olympus began making their way into the council hall, among them were Aphrodite and Hestia, while Earth-dwelling gods such as Poseidon and Ares ascended to Mount Olympus. The power of the trumpets filled Olympus's air and everyone present with renewed excitement. Inside the Parthenon, the euphony of lyres and harps welcomed everyone with melodious sounds to ease the souls of those troubled minds. Dionysus's servants walked back and forth along the hall to serve the gods wine and grapes from his own vineyard.

Everyone was dressed in togas arrayed in vibrant colors and evocative styles, it resembled a garden of rare flowers. Some wore togas of more red than ruby stone, sapphire blue, light silver, or midnight black, while the few kept it simple and elegant by wearing togas white as snow. Some gods wore short and revealing togas, while others wore theirs down to the floor that trailed with each step. Some of the togas' materials were thick in texture and shone with an array of colorful lights, while others were made up of sheer fabric and hugged the exceptional physiques of the Olympians.

Gathering such these on Mount Olympus was a time for the gods to show off their creative sides and display their high taste for fashion. No matter what they created and adorn themselves, it was always eye-catching for all. Hera, along with many other goddesses, looked forward to the council assembly for this exact reason; it was "toga extravaganza!"

The gods delighted in exquisite and elegant things of life.. The Parthenon on Mount Olympus was twelve times larger than its likeness in Athens. The temple towered over all other establishments on the Mount and stretched out into the mists. Before the gods could enter the temple, the sight of the massive, white, stone columns stood before them. Athena came up with the idea of combining the strength of a Doric column with the floral design of the Corinthian column to produce a hybrid column of grandeur, strength, and beauty. Each column was broad as four elephants and soared to the great height, while gold lines running along the edges of the Corinthian-style grooves and floral designs.

Marble mixed with gold dust was of significance to the gods on Mount Olympus, and thus it was everywhere, and adorned everything, from their majestic monuments to the clothing on their divine bodies. On all the four sides of the Parthenon, the gods saw full-body sculptures of themselves modeling in various positions in the pediment. Each god sculpture was forged in gold and silver by the hands of Hephaestus, the god of fire and metalworking.

Past the white, stone columns were four double doors on each side of the Parthenon. There were endless paintings that displayed epic moments and sculptures of the gods in their best poses. The temple's floors and interior columns were as shimmery as the blue Mediterranean Sea. With every step a god took inside the Parthenon, their lucid reflection followed them from every angle. Of course, many of the gods of Olympus started exhibiting symptoms of narcissism—but not one of them would ever admit to it.

To get to the council hall, every god passed through the "Hall of Olympians." This hall contained the most magnificent sculptures in the entire Parthenon. These sculptures had the distinguishable characteristics of each god. Zeus had his lightning bolt in his right hand, and the golden owl on his left shoulder. Athena was adorned in her armor, and she also had her owl resting on her left shoulder. There was a sculpture of Hermes flying in her winged footwear, racing to deliver a dire message. Apollo had his lyre in his right hand, and the power of the sun in the other. However, what made this hall the most spectacular was the array of colorful lights that shone out of the eyes when they entered the Parthenon.

The gods and demigods were flying and walking into the Parthenon by the dozens. The council hall where Zeus and Hera resided was teeming with gods born and raised in Olympus. They moved with no sense of urgency; instead of conversing here and there with one another. The council hall was massive and oval-shaped, with a theatre-style high-rise seating arrangement. The only seats that exclusively stuck out were those that belonged to the gods from the "Hall of Olympians." While the other gods sat on the main floor, these Olympians—the founders of Olympus—sat on colossal thrones above. Special assemblies, such as this one, were the only times when all the founding Olympians sat on thrones made of white, marble pearl Ionic columns. The top of each column had cushion-like clouds to soften their seats.[1]

---

[1] This assembly hall had a theatre-like architectural design made by Dionysus, which inspired Athena to guide the sons and daughters of Athens to erect the same theatre of Dionysus in Athens.

The trumpeters reappeared inside the center of the council hall and blew on their trumpets again, signaling it was time to officially commence. The crowd rushed to their respective seats to settle in, with a few still discussing pressing topics of concern. Zeus could feel and hear the anxiety from the voices among the mass, as well as their desire for something hopeful to come. The moment was now to put their minds to rest, but Zeus knew that everything that needed to be discussed would not satisfy all these troubled souls. Zeus's body tensed up enough for Hera to become aware of his laden thoughts. She leaned closer to her husband and caressed his face with her left hand while her other hand remained interlocked with his. The comfort of Hera's touch was enough to ease the troubled deity before the commencement of the assembly.

The topic of discussion was a pressing one—and it was unforeseen as well. The messenger god was the last Olympian to re-enter the divine council before Zeus gave Poseidon the signal for the call to order. Poseidon banged his golden trident three times, which shook the entire council hall. Zeus stood up over the massive assembly and said cryptically in a clear tone, "The rise of a new, and the fall of our own."

The assembly was made tacit by Zeus's sad words. The gods comported themselves to take in this fact once again. Before Zeus could resume his position on his throne and ask if there were any comments, the assembly became bombastic as they voiced various questions and concerns. As Zeus made his way back to the throne, he sighed, because he knew the trenchant words meant it was going to be a long assembly.

CHAPTER 2

THE UNANNOUNCED

R aising his voice, Zeus began again. "The death of the *Great Alexander* from Macedonia resulted in the division and fall of his empire. Foolishly, Alexander's generals and their remnants lost the specter of dominion, and now all the lands the Grecians once held dominion, a new nation now rules as *the* empire of world supreme." Zeus placed his hands on his face.

"What did you expect from man, brother?" Poseidon asked with his eyes focused on his right thumb as he rubbed his golden trident up and down. Poseidon ceased his action and turned to Ares with malice in his eyes to say, "Plus, we have your son to thank for these endless wars between the Macedonian generals and city-states throughout the Grecian Empire."

Poseidon's bold, candid statement left an uneasiness inside the divine council. All attention shifted toward Ares, which Ares felt when he simply looked around the council and saw their reactions to Poseidon's words.

"How dare you, uncle," said Ares with hostility. "That was a weak move for a god of your stature."

"Brother, be not overzealous as the Spartans of old," Athena said to her half-brother. "The ignominy of creating wars among our people will not fall on you alone, because I too share in the havoc of war with our people," she said with hopes of diffusing the tension.

Athena stood and carefully made her way to the center of the council room. She walked with grace across the marble floor, which reflected her elegant, light-silver, two-piece toga with streams of white-silver gems running along the edges. With every step Athena took toward the center of the Divine Hall, Athena's long, brunette hair swayed and glistened from the sparkling diamonds studs that flowed down the middle of her fishtail braided hair, while her toga rippled across her Junoesque stature as the wind moves across an open meadow—and revealing her shapely abdomen and her smooth back that was desirous to touch.

She took a good look at everyone around the assembly room and said, "I agree, father, that the wars were imprudent and impetuous—but they also seemed inevitable."

Zeus's eyes grew thin, as though he knew his daughter was heading down a path she was unprepared for. Athena observed her father's reaction, as well as Hera's, which was much the same.

Athena did not allow their shared reaction to dissuade her from voicing her thoughts and observations. "It is true that humanity has limited their worship and adoration of us and grown more dependent on their own merits. This disloyalty, we can assume, may have resulted in the fall of our empire," Athena said as she gestured around the council. "Please stop and think for a moment." Athena placed her left index finger on the side of her head while she gave the council a moment to consider her words.

"There seems to be a pattern here," she started again. "Please tell me that one of you has seen it?" Athena looked into the faces of the gods and goddesses who all sat before her with looks of incertitude. She shook her head and said boldly, "There is a pattern here; a pattern where great empires rose up and fell!"

The silence grew thicker. Judging by the facial expressions and body language of some of the other gods, Athena saw her words were not registering, but she continued regardless. "First, the Kushites stood up as a powerful empire with the reign of Nebuchadnezzar, but the kingdom fell to the Persian Empire through the remarkable leadership of their valiant kings, starting with Cyrus of Persia.

"However," she continued as her right fist clenched, "under our leadership and guidance, we helped our beloved Grecians through a series of wars to overthrow them. We witnessed many memorable leaders in times of great division—leaders such as Miltiades, one of the ten generals of Athens whose contributions led to the victory at the Battle of Marathon. From King Leonidas of Sparta and his few hundred Spartiates to Philip the Second of Macedonia, who not only united the Greek city-states, but also prepared the way for our beloved Alexander the Great." The divine council all cheered and uplifted the name of Alexander. "Yes, brothers and sisters," Athena said with exhilaration, "it was this man who took our nation to victory over the Persian Empire and the far territories of the east."

"Alexander's conquest also proliferated our teachings and mores to other cultures that required it." Athena's comment had all the gods nodding their heads in agreement.

"My child, a moment please," Hera said, cutting off Athena. "Yes, this proliferation of knowledge would not have been possible without our influence on the philosophers, starting with Socrates; with whom you, Athena, spent quality time morning, noon, and especially night," Hera said. She took her focus off the assembly and directed it to Athena. "You also spent time with the seven sages of Greece in the same way."

"This is true, Hera," Athena responded, looking back at her stepmother. "And Socrates taught Plato, and Aristotle produced a pupil who provided counsel to the young Alexander of Macedonia in the art of war."

The council of gods unanimously said, "Aristotle!" The male gods all laughed, while the female gods all shook their heads in dismay.

"Well, yes, Aristotle was partially an exceptional product of our educational system in my eyes," Athena said while rolling her eyes. "Moreover, the point is this," she said, redirecting the council's focus to the matter at large. "The same way Babylon and Persia fell in a matter of time, our beloved nation has fallen, and now a new empire is on the rise, and they refer to themselves as Romans!"

Athena's last words left the council of gods in a loquacious state. Every god present had something to say about Athena's observation, so they all tried voicing their thoughts and concerns at the same time. The divine council was in chaos. However, Zeus and Hera remained silent throughout the turmoil—but they were not the only gods who were quiet with their words. All the original Olympians were speechless, something Athena could not help but notice. However, there was more to be said on the matter, so she continued.

"This rise and fall of these empires are portents of something major at work," Athena continued. "I have a strong inclination that we ought to come together as one, just as the Greek city-states did during their perilous times. That way, we can help restore our empire—"

"Enough!" The voice of Zeus silenced Athena.

Zeus perused the council, while Athena hastened back to her seat, displeased. "Allow me to palliate your minds, please," Zeus said as he descended from his throne to stand where his prudent daughter had just stood a moment ago. Zeus turned to look into Athena's eyes, and then looked away. "The wisdom of my daughter surpasses me time after time, but it should never be overestimated. Moreover, we cannot allow anger to pilot our decisions, such as it has in the past."

Meanwhile, Ares had positioned himself in such a manner to make it easy for the new female faces to have a better view of himself. The

goddesses smiled with appeasement, while others nearby scorned Ares with their eyes and thoughts.

Ares, looking to impress even further, decided to cut Zeus in his talk to the council. "Father," he began, "I will say that I apologize for the civil wars I have caused among our people. However, what my dear uncle forgot to mention was that through these wars, men are more compelled to worship me rather than him." Ares then turned to Poseidon to say, "Even your most faithful followers find more strength and assurance in my name. Do they not, my dear uncle?"

Ares's words and facial expressions were enough to infuriate Poseidon. "I will teach this fool the concept of respect," he said with both hands on his golden trident.

"Whenever you're ready," Ares replied egotistically. "I'll make you see why they praise me more."

Ares responded to his uncle's challenge with his *aspis* in his left hand and *kopis* in his right.

Poseidon jumped off his elevated throne with insurmountable power, shaking the entire council floor and marring the glass-like surface as he landed. The power surging through the god's body emitted a potent energy that jerked every god back in their seats. This display of power made Zeus genuinely concerned for his son. Zeus knew Poseidon could demolish his son far more than Ares could perceive. Ares was no match for an original Olympian, but Zeus knew Ares's pride would blind him of this fact. Zeus had to do something quick.

Ares smiled maliciously, because he knew he was in for a challenge and he hungered for war. The two gods made their way toward each other, but Zeus raised his hands. "Enough, you two," he yelled in a powerful voice, and the two rushed into an invisible barrier which became visible when they slammed into it. The sound of the two gods hitting the barrier made a louder bang than Zeus's own thunderous call. Silence swept across the majestic hall as everyone waited to see what would happen next.

"Did you two not hear the counsel of Athena, or did it fall on deaf ears?" Zeus demanded to know.

Ares opened his mouth to defend himself, but his words were silenced when Zeus raised his index finger toward him.

There was something suddenly *different* and yet *familiar* in the presence of the council. Zeus turned his head to circumspect the source of this peculiar feeling, and then he saw a figure moving between the columns that held up the council hall. Zeus's eyes grew wide as though he had seen something troubling, and then he remembered the apple from the messenger god. He looked down into his daughter's curious eyes, which were searing into his own. Zeus knew Athena had seen his reaction, and how this was wood to her fire of curiosity. Zeus saw Poseidon's countenance mutate from belligerent to concerned. Zeus then looked at the other original Olympians and saw their troubling expressions, and he knew he had to act fast—and wisely.

"Ares, enough with your words, because this divine council assembly is over." Zeus clasped his hand into a fist. "Let us contravene when I schedule a new council assembly. Until then, please leave me to my thoughts, and build upon yours," Zeus said as he gestured with his hands for dismissal. Zeus made his way back to his throne beside Hera's while everyone else made their way out—except for Athena.

"Father—"

"Athena," Zeus said, cutting her off, "I know what you want, my child, but I gave my command. Please see yourself out. The son of your past love awaits you outside." Zeus looked at her.

"He can wait, but this cannot—"

"Athena, my child. Do as I say, and say no more, please!" Zeus's words were stern and calm, which meant to Athena that something direly important had come up.

Athena took a breath in and let it out as she turned to dismiss herself from the council hall. Overwrought by Zeus's authoritative position, Athena ran out of the hall in great discontent. She was unaware of the

presence of another deity—the one that had Zeus and the other Olympians in an uneasy state. She knew something was awry, and could not bring herself to so obediently depart without gathering more information. She knew what she had to do, and her new love was going to help her gather the information she desired.

With Athena finally gone from their presence, Hera turned to Zeus to say, "Is it who I think it is?" Oblivious to her surroundings, she stared into Zeus's eyes and saw the reflection of the same figure he was currently watching. Hera carefully turned to see the unexpected figure smiling at them.

"I hope I am who you thought it was, sister! Nevertheless, it is good to see you two again," the unexpected guest said to the two gods in a melodious voice. "I do come unannounced—but not without reason, of course!"

CHAPTER 3

BROTHERS AND SISTERS

This is unlike you, my brother." Zeus's voice resonated throughout the vacant council hall. "Normally, you leave *logos* in the stars for us to know that you require an audience with us." Zeus leaned forward on his throne and asked, "What is it?" Zeus stared into the soothing eyes of the being that stood boldly before him. "You would not come unannounced unless you had something urgent to say. Please, state your business," Zeus pleaded. When he received no response, he grew more unsettle. "Brother, I asked: *what is it?*" Fear swept across Zeus's face while suspense numbed his body.

The flawless being laughed inwardly. He shook his sleek, pearl-white hair from side to side with eyes fixed on the two gods sitting high on their thrones. "I was actually convinced that only your *daughter* was the one with the *real* wisdom on Olympus." The impeccable being placed his fingers underneath his hairless chin and rubbed it. "No, I know she is the only one with *real* wisdom on Olympus—"

"We ought to feel offended by your words, but somehow I feel nothing," Poseidon said. His words caught Zeus and Hera off guard; they were still in awe over who was standing before them, unannounced.

The unexpected guest turned as Poseidon walked toward him with a stern look on his face. The newcomer held out his right hand, but

Poseidon simply glared with disdain and raised an eyebrow. Then he shook his head in disgust at the being. "What's brings a distinguished figure such as yourself to our humble abode? Surely, our *elder brother* has more pressing matters that requires your attention."

"Humble!" The bemused being repeated, with his right arm still outstretched to greet Poseidon.

"You find fault in my description of this place?" Poseidon asked the unexpected guest while he gestured around the council hall.

Poseidon looked at the arm of the being that stood before him and saw no sign of retreat. He knew his long-time elder brother was one of persistence, so it was pointless for him to resist his modest greeting. Poseidon looked into the face of his elder brother and saw an indescribable smile on his face. Poseidon knew that his elder brother knew that he was going to give in, so Poseidon sighed and grabbed his brother by the forearm. The two smiled and embraced each other with an extensive hug and a well-deserved kiss, which resulted in the two speaking in their native tongue—a language that had been banished by the first Olympians before the creation of Mount Olympus.

"It's good to see you're doing well, Poseidon," the elder brother said.

"Yes, it is also a privilege to have you here, *Andragel*[2]," Poseidon replied, pulling away to stare into the exotic eyes of his brother, which displayed an array of colors from the rainbow whenever he blinked. "What brings you unannounced? This is not like you, so I'm going to assume something major has occurred."

Andragel gave his younger brother, Poseidon, a simple nod in agreement to his assumption. This was the same assumption running through all the Olympians' minds; even Hestia and Demeter had similar questions and concerns running through their own minds. This was why the sisters returned to the council hall, because just as Zeus and

---

[2] Andragel is the fifth of the seven elder gods created to guard the original seven stars (pillars) of the multiverse.

Poseidon were able to sense their brother's obtrusive arrival, they had also sensed his recognizable presence.

Welcomed or not, the sisters greeted their long-time elder brother with long hugs and courteous kisses.

"Brother," Hestia said in her soft voice, "why are you here so unannounced, especially at a time such as this?"

Before the Elder Brother could answer, Demeter interrupted by saying, "I assume you have answers as to why our empire has fallen, and why a new one has risen."

"That's it," Zeus said with life in his voice and legs. "Demeter, that makes sense," Zeus said while looking at his older brother.

Hera got up to stand beside Zeus, and she held her husband by his left shoulder. "Zeus, please," she said, trying to pacify her husband's unnecessary outbursts and persisting interrogation. Zeus turned to his wife with wild eyes. "Please," she continued, "let's give him a chance to explain himself. You're not giving him a chance to speak—just give him a chance, please!"

Hera's words of counsel were enough for Zeus to restrain himself and allow his brother to explain.

"Yes, Zeus. I advise you to listen to our sister for your own sake, brother." The elder brother's words were soft to the Olympians' ears, even though he looked stern when he spoke to Zeus. The elder brother turned away from his siblings to admire the beauty of the council hall, while the eyes of his younger siblings were glued to his every move and word. "I must admit," Andragel said while he circumspect the Olympian's Council Hall. "This is a spectacular place you have constructed over time. I can see the creativity that has gone into these fine establishments and sculptures throughout the entire Olympus." The elder brother turned back around to see all eyes on him. "Sadly, it's nothing compared to home." He then turned back around and said, "Suffice it to say, of course!"

The countenance of all the gods of Olympus instantly became downcast; their past life was a life they had to learn to leave behind them. The brother saw his younger siblings in dismay. "I apologize for taking you down memory lane, but you feel as though your lofty thrones and infinitesimal praises from humanity places you in the position of the Father of us all!" His voice was cold and stern enough to send a power surge through the bodies of all the Olympians. The Olympians became humbled by their brother's words, while their minds were left uneasy by the way he said it. Silence swept across the entire council hall because the gods knew their elder brother was right. "I need not remind each of you of who we truly were, and no new identity as an Olympian or Greek god will change this fact. I chastise you not, but I need us to be realistic." The Elder Brother knew that his words were laden with meaning and truth. Suddenly, a muffled laughter resonated throughout the hall, which evolved into a heartless laughter. The god-siblings all watched their elder brother hysterically laughing.

"I was admiring," the elder brother said as he gestured to the hall once again, "how the paintings in this establishment tell a tale of how the first Olympians defeated the mighty Titans with their effortless teamwork, and of course—how could I forget!" The elder brother clasped his hands together and then opened them. A divine light emitted from his palms. The Olympians' shielded their eyes until the light dwindled and they returned their focus to the sight of a small dagger floating in the center elder brother's hand. He then turned the dagger horizontally and opened his hands outward. The dagger grew into a full-length sword. The blade was polished silver with gold running along the edges. The sword also had an artistic engraving on both sides of the blade, while the hilt was solid gold encrusted with rare stones.

"The Sword of Olympus," the elder brother announced while he held out the sword with his left hand toward his siblings. "Isn't this the sword the Olympians used to *slay* the mighty Titans?" Andragel asked the Olympians. His right hand slid across the blade and the sword was

instantly set ablaze. The god-siblings hid their faces for the fear of their brother's true power. The elder brother knew that if he held on any longer, the power emitting from the blade would destroy the sword itself, and with it the pride of his Olympian siblings.

The elder brother removed his left hand from the hilt and left the sword afloat in the air. He allowed them the opportunity to recover from the sudden exposure to his familiar light. "The Titans were not defeated by your actions," the Elder Brother said candidly. "To have fought the Titans would have resulted in the nonexistence of this so-called 'Olympian Empire,' because the Titans would have annihilated you all."

The Olympians looked at the elder brother with shame in their eyes.

"Do you not understand what I am saying?" he asked.

Instead of a response, shame remained engraved on their visages.

The elder brother walked in circles as he continued. "What you Olympians did not know was that I encouraged the Titans to seek refuge inside a galaxy large enough to hold their very existence. A galaxy located inside the Fourth Pillar[3], *Pleiades*, a galaxy quite far from here, which will be hard to find inside a Megaverse such as *Pleiades*." He stared directly at Zeus and said assuredly, "And for your sakes, the Titans accepted the new realm I provided them."

The elder brother then pointed to Zeus in chastisement and said, "I knew this confrontation between the Titans and you all would draw unnecessary attention. Suffice it to say, it would have infringed on my objectives and disturbed my long-term goals." The elder brother clasped his hands together and continued, "I am grateful that your older siblings, the *Titans*, respectfully accepted what I offered to them. Therefore, your epic tales of a formidable battle with the Titans was a great *lie!*" He then turned his back to the sword and walked away, and the sword faded with every step he took until it was finally no more.

---

[3] Pillar is another term for a star; therefore, the Fourth Pillar, also known as *Pleiades*, is a part of the original Seven Pillars to ever be created and through these seven stars came the many multiverses and entire Omniverse.

"Please!" Hera called from her throne, to which she had returned. "Please, tell us why you're here, Andragel." Her voice was full of compassion and deep concern, but the elder brother knew her intention was to draw attention away from the Olympians' shame. He knew the drivel was becoming overbearing.

"Our exile was an unfortunate and unfair turning point for us all," the elder brother said. The gods felt their brother's distress, because they were all on the same boat.

"What happened, brother?" Poseidon asked as he dragged his trident across the marble floor to face his brother's back.

"There's not a moment that goes by where I don't gaze into the heavens to see the movement of the celestial bodies changing their courses as the time goes by," the Elder Brother said. His eyes revealed that he was reliving the days of their shameful defeat during the *Great War of Gods*[4].

"Everything!" the elder brother said before he started to chuckle. "Everything," he continued, as a grim expression appeared across his visage. *"Everything!"* he said with emphasis without opening his mouth. The gods were more than aware of their brother's mastery of elocution; it was how he had convinced them to join his side in the time of the *Great War of Gods*. Nevertheless, his calm voice was still potent enough to cause the Parthenon to tremble. "Everything—just gone, as though it never existed," the elder brother said with his fingers pressed on his chin. "I knew the cost was expulsion and I was willing to pay the price— back then of course! But now, I wish I'd approached matters differently." His vivacious eyes were lit with the fire of a thousand suns; the gods found themselves shielding their eyes once again from their brother's immense power.

"Andragel, please, restrain yourself," Hera said from her throne.

---

[4] The Great War of Gods was a galactic war which took place many light years ago inside the region of the Fifth Pillar, between the inhabitants of the Fifth Pillar and the guardians of the High Council of Alliance.

The elder brother gave his siblings his back while he placed his right hand on his chin to reflect on thoughts of the past. "I addressed unfairness, and my image becomes tarnished as a result, and now I'm on a never-ending trial to prove my innocence. But *no... No, no, no!* That's not the worst part," Andragel said as he rubbed his forehead. "The worst part is the High Council of Alliance has decided on taking away my birthright—*Arcturus*, the Fifth Pillar[5]," he said with a sinister chuckle. "The moment of expulsion by the High Council—I can hear their incompetent voices, mocking me in their speech." He opened his mouth and spoke in the old tongues banned on Olympus. "Oh, fallen star, whose throne now lies in the shadows of the deep, never rise to old or new heights!" He turned to his siblings and roared to them, "Fools, they all are, for they know not what I know—and witnessed. For everyone that speaks ill of my name lack understanding." Andragel continued, "Do they not know that I was among the first of the seven constellations[6] to shine across the many galaxies? It was I who traveled the many galaxies long before any of them sat at the *Table of Order and Justice*[7], and now they sit to pass judgement on me. How did this become my fate?"

Andragel glided his hands behind his back before he continued. "Once I have proven my innocence to the High Council of Alliance, my throne," he said with adoration, "and our place at the High Council will be established. I will sit to represent all of us who were cast away. I will be your voice when we have been without a voice for so long. We will be heard and acknowledged by all. We will be respected, and we will be new gods."

---

[5] *Arcturus* is the Fifth Pillar of the original seven Pillars and the Pillar Andragel was made lord over.

[6] The seven constellations refer to the seven original pillars, which produce billions of stars and through the connection of stars. Millions and millions of galaxies were formed with time.

[7] The Table of Order and Justice is where decisions are formulated, laws are created, and judgements are decided by the members of the High Council of Alliance to govern the entire Omniverse.

Speechless were the god-siblings as they earnestly listened to their brother's enthusiasm and ambition. He fell to his knees as though he had lost faith in his cause. The sight of their brother kneeling on the floor pulled their own spirits downward to where he was. However, his arms outstretched arms showed he was not giving up. It showed also the weight of his objectives were excruciatingly difficult to bear, but the determination to prove to the various galaxies far and near that he was in the right and more than fit to sit at the Table of Order and Justice. The Olympians knew their elder brother saw the complete picture of hope from all sides and angles, and it was this picture that kept him from falling flat on his face in surrender.

Still on his knees, the elder brother saw a new being when he looked down at his reflection on the glassy floor. This angered him, because he knew who he once was, where he had come from, why his life had changed, and what he was going to do about this change. He raised his hands above his head into a fist to slam the floor, but he stopped himself short. The thought of looking defeated is the belief in the idea of actual defeat. "*No!*" he said to himself with assurance. He set his gaze upon the artistry of the ceiling in the Divine Council Hall and said aloud, "The time will come when they will all recant their words and doubts about us. Yes! That time will come for all those at the High Council of Alliance to take all their disbelief back." He rose to his feet. "When they see us prospering like the gods were destined to be, yes, they will *all* see and declare our greatness before me." Standing firm and filled with self-assurance, he suddenly burst into shimmering specks of flickering lights before reappearing in the beauty of the light atop the throne where Zeus and Hera were sitting. Then he said, with a voice like a mighty trumpet, "The time will come when I will reestablish our names for all to know and *respect*! He then raised his hands to the air and said with full rage, "*This is our time—I will not let them take it from us!*"

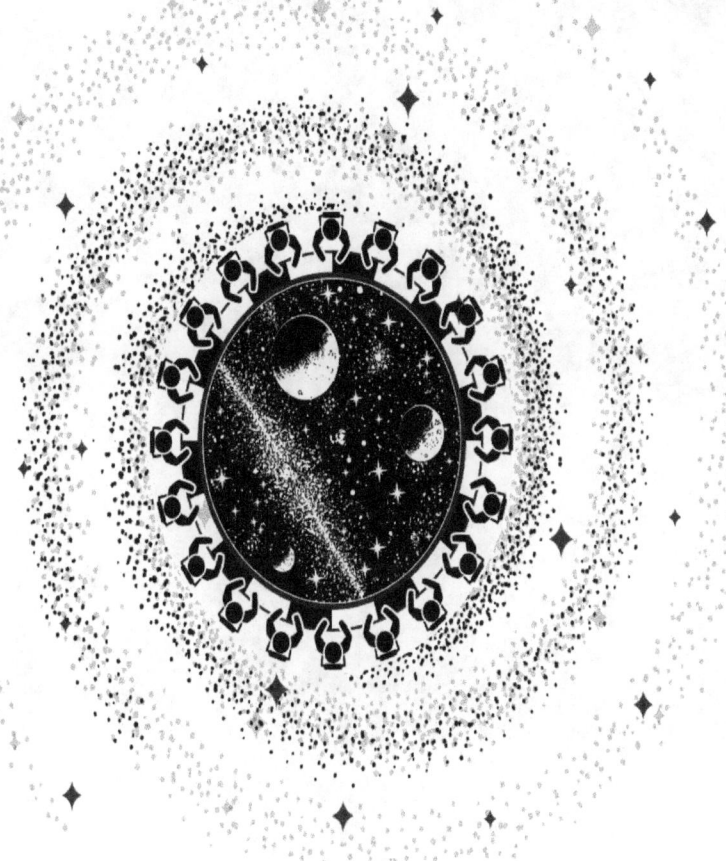

THE TABLE OF ORDER AND JUSTICE

CHAPTER 4

CHILDREN OF THE FALLEN

Applause filled the council hall. All heads turned to toward the entrance to see a familiar face.

"I hope I am the first to say that it is truly a blessing to hear the voice of promise," the newcomer said. He carried a strange ambiance with him as he strolled into the council hall.

"Hades, brother, all I do is for us, not just me alone," Andragel said to his younger brother. Hades maintained his clapping after his elder brother reminded him of his just cause. However, as Hades made his way to where his brothers and sisters were standing, it quickly became clear that he wasn't alone. A sudden scream of joy was heard from Hera when she saw who had just entered the council hall. She ran to greet the unexpected guests. The deities that walked into the council hall had the bodies of men and women, but their faces were not all those of humans. There were beings with the faces of a falcon, ram, panther, jackal, ibis, and other beasts of land and sea, and atop each of their heads was the powerful symbol of the sun.

Hera ran to greet her brothers and sisters who were worshipped by their followers residing in the holy lands of Khui, which can be found in the northeast regions of Kemet, which the Grecians called Egypt. The skin of the Kemetic deities resembled that of polished onyx, and they were adorned with gold ornaments from head to toe and their garments were of fine silks. Kemetic gods such as Osiris had a gold-and-sapphire crook in his right hand and a flail in his left, while others such as Amun-Ra had a golden scepter that was equal in length to Poseidon's trident. However, the ankh was the symbol of eternal life, a symbol this family of deities hung on to long before the Great War. The Kemetic gods were never seen without the ankh. This symbol was found painted on their bodies, carved on their sacred relics, or chiseled on the walls of their holy temples along with other pictorial symbols often referred to by man as the *Metu Neter*. Even the Kemetic gods' most devoted followers were never without the ankh around their necks, painted on their skin, and welded objects of artistry from precious stones and metals for decoration and spiritual worship purposes.

Hera greeted her Egyptian brothers and sisters with open arms and kisses. The bond Hera shared with the onyx-colored gods was unbreakable. If anything, Hera and the other Olympians were the closest gods of Kemet out of all the other Children of the Fallen. Even Zeus got off his throne to greet his family. The onyx gods also greeted Andragel, their elder brother, but they were all far from being ecstatic about his unexpected presence. The Egyptian gods were known for their candid and fastidious personalities.

Atum meandered through the crowd of his of banished brothers and sisters, and approached the elder brother with an easy smile across his face. "Brother! It is a pleasure to be in your presence. Such moments are rare," Atum said humbly. "Tell us the concerns of your heart, for I know time is sacred in your eyes." All the gods turned to their Elder Brother for a response.

"Patience," the Andragel replied to the curiosity of his younger sibling. "Let us wait for others to arrive. I hope such a request is not too

much to ask from your busy lives." The siblings sensed his sarcasm and tried to refrain from asking any bolder questions.

Hades turned to his brother, Osiris, and asked with a bewildered look, "Why does our brother, Amun-Ra, possess the "Swords of Ra" imprinted on the back of his skin? If I am not mistaken, were these swords not a gift toward his most faithful servant of the first empire?"

The Atef crown on Osiris's head turned with him to observe what Hades had pointed out. "Ah, yes," Osiris said calmly. "You have a keen eye, Hades. The Swords of Ra were a gift to his most faithful man servant, but his descendants misuse the power and increase the bloodshed throughout the lands," Osiris said casually with not a hint of remorse.

Hades interjected convivially by saying, "What's a world without death?"

A sudden cold and sinister laughter came from the two brothers, which sent chills through the souls who stood nearest to them.

"However," Osiris continued, looking stern and focused, "as the story goes, an assembly of the wisest and wealthiest in the early days of Kemet had all the remaining descendants of the faithful servant of Ra assassinated, or so they thought or hoped. Now what the assembly did next with the swords was quite clever I must admit. This assembly propagated lies by spreading false tales of mystery and adventure as to keep the desires of men away from the truth. The spreading of lies was successful for a long, long time, eventually turning the truth into myths and legends. Until someone was found using the Swords of Ra to the point that the power of the blades was becoming one with him, and soon he found himself no longer a man, but a weapon of vengeance for Amun-Ra—"

"So, he became a monster," Hades interjected again.

"No," Osiris replied, rejecting Hades's conclusion. "He became something of a 'mindless-soldier,' but little did Amun-Ra know this last descendant also had family ties to the gods of the Twelve."

"Oh, I see," said Hades thoughtfully, nodding his head in dismay.

"Exactly," Osiris said in a heavier tone. "The endless bloodshed by the hands of this mindless soldier caught the attention of the '*new... high ... guardian!*' With the new title, it was the responsibility of this high guardian to put an end to the bloodshed." Osiris and Hades both shook their heads because they both shared a lack of respect for humanity.

"What happened next?" Hades asked his Egyptian brother.

"Isn't it obvious? This newly promoted guardian took the swords back to Ra and warned him not to allow any man to possess these swords ever again, or else he would return with no warning nor mercy."

"Hmmm, I see," Hades said thoughtfully again. "There was a time when this *high guardian* was nothing more than just another brother, but sadly times have changed." The background noise carefully escalated with everyone in their small groups discussing all manner of topics of interest.

"Ra, just like any of us, didn't take the threat too easily, so Ra drew his swords, and that escalated the matter. The two fought in the skies, but as quickly as it started, it ended—"

"What do you mean?" Hades asked Osiris with a puzzled look on his face.

Osiris turned to Hades and said, "*Seraphina* stopped the fight."

Hades stepped back as though he had heard the name of a ghost. "No," Hades said, looking aghast while Osiris nodded his head. "So, it's true," Hades continued. "She returned home!"

Suddenly, smoke appeared in front of Zeus's and Hera's thrones, while the sound of drums resonated across the floor where the gods stood, and the wind howled with the sound of wolves under the starry night. The deities who were worshipped in the far northwest of the Earth's hemisphere made their entrance on Mount Olympus with soft, blue-and-white lights dancing and swimming throughout the hall displaying themselves in the celestial images of forest animals. These gods were spirits that had learned to adapt themselves to the elements

of nature, by combining themselves together to create a singular, hybrid host. In this same light appeared a tall being with the heads of many forest beasts. The wings of an eagle flared at the top of the being, while below had four legs as a brown bear. The presence of the combined spirits—thirteen in all—transformed the atmosphere of the council hall into the cool aroma of the northwest outdoors. Four animal spirits were facing in the direction of the coordinates—four in the lower region, four in the mid-section, and four near the top. However, at the very top was the head of a man covered in a long, feather headpiece. The faces stared at everyone present in the hall and became inundated with excitement, which caused them to disperse from their combined form and bloom into their true forms to greet their fellow brothers and sisters.

Feathers of every color started to rain down from the ceiling of the council hall. Through the raining feathers came a being with the massive wings of an eagle, but the wings were blue and yellow and his skin was fluorescent green. When the majestic creature landed, his serpent staff hit the glass floor with a deafening *thud* that bellowed throughout the council hall. All the gods looked at the flamboyant being and wondered his identity, but Zeus and Andragel knew who it was from the moment the feathers had fallen from the ceiling.

A surge of lightning started to flow through Zeus's body, and his eyes glowed white with rage. All eyes shifted toward Zeus when they saw the unexpected display of power. The eyes on the serpent staff started to glow, along with those of the one holding it. In the blink of an eye, Zeus's right fist was in the red-and-green painted face of the mysterious deity. The attack was faster than lightning, and it caught the mysterious god off guard. The god was flung across the council hall, but stopped himself by hitting against an invisible barrier that shimmered upon contact. The hall rumbled as he fell onto a knee, maintaining his balance with his staff. The deity looked up with the eyes of a serpent fixed on Zeus's head. Through these eyes, the rest of the gods knew the identity of this mysterious god. His followers knew him as "Huitzilopochtli," the hummingbird god known by his association to the sun and love for war. However, the god-siblings knew him as "*Loyal*." Huitzilopochtli was worshipped as the main god in the southeastern region of the Earth. Huitzilopochtli's followers were very faithful to him through their human sacrifices; the followers would literally give Loyal the hearts of men to prove their loyalty to him, and this greatly pleased him. Loyal enjoyed reminding Zeus of the fact of having more faithful worshippers than he would ever have in his time being the *god-king* of the Olympians. Such facts created strife between the two for a time now, thus making Loyal one of Zeus's many competitors.

Nevertheless, the eyes of the staff grew brighter, and every feather on the marble floor changed into serpents with wings which latched onto Zeus and constricted his movements. Loyal flew over to the constricted Zeus and landed a series of blows onto Zeus's face.

Hera looked up because she heard the rolling of thunder, and she knew what was coming next. "Everyone, get back," Hera cried out frantically as he turned away from Zeus. A gigantic thunderbolt broke through the root of the Parthenon and struck Loyal, propelling everyone to the farthest corners of the council hall.

When the other gods recovered, they found the elder brother standing in the same spot he was in before the thunderbolt fell from the skies. He was shaking his head at Zeus and Loyal. Zeus was on his knees and hands, panting, while looking at an upside down Loyal, who was attached to the wall of the council hall. Others appeared right after the brawl to see the aftermath of the damage to the assembly hall inside the Parthenon.

"You two had enough?" Andragel asked the brawlers, putting out the burning snakes by waving his left hand from right to left.

In a matter of minutes, the Divine Council Hall on Mount Olympus was teeming with banished brothers and sisters from the farthest corners of East and West of this new world. The deities worshipped from the far east of the world—the ones who ruled with strict moral

codes and taught men about the inner strength one can receive through cosmic meditation—were present in the hall. Some gods stood tall, towering over the others, while a few moved around the hall in the form of a mystical mist. Some gods had gaping smiles with fangs sticking out from the sides and on the bottom of their mouths, and arms that numbered up to five on each side of their body.

Whenever the gods arrived at the Divine Council Hall, their very presence was a rush of exhilaration and splendor for everyone to see how much they had changed. Some entered with an explosion of wildfire, others with the ominous cries of hastening winds, and a handful humbly walked through the main entrance of the hall. One god had the audacity to hammer his way into the hall with the roar of thunder. Zeus turned to Hera with his jaw dropped, which Hera carefully closed for him, for she knew the disrespect was too much for him to bear. Amid Hera's comfort, another being mystifyingly fell from the heavens with the human embodiment of the starry night sky mixed with celestial clouds of many colors. The presence of this god was so powerful that her ascension into the Divine Council Hall brought down the celestial night skies all over Mount Olympus.

From inside to outside the hall, everyone marveled at the grandeur of the night sky. The gods saw colors they never thought could exist in the sky. Some saw indigo blue and crimson red mixed with magenta pink and pure silver, while others saw turquoise and gold mixed with orange and harlequin green. No one saw the same color twice, which was all due to the celestial clouds constantly moving and fusing with each other to create new colors.

Everyone inside the hall was so mesmerized by the array of colors that they forgot about the god that had made it all happen—that is until she opened her eyes, which were like gems in the sky. The *Children of the Fallen* watched as shooting stars flashed across the colorful sky, filling the god's eyes with countless shimmering lights. Her entire figure was decorated with tiny specks of sparkling stars, while the movements of the celestial clouds in the sky matched the movements of clouds in her body.

All those around this goddess greeted her right way; even Hera left Zeus's side to greet this beauty of the night. The god of the night took her time to greet everyone she came across, from Ra to Hades, as well as the sagacious Spirits from the far West to the honorable gods in the far east.

"It's been too long," said the god of the celestial skies.

"Yes, it has been, Lunesta," replied the elder brother before he was embraced by the coolness of her celestial body. Lunesta's eyes shone bright like full moons in the presence of the elder brother as the two caught up on an overdue conversation. Her celestial presence was so monumental that the spellbinding beauty of the night remained unchanged inside the hall and throughout all of Mount Olympus. All the inhabitants of Olympus saw the majestic changes in their skies above, causing many to marvel at the opulent splendor of the celestial skies, while others grew suspicious.

However, this did not stop the other god-siblings from making their grand entrance; Lunesta's presence even paved the way for one god who fell from the starry sky like a star on fire, landing right in the center of the hall, which created a massive campfire. The flames from the massive campfire burst into every vibrant color as they scattered themselves all over the assembly hall.

Some of the god-siblings were aware of the many dangers within these exotic flames if the flames continued to burn near them, so they wasted no time in moving away from them. To the average third-eye being, a simple fanning of the flame would not suffice, nor would the pouring of water. The technique in extinguishing these flames required skills that few of the siblings possessed—but that was the beauty of it all. Depending on the color of the flames, each god possessed the ability to extinguish the flame. Unfortunately, few of the god-siblings were unaware of this special skill hidden inside of them; it was like a buried

treasure. The elder brother, on the other hand, knew about these talents hidden inside each of his brothers and sisters. He even knew what it took to uproot this potential treasure: *self-awareness*! Self-awareness was the answer, the key to opening other treasures hidden from within, but self-awareness was not enough to take them through the door where the vast treasures were laid.

Nevertheless, Andragel knew today was the day that his brothers and sisters would witness and experience what happens when the "Children of the Fallen" embarks on a journey to not only open the door of self-awareness, but walk through the door, and keep walking until all glory is obtained. It was then that from within the center of the hall, where the flames burned massively bright, a colossal being with the body of a man ascended out of the towering flames and sprouted massive wings. These wings were mightier than those of a thousand eagles, large enough to cover the tops of snowy mountains, and dark enough to blend with Lunesta's night sky.

The outstretched wings rained down tiny specks of sparkling, black diamonds all over the council hall. Instantly, every burning flame turned into a sacred nightglow.

"Black fire, huh? I haven't seen that in a while," Lunesta said to the elder brother as the murmuring and mumbling of voices increased in the background when they realized the black flames. The black flames had every god on edge. Some even ascended into the roof of the council hall to avoid any possibility of making contact with the black flames. Lunesta pulled a star from her own body and rubbed her hands together over the black fire. "I can't lie to you," Lunesta said as her hands began to illuminate celestial lights. "This black fire is tempting me." Andragel said as he curiously watched the way Lunesta rubbed her hands for less than ten seconds, and out came a cascade of colorful, crystallized diamonds. The multicolored diamonds fell into the black flames, which caused the flames to snap, pop, and crackle.

"Would you look at that... that was fast—"

"Yeah, the black fire incinerated the diamonds," the elder brother explained to Lunesta as he continued to examine the flames for any sight of the diamonds. "This kind of fire is a true mystery," he continued. "It amazes me how this fire gives off no heat whatsoever, yet it chooses what and when to burn." Andragel had his eyes on the flames in front of him, trying to analyze it properly, when a sudden gust of wind flashed across the council hall, commanding everyone's attention, and igniting the flame. Lunesta grabbed Andragel and swiftly pulled him back in time to prevent the black fire from touching him.

"Thank you. That was too close for comfort," said Andragel maintaining his composure.

"Look... this is new," Lunesta said, with her eyes glued on the god hovering over the black flames, which now shone golden at the tips. It was through the golden light of the black fire grew brighter in the company of this new god.

"A *black phoenix*! How could this be?" Lunesta asked in awe.

The elder brother heard the shock in his sister's voice and knew she was not the only one who was unaware of this transformation. None of the Children of the Fallen had ever seen a black phoenix; it was almost unheard of—a complete myth or legend. However, today was the day that every fable was put to rest, and the god-siblings were among the first as a family to witness this crucial moment. The black phoenix wore metallic black armor with gold designs traced across it. The designs were symbolic of her family's crescent and house. Her beak, along with her talons and claws, were polished gold; even her massive, onyx-colored wings were lined with metallic gold.

The entire council hall was suspended in silence, taking in the rare moment. The god-siblings saw the eyes of the black phoenix as they began to open. Instantly, every face present flushed with a sudden wave of mixed temperatures that were expelled from the phoenix opening her eyes alone. The intensity of these mixed temperatures flung itself to the farthest corners of the council hall and dispersed itself through the walls

of the Parthenon, changing the temperature throughout Mount Olympus. The temperature of the council hall became a furnace for some, while others felt horrific chills. Some felt soothing temperatures, while to others they felt an unbearable up and down in the temperature. Few felt nothing at all, which was what Lunesta felt. Meanwhile, the rest fainted.

As the phoenix spread her massive wings, the black flames grew in height and width. The gods jumped, flew, picked up, and pulled each other out of the way in time to evade the unexpected growth of the fire. The massive, black flames created an uproar of frustration among the godchildren, since nobody seemed ready for this display of firepower. However, in the midst of the gods' frantic complaining, the black phoenix raised a golden claw-like hand into the air and said with authority, "*Renascentia!*"

Many of the god-siblings were confounded by the word, since this was the first time, they had ever heard it.

"What is this language that was spoken?" Lunesta asked.

"*Renascentia* is Latin for rebirth," Andragel explained.

"Rebirth, huh," she replied as she continued to observe the phoenix's eyes as they burned with the fire of all the phoenixes across the galaxies. "Nevertheless, this transformation is splendid... I mean, just look, just look... a *black phoenix* is right in front of us!" Lunesta said enthusiastically.

"Yes, she is breathtaking," said Andragel admiring the phoenix deity. "She is the first of her kind—a phoenix forged in the depths of the galaxies, a fusion of many stars. 'Magnetar Phoenix' is what I will call her, for she is a new star."

The black phoenix raised her massive wings and absorbed all the black fire around the council hall for the sake of her god-siblings. She could hear their excessive complaining and understood why. When the black flames were gone, those gods who had fainted regained consciousness within a few minutes. Meanwhile, those who were worshipped in other regions of the Motherland entered the council hall with all savannah drums and ivory horns, as well as dance moves that matched the beat of the drums. In the midst of the music and dancing, there were other gods who rained down with their own rich, angelic melodies, filling everyone both inside and outside the council hall with the comforts of home and promises of hopeful tomorrows. The spirit of every godchild in the council hall was lifted up with melodies and tunes they had never heard in their lifetimes.

A true legendary composer and singer, the elder brother was taken away by the way these gods came in with their symphony of sounds—melodies he had never even dreamed of composing or singing himself. The tunes and rhythms combined in a way that filled the council hall and blessed everyone inside and outside the Parthenon. As he found himself submerged in music from his younger siblings, despair and regret suddenly entered the elder brother, because he knew it had been some time since he had dabbled with his own musical instrument.

In the mix of gods now present, there were some who were happy to see one another, while others, if permitted, would have preferred to take the life another's. However, they were all there at the elder brother's request. He watched at the way some of his family entered into the massive council hall adorned in their new, transformed bodies. Andragel's eyes shone brightly at the spectacular permutations his god-siblings had recreated for themselves—all images of their choice—which created a collective, cosmic beauty that could not be comprehended by average minds. The god-siblings were a new age of majestic beings; a mosaic of true beauty and artistry that no artist could draw. A remarkable sight that no man's eyes could ever behold. The deities' very presence was glorious, and their spirits burned with the essence of new greatness.

As every new face arrived, Zeus, along with the other god-siblings, knew with growing certainty that their elder brother had invoked this great assembly for something pressing. "So... something massive is

coming and it involves all us," Zeus said candidly, while gazing wearily around the hall in hopes of finding an answer to suffice. Hera, who stood beside him, nodded her head without even looking up at her husband.

Poseidon walked to them and said, "I think our reign in this new galaxy is coming to an end."

"I'm afraid you might be right," Zeus said with a despondent tone, while he watched Andragel ascended into the air so that every eye could see him. Then, he said with a calm voice, but loud enough for all to hear, "Shall we begin!"

He clasped his hands and then carefully opened them up to reveal a bright, spherical light that resembled the farthest star in the night's sky. He stretched his hands apart, both shining with a gold aura, but the star remained the same size. The gods watched with uncertainty to see what would happen next.

The elder brother swung his hands toward the small star, and the very instant his hands made contact with the spherical light, every ear heard a quick, vacuum-like sound that swallowed the air around the him. Eyes eagerly watched as he held his hands firmly together, while the crushed starlight began radiating streams of golden lights through the cracks of his fingers. His hands then began shaking aggressively as he fought persistently to keep them together and away from his chest.

Suddenly, Andragel realized his own power began disseminating throughout the entire council hall as he tried to contain light in the palms of his hands. The very essence of his power was cool and invigorating in the sight of the god-siblings, as it filled the council hall with memories of the past. What was so familiar to the god-siblings turned out to be something they hadn't felt in some time; that's when a rush of wind began expelling itself out from the pressure building up in his hands, which could no longer contain the power within. Andragel began steadily opening his hands to release it, and it pushed itself through the entire council hall to the outer regions of the Parthenon.

Below, the inhabitants of Mount Olympus saw light waves engulfing the Parthenon. This burst of energy made the inhabitants uncomfortable, so some tried to approach the source of the strange light and quickly discovered they were unable to even approach the Parthenon. There seemed to be a visible barrier surrounding the Parthenon, which meant no one could go in or out.

* * * *

"I am grateful to have every one of you here." Andragel said while he placed his hands behind his back. "I know it's not everyone, but we have to keep pressing forward and hopefully word reaches them. As most of you know, I am here as your ambassador, your *voice* at the High Council of Alliance. As your representative, it is my responsibility to always look out for my brothers' and sisters' best interest. With that said, I must forewarn you all that there are changes in the cosmos. Changes decided by the High Council, and changes that will affect us sooner than later."

The last statement did not settle well with the god-siblings. They started to voice their concerns to one another, confused by what they were hearing from their ambassador—their representative.

"Did you voice your opposition to these changes proposed by the High Council?" Lunesta questioned the elder brother.

"Of course, I did Lunesta," Andragel replied in an offensive tone. "The members of the High Council gave me the opportunity forewarn you all of their decisions."

"You sound more of a messenger for the High Council than a representative on our behalf," Poseidon said out loud, which many agreed with his comment. Andragel sighed heavily and slowly nodded his head in agreement.

"Unfortunately, it does appear so, I will admit, but this is not the case. Patience is the name of this game; it is the only way we have a fighting chance to live out a life of promise and comfort. The *Great War*

of Gods closed more doors rather than opening them, and now, we must play this very long game that requires our patience. So, I ask you all to hang in there and wait for my seat at the High Council, and please be mindful about drawing any unnecessary attention to yourselves."

"Brother, you speak of unnecessary attention as to say this is of our own doing," Lunesta said aloud. "The guardians[8] travel throughout the galaxies causing problems by waging wars on us. What will you do about that?"

Andragel rubbed his hands over his face while the crowd of voiced their concerns louder than before. The elder brother was well informed about the dilemma Lunesta brought up before the sea of gods, and she was not alone. Many others related to being terrorized by the acts of the guardians. Andragel knew the High Council approved these activities of the guardians, long before he stood before the table of the High Council, and now he was trying to repeal an old decree before it was too late and another galactic war erupted.

"Ever since I lost my position as the first of the seven constellations, the High Council of Alliance has slowly and steadily taken away large sections of the galaxies, which I once presided over since the dawn of my very existence. With such a large subtraction, my *natural light* is steadily diminishing, which means soon I will lose dominion over multiple galaxies and in time there will be no realms for some of you to reside in. Especially this newly created galaxy, which has attracted most of you here due to its yellow pillar that is bursting with youthful energy. Even though this young star is appealing, I must warn you to keep eyes on the growing presence of the guardians on the moon. I say these words not lightly, because at the assigned time. When the moon is darkened and the yellow pillar stands at the highest point in the sky, the military presence of the guardians will invade this new galaxy. However, before

---

[8] The guardians are the military force for the High Council of Alliance—as well the High Council's eyes and ears throughout the galaxies.

such an invasion comes past, I suggest that all of you residing in this galactic realm to flee and do not fight, nor get involved. For this galactic warfare does not involve us in any way possible, so I repeat. Do not get involve and flee! Flee now if you can, this new galaxy is to be taken from me, since it has been prophesied in the movement of stars and in the writings of the prophetic gods of the Twelve."

The words of the elder brother left many laden with thoughts to voice and thoughts to consider. Andragel raised his hands to silence the clamoring of his brothers and sisters. He knew what this meant to them, but he had to be honest with them and reassure them that things were going to get better.

"The guardians are traveling throughout the galaxies, expelling us from galaxy to galaxy, even when we are doing good by contributing to the development of the galaxies. They expel us with no remorse, and now you tell us this brother!" Lunesta said aloud, then she looked upward at Andragel to say. "At the rate guardians are moving, where will we go to reside comfortable enough to call home?" Lunesta's question raised new questions and concerns. Andragel tried to say something, but he was cut off with more pressing thoughts of the god-siblings.

"We are still losing in this war," shouted Amun-Ra to the sea of gods. "And it will only end with us dead or returning back to our state of oppression."

"I agree," Poseidon said unexpectedly. "I say we stay in this galaxy and fight to make our stand here." The last comment sent the gods in an uproar, splitting some in agreement with what Poseidon said, while the rest disagreed with his proposal. Andragel placed his left hand on his forehead and sighed because he just cautioned his siblings not to fight and here some of them were shouting for galactic warfare. Again, Andragel raised his hands in an attempt to pacify the rage of the crowd, but he was again cut off.

"I say we stay and fight—or else we will always be on the run," Auset said, while flying with her colorful wings carrying upward for all to see. "Plus, we have an advantage—we have the black phoenix." Everyone turned toward the black phoenix, who stood towering over many of her siblings, and looked at everyone steering at her.

"No," she said plainly.

"No to what?" Auset asked the dark phoenix.

"No! I will not participate in this sudden call for warfare involving the guardians."

"The guardians will fear the black flames—"

"Yes, the power of the dark fire could potentially change the fate for our sake, sister, but the dark flames should not to be used for warfare. This fire has life."

"All fires have life," Zeus replied to the black phoenix.

"No, brother, the black fire is not another fire with life. It breathes, thinks, and grows just like us. It is an actual being, a spirit, which existed long before any of us danced across the celestial skies. The dark flames have seen many things beyond our comprehension and taught me many mysteries that could never fall into the wrong hands, but the dark fire saw it fit to teach me these mysteries of eminent power. A daughter banished with a disgraceful name and nowhere to call home, and yet the dark fire made me one of the few disciples in the Omniverse and the first phoenix to ever possess black fire. So apologies, I cannot be a part of this warfare. For my participation will not only consume me in the process but bring great shame to the spirit of the dark fire and a new disgrace to my name. Again, forgive me."

"That will be just fine sister," Andragel replied to the black phoenix. "Because there will be no warfare of any sort. Must I remind you all, again, we are still under the laws of the High Council of Alliance, which govern the many galaxies, far and nigh. For these laws are the sole reason we are all still alive and able to travel to certain galaxies for temporary refuge."

Andragel sighed to himself as he looked around at the fallen brothers and sisters and felt rush of regret. If only he could go back in time and go about his pursuit a bit different, but such was not fate. The elder brother looked into the eyes of all his siblings and saw a flashback to the moment leading up to the War of Gods—the Great War that changed everything and everyone. A war that turned children into gods, a war the gods continued to fight internally to this very moment.

Andragel knew this war was far from over, even though deep inside he wanted it all to end. To end fairly, of course. However, this *end*, they were heading toward was not the ending that he nor any of his fallen brethren wanted. It was going to end in the favor of the High Council, and not in the favor of the Children of the Fallen. Andragel looked into the eyes of those who had courageously fought with him in the Great War, and he saw their fates. The spirit of fear crept into Andragel's body and mind. He could hear the voices telling him to give up, but when he looked out into the crowd and saw how much his siblings have grown since their expulsion. A sense of hope flickered inside him. This fight was bigger than him, which meant he had to be more patient for their sakes. He knew that fate itself could not be trusted, so it was time to take matters into his own hands and steer fate in the most promising direction. Andragel looked at all his siblings and felt a new life surging through himself, because he was too close to introducing a new era of gods where his banished siblings could live in peace, and all he had to do was secure his permanent seat at the High Council.

"The time for change is now," Andragel said breaking his silence, causing conversations to cease. "The time for change is now and no one is going to give it to us, so this is why we must stay on our course and not draw too much unnecessary attention. It is time we change the narrative of the High Council whenever they discuss any topic concerning us, they will speak of the rise of gods rather than rebels. The High Council will not only learn but proclaim how we stood up to the injustice rather than allow 'the Head of High Council' to govern our

every decision. We will be the lights in this dark and vast Omniverse to reveal the surreptitious lies of the High Council—especially the Head of the High Council. The time has come for us to converge as we once did in the days leading to the War of Gods and continue this fight till the end. This path was not an easy, nor desirous, but it gave us the motivation to keep moving forward and become who we are today at this moment. We have shown the other realms in the many galaxies that we would sit quietly on the injustices, but stand up boldly for what is rightfully ours. There was a time when we were once a family that shared similar values with the High Council, but now, I say look around at your new family. A family that requires unity in order to survive this ongoing war and see it to a satisfying end. It is time to rise up again and take control of our fate." The elder brother picked his head to point upward and said, "The whole Omniverse, along with the High Council, must know of our renown." Then he bowed his head and said, "Let's not disappointment each other."

The words of hope gave the god-siblings the motivation they needed to stay strong and be patient, while they placed their faith in their new ambassador. Androgel was their only hope to find a galaxy to call home, and he was their hope to prevent war across the galaxies. He watched as his brothers and sisters made their departure in cheerful spirits, it dawned on him. His mission was possible as he reflected on how far he came from the days of the Great War. Andragel knew that he was almost there, just had to be a bit more patient. He knew this as more of the Children of the Fallen took their leave from the Parthenon, and the Olympians remained.

"I take it that you could explain the fall of the Grecian Empire and the rise of the Roman Empire," Hera said to Andragel as he drew closer to her.

The elder brother looked at Hera and then at the other Olympians. "The rise and fall of these empires are distractions for you all. Do not get so caught in humanity's affairs, for their matters are futile compared to us regaining a new status—which is something I am trying to change with my seat at the High Council." He turned to walk out of their presence, but before he could, a new thought entered his mind. "Oh yes—among the various realms, I've heard much chatter about this god and his interactions with the guardians in different galaxies. For his defiance to respect the galactic laws is drawing unnecessary attention."

This new information caught the Olympians off guard. They all searched themselves, but no name of such a god came to mind.

"An anthropomorphic being your daughter, Athena, was intimate within time's past to be more precise," their Elder Brother continued, with a smile on his face. "I believe the correct term is—*new gods!*"

Zeus sighed and nodded his head. Hera turned to Andragel and asked, "I believe you seek after the god that wields the *four serpents of time?*"

PART II

AMONG FAMILY

CHAPTER 5

MOMENT ON A CLIFF

[Mykonos Island / Aegean Sea, 29 AD]

As Teraditus reached down to pick up his golden lyre, he thought to himself, *Life truly comes with its share of ups and downs.* Teraditus's mind slowly slid back in time while his eyes and hands admired the godlike artisanship of the cleverly designed instrument. At this time of the year, the Mediterranean Sea tended to have a gentle roar as it grasped at the rocks near the cliff. It was the calm moments such as this that drew Teraditus, on numerous occasions, back to the cliff in order to enjoy the serenity and beauty of the isles of Mykonos. With his mind meandering down memory lane, his fingers began playing a musical selection that no human ear had ever heard. However, this piece was not of Teraditus's own creation; it was a sound familiar to the inhabitants of Olympus.

The moment of peaceful contemplation came to a stop with the sudden presence of a strong sea breeze. Teraditus placed his lyre down and staggered to his feet to have a better view of the light blue sea.

A MOMENT ON THE CLIFF

"There's something in the air," Teraditus said to himself with eyes still on the horizon. "Something… doesn't feel right." This was the thought on Teraditus's mind as his spirit sensed something in the distance. He used his right hand to shield his eyes from the sun's rays, which gave him have a more lucid view of a small boat moving closer to the island. Happiness sprang up inside him like the sunflowers looking to the east to be kissed by the light from Apollo's sunrise. For he knew on that boat had precious cargo that sailed all the way from the shores of Rome.

Teraditus's eyes were still fixed in the direction of the sea as he snatched up his shepherd's staff. Then, again, he felt it: something dauntingly familiar, a past that would not depart from him. No matter how many times he tried, this feeling was a part of him. Suddenly, a serpent slithered up his right arm, and another up his left. Then, a third serpent slithered up his torso while another moved up his back. Teraditus watched as all four serpents converged around his neck. Four serpents, each with their own distinct color — onyx black, shimmering gold, emerald green, and ruby red — were revolving clockwise around his neck in perfect unison. One after the other, the serpents luminated from the radiant touch of the sun, which felt like a burning rope rotating around his neck.

A perplexed expression appeared on Teraditus's face. His muscles clenched in response to the burning sensation coiling about his neck. "Not again," he said incredulously while shaking his head from side to side with eyes closed. Suddenly, his head stopped swinging from side to side and he looked upward to see a man standing at the edge of the cliff. The man was adorned in white garments that majestically floated off his body without the touch of the sea breeze. "*Ah-ra-ma-nah*," Teraditus whispered with disdain and contempt. With one step, the being vanished from the edge of the cliff and reappeared right in front of Teraditus, then the man placed his right hand on the center of Teraditus's chest where all four serpents converged in cyclic unison. The being looked at Teraditus with eyes glowing like the sun, and said in the tongue of their mothers, "I will return, my child."

Suddenly, he was gone, leaving Teraditus with no strength in his legs. He collapsed to his knees, but the shepherd's rod he held broke his fall. Teraditus felt something dangling from his neck and realized the four serpents had become an amulet sitting on his chest. He took it off and examined the spherical, stone object, and saw his reflection inside the clear crystal quartz. With the amulet in his hand, he looked up and saw three slender clouds moving west across the sun. A sigh fell from his mouth as he stood up and returned the serpent amulet around his neck. He looked up to the sun again, and the same three slender clouds were still sailing to the west.

"Yes, he will return, but I can delay his return," Teraditus muttered. He began his journey back home while the sun continued its steady journey westward.

CHAPTER 6

OLD AND NEW FACES

Three hours had passed since that unexpected moment on the cliff, and still the house was not to Teraditus's satisfaction. "This isn't right," he said to himself. The table was embellished with orchard-picked fruits, wheat bread, scented-oil candles, a vase from Athena filled with fresh-cut lavender flowers, and silver utensils to complete everything. However, something was missing, even though the table was overflowing with items. Teraditus stepped out of the cellar with a feeling of reprieved because of what he held in his hands: two dark glass bottles plugged with wooden corks. The corks failed to smother the potent smell of the fermented grapes, which now infused Teraditus's clothes and hands. *It's no Dionysus's wine, but it will do,* Teraditus thought to himself as he made his way back to the table.

Teraditus placed the bottles on the north and south ends of the table. He adjusted the vase and scented candles in the middle of the table, and yet something *still* felt like it was missing. This seemed crazy since the table was already full, but Teraditus still felt something was missing. He looked around, but still couldn't figure out *what* that was exactly. That's when he knew his paranoia and stress had finally kicked in, so he took a seat at the table and closed his eyes to breathe in and out. He did these five more times: a common calming technique that Teraditus's wife often reminded him to do when the stress of life overwhelmed him.

His eyes still closed; the thought of his wife brought Teraditus back to a time when his whole family was all under the same roof. He started to recall moments: when each of his children had learned to walk, their first words, and all the interactions his children had with their mother. He remembered how, in their juvenile days, his children would cry out in agony for her whenever they got a bruise or a cut. Bedtime stories had been some of the best times in this house, especially with the stories their mother knew. Those moments were some of her favorite times with the children; it was her chance to tell her imaginative stories based on real-life events, and no matter what the story was about, she always had the children's full attention.

Teraditus sighed as he opened his eyes and said to himself, "She even had my full attention, and I never told her." With his hands covering his face now, he broke out in a soft chuckle as he remembered a time when he had to save his wife from a spider she had sighted while tending to their olive and peach orchards. She was hysterically frantic over it. Her reactions often amused both him and the children, especially as she had a reputation of placing fear in the hearts of numerous men in her past life when she was a prisoner of Athena. However, she was truly something special like a rare diamond. From the sound of her voice to the touch of her skin, Teraditus knew not of a moment wasted with his wife, for he understood the value of life and how unwise it was for man to not take advantage of it.

Teraditus remained in his chair, now staring aimlessly at Athena's vase in the center of the table. Teraditus's mind, still preoccupied with his wife, wandered into a new direction. This memory took Teraditus to a moment when she would bring freshly picked lavender flowers into the kitchen to be trimmed and pruned for Athena's vase.

Teraditus remembered how he would walk over to where his wife was with the flowers and hug her by her waist. With his hands tenderly embracing her, Teraditus would bury his face on the side of the head — where hair often covered her ears — in order to smell the rich aromas of frankincense and myrrh from Assyria on her fair skin. His wife would giggle and try to show him away. He would take a few steps away before she grabbed his hands and yanked him back toward her for a more sensual embrace.

The tenderness of his wife's embrace kept Teraditus in a trance. He recalled the sensual games she played by having him figure out which scented oils she had put on her skin. In these games Teraditus was never able to get the scent right, except for one afternoon. Fate was in his hands and he figured out the scent, and on that day their fourth child was conceived. The aroma was a mixture of scented oils, but the main ingredient was a flower called *Cassia*. And it was from that flower that their second child was named Cassiani.

"Grandpa!"

Teraditus snapped out of his trance and made his way to the main entrance of the house. Before he could open the door, Teraditus heard a baby crying and a young woman trying her best to calm the flustered infant.

Teraditus swung the door back and examined the image of his younger self in his grandson. "Grandfather, how have you been?" asked the smiling teen.

"Rellos, my boy, you've grown so much," Teraditus said to the young man as the two embraced each other with a hug and a kiss.

"I want you to meet my new wife, Allidephi, and our baby boy, Diodotus," Rellos said as he guided the mother and child to greet Teraditus.

"It is truly a pleasure to finally meet you," Allidephi said as she handed over the infant to Teraditus. He took the baby into his arms and stared tenderly into the child's glassy, hazel eyes.

Diodotus peered back with great curiosity, as if to ask, "*Who are you?*" Teraditus placed a finger into the child's palm, and the child instantly held onto it.

"Diodotus—*Giver of Zeus*! I must admit, that's a creative name," said Teraditus as he looked into the mother's bright blue eyes.

"Father, how's life treating you on this island?" a voice asked.

Teraditus looked up to discover the youngest of his children, his son Apollos, struggling to take some bundles off a cart. Teraditus carefully handed the infant back to the new mother and walked outside. As he approached the cart to lend a helping hand, his daughter-in-law leaped out from behind it and greeted him with a hug and warm-hearted kiss.

"My dear Seleni," said Teraditus as they were still in each other's arms.

After the hug, Seleni held onto Teraditus's arm and said, "You look very well for a man of your age. It's truly been too long."

"It truly *has* been too long," Teraditus said, followed by another hug.

Their embrace ended when a crate fell from the cart and briefly startled the brown spotted horses.

"Father, please help before something really breaks," Apollos said at the back of the cart, while the driver rushed over to check on his horses.

"Hey, Rellos, come over here and help too," Teraditus said as he lent a helping hand to unload a rather ancient cherrywood chest covered in a white cloth.

"Thanks, Father—Rellos is no help all time..."

"He's just excited," said Teraditus as he reached for the crate. "Apollos, my son, I didn't know you'd become a grandfather."

Apollos leaned in closer to the cart and lowered his voice, "I'm still not used to it myself. Rellos is barely in his twenties, and he thinks himself a full man. He can barely hold a job because he lives life too carefree."

Rellos finally made it over to the cart with a credulous smile on his face and picked up a crate near the ancient chest. Then, he said to both

Teraditus and Apollos, "Man, this is heavy, if only there was an entry section where we could bring the cart inside the house, offloading would not be so strenuous."

Teraditus raised an eyebrow and stroked his white beard. "That's not a bad idea, if you help me build this new idea of yours. The house can be yours when my time is no more in this realm," Teraditus said as his son looked at him with an air of disbelief.

"Grandfather, are you serious?" Rellos asked.

"Are you serious?" Apollos echoed before Teraditus could respond.

"Yes, I am serious," Teraditus said with a smile.

"You know what? I will consider this offer, just... just let me speak to Allidephi," Rellos said before running off empty-handed.

Apollos looked at his father, who was still stroking his beard. "The offer will not come to pass, since Rellos is not committed to anything that requires laborious work. Nevertheless, Seleni was right about you aging well. Is the touch of Olympus still with you?" Apollos asked.

The question caught Teraditus off guard as he turned to look at his son's light gray eyes. "I was touched long before I walked the grounds of Mount Olympus," Teraditus explained to Apollos. "I was touched in the days when gods and giants roamed the world and ruled from the land of Mesopotamia."

Apollos stopped what he was doing and looked at his father. "The days of Mesopotamia were a long time ago..."

"They were."

"And you're telling me that you were there when Mesopotamia was an empire?"

"In another body and time," Teraditus answered.

Shaking his head in disbelief, Apollos said, "Some of these tales sound like myths or tales mothers tell their children before bed—just like the tales of the *First Five*."

"I tell you, Apollos, those are no tales of myth," Teraditus replied with conviction. Then he added, "Time truly flies."

Teraditus reached out to grab a woven basket that was on the crate and placed it on the ground. Then he looked up at his son to see a hint of brown surrounding the pupils of his eyes. "Truthfully, those gods will be good to you as well, as they were to your mother and I. Keep in mind, Son, that Telus now walks among these gods now. Life has been good to this family, I can say with certainty. Trust me, time will tell. It always does." After a minute of reflection, both men sighed to indicate they accepted these words of assurance.

After a few minutes, all the necessary items were off the cart and the driver walked over to hand a crate to Teraditus. Teraditus took the crate from the driver and had a few words with him. They laughed and hugged, and then the driver said his farewells and disappeared down the path. Everyone started carrying items inside, including the new mother with her son in her arms. In the midst of this activity, a young, white-haired woman with soft, green eyes came jogging up the path and yelled her greetings to the family.

Apollos and Seleni raised their arms and waved to the young woman approaching them.

"Hey, Priscilla, you came just in time, my love," Teraditus said to her. "Did you get what I sent you into town for?" he asked while she was still panting.

Priscilla answered breathlessly, "Yes... I did. And, I got a special treat... also." The smile on her face brought joy to everyone, especially Diodotus. "That's good, my child," Teraditus said to her. "Okay, everyone, let us get settled indoors." Everyone grabbed what remained and made their way inside, and Teraditus closed the door behind them.

CHAPTER 7

FELLOWSHIP AMONG FAMILY

O nce everyone had settled into their various accommodations, Teraditus shouted for everyone to sit at the overcrowded table. Priscilla was already there with him, a welcoming smile was on her face. The sound of footsteps became louder as everyone approached the dining area. In the blink of an eye, the family was eating, drinking, and socializing. Teraditus sat at the head of the table, watching and listening to all that was transpiring around him, while Priscilla scurried back and forth, aiding those as best as she could.

The atmosphere quickly filled with a sound Teraditus had not heard for a while: family laughter. "Father, father, remember when the skunk chased Mother, and you ran out to see what the commotion was about? And once you saw what it was, you quickly did an about-face and ran away from Mother to head back into the house."

Teraditus shook his head while the sound of laughter increased.

"And then, and then... Mother screamed out." Apollos's voice rose in tone to reflect that of his mother: "*Noooo, don't go in the house, don't go in the house!*"

Teraditus covered his mouth with the back of his hand to prevent the food from flying out. It was too funny to see how Apollos was able to emulate his mother's voice so easily; he had truly inherited her skills of telling a captivating story.

"Somehow, somehow," Apollos continued, "you two made a quick dash into the peach orchard, and all we could hear were the screams of Mother, and you yelling at her to keep running."

The laughter and banging on the table became so tumultuous that it shook the dining room. "Please, Apollos, you're killing us. I beg you, stop, stop," Seleni said with tears in her eyes.

Teraditus turned to Seleni to say, "The story isn't done—"

"Yeah, there's more—please, I am almost done," Apollos said after cutting off his father. "Now, we were all laughing in the house when we realized what was chasing Mother, and now Father. Next thing we knew, Telus — who was beside us the whole time, staring at the distress outside — suddenly ran outside with a bucket of water. Telus moved so quickly that no one noticed when he left our side, or where he had even gotten that bucket. Nevertheless, he was outside with a bucket in his hand and yelling at Father and Mother to run in his direction. Both of them ran around the house one time to see if they could gain some distance, while the skunk trailed them all the way to the front of the house again, where Telus was waiting. As soon as he saw the skunk, he threw the murky water—as well as the bucket, by accident—onto the skunk."

Everyone in the house stopped laughing and opened their mouths in amazement. The story had taken a new turn, and everyone at the table except for Diodotus were riveted in suspense. Apollos continued, "Even Mother and Father's turmoil ceased when they realized what Telus had done. He later said that he watched the skunk's pupils expand and all the hairs on its body stood up like a terrified cat . We couldn't see its crazy eyes, but we all saw the skunk's hairs standing upright, Father?"

Teraditus nodded slowly in agreement and said, "When your mother and I saw that, we knew Telus was in danger. That's when your mother screamed out, '*Run, Telus, run!*' That boy sprinted so fast around the house two times with your mother now chasing after the

skunk, who was now chasing Telus. Unfortunately, mom was no match for the speed of either of them. We all watched Telus sprint down the path that led into town with the skunk on his heels and your mother running behind them."

The table was filled with laughter as they visualize the entire scenario. "I decided to chase them down using one of the horses, but by the time I found them. It was too late, since both Telus and your mother were soaking wet and smelled awful. I asked your mother what happened, and she told me while still laughing with exhaustion: Telus decided to jump into the sea, and the skunk jumped in after him. It was in the water, Telus saw that the skunk was not going to make it, so he helped the skunk back to the shore where your mother was waiting. Soon as he made it onto the land, your mother ran to over to them and the skunk sprayed them both before it walked into the sunset."

Teraditus took a slip of his drink and said, "Your mother broke into tearful laughter as she held onto Telus outside the house," Teraditus said as he was finishing the story. Laughter soon filled the room again, while the house was vibrating with life once again. Teraditus tried to catch his breath when he suddenly felt another presence in the room. Teraditus turned his head to the doorway leading to the kitchen, where he saw Telus smiling at everyone.

"This tale never gets old, huh, Father? Nevertheless, it is incredibly good to see everyone," Telus said. Priscilla flew off her chair and quickly wrapped her arms around the well-built body of the man.

"Telus, it is so good to see you! My goodness, you look well," Priscilla said as she turned to everyone at the table with her arms still tucked in Telus's arms. "Doesn't he look well?" she playfully asked everyone. Murmurs of agreement filled the room. Telus broke the awkward moment by freeing himself from Priscilla's grasp and greeted everyone one by one. Priscilla gave Telus the chair she had been sitting on and disappeared through another doorway, only to return with another chair in her hands.

"Father, you're filled with endless stories," Telus said with his sturdy voice resonating throughout the table whenever he spoke.

"No, Apollos was the one telling the story—I just jumped in for a while," Teraditus replied. "But you have to admit, it's a fitting story," he added with a smile. That's when the expression on Teraditus's face changed. "Plus, you seem to be missing your better half."

Telus tried to hide his smile and responded, "She had to take care of a matter with the Alpha of the Omegas—"

"I see, say no more," Teraditus replied. "Furthermore, I'm sure we all spoke and ate to our hearts' content—"

"*Wait, no!*" Allidephi screamed out unexpectedly, which caught everyone by surprise and startled her child out of slumber. Diodotus had managed to sleep through all that excessive laughter, but he woke up the moment he sensed his mother's distress. "I'm terribly sorry, everyone, but I want... no, I need to... I heard so many tales about you, Teraditus, so I'm just a bit anxious to hear more. Apologies if I seem overbearing."

Something in Allidephi's voice made Teraditus smile inside. "I understand your curiosity—it reminds me of my wife." Both sons raised their left eyebrows the same way Teraditus did when he heard or saw something unusual.

"I know that I'm someone new, along with my son, but it's not every day I get to meet someone such as yourself," Allidephi said quietly.

Teraditus nodded in agreement.

"Please," she continued, "you must understand why I am eager to hear more of these tales. I'm a bit of a scribe, and these are the kind of tales. I want to write them down, so that they never die and continue to live on long after we're gone."

Her passion to hear these stories left an impression on Teraditus and the others. "Since the sun is down, let us call it for the evening," Teraditus said. "Tomorrow will be a new day, with new tales to tell."

Everyone agreed as the sun dipped below the western horizon.

CHAPTER 8

THE STORY BEGINS

The next day arrived with the sun slowly peeking its head out from the east. At that very moment, a rankled rooster flapped its wings in preparation to give its morning call. However, the rooster sensed another presence in the midst, so he looked down to see Teraditus with a grin on his face.

"*Puccccaaaaaac!*" the rooster screamed, as to say, "*Noooo!*" The rooster flew off the top of the house and stared firmly into Teraditus's eyes before strutting away.

Allidephi heard the excitement from the rooster and dashed outside to see Teraditus watching the rooster walking away. "What happened to the rooster?" she asked.

Teraditus, still facing the feisty rooster, laughed before he said humorously, "This rooster is a part of a long line of many roosters that have tried to sound their morning call before I, or anyone else, woke up; but I always beat them to it." He turned around and smiled at the young mother. "They have greatly despised me, because I always know when and where they're going to sound their morning call." Teraditus laughed as he approached Allidephi. "They are probably thinking this behavior is outlandish for a human, and it is—but there is just a sense of satisfaction from seeing the rooster's frustration, which makes my day."

Allidephi now understood the reason for the rooster's loud shriek; however, she continued to listen to Teraditus's words. "I ought to stop doing that, since I'm getting too old, but it is too much fun," he said and laughed, while he near to Allidephi. "My behavior has driven these roosters insane—once to the point that it actually *killed* the very first rooster who noticed my peculiar behavior. At first, this rooster interpreted my early morning appearance as just an amusement. Then, slowly, he realized that months had passed, and I was still out every morning before he could sound the morning call. The rooster decided to change his location, but I always knew where he was. Then the madness slowly grew, because the message was becoming clear about the one thing that made him feel useful: *We don't need you for the morning call!*"

The two made their way inside and toward the kitchen area to have a seat at the table filled with so much, but two oinochoe pitchers were the only items that stood out. Particularly for Allidephi, who undoubtedly noticed the ancient Minoan artwork painted on the ebony colored pitchers. "I tell you, the very first rooster started coming up with creative ways to outsmart me," he continued, "but it always failed. One time, he went as far as breaking into the house in the middle of the night, but he often fell asleep, only to be awoken by my angry wife shooing him outside. The rooster even involved other roosters to help him with his dilemma. They quickly picked up on my odd behavior, and thus began the linage of the roosters' movement.

"The first rooster, along with a group of other roosters, came up with insane and yet creative tactics. They broke into the house to eat up our food, hide garments, break glassware, attack Telus on a regular basis, play with Cassiani, steal and hide silver utensils, and basically frustrate us every day. My wife lost it when these mad roosters broke into our home every night for a week, shrieking all night long. Nobody got to rest

that whole week. These roosters came from all over, even from the neighbor's yard. The next week, my wife made sure I stayed in bed while all the roosters sounded the morning call. For the remainder of that week, the entire house shook every time those mad roosters sounded their call. The mad rooster had won that battle."

"These tales will never grow old, especially when you're telling them." Telus's powerful voice caught Allidephi by surprise, but when she laid her eyes on him, she blushed. Telus was shirtless and very muscular. She opened her mouth to greet him, but when she beheld Telus in the sunlight. She saw a glimpse of something that seemed godlike or supernatural: his defined muscles throughout his sculpted body; his sleek, midnight-black hair; and something else unexplainable, like a breath-taking aura that intensified with each step Telus took toward them.

The closer Telus got to Allidephi, his presence was becoming more and more overwhelming for her. However, her eyes never left his white, porcelain teeth and smooth caramel skin. Telus sensed the amorous attention and caught her before she slipped off her chair. Allidephi was a bit in a daze for a minute or two, only to recover to see Telus's full, tricolored eyes staring back at her.

"Are you okay?" Telus asked Allidephi, as if his voice was vibrating through her entire body.

Before she could reply, she felt the sensation of his tender-yet-firm skin as she tried to adjust herself in his arms. When Allidephi saw a peculiar symbol of a female deity with wings on the right side of Telus's chest.

"Is this the goddess Isis?" she asked.

"Yes, our queen goddess, Auset, is what she is also called," Telus replied.

The young mother carefully examined the tattooed symbol on his chest; her fingers gliding across the rainbow-colored wings of the Nubian goddess. "The design of this image is so flawless. Never have I seen such exceptional artwork before. It's as if her power beams through this very image," Allidephi said without thought—just pure observation.

Telus picked up Allidephi to place on her feet, but the intoxication of Telus's presence had already engulfed her. However, she sensed that she had said something wrong, judging by the expressions on the faces of both men. "Apologies, I have crossed the line—"

"No, no," both men responded to her apology with a smile.

"You're a very intuitive young woman," Teraditus said to her, "but it is vital to remember that your intuitiveness is limited to this time and place."

She nodded in agreement, and then turned and whispered to Telus, "Apologies, again."

Telus smiled and laughed at Allidephi and whispered back, "It's okay."

His words provided a temporary moment of solace; however, it did not take away her feeling that she had overstepped some boundaries again as she sat back down in her chair.

"I recall the days when I continuously sought counsel from one of the many high priestesses who sojourned from the Oracle at Delphi in Corinth," Teraditus began. "These Venuses, who were also referred to as the 'black doves of the gods,' were all daughters of the Nubia, Kush, and Egypt. Therefore, their counsel was most required at a particular point in my life in Sparta. These were the days before King Leonidas and his three hundred Spartiates, the elites of the royal guards, fought King Xerxes the First and his Persian armies at Thermopylae."

When Allidephi heard those words from Teraditus, all guilt departed from her, and the curiosity to know more was rekindled. "Wait, what did you say?" she questioned. Teraditus laughed to himself. "You speak of days long before Alexander of Macedonia," she continued, which caused Teraditus to nod his head in agreement.

"I remember his days of reign. His armies were swift, and he made his gods on Olympus proud," Teraditus shared with the yellow-haired mother.

"How could you," Allidephi whispered at first. "How could you have possibly been around in those days, and still be here?" she asked in awe.

This was the question Teraditus was waiting for, and he had an answer. "I walked among *gods*. That's the quick answer, or would you prefer to hear the story from the beginning?"

"The second option of course," Allidephi responded without giving herself a second to spare. Teraditus laughed for he knew she was in for a long, long story.

"Your son needs you," said Telus randomly.

Allidephi turned in the direction of the doorway in time to hear the crying baby. She glanced back at Telus, who had a smirk on his face as he drank from his copper cup, while Teraditus closed his eyes and laughed softly.

"How did you know?" she asked with a mystified whisper.

Allidephi excused herself from the table, while Telus said to his father, "Might want to get the door."

Now a bewildered expression was on Teraditus's face as Telus left the room. Teraditus walked to the front door to open it, and immediately sensed something in the air. He took a deep breath, opened the door, and then opened his arms wide with his eyes closed. Before he could exhale, someone rushed into his arms and held on tight. When he opened his eyes, he was met with the sight of a stunning young woman in his arms. "If Telus did not say anything, you would've never known. You're really losing your touch, my love," the young woman said to Teraditus in a silky voice as she batted her eyelashes.

Teraditus just stared at this woman, deep into her blue, green, and gray eyes. "Speechless?" the young woman asked him.

"It's good to see you, beautiful," he replied. "How are you?" The young woman squeezed Teraditus tighter as she blushed and laughed.

She buried her face into his chest as the sunlight lit her brunette hair with a golden sheen. She sighed as her head rested on Teraditus's chest and massaged his back. "I remember when you enjoyed my back rubs," she said. "It seems like you could use one right now."

Teraditus calmly laughed and replied, "Another time, my love."

The young woman broke out into giddy laughter and sighed again. "It's so good to see you," she reiterated.

Teraditus took his two hands off the young woman's back as he stepped back to give his hands the chance to hold her chin affectionately. As Teraditus stared into her tricolored eyes, he said, "I've truly missed you, Ena."

Ena smiled and blushed when she heard those words, because the feelings were mutual. Teraditus bent his head closer to Ena's face to kiss her caringly on her forehead—the same way a mother would do with her newborn—while a light wind passed by that blew her fishtail braided hair.

When the moment of shared memories ceased, Ena sighed with her eyes closed and said, "I despise how moments such as this one can so easily come and go." Then she opened her eyes, which now had a longing in them, and she said to Teraditus in a bothersome tone, "It always seems so temporary for us. The moments we shared always seemed so minimal, as though fate did not want us together." She sighed again and without a plan or much thought, they both said together, "*Fate!*"

The two glanced at each other before they started laughing sincerely. "I miss this," Ena said to Teraditus with a hint of care in her eyes. "I miss the whole unison thing... I miss *us!*"

Soon after, a sigh fell from Teraditus's chest. "Ena," Teraditus softly. Ena calmed herself by closing her eyes, and Teraditus did the breathing technique his past wife would often remind him to do in stressful situations.

When Ena opened her eyes, she smiled politely at him. She held on to his hand and lifted it to her nose to smell the familiar scent of his skin. She caressed his hand with the warmth of her cheek.

"I don't think you understand how it feels to see you again, and to hold you, too," Teraditus told her.

Ena blushed as she pulled herself closer to Teraditus's body to rest her face on his chest again. "Do you still love me, Teraditus?" she asked. Teraditus was unprepared for this question, while both of his eyebrows rose up. Ena could not see the surprised expression on his face, but the jolt from his body she felt was enough. She decided to look up with a longing to know. "Well, do you, Teraditus?"

Teraditus knew the kind of response she wanted to hear—the truth—but would his truth suffice? "Yes, I do," he began.

"'You do' what?" she asked.

"I do love you dearly. We both know our story, and only we could tell it, my love. For I was and will always be there for you as long I live. What you've done for my family and I... we are truly grateful for it. And if I could repay you, it would be through Telus."

They both laughed hysterically at the truth behind the last comment.

"However, I do... I do love you," Teraditus said caringly. Serenaded by these words, Ena extended herself forward to kiss Teraditus, and he kissed her on the forehead once more.

Telus came outside on time to see more than he wanted to see. "Hey, Father, can I have my woman back now?"

They both turned to see Telus with his arms folded into each other and a displeased expression on his face.

"She's all yours, Son," Teraditus shouted cheerfully to Telus. "Just finishing up my greetings."

Teraditus finally unwrapped his arms from Ena's body, and made his way inside the house. Ena started to make her way to where Telus was standing with a look of simplicity on his face. "Are you sure you're done?" he asked.

Ena smiled coyly, wrapped her hands around Telus's muscular shoulders, and leaned in close to whisper, "I'm never done with him— that's why I have his son now."

Inside, Teraditus saw Priscilla gathering things here and there for the daybreak meal, so he quickly lent a helping hand. It didn't take long for Telus to make his way inside the house, but he was alone, with no Ena following behind him.

"Strange, where's Ena?" Teraditus asked Pricilla, but she was too busy body to hear him. Priscilla handed him a platter of sliced melons before moving on to her next task. However, Teraditus was lost in his thoughts, unaware that Priscilla was staring sternly at him with the platter of sliced melons in his hands.

"Oh, apologies, my child," Teraditus said to her, since he knew she knew he was daydreaming again.

Priscilla took the platter from Teraditus and handed it to Seleni, who smiled and said, "Rise and shine," before making her way to the table.

Teraditus made his way toward the table to see everyone already eating and drinking—everyone except for Ena, who was nowhere to be found. Priscilla was scurrying about, arranging the final few items on the table for the daybreak meal when she remembered one more item, so she returned to the kitchen area. Out of nowhere, an unexpected pitcher was handed to her, which startled Priscilla. However, the fear quickly turned to a smile, and she took the pitcher and returned to the table. Ena decided to help Priscilla, which Priscilla needed.

Ena slipped in and saw most of the family at the table eating. She said her formal greetings to all the recognizable faces from a distance. However, her focus was on Telus holding the baby in his arms, teasing him with a piece of breadfruit. Diodotus did not take the Telus's taunting too lightly. The infant's face scrunched up and he said a couple of baby words, which made Telus and Ena gasp in horror. The gasp caused everyone to redirect their focus to Telus and the baby, but Telus did not want any more tension between him and Diodotus. He gave the baby the piece of bread, and Diodotus bit it right out of his hand and growled like a baby pup. This shocked everyone—especially Telus.

Ena saw her chance and quickly swooped in right next to Telus. She took Diodotus into her arms. The touch of Ena's skin reminded Diodotus of his mother's touch, so he instantly gravitated toward her, and she to him. There almost seemed to be some type of spark between the two. The affection Diodotus received from Ena made him more jittery and talkative each time she fed him. Ena would respond back, which made Diodotus react with wild excitement.

More and more the baby boy was growing fonder and fonder with the new motherly touch. Allidephi, who sat across the table a few chairs down, was not impressed by the bonding; if anything, she was bothered by it all.

Ena looked at Allidephi and said, "This little man is a bundle of joy. I just want to eat him up and kiss him all day long." The baby started speaking to Ena, and she responded back with baby chatter. It brought smiles to everyone watching the two conversed back and forth. Allidephi, on the other hand, grew irritated with every passing second Ena held her son. She wanted her child back in her arms, but he seemed happier than he'd ever been with her, and that made her spirit uneasy.

"Greetings, my name is—"

"Allidephi! I know, your beautiful baby told me. Yes, you are, yes, you are," Ena said to the chatty baby. Allidephi was thrown off by Ena's statement.

"Ena was joking, she was joking," Teraditus said to Allidephi to make sense of things—when, in actuality, he knew Ena was not lying. Again, Allidephi sensed Teraditus's attempt to placate her. However, the mystery of who Ena was pressed on Allidephi's mind, and it was aggravated by how naturally Diodotus clung to her.

Allidephi sighed, and just assumed that Ena was an expert when it came to children. "You're very good with him—I guess motherhood is nothing new to you," she said to Ena.

"No children of my own," Ena replied before giving Teraditus a slightly judgmental glance. Allidephi, even more confused now, simply stared at the woman and child. What Allidephi did not know was that Ena had never had a child in her lifetime, but Ena's mother was the wisest when it came to infant care.

"How's the rise of the Amun-Ra's star going for everyone?" Apollos asked to strike up a conversation at the table. However, the silent feedback Apollos received was quite unwelcoming.

Teraditus picked up on the insipid response Apollos was receiving from the table, so he quickly brought up a familiar topic. "You know, I caught the rooster again."

Apollos shifted his head in his father's direction. "Father, no, not again. I thought we got rid of this problem." When everyone else at the table noticed the way Apollos had turned his head and responded to Teraditus, they knew another story was on its way.

"Earlier at sunrise, I was telling Allidephi about how it all began with the rooster, but I didn't delve into it much," Teraditus replied, then turned to Telus, who was shaking his head from side to side with an expression of annoyance.

"I'll never forget the passing away of the first rooster. All of Hades broke loose, and the wrath of the roosters was unleashed," said Apollos.

"That's not even the worst part," Telus followed after. "Father went to the burial ceremony surrounded by all the roosters and other birds on the island to watch another farmer bury this first rooster."

Those gathered around the table started laughing, and someone asked why Teraditus was at the burial ceremony. Teraditus laughed and said, "It was just amazing to see how this one rooster had united all the roosters against me."

A confounded expression appeared on Telus's face. "That's an understatement, Father," he said sarcastically. "All those roosters after the first one plotted against all of us in the house—especially me."

Apollos nodded his head in agreement and laughed. "Hate is an understatement— the roosters despised you the most, Telus," Apollos said and laughed again. "Whenever Cassiani fed them corn grains, they would chase her away instead of eating the grains. They walked over the corn bits and ate boldly from our orchards."

Everyone laughed except for Allidephi, whose focus was still on Ena and her son. As Apollos and Telus continued their humorous tale, Teraditus could not help but notice Allidephi's distant behavior; mentally, she was elsewhere. Teraditus reached over and touched Allidephi on her shoulder. She jumped and snapped her head to face him.

"Why don't we go somewhere else and talk more of what you've seen and heard since you arrived here?" Teraditus whispered in midst of laughter in the background. "Plus, you already heard the gist of this tale, and your baby boy is in good hands."

CHAPTER 9

HUMBLE BEGINNINGS

Teraditus and Allidephi got up and made their way to the back of the house. The sound of the family interacting with one another followed them until they reached the backyard. As soon as they stepped outside onto the open patio, the sunlight embraced them with its warm touch. The sun was two hours away from reaching the highest point in the sky, so life in the backyard was fully awake and tending to their daily activities: birds were singing in the trees, small creatures scurried around in the underbrush, and all manner of insects swayed from flower to flower. Moments like these calmed Teraditus's mind. "I always come back here to get away and remind myself to take it easy now and then," Teraditus said while Allidephi walked to the end of the patio and sat down on the edge of a stone wall, inhaling the splendor of it all.

"It's beautiful," Allidephi said calmly. "This view can make you forget about the problems of life and reflect on everything that's right."

"Father, Father," Telus called as he made his way outside, "I need you to clear up Apollos's vapid mindset. Who was the fastest runner among the five of us when we were growing up? Wasn't it me, Father?" Telus asked, while heavy footsteps made their way outside.

"Don't answer him, Father," Apollos objected. "He likes it when his ego is stroked."

"This is very true," Ena said, strolling outside, still carrying the baby, while Seleni stood near the patio's doorway, listening to everything. "But it's fine, I like stroking it," Ena continued as she winked at Telus. Telus smiled and shook his head from side to side, while everyone else started to laugh.

"Well, I'm not going to stroke his ego," Apollos replied to Ena before the two started bickering at each other to prove who was right and who was wrong.

Teraditus decided to sit down in his favorite outdoor chair while his sons debated endlessly. He simply wanted no part of this conversation, so waved his hand dismissively at his two sons, indicating just that. However, Teraditus knew that Telus had been the fastest runner, but when Luciano and Apollos became older. They fought endlessly to claim the title, which Telus tried relentlessly to maintain it—and he wasn't always successful.

Teraditus sat back in the sunlight and enjoyed the soothing breeze. Allidephi joined Teraditus in an adjacent chair, while Ena and Diodotus sat next to Allidephi. Ena held Diodotus by his waist with her hands, while the friendly Diodotus danced on Ena's lap with his stubby fingers in mouth, mumbling all manner of things. Diodotus then turned his head to see his mother, and he extended his arms, indicating that he wanted to be picked up by her. The sight of Diodotus desiring her attention melted Allidephi's heart. Ena observed this and handed the baby boy to his mother. Allidephi decided to take advantage of this opportunity to cuddle and kiss her son as much as possible before he desired Ena's touch again. With the baby out of Ena's arms, she decided to remove the diamond studs in her hair to make it easier to unwind her feathered fishtail hair braid, which was long, brunette and gleaming

under the early sunlight. Once Diodotus saw the new Ena, he started to stretch his arms to Ena again. This excited Ena, so she stretched herself over and took the baby boy from his mother—who just gave in to her son's desire to be with another woman by handing over to a very peculiar woman.

Allidephi watched her son bursting with new joy as he played with Ena's hair. A sense of abandonment from by her own son caused Allidephi to feel despondent and envious of Ena.

"Try not to look as though you were cast aside by your son. Ena has a way with children, because of who her mother is," Teraditus told Allidephi, while Seleni drew nigh to Allidephi's side and gave the young mother a comforting smile and hug. Ena got up with the baby to see where Telus and Apollos had disappeared to into the orchard, but before she walked away. She tossed Allidephi the diamond studs which she removed from her hair and in a charismatic tone, Ena said, "I hear they're a girl's best friend."

Teraditus was silent for a moment, gazing out at the landscape before him, while the two women examined the authenticity of the diamonds Ena gave to Allidephi.

"Now that I think about it, if someone had told me where my life would lead me, I would not have believed them," he eventually said.

"Why is that, Teraditus?" Allidephi asked as she looked intensely into Teraditus's face.

"I hope it is obvious to you that I am not fully Grecian," Teraditus said. "I mean, just take a good look at me. Have you ever seen an everyday, natural-born Greek man look the way I look?"

Allidephi and Seleni stopped to admire the darker skin tone of Teraditus's skin. "Well, the first inhabitants of the Greek lands were dark in their skin complexion, which is evident in the artistry of the Minoan civilization," Allidephi explained with self-assurance.

"You may have a point on that part," Teraditus replied with a simple nod.

"So where are you originally from?" Allidephi asked Teraditus in hopes of avoiding any irrational assumptions.

"He was born in the land of what Greeks today call Egypt, so he is an Egyptian," Ena responded, with her full focus still fixed on the playful, baby boy.

"Wait! Where did you come from?" Allidephi asked Ena, who she recalled disappeared a few minutes ago, but now sitting with Diodotus. Horrified as Allidephi was, she was still amazed at how Ena could be so engrossed with the baby, while staying in tune with the conversation. Allidephi stared at Ena for a good minute before she suddenly realized that there was more to Ena than what her eyes were showing her.

Teraditus noticed Allidephi observing Ena, so he quickly redirected her focus back to him. "Yes, I was born in the land of Kemet, just like my mother." Teraditus proceed to clasp his hands on his head and closed his eyes. "The Greeks are known for changing the names of people, especially when they cannot understand the tongues of a different nation," he said with a great burden. Allidephi nodded her head to indicate that she saw his point. "My father, on the other hand, was a traveling merchant from the east to the west, and to the north and the south. He told me he spent ample time growing up in the city of Zidon, which other Greeks call Phoenicia, meaning 'the land of the palm trees.' He also spent time in the city of Tyre as well, since Tyre and Zidon were neighboring cities. However, he never talked in great detail about his past life as a merchant, even though he was well respected by many other merchants by land and sea. However, it seemed he was not proud of about his past life being a merchant, as if he had sins he could not atone for, but in his days of fatherhood he was an exceptionally good man to my mother and me."

Rellos walked up a set of stairs leading up to the patio platform with a bucket of pears and peaches and placed them on the patio table. He sat next to his wife and offered everyone on the patio table a fruit of their choice. Both Teraditus and Allidephi refused Rellos's fruity offerings, but not Ena. She took a peach and bit into it, so she could chew the peach into smaller pieces for the baby to eat. Then she stuck the piece of chewed fruit out from between her rosy lips and offered it to the infant boy. Diodotus extended himself in order to reach Ena's lips so he could receive the peachy fruit. Diodotus squeezed his face and did a squirmy dance of joy, in reaction to the fruity sensation of the peach. The expression Diodotus exemplified was most the adorable sight for everyone, but Allidephi. Allidephi was not pleased since she had never thought about doing that with her beautiful, baby boy.

Rellos turned to his wife and said, "How come you don't do that with me?"

Allidephi looked into her young husband's eyes, and then reached out and held onto his face. "Now I know about it, I will, but Diodotus first."

"Fair enough," Rellos replied before he shared a kiss with her.

"Getting back to the topic, as I said, I was born in Egypt, or Kemet. However, in my early days, I grew up in the country of Libu, but near to the city you may know as Cyrene. Moreover, we lived a simple life, my father was a skilled fisherman, and that was how he supported his new family. Fishing was popular around those areas. I personally think that was another reason why the Greeks came to the city area. He taught me how to fish by observing the tides. He also recommended that the best time to fish was before sunrise. My mother taught me how to speak the tongues of Kemet and interpret their pictorial images often referred to as the *Metu Neter*, while my father taught me how to compose the letters of Zidonian." Teraditus sighed and continued, "Life was good growing up there. We had everything we needed and wanted, and it was a humble start to life. What more could a young man ask for? Anyways, where should I begin my story? Oh, yes! I know exactly where to begin— *on the shores where life and death met.*"

PART III:

THE SHORES OF LIFE AND DEATH

CHAPTER 10

ON THE OPEN SEA

[Cyrene/Libu - Ten Years Before the Battle of Thermopylae (480 BC)]

Teraditus, sweetheart, wake up! Your father is ready to go fishing. Get dressed quickly—you know how stern your father can be when it comes to being on time."

My mother's voice had the power to not only wake me from any slumber, but to rearrange my focus and, most of all, comfort me in my darkest moments. I knew my father's fishing routine like clockwork. He fished every weekday and took me with him every other day, starting with Monday. He never fished on Saturday, and rarely on Sunday. Today was Wednesday, and my father always got up extremely early in order to be on the Mediterranean Sea an hour before sunrise; his theory was the average creature begins their day at sunrise.

I quickly assembled the appropriate clothing to keep me warm on the open sea, and then gathered the remaining fishing gear my father often left to my care. Before I could reach the door leading outside, my mother called out to me.

"Ah, my young love, you know none of my men leave this house without giving me a kiss first. You know the deal."

"Ahh, mom, I'm too old for this," I replied as I dragged myself over to her. "One kiss," I proclaimed. My mother nodded before she wrapped her arms around me tightly, kissed me one, two, three, four, and five times. That's when I started squirming to break free.

"Hey, are you giving my sailor a hard time over there?"

My father's voice caught both of us off guard, and I struggled to reply, "Yes!" to his question, since I was still trapped in my mother's arms.

"So, what if I am giving this little sailor a hard time?" my mother asked. "Would you rather I give *you* a hard time?"

"No, I am good. The last time you gave me a hard time, my crew left the docks without me, and then your stomach grew," my father answered.

What my father said was very strange, because now that I was in my mother's arms, I could feel her stomach sticking out. When she freed me from her grasp, I saw that her stomach was bigger than unusual, and this was a strange look for her, since she typically had a tall and slender shape. I was quite amazed that I hadn't noticed until now.

"I wanted to tell you when the time was right, but now it has been brought to your attention," my mother said to me. "You're going to have a baby sister."

"What!" I replied in shock, my left eyebrow raised higher than the right. "How do you know it will be a girl and not a boy?"

"That's a good question, dear. Well, remember when we went to the city of Thebes in the land of Kemet last year, when my mother passed away and you saw your great aunt, Zipporah? Well, she was a midwife, and she taught me the basic procedure of childbirth. She also taught me an old wives' trick to observe a mother's stomach and see if it sticks out or drops down. If the stomach sticks out, it tends to mean the baby is a

girl, but if the stomach extends downwards, that tends to mean the mother will have a boy."

I nodded my head and just accepted what my mother told me, because she always knew best.

"Okay, my love, I think this young fisherman has heard enough about childbirth for today. Plus, it's time for the fish to have meal before sunrise," my father said to his wife. Mother smiled at us, and we all said our final farewells.

My father and I both made our way to the docks, and it only took an hour to get there. Once there, we saw our crew of five. Together, we were called "the *Wonders*," because of how abnormal our crew was and what we were always able to catch on a weekly basis. The crew had an old, retired Grecian captain who had lost his leg at war— as well as his voice, so we were told. Therefore, the crew called him Captain Mu—or, just for short, we called him Mu. He also had a wrinkled tattoo of a six-headed sea serpent that revolve clockwise on his right shoulder, which made him appear tougher than what he already was. We had another crewmember who was deaf in his left ear and blind in his right eye. We called him Blade since he was very skilled with knives, which explained the missing right eye. I assumed that at least, but deep inside I knew my assumption was probably wrong. Blade wasn't much for a talker, so any story revolving around him came from overhearing what others had to say about him. Stories that could never be confirmed, especially not from Blade himself. Nevertheless, the remaining crew consisted of my father, my mother's brother—my uncle, his son, Gershom, and me. Gershom and I were both ten years old, and thus the youngest crewmembers.

"We were *this close* to leaving without you guys," my uncle said while pinching the air with his right hand. Mu gave us a hard look, and then he too raised his right hand and pinched the air just like my uncle.

"We got it, Cap," my father said with his head moving up and down to show Mu that he understood his faults. In a span of two minutes, we had left the docks and were traveling to an area that Mu had directed us to since he knew the sea the best. The crew sat and chatted about their afternoons the day before. We sat till we saw the sun begin to poke itself above eastern the horizon.

"Here comes Ra! Guys, you know what to do—it's time for the good stuff," Gershom said with his head nodding up and down.

Then the crew started moving their heads the same way as Gershom, and they all shouted together, "*Oh yeah!*"

The "*good stuff*" was how Gershom referred to the chum, which my uncle and father made differently every week in hopes of outdoing the other. This competition between the two men made our crew's gave us edge and kept us thriving in the fishing business. The special concoctions of chums my father and uncle made had most fisherman on the costal line envying us, because they never understood fully what we put inside our chum that made most of our catches so successful. It's just a secret, a secret we vowed to take to our graves.

With the sun steadily ascending, the nets were cast into the Mediterranean Sea to sink to an adequate depth, and the chum followed afterward. We then waited, shivering cold, to see how long it would take until the tuna came up to feast; it usually took fifteen to twenty minutes.

My uncle had made the chum this time, so he was resolved to beat my father's record time of ten minutes and eighteen seconds to attract the first set of tunas. The countdown had begun as soon as the chum hit the dark sea. Everyone's eyes were steadfast on the swaying waters, especially my uncle and father, to see any sudden movement from one fish or a school of them. The moment one fish bobbed their head or opened their mouth, the time stopped and a winner was announced. The suspense was so intense that even sea fowls like the pelicans and seagulls often landed atop our boat to watch and see which fish would serve as their first meal of the day.

The net used was one of Blade's special designs. The net had miniature sized hooks on them that would catch and hold the massive

tunas from hopping out of the nets. Blade was another mastermind behind all the boat's peculiar apparatuses. As I came to think more about it, Blade was the mastermind behind all—if not all, then most—of the boat's peculiar apparatuses. He came from a long linage of metalworkers, artisans, and engineers. He had learned all his craftsmanship from his father and later on, swordsmanship from an uncle with a double life in Babylonia—a life which my mother shared with us last night. As the years progressed, for Blade, his inventions started to reflect his creativity and intelligence. He started making devices that made life better for himself and those around him. The story of Blade is truly a rich one that it needs its own chapter or two. "*Maybe three!*"

CHAPTER 11

FISHING CONTINUES

The breaking of dawn grew steadily brighter with each passing minute as we waited for the tuna to arrive. The sea breeze was firmly brisk that it made me long for the sun to warm these cold, stiff limbs of mine.

"*Thump!*" That was the seventh thump from Mu to let us know seven minutes had passed, and no sign of a jittery tuna. I turned to my left and looked up at Blade in awe. Blade was the closest person to an older brother figure for both Gershom and me. My father and my uncle knew, to a certain extent, about Blade's family's legacy of artisanship, as well as their dark history. However, this dark history was never held against Blade, nor blinded my father and uncle from his true potential and gifts, which is why they asked him to join them on their adventures on the open seas some years back. The addition of Blade to the crew, with his special abilities, was key to our success. We all knew it, and even Blade knew it, but he was too humble to admit it.

After twelve thumps from Mu's wooden leg, the massive tunas began springing up in the water with their gaping mouths and their tail fins fanning each other.

"*Blast*! You win again... yet again," my uncle admitted bitterly to my father while walking away and shaking his head in disbelief. "These losses of mine are adding up, aren't they?"

My father laughed, and then he turned to Blade and said, "Get ready." The net was on the side of the boat, connected to iron poles that worked by spinning the apparatus in a circular motion to pull the tunas into the boat. Blade had also made spears with very sharp hooks on the end, which were used to hold and pull the caught tuna into the boat. It would be years later in Athens where Blade's clever invention would finally become popular and inspire other fishermen to be more creative in designing their fishing spears.

Both my uncle and my father worked on revolving the net upward to scoop the tunas into the boat. Mu and Blade stood near the poles that pulled the net upward to help guide it, and they also kept the fishing spears nearby. Once the net scooped the tunas out of the water, my cousin and I would use our spears to guide the massive tunas onto the deck of our boat. Today's catch was bountiful, which meant the pay would be satisfying.

Twenty-four minutes later, the crew found themselves approaching the mouth of the bustling docks of Cyrene, where the cries of men were louder than any sea fowls. In the distance, our eyes beheld a peculiarly large sea vessel on the sunlit horizon. Still, some distance away from the docking port, the strong sea breeze noticed our presence on the open waters and quickly shifted itself to throw us off our course. My father at this point had two hands firmly clutched to the tiller of the fishing boat to steer the boat away from the opposing winds, while Blade controlled the boom of the mainsail by adjusting on the line of the mainsheet. The two men battled the fierce winds as the boat, with great determination, shifted right to left and left to right, but never straight.

"Hey, get the oars ready," my father yelled to us, "we may have to drop the sails in the next minute if I see no sign of the winds dying down." Gershom and I ran to the left side of the boat, while Gershom's father ran to the right side. There we loosened the oars from the inner walls of the hull to attach a rope to the handle of the oar, in order to prevent the oars from slipping off the edge of the hull to be lost at sea. Normally, my father would wait until we finished attaching the rope before dropping the sails, but the high winds forced his hands to drop early and the sails were no longer in use. That's when the winds started spinning the boat around and around. Blade rushed over to Gershom and me to lend a hand, while my uncle on the other side already had his oar in the waters, trying to prevent the boat from spinning back out to sea, but it was futile. The winds refused to let us journey to the docking ports.

Blade secured the oar to the hull and started to row along with Gershom's father. Mu, making sure the catch of the day remained on top of the net attached to the boat's floor and the mast. Mu snapped his fingers and Gershom and I turned to see Mu pointing to my father before indicating to the left. We gave Mu a nod and carefully maneuvered ourselves to where my father still held onto the tiller.

"Mu is suggesting we go left!" Gershom shouted to my father.

"I know," my father replied with his eyes slightly open, "but the winds won't let us go left. Instead, they are pushing us back out into the sea. So, it is up to Blade and your father to row us outward to the left. You two ought to give them a hand."

Gershom turned around and made his way to his father, with his hands shielding his face, and I did the same as I made my way to Blade. Before I reached Blade, he had already made room for me to sit between him and the hull of the boat. Since my head was more exposed than my body, my face received a breezy beating, which forced me to close my eyes and clamp my teeth to bare the loud roar.

"Hey, open your eyes and row," Blade said before he shrugged me to my senses.

I opened one eye first and felt the mild winds brushing across my face.

"What happened?" I asked Blade.

"We're moving to the left," he replied, while my feeble arms held onto an oar that Blade kept on rowing.

Blade was right, my father managed to steer the boat to the left by taking us back out into the open sea. Once he reached a certain distance where the winds were no longer a hindrance, the boat shifted back toward the docking port. But this time, the boat bearded to the left where the winds were not too harsh. A moment drew by as the wind permitted us to draw nigh and nigh, until the winds and the current decided to carry us inward. This gave Blade and my uncle time to rest and regain their strength once the mainsail was back up.

I got up from where I sat, and my attention was again directed to this peculiar ship docked at the port. It wasn't the largest boat I'd ever seen, cause I'd seen larger, but it was a ship I've never seen before. Mu snapped his fingers to get my attention and signal for me come over to him, so I could help him up from where he sat on the boat's floor. Once on his feet, I reached down to retrieve his walking staff, but he refused it and tottered over to the front of the fishing boat to rest both hands on the bow hull of the fishing boat. As we drew nearer, not only did the ship become clearer, but the sea breeze carried all manner of colorful scents. This was how we knew we were close to the docking port.

However, Mu looked deep in thought, as if he was reliving a life he once knew. I saw this behavior quite often with my own father to know this was happening to Mu at this very moment. A walk down memory lane was something all men experienced once their days of adventure were no more, and this was the case for everyone on this boat except for Gershom and I. With each rock and sway of the waters below, we moved closer and closer to examine this strange vessel. The first thing that caught my interest was the insignia of the six headed sea serpent revolving counter-clockwise on the mainsail.

THE GRECIAN NAVAL WARSHIP OFTEN REFERRED
TO AS *TRIREME*

The insignia was a fierce one, instilling a sense of fear to all those that saw these horror-stricken sails of a six-headed sea beast, which was similar to the tattoo on Mu's right arm. I turned back to Mu, who was more than unusually quiet at the sight of this ship. I couldn't understand why until I saw the Greek Key designs, also referred to as the *meandros*, that was visibly craved on the body of the ship.

"It's a Grecian ship," I said to myself, while taking a step closer on our fishing boat for a better view.

"Not only a Grecian ship, but a Grecian military warship called a *trireme*," my father said, standing on the left-hand side of me and steering intently at the ship.

"Is this a naval fleet from Athens, Uncle?" asked Gershom making his way to the right side of me.

"No," my father answered suddenly, "this one's from Sparta, but the Athenians are known more for their speed and strength with their own naval sea fleets, I should know firsthand."

"What do you mean?" asked Gershom.

"I had some unpleasant encounters where I could not outrun the fast and agile triremes of Athens, so the Athenian captured my crew and on all that I had on my boat."

"What happened? How did you escape? Did people die?" Gershom questioned with bright interest, but my father's smiled looked painful as he recalled such moments. Whenever I saw that expression on his face, I knew better than to be persistent, and wait until he wanted to share.

"Let's just say, I offered them a deal they could not resist," my father said with a wink to Gershom.

"What deal?" asked Gershom inquisitively. My father gave Gershom a questioning look, then me, and back to Gershom to answer his question with laugher.

"You boys are way too young to know in detail what that deal consisted of," he replied to Gershom's question with a smirk. "However, I will leave you two with words to remember. Always remember, when men have been at sea for so long, there are two things they long for—*rum* and *women*! Keep these words in mind as you two get older, it will open new opportunities and allow you to live another day, trust me."

"Did this deal with the Athenians have something to do with rum and women?"

"Like I said before, Gershom, it opens new opportunities," my father answered, self-assured. "And don't tell your mothers I told you these things, because men talk is for?

"Men!" All three of us said together in unison.

Gershom looked at me and shook his heads at my father, while he laughed to himself behind us.

"Anyway, it makes sense why Mu is acting odder than usual, these men of Sparta might be his comrades," Gershom said before Blade called for him, leaving to me to my father.

"Father, does this ship not resemble some of the merchant ships of Tyre?"

"They do, son," my father replied thoughtfully. "The Grecians have learned many things and replicated many things from the great cities and nations throughout the land of Canaan."

Since the trireme was a large sea vessel, it had a special docking site design for bigger ships. Therefore, the trireme had to be docked horizontally as opposed to the vertical docking the smaller sea vessels such as our fishing boat were accustomed to when it was time at one's assigned docking station.

"Take a look at the bronze ram right below the bow of the ship," my father said, pointing. "That part of the sea fleet is used to ram straight into other boats, sinking whoever stands to oppose them in the open sea." Gershom ran back to us in time to hear more of my father's vast knowledge, which had unknown depths.

"Can you two see the three levels of open spaces?"

"Yes!" replied both Gershom and me.

"All those open spaces are where oars extended out for the slaves, who they referred to in Grecian tongue as *helots*, to row the trireme at maximum speed, so they could slam straight into other boats—*BAM!*" yelled my father, while slamming his right fist into his left palm. "Down the ship would go, sinking into the deep sea."

"Whoa!" said Gershom, "those oars must be really long."

"Yes, the oars are very long and made from the strong timber of an oak tree."

"Look, I can see the helots from here," I said, pointing to the two men standing visibly to the edge of the trireme. "You see the sun reflection on their helmets?"

"No, son," my father said, taking a closer look, "Grecian soldiers are known as *Hoplites*, but these soldiers you're looking at right now are called *Spartans*." The word "Spartan" sent a startling chill down my spine. I wasn't sure why, but the moment I heard the word spoken by my father. I immediately sensed an unsettling familiarity with the word, but why?

"The trireme has eyes in the front and the back too," said Gershom, pointing in both directions. "What does it mean?"

"The ship has six pairs of eyes, two in the front, back, the sides of the hulls, and on the dock floors to represent the six-headed sea beast the Grecian often referred to in the Grecian tongue as *Hydras*."

"Fishermen," shouted Gershom's father, which drew our attention toward him. "We're about to dock, so get ready."

My father left us to help Blade, who was bouncing anxiously on the edge of the bow hull to jump onto the dock floors. I redirected my focus back to the Grecian warship, and wondered why were these Grecians here? I recalled some of the tales of my father's encounter with the militaries of various nations and empires in his early days as a traveling merchant. Tales of how he barely made it out alive and how vile men promised to seek vengeance on his name. I wondered if these men of war on their daunting naval fleet were here to fulfill their promise of vengeance. For I knew my father was a well-known merchant for his success on deliveries, but as my father would say, "Such successes did come with both friends and enemies, far and nigh—this is something you will come to learn in time."

My father would often remind me that all things would be revealed to me in time, but time took too long and waited for no one. My mother would often say this in response to my father.

"Hey, daydreamer, come and help us," Gershom shouted before he stooped down to pick up two tunas by the tail to place into the wheelbarrow to be wheeled off the boat and onto the dock floors. Instantly, I rushed over to my cousin to load the tuna when I heard the snap of Mu's fingers, so instead of reaching for the tuna's tail. I reached for his walking staff and tossed it over to him. Mu caught the staff with his outstretched arm and walked boldly off the boat onto the dock floors.

With the sun warmly resting on our backs, we all stopped what we were doing and watched Mu make his way over to the two men dressed in full military armor. From the red crests on top of their helmets to the bronze greaves that protected their shins and feet, the two men stood side by side in the spirit of oneness. The moment Mu stood in front of the two soldiers with their crimson cloaks proudly soaring off their shoulders, the two men tensed up in unison and tucked their nine-foot spears into their left arms — which held their massive, circular shields made of bronze — and greeted Mu with their liberated right hands by balling them into a fist and slamming them on their breastplates. Thus, revealing the muscular built in their right arms. Mu greeted them back in the same manner before their conversation began. During that entire encounter, I failed to notice the trade between Blade and a nearby fisherman known for hunting sea scavengers. Blade gave him two full crates of tunas for four crates mixed with lobsters, crabs, shrimps, clams, and scallops. Once the trade was over, Blade returned to our fishing boat so he could help in the filling up of the first wheelbarrow with the tunas before my uncle went away to fetch another wheelbarrow.

"Is that the lambda symbol on their shields?" Gershom asked openly.

"Yes!" replied three men as one.

"That symbol means they are fully inducted soldiers and citizens of Sparta," my father elaborated.

"Make sense why Mu was so quiet, they're his people," Gershom made his observation.

"Indeed, they are his people or probably soldiers that were once under him when he was a captain over this very warship, and many more just like this one," my uncle replied informingly to his son. "Moreover, we ought to focus on getting this catch to the shop in town and then to the restaurant. Mu has some catching up to do with old comrades, but when he's done, he will know where to find us, so let's move out, men."

After hearing those commands from my uncle, my uncle wheeled the first wheelbarrow full of tunas off the boat and onto the dock floors and made his way to our ass-driven cart. Blade made his way onto the fishing boat with another wheelbarrow where Gershom and I started loading more tunas into this one, so it could be offloaded from the fishing boat. After the second wheelbarrow was full and wheeled off, my father came with the third one and again we filled it up with fish. Once the third was wheeled off the boat, my uncle and Blade came back with their wheelbarrows to be filled back up again, and on the sixth trip, all the tuna was removed from the fishing boat.

Once the catch of the day was securely stored on the cart, it was time to head into the heart of the town. However, there was no room for all five of us to travel on the cart, so only two riders could travel on the cart. This meant Blade, Gershom, and me had to walk into town. Something our fathers had no problem with, so off the fathers went, and we followed after them. I remembered Mu and what would become of him since we were leaving, so I turned back to Mu. I noticed the soldiers' helmets were removed from their heads.

"Wow, the helmets made a difference," I said to Gershom. "They don't look that tall anymore."

"You're right," he agreed. "But look how long their hair is. I wonder if that gets in the way when they're fighting other soldiers?"

Gershom pulled out an imaginary sword from his right side and said in a manly tone, "Let's fight." Quickly, I pulled out mine and readied my stance for defense.

"Wait, wait," pleaded Gershom. "Let me fix my hair." I laughed as he pretended to comb his long hair from his face.

"I'm ready, I'm ready," he said, flinging his pretend hair back every five seconds. I laughed some more, while Blade walked ahead and disappeared in the crowd of people unknowing to us since we were busy distracted from our silly bantering.

"Wait, stop," Gershom said to me, so I did. "Where's Blade?"

We turned in all directions and saw no one that resembled Blade, only the anxious faces of men hurrying to their affairs for today.

"I think we are in—" said Gershom before someone picked him up and ran off with Gershom in their arms. Shocked by it, I stood frozen with fear as Gershom disappeared from my sight.

"Gershom," I whispered to myself

Run after him, run, said the voice in my head, so I started walking at first, trying to see where exactly Gershom was taken, but there was no sign of him.

"Gershom, Gershom... Gershom!"

Gershom was nowhere to be found. I grew more frantic with each turn I took and saw no one familiar. Nothing was making sense while all manner of thoughts deluged my mind. Thoughts of my father's old foes seeking revenge or was this the works of Grecian soldiers from the naval fleet at the docks? That's when it hit me. "The docks!" Mu might still be at the docks, and he'd know what to do. Since I was nearby, I turned and made a run for it, but then I heard footsteps and the laughs of a young person approaching. I turned to my left in time to see a massive, mahogany-skinned arm scoop me up and sprinted away from the docks. Blade spun Gershom and I around and around, while Gershom held out his arms like he was flying and laughed jubilantly.

"Hold out your arms like this," said Gershom joyously. "It feels more real."

I did exactly what Gershom was doing with my arms outstretched, and he was right. It did feel more real. The cool air flowed through my little fingers as the world seemed to go round and round before Blade sprinted off into to the sea of people, making air noises to add to our enjoyment, while he dodged and cut in front of the busy bodies making their way to a destination of choice. We couldn't see the angry faces, but we heard their cries of frustration with each step Blade sprinted away. It made all three of us laugh harder considering how it only added to our excitement.

I worried about Blade. Yes, he was the strongest in our crew, but he ran for so long with both of us now on top of his shoulders and yet he showed no signs of weariness. He just kept moving, slipping in between moving carts, jumping over those pushing wheelbarrows, outrunning both man and beast, and cutting in front of the skittish horses. Blade wanted us to feel every second this moment brought us a sense of rushing exhilaration. That's when he started rocking us from side to side, shifting the way we saw the world around us. Suddenly, Blade turned around and started jogging backward. Gershom and I started screaming and waving our hands frantically, while trying to convince Blade to turn back around as the excited winds swam through my bare legs. However, Blade refused and kept moving backward, all the while laughing and telling us to direct him.

Gershom and I turned back wide-eyed and shouted, "Left, right, stop!"

Blade stopped instantly and spun around to see confuse ox chewing away at his watery reed, while attached to his owner cart.

"I thought you two would be better at directing me now," said Blade. "We've been doing this for a while now."

"Apologies," we said to Blade.

Blade walked away from the clueless beast, whose black coat shimmered brightly from the sun above, and sprinted away deeper into town, and he ran all the way with both of us still on his shoulders. I assumed all this was a form of workout for Blade since he took remarkable pride in his muscular appearance and his hair—especially his hair. Nevertheless, Blade wanted us to laugh and grow up in the environment children ought to grow up in. Something he never truly experienced, so he took up the responsibility of being an older brother to Gershom and me to make this possible for us. A duty our family appreciated, but it was more appreciated and treasured by Blade.

In the distance, I saw our shop through the thickness of the crowd, which was a mix of many odd faces. By this time, it was no surprise we were in the heart of the town and all the vendors were rushing here and there to get their shops set up. Therefore, Blade had to slow down in his movements, fighting through the coming and going by carefully avoiding bodily contact, until we stood in front of our shop.

The shop or the market stall inside the town wasn't far from the docks. It only took less than fifteen to twenty minutes on the cart to get there, depending on how crowded the market square was, but on foot, it rounded out to thirty to forty minutes. However, this time around, the journey by foot seemed too short when we were having this much fun. Normally, the journey into town was always an experience filled with adventure, especially when Blade was around, because we knew he was going to make the moments unforgettable. For this was one of Blade's missions in life.

"Good, you boys are here," said Gershom's uncle. "Let's unload and start preparing the fish for to be cut."

This small shop in the market square of the town was where my father and uncle sold what they had caught during their fishing

ventures. Blade would cut and clean the fish with the help of Gershom and I by his side, while my father and uncle sold the fish to the various consumers. The customers would come to us and request the strangest fish parts to purchase. There were those who purchased the fish heads, while others wanted the fish whole and uncut. The weirdest purchase from customers was that of the fish's insides, and they wanted it by the *gallons*, and they weren't even fishermen. However, many of the customers would come to our shop to buy the fish in various cuts and pounds. Most of our profits came from the sales of the fillets.

Today's catch on the open sea was truly paying off. People were lining up with looks of anticipation to leave with a fish of their choice. We had to move fast in order to supply their demands, so it was a good thing Gershom and I were better now at using a knife to cut the fish in properly. Customers even came into our shop looking for the previous day's catch of crustaceans; they could be quite impetuous about obtaining pounds of the various crustaceans we had for sale.

The sale of seafood was a massive industry in the city, especially because we were so close to the coastal line. The competition was fierce, and there was always demand. This was the environment in which my father taught me business. The appearance of the Greeks in our city made the sale of seafood into an *international* business affair; there were faces from other countries who were willing to pay gold and silver by the pounds for what we had in our waters. The Greeks knew one another and typically did business with one another. I figured this must be the reason my father and uncle had Mu in our crew. Mu, a native Greek and somehow highly respected by other Grecians, was able to find Greek businessmen looking for a shipment of a variety of marine life that was either dead or alive. Mu's connections were one of his many attributes that he offered our crew, even though he looked a bit of a lout each time he moved himself from place to place. Overall, the crewmembers appreciated Mu's connections because of the tremendous amount of coins it put into their pockets.

Three hours had passed since the sun left the highest point in the sky. My uncle told Gershom and I to go and gather the three crates filled with pre-cut tunas, as well as four other separate crates: one with live lobsters, two with live shrimps and clams, and the other with live crabs. We were to take them to the restaurant before the noonday rush when the sun reaches the highest point in the sky. Gershom's mother ran a food establishment where people could pay and received strong drinks, hot and cold meals, baked cakes, and an atmosphere to socialize with new and old faces. The restaurant had an all-women staff, which included Gershom's sister and a very interesting cousin.

After the large crates were secured on the cart, we began our thirty-minute journey through the sea of people in the city streets. Before we could pull up near to the family's place of business, we saw Gershom's mother waving to us with a welcoming smile on her face.

"My darlings, how are you?" she asked us in a tone quite similar to my mother's voice. Then she reached in to grab us both and hug us tightly.

"Hi, Aunty," I said.

"Alright, Mom," Gershom said while pulling himself away from his mother's grasp.

"Come on, then, I'll give you boys a hand," my aunt said with purple head wrapped and navy-blue apron From her smile to her gentle, maternal touch, my aunt was the second closest person who resembled my own mother—in short, she was my second mother. My aunt inspected each crate and handed them to Gershom and then me. There was a crate with a rather pungent scent; she took it in her hands and led the way inside the restaurant with a strange look on her face. I assumed it was due to the smell.

Inside the restaurant, the atmosphere was quite affable. The customers were eating and enjoying one another's company, while the female servants, along with JuJu, tended to every need. JuJu now was a slender, sassy young man who took exceptionally good care of himself for a man. He always smelled fancy since he made and sold his own fragrances, and his hairstyles always stood out. Women loved him, and men envied him because of his effect on women. Even though JuJu never seemed interested in women whatsoever, except for gossip and doing their hair.

"Seems like the *fishermen* are back with the catch of the day," JuJu said to Gershom and me with a wink. "What do you boys have for me?"

"Your favorite."

"*My favorite*? What do you know about that, Teraditus? Who have you been talking to?"

"Take a look for yourself," I replied to JuJu, bringing the crate with shrimp and clams for him to take a closer look. "Little man, you *know* what I *like*," JuJu said to me, while nodding to me with a sassy attitude.

"JuJu, go back to work and leave these boys alone," said Gershom's mother before disappearing into the back.

"You got it, Aunty," JuJu replied while rolling his eyes and waving me off in an effeminate manner. I walked over to where Gershom stood in front of the entrance to the back, and he said to me in disgust.

"So extra for a man," Gershom admitted with disdain. "I can't believe he's related to me."

"And me—"

"No, he's not related to you, Teraditus," Gershom snapped at me, "since he's my cousin from my mother's side of the family, and you're my cousin from my father's side of the family. You see where I am going with this?"

"Yeah, I do, you just broke down how we're all one big family," I replied to Gershom's comment. He sighed and disappeared through the entrance leading to the back of the restaurant. I glanced back over to where JuJu was standing laughing with two of the girls behind the counter where the drinks were sold and stacked high on the wooden shelves. JuJu was truly the life of this restaurant. If he wasn't serving, putting on a show through his singing and tribal dancing, he was making someone laugh and making them feel good about themselves after a rough day. JuJu was genuinely a good soul; something rare to find in people these days, as my mother would often say.

The back of the restaurant was the place of creative mayhem, and of course where all the food was prepared. It was also where all manner of food items were constantly tossed around in the air, from one side of the room to the other. All the while, the cooks and servers sang catchy tunes, while the rest swayed to the rhythm.

"Think fast, Teraditus," yelled Gershom as a red onion was flying toward me. I was about to drop the crate when another hand appeared in front of my face in time to catch the red onion.

"Someone is not fast enough," said Gershom's mother to me before she turned toward Gershom. "Please wait until he puts the crate down first. You know the rules, Gershom," she said with a motherly tone. Gershom gave me a troubled, devious smirked.

I placed the crate down and took two clams out, and quickly tossed the two clams toward Gershom before I could say, "Gershom, think fast!" Gershom looked up to see two clams soaring towards him and a horrified expression appeared on his face.

"Not fast enough, huh?" I said with a smirk on my face, but my joy ceased when he caught the first clam and threw it back toward me. I caught the first clam on time, but failed to see the second one was on its way back to me, too.

"Got it!" The same hand from before was in front of my face with the second clam inside the palm of her hand. "You have to move faster than that," said Gershom's mother, my aunt. I shook my head and sighed because she was right. I was behaving like a beginner, considering how much exposure Gershom and I were accustomed to with items being tossed back and forth inside the kitchen area of the restaurant since the ages of four. Gershom laughed at me, while JuJu burst through the entrance doorway and stood, tapping his right foot, waiting to see if his order was ready to be served.

"JuJu, come inside. I don't want people looking inside here, especially when we are tossing food around," said my aunt without even looking at JuJu once.

That's when JuJu rolled his eyes at his aunt and stepped inside. "Keep rolling those eyes and see what I do to you," she warned him assuredly. JuJu put his hands on his hips and rolled his eyes again intrepidly. Gershom's mother snapped around with a knife in her hands, waving at JuJu. "Keep testing me, and see what happens," she said sternly before JuJu gasped in fear and burst back out the entrance doors dramatically. Everyone inside the kitchen laughed except my aunt. "And keep my doors closed," she yelled at him, while the doors swung closed. My aunt had a strict rule about keeping the doors closed to the kitchen area because she wanted to keep this jaunty life in the kitchen hidden from the customers. Some customers were more than aware of the festivities in the back, while the majority remained ambiguous.

"Would you look here, my two youngest fishermen— how did fishing go today?" a young woman asked while entering the kitchen. I knew that voice right away, and so did Gershom. It was Nephtali, Gershom's older sister.

"It was a great catch! Come and look for yourself," I replied. I held out my crate toward her.

"Wow, look at that, it does look good, my love," Nephtali said taking a closer look, while her hair nearly fell into the crate.

"Nephtali, your hair... it has grown so long," I pointed out.

"Oh yeah, Blade hates it when I cut my hair," she said, swinging her three-stranded ponytail in front of her face. "And trust me, he would notice if I did. Even with his one eye!" My aunt laughed at Nephtali's comment, while I smiled silently.

"And where is your purple head wrap?" Gershom asked. Nephtali glared harshly at Gershom without replying to him; meanwhile, my aunt had her chastising eyes on Nephtali, giving her the look that a mother gives to her child when she expects better from the child.

"I expect better from the one who will one day take over the family business," my aunt said.

Nephtali looked away from her mother and rolled her eyes. "Okay, okay, I just took it off for a minute to let my hair down in the back. I'll put it back on," Nephtali told her mother before walking away.

As soon as Nephtali disappeared to put on her head wrap, my aunt sighed and made her way to one of the crates. She then called out for two of her workers to assist her with them. Once the two ladies saw what was inside, all three looked at each other and conversed for a while. Then, they synchronized their movements as they went to their various stations with the crates' contents.

Nephtali returned from tidying herself up and a purple head wrap on her head. With her appearance refreshed, she looked more stunning than she had before she left. It was strange, but I found myself attracted to Nephtali. She was the first woman I had ever been attracted to, but the feelings were futile. For one, she was older than me by a decade. Secondly, she was my cousin. And lastly, Nephtali was in a steady relationship with Blade. Blade was the kind of person to confront a man if they came near someone he cared about dearly. And Nephtali was number one on Blade's list of people dear to him.

Nephtali was an attractive twenty-five year-old with a curvaceously slender body and sleek, long, black hair. Her complexion was quite similar to her baby brother's and father's: a soft, brown skin tone. Her eyes were bright and brown like her mother's, as well as my own mother's eyes.

As I looked at her, Nephtali pulled a knife from behind her and began to spin it by the hilt with her left hand. She looked at me to see my curious eyes amazed by her performance. This motived her to be more creative with her knife techniques, but she behaved herself every time her mother turned around to look at her. This made her performance all the more fun. The more Nephtali moved the knife

between her hands, the more I saw the influence of Blade on this remarkable woman.

"Get back to work before Mother sees you," Gershom commanded his sister. Then he made a face and stuck his tongue out to Nephtali. Both Nephtali and I gave Gershom a disdainful look.

Nephtali turned to me and smiled. The next thing she did was more than I was prepared for: She used her left index finger to signal me to come near her, and when I made my way over her, she said in a quite tone, "The thing about knives is knowing when and where to use them. You never know what situation you may run into, and having a knife stored securely for your disposal can be a major factor in determining whether you live or die." Meanwhile, she continued cutting a piece of fish into meal portions. "Can you guess where I keep my most personal knives?" she asked.

I thought about it carefully, and said with excitement in my voice, "Somewhere one would least expect it—"

"Like your butt," Gershom said, suddenly behind me, trying to be humorous.

I turned around to give Gershom a disappointed look, while Nephtali said, "You're close, so keep guessing." Gershom wandered off. Then she returned her focus back to me.

Nephtali turned to see if her mother was looking at her, and she was not. Then, she picked up the edge of her dress and exposed her silky, brown leg, revealing a leather strap around her inner thigh. The strap had a blade attached to it, and the blade was seven inches long. Nephtali's exposure not only revealed the leather strap—it also revealed the color of her undergarments. This revelation was extremely exhilarating for a boy of my age. It was the first time I had seen that much of a woman's body.

Nephtali wasn't finished. She bent down to open her top, which exposed her soft, buoyant bosoms. *The excitement is too much,* I thought to myself. Caught up in the sight of the exquisiteness of her breasts,

Nephtali pulled a knife out of the inner garment that held breasts together. "You have to be creative, Teraditus," she said, "especially when you don't know what life will throw at you." Nephtali smiled at me while looking into my eyes.

She is so beautiful! I admitted to myself, but she had Blade's influence all over her. Nevertheless, if only Nephtali knew what she was doing to me... or maybe she did know, to a certain degree. All I knew was that I could never tell her about how I was feeling about her at that moment.

I smiled back at her while she returned back to her work. Gershom threw linen cloth at me to indicate that we had to return to the crew, so it was time to cease from the old talk and throw in the towel. We both gathered the meals the women typically prepared for our crewmembers. We gave them our gratitude and bid them our farewells. Then we began our journey back to the crew.

CHAPTER 12

LIFE ON THE SHORE

T he journey back to the crew with their meals felt odd this time around. Gershom and I often pointed out things of interest far and near to keep us busy on the ride back to the crew. As we rode through the vibrant streets of Cyrene, there were always people coming and going. However, on this afternoon, some of these new faces had ominous spirits about them as they glanced dubiously at our ass-driven cart. I didn't believe I was a seer or anything, but if you lived and worked in this town for as long as we had, you tended to notice the strange intentions on new and old faces, and something felt off course as the unfamiliar steers appeared more and more.

In times past, Gershom and I came to learn through eavesdropping on our fathers' *adult* talks, some of the concerning intentions of these new and unfamiliar faces of men. Intentions of men involved in questionable business ventures through deceitful acts were by far the most concerning for our fathers. Instead of using actual gold and silver to buy from the local merchants, deceptively designed stones and coins to look and feel like actual gold and silver to the average man. This kind of deceit fooled many local merchants, we included, in the past.

However, for those businesses who were not able to detect the foul play of this new kind of fool's gold, eventually lost their business. Hence the reason why my father and uncle always handled the financial part of selling the fish at our shop. Our fathers, along with Mu, developed their own skills in detecting when someone was using fake as opposed to the real. I, on the other hand, struggled from time to time to figure out the difference between the real and the fake, even though my father would often practice with me. I simply struggled, while Gershom was steadily figuring out the difference.

Still lost in my own thoughts, Gershom suddenly made a random observation that matched up with my thoughts about these new faces.

"Are you sensing that something is off?" he asked.

I turned to him and said, "I knew you would sense it too—but what is it?"

Gershom tried to think of a pragmatic response, but he realized he had no answer; it was all intuition. "Let's just assume it's nothing. Maybe we're overanalyzing and assuming too much about these people Let's hurry back to the crew. I'm sure they have been waiting for us," Gershom said in a reassuring tone. I knew Gershom was like his mother when it came to observing when something was not right; he could sense the storm in the quiet of the day. However, he still tried his best to not overthink it. Therefore, when Gershom's concerns mirrored my own, I had an escalating feeling that something terrible was about to occur. But like Gershom, I tried to not allow it to overladen my thoughts.

Our minds were lost in their own interpretations of our observations, while our ass eventually pulled us right up next to the shop, where both my father and uncle were waiting for us to come to a full stop. Gershom was the clever one out of the two of us, so he looked at the beast first and then turned to see our fathers staring at us with questions to ask.

"Oh, we're here! We apologize for taking so long, but we got what you need." Gershom turned to me and said. "Hey, Teraditus, we're here."

I turned to meet the eyes of the two familiar men. "The food is here, so come and get it," I said for all the crew to hear. Blade immediately walked out with a limp to the cart to gather the boxes which contained various food items. The four of us carried the boxes to the back of the shop where we saw Mu and a strange man, who was undoubtedly a Grecian.

Mu smiled at us and placed his left hand on the blond-haired fellow on his shoulders. The young man looked at Mu and jumped in surprise, which I interpreted as him trying not to be impertinent in front of Gershom and me. It was obvious that this man was a Greek soldier by the armor he wore, which was quite similar to the two soldiers we saw earlier in the day, except his panoply was more dignified as if he was a man of great importance. The blue-eyed, well-built, and clean-shaven man stood to his feet and said, "You two must be Teraditus and Gershom. I heard quite a lot about you boys from my father and your mothers."

That last comment about our mothers caught me off guard.

"I go by the name of Myaneus, just like my father in his time. I am the captain of the naval fleet you probably saw at the docks."

He speaks the tongues of our mothers very well, I thought to myself.

"The pleasure is ours to meet you, son of Mu. We too heard much about you from him," Gershom said emphatically. Everyone in the room laughed, because we knew Mu couldn't talk—Gershom was just trying to impress.

We all sat down together, and there was a sense of fellowship among us. Every man ate voraciously without any judgment, which was typically the case among us men dining with one another. These moments of communion with men were moments I grew to treasure, because of the relaxing atmosphere it tended to bring, and mostly because of the life lessons that could be learnt. We talked for hours, but somehow my father and uncle kept selling fish. They took turns going to the market stand to take care of the customers who came to buy our catch of the day, but when the late afternoon hours were upon us, we all had to get back to our routine of supply and demand. The rush of customers typically came around the mid-to-late-afternoon hours, when people were heading home after a long day of work. Around this time of the year, the sun would set earlier, thus making the day shorter. Since Mu's son was in town, we stayed at the shop a bit longer.

Myaneus walked outside and looked into the sky. "The sun is about to set sooner than I hoped for; however, the day was well spent. Thank you for the fellowship, and I hope to see you men for the remaining week. Come on, Father, let us retire to our home." Mu walked over to his son who stood near his cart and the two men waved us a farewell. We bid them farewell, and then we too gathered up our belongings and made our way home.

On the way home, the sun was disappearing into the west. It was beautiful how the sky filled with an amber glow, a color that eventually faded into an unforgettable memory for us all.

As we traveled, we discussed the highlights of the day, while we made plans for tomorrow. Blade—with the help of my father and uncle, of course—had built his own home on the same land as my uncle and father. We all lived along the same path, but my house was a good ten-minute walk from my uncle's house.

My father and I continued our journey home to meet my mother, who was feeding the fowls in the yard. The smile from my mother was enough to feel the serenity of being home. My father felt it too, every time he came home. He kissed my mother as though they'd been separated for days—no, *years*. It was enough to believe in their love and a marriage bond that seems unbreakable. I vowed at that very moment that I too would have a love and marriage just like this, just like mother and father.

* * * *

The night was young, and it was time to see what the evening had in store. I wondered what Gershom was doing, so I decided to head over there after our meal in the evening. Gershom was the brother I never had and always needed. Before I left my household, I told my parents where I planned to be for the night. My mother was skeptical, since our dogs were over by her brother's house. She preferred that they were with me while I was walking to my uncle's house. My mother's insistent concern was overwhelming from time to time. It was a daily to weekly battle trying to convince her to let me leave the safety of our home to travel ten-minutes down the perilous road to Gershom's house.

I wasn't in the mood for it tonight, so I used my head and yelled, "Gershom is outside with the hounds, so talk to you later." Those were my last words before closing the door behind, however, the closed door did not stop her from yelling back something, even though I understood not a word. I failed to understand why my mother was acting this way, which was unnecessary. Considering last night, we all stayed inside to hear her tales concerning Blade's life in Babylonia during the reign of King Cyrus of Persia.

In silence, I walked into the stillness of the late evening. As the moon above professed its dominion as lord of the night, the creatures of the night were slowly waking up while the fireflies danced in the open fields. The nights in this part of the country were dark and mysterious—the way Gershom and I preferred it as we explored the dark landscapes, since it is evident that the strangest things came out at night. Nevertheless, as I drew near Gershom's home, I felt the vibration of giddy footsteps approaching me. Without giving it a second thought, I stopped just in time to embrace the full impact of excited hounds jumping all of over me and casting me into the ground. The weight of all the hounds was a bit much for me, while I tussled to break free from their tongues in my face.

"Come on, boys, give him a break. Come on." I heard Gershom's voice, but it took a minute before I felt him reach down and pick me up with a feisty puppy in his other hand. Gershom was right behind them, but I failed to see him at first.

I laughed and asked, "Did you feed them?" while I swiped the saliva from my face.

"Yeah, I did, but you know how they can be from time to time," he replied.

I looked around to see a sea of pharaoh hounds. They were all-natural breeds from Kemet. My family had seven of them, while Gershom's family had nine, and the puppy he had in his hand made ten in all. Of course, we had more hounds when Gershom and I were much younger, but Blade — along with our fathers — gave them away to locals willing to buy hounds for hunting. Often, these hounds came back to visit us, or they would join us out in our wilderness ventures or go out on their own. It was a family thing for the hounds.

My mother had told me stories of how the hounds were descendants of the Tesem. Tesems were the scared hounds of Kemet, long before the days Kemet became a nation of utmost power. These magnificent beasts were great hunters for the farmers, hunters, and the great Pharaohs of the old days. This was true about our hounds, too, because they could hunt on land and in water. Occasionally, when we took them to the shoreline, they would attempt to catch the seabirds, and most times they were successful. Mother had also pointed out that the hounds were sacred animals because they had the appearance of Inpu,[9] the Kemetic god of the underworld.

"So, what's the plan? I mean, you were about to head over here," Gershom asked.

I turned to him and said, "Well, you were heading over to my house, so I should ask you the same question."

---

[9] "Anubis" is the Greek translation.

Gershom pushed his lips in an upward motion and nodded his head. "Fair enough. Plus, I figured your mother might be giving you a hard time, so I was on my way to lend a helping hand."

"Yeah, she was, but I did what you suggested, and I told her you were outside," I said regretfully, for I was not sure if Gershom's suggestion was the best suggestion.

"You see, my suggestion worked since I was already on my way over to save you, so you're welcome," Gershom said, looking forward to some appreciation of his goodwill, but I remained quiet. Even though, his suggestion somewhat did work, I refused to give him such satisfaction because it would go straight to his head.

"Wow, no response," Gershom said, almost offended. "Anyway, the night is still young. We have our hounds and two young minds, so let's go exploring since we did not go exploring last night." Gershom was right, we did not go anywhere last, while he walked away from me with some of the hounds following him.

"Hey, Gershom, there was another reason why I was making my way to your house. I wanted to speak to Blade about the leather strap your sister showed me earlier today."

Gershom chuckled and said, "Let me guess, you also want a knife to be hidden in your upper inner garments like a woman—"

"No, that's not what I meant," I responded, irritated by his comical assumption. Then it struck me: what Gershom had said was not a bad idea—for a woman, of course. However, I knew better than that to say anything like that in front of Gershom to hear.

We pulled into the yard and made our way to Blade's house. I knocked on the door, and Nephtali answered with an attractive smile. She was wearing a sleek, purple-and-green embroidered garment that hugged her affectionately, and around her neck was a wesekh made up of matching stone beads. In the center of her neck jewelry was a golden image of the goddess Auset, which was an image always seen painted on the back of my own mother's brown skin. This painted image of the queen god on my mother's body connected her to a past life as a priestess at one of the many sacred temples in Memphis and Thebes. A life she abandoned to be with my father, but a life she rarely talked about in detail—until last night. However, Nephtali took a special interest in my mother's past life as a priestess of the goddess, Auset, which was seven years ago when Nephtali was eighteen years of age.

Therefore, it made sense for the image of Auset to be visibly displayed on Nephtali's wesekh. My mother's influence undoubtedly shaped Nephtali's life, which also created an unbreakable relationship between the two. A type of mother-daughter relationship where my mother shared with Nephtali many secret things, specifically in the spiritual/mystic arts of Kemet. Something she often told me I was too young to learn about at the moment. However, little did my mother know Nephtali was teaching me the fundamentals of Kemetic sciences and the laws of nature, which I always put into practice whenever I went out exploring with Gershom.

"How can we be of service to you boys tonight?" Nephtali's words were full of life and curiosity. Not caring to know what she would say next, Gershom pushed her out of the way and made his way to the master blacksmith. Suddenly, Nephtali's appearance changed from a summer night's breeze to a violent dark storm. She was going hit Gershom for his impoliteness, but I quickly reached out and grabbed her arm, and the storm calmed. She looked at me and sighed with dissatisfaction, because she wanted to hit her little brother. "You come to his aid too much," she said before drawing me closer to kiss me on the forehead. "He doesn't deserve it," she continued after she had closed the door and we made our way to where Blade was in the house.

"This guy wants one of your special upper inner garments to borrow for himself, you know," Gershom said to his sister. "The ones where you can store your knives."

Gershom's unexpected words made both Nephtali and Blade burst out in laughter. The embarrassment I felt inside started to show on my

face. I wanted to turn around and hit Gershom in the face for his ludicrous comment. However, Nephtali hugged me and negated the idea.

"Don't worry, dear, I know what Gershom means. However, Blade may have what you're looking for."

I turned to Blade and asked him, "Blade is this true?"

Blade chuckled for a while and gave us a smooth smirk. "I have some leather straps over there in my craftsman's room. I can show you how to customize them to whatever you want, so you can have a set of your own hidden knives," Blade said to me in the raspiest voice I ever heard from him; it may have had something to do with the dark bottle in his left hand.

However, I freed myself from Nephtali's grasp and made my way to the room where Blade had pointed to, but I caught myself. When Gershom asked, "Hey, does this mean that our night expedition will be in here?" I stopped and looked at him and shook my head from side to side, because I did not want to stay inside when there was much to explore outside. Plus, I was sure Blade and Nephtali would prefer more alone time.

"Come on, Gershom, we can create our own straps and then we could head out for the night. It won't take long," I said. I turned to Blade. "Right, Blade? It won't take long?"

Blade gave me a nod before turning to Gershom to say, "Come on, you two, the faster we move, the more time I can have with Nephtali."

Gershom sighed and walked out to place the puppy he was still holding outside with the other hounds to eliminate distractions. After such, Gershom returned inside the house and lethargically walked back to the room where both Blade and I already begun working on the project at hand. Gershom walked into the thoroughly lit room where Blade and I sat at one of Blade's workstations, and suddenly his face expressed something he remembered to say or ask.

"Blade take a look at my hairline, please," he said moving closer to Blade for him to take a closer look. "I messed it up, right?"

Blade turned in his chair towards Gershom to place his left-hand underneath Gershom's chin and shifted his head left and right.

"A little uneven," said Blade, carefully inspecting Gershom's hairline with his one eye. "It's uneven because you keep shaping-up your hairline every week, which prevents the natural hair from re-growing. How long are you supposed to wait to shape-up your hairline?"

"Two weeks or eighteen days," answered Gershom.

"How long to cut your hair?" Blade questioned Gershom.

"A month," Gershom whispered his answer.

"That's correct, Gershom, a month—but no longer than eight weeks to cut your hair," said Blade while removing his hand from the young boy's face. "I've taught both Teraditus and you," said Blade as he indicated to me, "how to cut hair almost two years ago, but Gershom, you've had more practice in cutting hair than Teraditus since you live closer to me and yet you continue to break the basics rules I set up as guidelines."

"So, you can't fix my crooked hairline?" asked Gershom, making his way toward the station where I was already working on my leather strap and listening to the conversation.

"I can fix it," Blade responded assuredly, "but I won't. You need to let your hairline grow back, like what I am doing with my hairline. I have a week more to go before I shape-up myself again."

I took a glance at Blade's hairline, along with his full beard, and everything was still pristine and neatly cut.

"It still looks sharp," I complimented Blade. "Maybe you can wait for more than a week."

"Do you see how Teraditus is thinking?" asked Blade, while looking at Gershom. "If a week or two has passed and you notice your hairline still looks neat and sharp, just wait another week."

Gershom nodded his head in defeat after receiving his unpleasant counsel from Blade. He did not take criticism well, even though Blade constantly had to remind Gershom of staying true to the basic rules of hair grooming. We both knew Blade took pride in his appearance and the appearance of his crew as well, and he wanted Gershom and I to have the same mentality since it will reflect in our hair grooming skills when the time finally comes to groom others. Blade took up the responsibility of grooming our hair and the full beards of the men in our crew by making sure we were always neatly cut and trimmed. The artworks from Blade's grooming skills were eye-captivating. Mother always said it was one of the best features that made our crew stand out, besides our skills on the open sea, we were a well-groomed and good-looking crew.

She had a point since other local men and young boys would often come to Blade to pay him for his grooming services. Occasionally, both young and mature women would also show up to Blade to have their hair cut in similar styles to men, or simply cut it clean off, which Blade despised greatly. However, with time, the grooming service eventually became overwhelming for Blade, so he started teaching Nephtali first before he taught us the ways of cutting hair and shaping up beards. That way we could make additional coins on the side, which Gershom and I were anxiously looking forward to.

Blade reached over to grab a leather skin for Gershom to start working on for himself. Gershom stood in between Blade and me, so I turned to my left to see Gershom's uneven hairline and I could not see what Blade saw, even with my two eyes. That's when I shifted Gershom's face by his chin to face me directly, but he slapped my hand away from his chin.

"Don't touch me like that," Gershom snapped at me, which made Blade laugh.

"So hostile," said Blade, while shaking his head. "I'll be back, you two behave and work. You two have everything you will need in here."

Blade got up and left us in the room to check on Nephtali, I assume, but when he was no more in the room, his last words started to repeat in my head, and a smile appeared on my youthful face. For I enjoyed being in Blade's room, it was one of the many places where I was able to witness first-hand his creativity manifesting into something realistic. All you had to do was look around the room and see the visual displays of ingenuity. In front of the workstation, there were shelves on top of shelves on all sides of the room, holding all manner of tools, strange artifacts, jars containing mysterious possessions, and rolled-up papyrus scrolls. These roll-up scrolls were everywhere, varying in sizes and length, it was where all his ideas were composed before they were constructed. Blade had many ideas, and not all of them had been invented yet.

One would have the assumption that this room would be chaotic, with all manner of things all over the floor, or markings of some sort on the four walls. However, this was not the case, and quite the opposite in describing Blade's room. Wherever I looked, the room's set up was neat, clean, and in order. The walls of the room were tan-colored, and on one side were sketches hanging from hooks attached to the wall. The side opposite was the best thing about Blade's room. The wall of *sacred justice*! In our more youthful days, Gershom and I were not even allowed in this room, but time has altered that rule to no touching anything on the sacred wall. Something hard for boys our age to do, considering how everything that hung on that wall glitter and shiny in our eyes. This wall displayed the best of the best from Blade's personal collection of artistic weaponry. Most of the weaponry he made, and the rest was earned through various means he refused to talk about. He decorated the wall with swords, knives, daggers, spears, shields, and bows and arrows.

The creativity of Blade's weaponry collection was enough to inspire you to be a hired swordsman or start your collection.

"Good, he's gone," said Gershom, making his way to the forbidden wall.

"Gershom," I whispered fearfully, while looking at the entrance to the room.

"Would you relax," replied Gershom anxiously. "I need to see how Blade made this dagger. I want to make one like it. You do know next week starts our next stage of training to learn the skills of a craftsman? I just want to get a head start, that's all."

"I understand, but Blade was very specific not to touch anything on this wall." I tried to remind him of the stern rules set up by Blade. "Plus, we have yet to master the hand-to-hand fighting styles of the ancient art of *Montu*, but you're already have your mind on the craftmanship."

"Yes, yes, I know we're an embarrassment to the ancestors for not learning the basics of *Montu*, but maybe we can redeem ourselves by making a decent sword—or a dagger, I could settle for dagger. However, Blade said to be a good craftsman, one's hands must see what the eyes cannot see, so that's what I'm doing. I want to give my hands the chance to see what my eyes cannot," said Gershom, still focused on this black hilt dagger that hung on the wall of scared justice.

The anxiety was high in the room for both of us now, or maybe it was just me. Gershom's curiosity drew me to him as I sat in my chair, but the fear of Blade catching us in a wrongful act had both of us on edge. I pushed back on my chair and slipped out to make my way over to Gershom. It was pointless to remain in my chair when Gershom was getting himself into trouble. The blame always spilled over to me, even though I did not participate in the act. Somehow, I still had some part to play, and the worse part about it all. Gershom knew this to be the case and took advantage of it quite often.

"Why don't you do as you are told and look out?"

"Why don't you do as you are you are told and get away from this wall," I snapped back at Gershom.

Gershom sucked air through his teeth in frustration and reached for the dagger that captured his attention.

"Wait, wait," I said, holding Gershom's arm reaching for the hilt of the dagger.

"What is it this time, Teraditus?"

"You ought to use a small cloth to hold the dagger, so Blade won't see your fingerprints on the hilt or anywhere else." Gershom nodded his head in agreement to my suggestion.

"Well, where is this small cloth you suggest I use?" Gershom questioned me.

"Why not use this one?" Blade said from behind. Quickly, we turned around and saw Blade holding a small, wheat-colored cloth extended toward us to use. We stood there, petrified like a cat seeing its shadow for the first time. Nephtali burst out with laughter, while taking the cloth out of Blade's hand and walking to the wall where we stood closest too. she handed the cloth over to Gershom. Gershom looked at the cloth and slowly took it from his sister and looked back at Blade.

"Pick up the dagger by the hilt, firmly," Blade commanded. Gershom turned around and used the cloth to grab hold of the black, stone hilt in his left hand, and suddenly he became suspiciously still the moment he turned back around to face us. A smile appeared on Nephtali's face when she glanced over to Blade. She knew something about that dagger and what it was doing to Gershom.

"What's going with him?" I questioned Nephtali breathlessly, then I turned to Blade, who kept his eye on Gershom.

"Guys, help him," I begged eagerly.

"Teraditus, relax, we're here," she explained with a simple smile. Suddenly, an unexplainable vibration came from Gershom holding this dagger, which the hilt started to gleam and glitter. Gershom's eyes grew wide as he struggled to retain the air inside.

"Nephtali!" I screamed.

Nephtali reached out to take hold of another dagger on the wall, while Blade pulled me backward and she knocked the dagger out of Gershom's hand by hitting the blade of his dagger with a heavy swing.

The dagger fell straight down, blade first, and sent an ominous vibration throughout the room. I placed my hands over my ears and closed my eyes and waited until the vibration was no more. When it was over, I looked up and saw Gershom on his knees with his sister embracing him and massaging his back. Nephtali was saying something to him in a song. A song of strength.

Blade walked over to the siblings on the ground and reached downward with his right hand to pick up the dagger Gershom once held in his hand by the hilt.

"Take a good look at Gershom, Teraditus," said Blade, pointing toward Gershom. "This is another example of what happens when you two continue to break the rules I set up for you two. This is the price you two will have to pay."

"What happened to him?" I asked Blade, while still searching for an explanation.

Blade looked at Gershom, who was steadily coming back to his senses in the embrace of Nephtali. Gershom's breathing had returned, but it was slower and louder. He freed himself from his sister's embrace and struggled to his feet. Quickly, I rushed over to help him stand on his two feet. Gershom grunted at the thought of me helping him stand up, but he knew better to resist. He had not recovered fully from whatever the dagger had done to him, which was evident in the way he was shaking as I held him up.

"Tell Teraditus what you saw," Blade demanded from Gershom, but Gershom shook his head.

"It's hard to explain, but I felt so unbalanced," explained Gershom with uncertainty. Blade started laughing.

"The word to pay attention to is unbalance," said Blade, still holding onto the black hilted dagger Gershom once held. "You see this dagger you were unable to hold. You need balance, both of you, to ever hold this particular dagger. A balance of mind first, and once that mental balance is achieved, then the spiritual balance is next, and that kind of balance is offered to many, and yet few can achieve spiritual balance."

In such a moment as Blade spoke, a cool draft entered the room we all resided in, like an unseen presence was steadily entering into our midst. Clearly, I was overthinking things, or so I thought—until I saw the bumps raised on my right arm, and that caused me to wonder more. *We're not alone*, I thought to my myself.

"I just wanted to get a feel of the dagger, so I can replicate it for next week when you start teachings us the next skillsets of a craftsman," Gershom said confidently, which made Blade nod his head with acceptance. However, that weakness left suddenly, while a new strength seemed to emit from his countenance.

"You first must learn about the basic rules of nature when it comes to certain elements and how to combine them in order to achieve balance. For everything in life is made up of elements, including all of us in this room, and knowing which elements go together will be the key to finding balance or sometimes unbalance. And we now know you, Gershom, are too unbalance for this dagger, even though you, Gershom, and this dagger are combined with the same elements."

"So, when will I be ready to hold this dagger?" Gershom asked Blade.

"That's all up to you and how you can find balance within yourself," said Blade, while he squeezed on the hilt of this dagger and tilted in a way that the blade of the dagger glowed a silver-white color, almost resembling the light from the moon. The glow from the dagger even changed the lighting in the room to silver white and the temperature into something cool and refreshing. That's when the garments on Blade's body slightly started to float from the surge of energy emerging from the dagger he swayed left to right in his hand as a trail of light followed.

My eyes could not believe what they were seeing from a man we knew our entire life. I knew Gershom, who was just like me, had so many questions, but all we could do was steer, while Nephtali just sat still on

the ground with a satisfying smile on her face. She gracefully sat there and watched with no fear. Like none of this was nothing new to her, which troubled me. It caused me to wonder what other things were these two up to when no one else was around.

"I don't understand, what we're looking at and how are you doing this?" I questioned Blade ghastly. "Does all of this involve all the mystifying arts of the Kemet sciences you've learning from my mother's teachings?"

That's when he removed the headband that covered his right eye and opened his eyelid.

"Whoa!" Gershom and I whispered. Blade's right eye glowed like the dagger.

"This is what balance looks like," Blade said while looking individually at us.

"Alright, enough show and tell for one night," Nephtali said, while standing to her feet and covering Blade's right eye with his headband, causing the glow of the dagger and eye to cease. "Let them finish up what they're doing so we can have some alone time."

"Wait, wait—no," I said immediately. "You can't possibly kick us out after what we just saw. We must talk more about, about... about what we just saw. Like, are there other daggers with this kind of power, can we obtain this power, and how do we achieve this balance you keep speaking about?" I paused suddenly when a new a question entered my mind, making all other questions irrelevant. "Does this mean the tales are true?"

"What tales are true?" asked Nephtali.

"The tales of the swords of course—*Swords of Ra*." The young couple laughed calmly at me, while Gershom's face grew stern from their laughter.

"The Swords of Ra," Blade said in a low and heavy tone.

"No, no," said Nephtali randomly, before she bellowed out, "*The Swords of Amun-Ra!*" Nephtali roared like a man in the battle, while swinging imaginary swords around, as though she was fighting an unseen man. She even made the sounds of swords clashing together before she broke out into more laughter.

Blade laughed and smiled before they shared a kiss.

"Oh, Queen of the Heavens, can you two just wait till we leave?" Gershom said in a nettling manner.

Blade gave Nephtali a nod to do something and she nodded right back at him. Nephtali walked over to the wall of justice and stretched out her right hand as high up as she could to reach for the hilt of a broken sword. Once she had a full grip of the sword's hilt, she turned the hilt to the left, taking it from a vertical to a horizontal position. Suddenly, two doors slowly creaked open and we all saw them. The Swords of Amun-Ra hung dynamically on the walls of the open doors, gleaming with raw, unearthly power, as if the best of men had not the aptitude to craft such a breathtaking weaponry.

The longer I steered at them, I could see the symbols of the Metu Neter on the golden blades mystically appearing and disappearing under the reflection of the light in the room.

"I see the writings," I said before pointing to the swords. "I see the images of the blades of the Swords of Ra."

"Are you sure?" Blade questioned me with disbelief.

"I'm certain," I replied with my eyes still fixed on the swords. Blade and Nephtali glanced at each other as though they developed the ability to converse with each other with their eyes.

"What does it say?" Blade questioned me in an austere manner.

"Well, it's hard to tell, but I think it says—*the fire is within*," I explained to Blade.

"The fire is within what?" Blade's questions persisted.

"I, I could be wrong—it's hard to tell, the reflection keeps appearing and disappearing," I said anxiously to Blade. The couple looked at each other as if they knew my eyes were not fooling me.

"*The fire is within the one who is willing to be a symbol of light in a world of darkness*," Blade said firmly. "Very impressive Teraditus, your spiritual eye is opening." Blade's words redirected my focus to the Sword of Ra and that's when the reflection reappear, and it read, "The fire is within—*me*!" I shook my head from side to side in disbelief, so I stepped closer and leaned in for a closer look since that did not make any sense.

"You see something else, don't you?" Nephtali asked me.

"I'm not sure, I think my eyes are playing tricks with me," I replied to her.

"You get this from your mother, Teraditus, and it will get stronger with time," Nephtali said with a smile.

Meanwhile, Blade walked over to the sword on the right with an oil-clay lamp and extended the lamp toward the sword on the right side of the door. The moment the small fire saw itself flickering in the golden reflection of the blade, it magnified itself in size and brightness. Blade had to look away, while carefully moving the oil-clay lamp away from the Sword of Amun-Ra. The massive flame forced us to shield our eyes from the awful brightness, while it roared vigorously in our ears.

"Blade, quick, move lamp over to the sword on the left," Nephtali informed him. Blade did just that because the roar of the open flame hushed, and we saw the oil-clay lamp flickering in front of the sword on the left side of the door.

"I hope that answers your question on whether the tales are true or not?" said Blade, while Nephtali laughed in a subtlyThe Blade placed the oil-clay lamp down at the workstation and sighed a sigh of relief.

"If the tales are true, why do you have the swords, instead of a powerful King with the means to keep it properly hidden from the wrong hands?"

"That's a good question, Gershom," admitted Blade with a smirk, "keep in my mind you two—that the greatest treasures are more than often hidden in plain sight. With that said, you two finish up for the night is still young."

Gershom and I looked at each other with frustration before returning our focus at the Swords of Amun-Ra. The blades of the swords were pure gold with ivory-and-sapphire hilts. On the two curved blades were pictorial designs that told the story of Amun-Ra giving these swords to a faithful servant for his unshakable loyalty. The story also extended to the ivory-and-sapphire hilts, which helped the wielder to know which sword belonged in which hand. However, it didn't matter if one knew which sword belonged in which hand; the true power of the swords would only ignite in the hands of that faithful servant and his bloodline, and fortunately and unfortunately, Blade's family lineage connected him to that same bloodline. The creation of these swords was remarkable and filled with a rich history. However, what I wanted to hear the most was the tale of how the swords became a part of the Blade's linage, which he refused to share in any particular detail, nor would anyone else for that much. It was a very hush, hush topic for everyone, especially for the parents.

When Gershom and I were much younger, Blade told us tales of how Amun-Ra had given the sun swords to the very first ruler of Kemet, which were before the days of the known Pharaoh Kings. This first ruler's undying devotion to Amun-Ra pleased the sun deity so much that Amun-Ra blessed his faithful servant by taking his two curved iron swords, which he constantly fought with side by side, and dipping them into the sun. When the sun deity returned with the swords, they were made of pure gold. However, the moment the servant held the blades, they shone with the brightness of the sun. He used these swords from Amun-Ra to fight all those who desired to harm him and his village. However, as time would see it, this servant used the swords to unite all those closest to the Nile and the Red Sea, thus creating a new nation that Amun-Ra's faithful servant ruled over.

As the other three conversed amongst themselves, my eyes never left the swords, as my mind recalled these old tales—tales of how the swords drew much of their power from the sunlight during the day, and the

moonlight at night. The power from these swords would increase to the point that they could cut a man's sword clean off, blind men far and near, and burn lands and men alive. With such intense power, the faithful servant became a new entity to feared by many—but ruling with the spirit of fear was not his mission. Instead, he built many cities, temples, and monuments for Amun-Ra and other deities. He set aside large acres of land for agriculture and constructed new inventions for better living based on the science of the combined people throughout the region of Canaan. His reign transformed this new nation into a magnificent kingdom, and his people worshipped and adored him by calling the "Son of Ra."

However, the corruption of his reign did not come until his children's children became rulers and grew more insatiable with power by expanding this new kingdom beyond the regions of Canaan. It is unknown how far the influence of the kingdom expanded since some did not return from their journey. But what is known is the corruption that overtook the new rulers, and how far their tyranny spread throughout the mainland of Kemet. Various wars and civil wars broke out as others pursued these weapons of mass destruction. The Kingdom of Kemet was nearly torn apart, forcing some residents to move up north and others down south. The split was the pushing point for wise men to come together to overthrow the descendants of the Son of Ra. Blade told Gershom and I how it was in the days of a young Imhotep when the wise gathered together to expel the corruption from Kemet.

Personally, I believed that Blade wasn't too sure about whether the great Imhotep was a part of such a gathering of the wise, but he was certain that the descendants were expelled from their rulership, and that the divided kingdom was no longer divided until another came and split it again. Nevertheless, the whereabouts of the swords was the real mystery. Some say the Swords of Ra were hidden by the wise men to never be found again; others say that the priest and priestess gave them back Amun-Ra; and others say that Amun-Ra took them back in order to return them to the true heirs of his first's faithful servant. This part may just be true, since Blade's family has held onto these swords for quite some time now. Again, this was not a topic discussed in great detail when it involved Blade's past and his family. All these tales flooded into my head every time I entered this room in Blade's house.

"Come on, you two," said Blade beside the workstation. "Teraditus, stop daydreaming and hurry up—I need my alone time."

Nephtali pushed us over to the workstation and started helping us in order to move faster. Blade showed us systematically what to do in order for us to craft it on our own. I keenly watched every step Blade took with bending and making holes in the leather pieces, but somehow, I managed to mess it up along way. Gershom, who was not as lively and attentive as I was, did not follow Blade's steps correctly, but he was somehow still clever enough to successfully finish before me, and he began customizing his new leather strap.

"You make me wonder at times," I told Gershom with indignation.

"What's your problem?" he retorted. "If you need help making the inner garment, you can always ask my sister in the other room."

Nephtali made a soft chuckle, even though her mouth never opened. I was still abashed by the whole idea that Gershom had said this aloud for all to hear. The urge to hit Gershom right in the face was stronger now, so I placed my utensil and leather piece down at the same time Nephtali tenderly guided me to pick up what I just put down.

"Focus, focus," she whispered to me, while helping me add the finishing touches, here and there.

However, Blade saw Nephtali's assistance, which he did not approve of.

"No, no, my love," Blade said to Nephtali. "He needs to do it, or he'll never strengthen his craftsman skills."

Blade's assurance to Nephtali was of course right, because my shortcomings were not serious enough to start over. It only required a little strength and ingenuity to fix the setback, but Blade made sure I

fixed it correctly. This way, I would develop a habit of fixing problems on my own.

"Nephtali, um, in our next one on one session, will we discuss all that we saw tonight?" I whispered cautiously to her.

"What *one on one* session are you referring to exactly?" Blade questioned Nephtali and me in a prying manner.

Both Nephtali and I looked at Blade before Nephtali replied to him to say, "I believe he was questioning me and me only, my sun-kiss god." I glanced at the couple as they gave each other a simple stare down before Blade left it alone.

"Teraditus, what did I tell you about time and place," Nephtali whispered her question.

"Forgive me," I replied to Nephtali. "I just have so many questions."

"I know, and I will answer them in our next session this weekend. I promise."

"Then I will wait until this weekend," I whispered to Nephtali and she nodded.

Once I was done with my leather piece, Blade went to one of the cabinets on the wall and pulled out a medium-sized, wooden box. The box contained bronze knives ranging from six to seven inches in blade length. Blade made us design leather straps to pocket two knives. Gershom and I took two knives and securely pocketed them in our leather straps. I placed the leather strap on my left arm on the bicep muscle, and Gershom placed his own strap on his right arm.

"This feels good," I said to Blade, while Nephtali gave us nods of approval.

"I cannot lie—it does feel pretty good," Gershom agreed as we both admired our new concealed knife holders.

"Now you guys are ready to explore the night. Just be careful not to hurt yourselves and try not to let your mothers see these knife holders. Just be careful you two… and have a good night."

Blade's counsel to be careful was the last thing we needed to begin the night's expedition. Gershom and I walked outside and whistled for our hounds, who quickly returned to us, and we left the couple to enjoy the remaining night hours. A sense of readiness ran through me now that I had my hounds, Gershom's annoying wits, and lastly, my concealed weapons. I felt prepared for the unexpected—or so I thought.

CHAPTER 13

THE FACE OF DEATH

The cool wind brushed against my face and filled my lungs with fresh sea air. It was starry night in the skies above, filling the dark, blue skies with new life and my mind with colorful thoughts of endless adventures. Gershom walked over to the side of his house and gathered his wilderness gear, then we made our way to my house to gather my gear. In our swift journey to my home, the sea wind howled strange thing while the moon shone a pale light on the open pasture, thus giving the trees and bushes an eerie appearance.

Gershom pulled two flint stones out of his bag, and with those stones he ignited my torch first and with the fire from my torch, I lit Gershom's torch. Together the new flames danced from the sway of the passing winds, while giving us the limited light to only see as far as five feet away. In order to see the full path ahead, we were going to need the light from the moon, but the drifting clouds from the sea would often cover the light of the moon. Nevertheless, our minds were set to explore the night, light or no light, we were going to explore the night. With our sacks over our back, staffs in our hands, and a pack of hounds covering our every side. We made our way into the pasture of sparse trees to see what night had in store for us.

As we journeyed deeper into the pasture, I started to have flashbacks of the time when all four of us—Gershom, Nephtali, Blade, and I—had found orange, crystallized stones on our first expedition. Nephtali and Blade had told us that these stones were precious stones; it wasn't till later that I learned the Greeks called them "diamonds." Nephtali gave us each one stone, which we carried in our bags to maintain positive energy. Nevertheless, on our last expedition, we went deeper into the pasture and found the bones of an unknown creature. We left the site in hopes of returning to it later to find out more about these mysterious bones in the pasture.

Gershom told Blade about the last expedition in full detail, hoping to receive his words of wisdom. Blade informed us of how the sea breeze, over time, had the power to move the ground south, thus revealing the hidden treasures of the land—like diamonds, and the bones of men. Therefore, it was up to Gershom and me to find more of these hidden treasures of the land.

Since our time inside Blade's house, the silver, white light from the moon paved us the path across the open horizon. While the night winds blew against the less than verdant trees and bushes, the winds howled soothing sounds of the summer night in our ears.

"Do you think we will find more of those mysterious bones?" I asked.

Gershom was about to answer when three of the hounds ran after something in the bush. Both of us ran over to see what the hounds were after. One of the hounds had a lifeless rodent in his mouth.

"Good one, Tum-Ra," Gershom said to his hound. The hound dropped the dead field rodent, and he received barks of praise from all the fellow dogs, except for my hound, Akhen-Inu. Both hounds were the alpha dogs in their own pack, so they were always competing for the top alpha position. Often, they tried to impress the two mother hounds by showing which one was the dominant alpha male. There were even times when the two alpha dogs were forcing their adolescent pups down the same path of competitiveness by encouraging them to fight and race each other. When it was obvious, the pups, who were now older in dog years, just wanted to play all the time.

The journey continued as we eagerly walked deeper into the dark pastures. I was glad that the hounds had sensed the small rodent in the darkness because it meant they would have no problem detecting bigger creatures in the darkness.

The chilling sea winds intensified as the night hours drew on, while the eerie clouds trailed our every step from above. The night could be deceptive and daunting to the human senses, but not for Gershom or the hounds. Gershom pointed out with his torch in his hand that we had been here before, because the marks we had left behind were two lines overlapping each other on the trunk of a tree. The two lines must overlap each other wherever and whenever we went out into the vast pasture alone. This became an unbreakable rule Blade wanted us to remember on our first night out together. So, every time we explored the pasture, night or day, we always left the Canaanite letters such as 𐤀 and 𐤕 to show that we'd crossed particular paths with trees standing tall or slanted, while these letters 𐤉 and 𐤆 we used to describe the paths near streams and smaller bodies of water. As I took a closer look with my torch, I saw that this tree had marks on it, so I decided to place another set of marks on the tree.

"No more marks," said Gershom with his blocking me with the sharp end of his staff . I gave Gershom a simple nod, and we kept on moving ahead. Our journey continued in the direction we had gone the last time. The anxiety of what we would discover made me shiver—not to mention, the night's air continued to blow a chill through the pasture and against my back. Our footsteps took us deeper, while my mind drifted to various thoughts of the day: the thought of the Grecian trireme at the docks, the Grecian soldiers, the strange faces in town, meeting Mu's son, and our time at Blade's house. To be honest with myself, the moment at Blade's place was still pressed on my mind. There were so many questions to ask, and yet Blade and Nephtali threw us out into the dark without feeding our curiosity at all. I looked up into the moonlit sky and felt relieved as I stood there and wondered why was this journey we called *life* was such a mystery.

We began to see more marks on the bodies of fallen trees and knew our search had taken us far from home. This also meant we were closing in on our previous findings. Gershom was ahead of me with Tum-Ra and his pup beside him as they led the way. The two mother hounds covered the east and west sides, while I remained in the middle with Akhen-Inu and his pup following behind me. The other pups covered the remaining outer coordinates in our pack. Blade was a mastermind in training the hounds to move in this special formation. He had trained these hounds to always obey a command, and to always take down a prey animal from different angles with one attack at a time, especially when the prey outweighed them. The hounds were also trained to make certain growls and noises when danger was ahead, but never to bark unless the threat was very serious, and it was time to run.

The two hounds in front of Gershom made whimpering sounds to indicate that they sensed something ahead. Carefully, I pressed forward to be side by side with Gershom, while the Akhen-Inu and his pup followed after me. We both pressed forward until we stood near Tum-Ra and his pup and saw what caused the whimpering from the hounds.

"There it is, Teraditus, we've made it back," Gershom whispered while staring into my half-lit face. In front of us lay the bones of some unknown creature.

"These bones kind look like ribs," Gershom observed while bending down.

"If so, then down here must be the legs of the creature," I responded. Suddenly, the female hounds made simple yelping sounds to signal us to over where they were digging up something.

"I love these hounds," Gershom admitted, making his way over to them. "Where would we be without them?"

"We wouldn't be out here exploring, that's for sure," I replied to Gershom, while he showed them his appreciation by petting them on their heads. We stood up to watch the two hounds dig eagerly until something caught Gershom's attention.

"Okay, okay, good job girls, good job," Gershom told the two mother hounds as he bent down to inspect the mysterious bones they had uncovered. Gershom placed his staff down and handed me his torch in order to pull out the special utensils we'd need to aid us in digging. Gershom started to dig around these bones and then began brushing the dirt off them. "These bones extend almost six to seven feet long," Gershom said as I bent down in front of him.

"What kind of creature could this be? Gershom questioned me, while gesturing for me to come closer with the torch for better lighting.

"There might be more bones just as long on the opposite end," I said to Gershom before I handed him his torch and I decided to dig on the opposite end of Gershom.

My set of younger hounds followed me. Meanwhile, the alpha dogs maintained their posts north and south of each other to keep watch for anything that was a threat. However, the rest of the hounds, the pups, and the two mother hounds, started digging and digging, and in a couple of minutes, more bones started to appear until we stood in front of a massive pit of dry bones.

"What exactly am I looking at?" Gershom stood up, dropped his digging tools, and examined the dig site. He was bit frustrated as he moved the torch side to side. "I'm looking at this from the wrong angle," Gershom said to me as he walked around the gravesite, searching for the right angle for a better view. "This is the angle," he said to me with certainty. "Come over here and see what I mean," Gershom with a hint of enthusiasm in his voice—so I hurried over to his position and that's when I realized this creature had a large wingspan.

"It's a bird of some sort," I proclaimed my observation. "This is no ordinary bird, Gershom," I said.

"Maybe," Gershom said while deep in thought. Gershom walked over to the center and signaled me to come near him, where it was easier to see the rib-like bones of this creature. There he gave me his torch and took out my digging tools from my bag, since he was too lazy to retrieve his own. He moved north of the rib-like bones and started to dig steadily. I signaled for the pups to aid Gershom, which they did. In a matter of minutes, Gershom stood up and moved to where I stood. I gave him back his torch after he returned my tools to my bag.

"Okay," Gershom said after a pause. "Let's return to the spot where we were first standing to observe the creature as a whole." I did as Gershom said to get a better view of the creature.

"What is it?" I asked Gershom, but I got no response. "What are you thinking about, Gershom?" I questioned him again. The suspense was killing me.

"Have you ever seen a bird with a crocodile-like head such as this one?" Gershom asked.

"Gershom, no one has *ever* seen a bird with a head that resembles a crocodile, so that's a stupid question from someone like you," I told him.

Gershom looked into my half-lit face, speechless, and then returned his focus to the unknown creature. "Maybe it came from the underworld, and men fought it till they killed it. We've heard of the tales from our mothers about how fearless men traveled to the underworld to save their loved ones."

I knew the exact tales Gershom spoke of, but what bothered me about some of these tales from our mothers was how they ended tragically. "There was a tale of a man who traveled into the underworld and forgot to close the door when he returned back to the land of the living," Gershom said. "Many spirits escaped and made life difficult for humanity. Then it was up to the man—"

"Yes, I know the story," I interjected. "It was up to the man to close the door of the underworld. Unfortunately, he had to close it from inside and trap himself in the underworld to save humanity. All these tales had a tragic end—"

"The tale doesn't end just there, Teraditus," Gershom, said cutting me off the same way I had done to him. "The man did, in fact, sacrifice his life, but the task of getting rid of the remaining evil spirits in the realm of the living was up to his children." I let the air out of my chest and gave Gershom a simple nod. Gershom saw that his story was leading me to believe this might be one of those spirits, which was making sense to me at the moment since we had no other logical explanation.

"Teraditus, don't you see what this is? This creature might be one of those evil spirits which escaped and probably killed by one of the man's descendants."

"Wait—I never heard anything about the man's descendant and whatnot. Who exactly told you about this additional piece of information?" I asked.

Gershom looked at the unknown creature and said, "Blade, of course!" We both knew better than to question Blade's word.

"Fair enough," I said to Gershom. Gershom walked over to retrieve his tools. I could see the enigma on Gershom's face; it as though he was trying to figure out what the next move should be. "I think we should tell Blade about what we found. He would know what to do. Don't you agree, Gershom?" Gershom gave a nod, agreeing with what I recommended. His body and face were impassive as he placed his in tools his sack and walked over to stand next to me. It was clear that Gershom was mentally processing what we had discovered.

It wasn't too often I would see this sort of expression on Gershom's face. When his own wisdom failed him, it made me smile a great deal. First, Gershom would become speechless, but somehow, he remained lucid enough to respond to every question, even though his mind was laden with thoughts. Odd facial expressions followed after the silence, and then he would make strange noises. By this point with Gershom, you had to wait until his noises became words that actually made sense.

"Underworld, mystery creature, man, descendants— *crocodiles!*" It would have seemed Gershom lost his mind. I do enjoy such a rare moment, but I could not afford him to lose his mind this far away from home in the height of the night. I knew quite well not to underestimate the darkness, because it had the potential to kill you with a calmness just like the open sea. So, I needed Gershom back to a state of mental stability.

"Okay, Gershom, come back to me, come back," I told him.

He turned to me to say, "Teraditus, we need to tell Blade about this as soon as possible. He'll know how to handle this."

Of course, he was simply repeating what I had recommended first— but I knew he would never admit to it. I shook my head and redirected my focus back to the unknown creature. There I began to ask question to myself: *What is this creature or was it some vile spirit that escaped from the underworld? Why would a spirit have bones—wait, does a spirit have bones? I think it will be wise to say that Gershom was onto something with his tale. However, let's run it through Blade first to be sure, of course.* My inner voice reassured me. A heavy sighed fell from Gershom, while his body shifted in the direction for us to head home.

Suddenly, the winds came to a momentary hush, which gave all of us the chance to hear something in the distance. Our heads turned back in the direction of the bewildering sound. Gershom and I glanced at each other, as if to say, *you heard that too!*

"We should head back," I admonished Gershom.

However, he absolutely ignored me. He said to me, "We have to check it out."

I wasn't surprised, because we always seemed to see through the looking glass from opposite sides.

"Perhaps, it is foolish for me to ask," I said, "but tell me why we should head in the direction of the peculiar sound?"

Gershom opened his mouth to answer, when we all heard the strange sound again; just like the first time, and we all turned our heads in its direction. Akhen-Inu made a whimpering sound of concern, while Tut-Ra followed shortly after.

"Even the hounds know better, Gershom. And somehow, you don't." I said with distress, but Gershom remained speechless and fixated on the noise. He seemed practically drawn to whatever that mysterious sound was, as though he sensed there was something that required his attention.

"Listen," he began, "the strange faces we saw in town gave me a cold feeling. I know it bothered you, too."

I sighed and gave him a nod of agreement.

"Okay," Gershom continued. "Who's to say that's not them? Plus, they are so close to our homes—I say let's check it out to see if we have anything to be concerned about. Perhaps lives will depend on it."

"*Queen of the heavens,*" I thought to myself, because I knew he was right.

"Quickly now, put out the flame from your torch," Gershom said hastily, while quelling the flame with his left hand. Something I failed to have mastered as of yet, but Gershom mastered it without any practice. I believe it had something to do with Gershom being left-handed; mother would often remind me that left-handed people were considerably gifted and rare, all the while possessing unimaginable talents they had yet to discover. Every word my mother said concerning left-handed people described Gershom perfectly. Suddenly, Gershom walked over to where I stood, lost in thought, and oust the flame from my torch with his left hand before he said to me, "You need to focus and give the command to the hounds."

I looked to the hounds, and I gave them the command they knew best. "Hunt!" The hounds quickly assembled into their positions. In this formation, their awareness of the surroundings heightened as they centered all their raw animal instincts on anything that presented a real threat to our lives—and their lives, too. However, the protection of Gershom and I was the hounds' primary objective, and they were willing to kill and sacrifice their lives to make sure their objective was fulfilled. The hounds were the closest and best experience of being a part of a military unit. This was all thanks to Blade's training, which typically took place every weekend—a training which Gershom and I were obligated to be part of. It was through these training sessions, Gershom and I thought Blade wasn't human, especially from all the *Montu* exercises and drills he would have us and hounds perform in order to develop survival skills. But after what we encountered tonight, our thoughts about Blade's training sessions were under appreciated. Blade was trying to prepare us in many ways, as if he knew the days were coming when we would have to depend on these survival skills. It was enough to say, there's nothing Blade couldn't do, or any topic he had no knowledge of. For a man his age, he knew more than both our fathers put together. Nevertheless, Blade always remained humble about everything, and I mean everything.

The wind pressed against our backs, and our hounds were by our sides. We set out underneath the shadows of the drifting clouds above, which we used to hide our very existence from the brightness of the moonlight. Every step we took, the ground below changed from coarse to soft and then it felt mushy. I could only assume we were approaching a creek of some sort, since bushes appeared more abundant in size, enough for us to hide behind. We stealthily meandered through the pathless horizon, often ducking in and out of bushes whenever the shadows from above could not hide us any longer from the silver light of the full moon of the moon. On my far left, more trees started to appear in the distance, standing tall over the dunes, with leaves thick enough to hide us from the light of the moon, but not strong enough for young boys like us to climb. I watched the trees swaying from side to side in unison.

The quest to discover more mysteries of the night increased my heart rate with every step we took. I was sure my heart was going to break itself out of my chest. Gershom and I tried our best to move swift, but smart. Gershom raised his left hand with the staff, which meant to stop. He bent down and looked around as if something suspicious caught his attention. Gershom looked up and saw the trailing cloud was soon to give way to the moonlight, so he ran over behind the closest bush before he signaled to me with his bird whistle and I hurried over to him with my hounds by my side.

"What happened? Did you see something?" I questioned Gershom, while we looked frantically through the bush for anything alarming.

"I heard something in the wind," he replied, while he kept his eyes looking through the bush. I close my eyes and listened, but the winds spoke nothing strange.

"What did you hear?"

"It's nothing," Gershom said firmly. "Listen, we're getting closer, so you know what time it is. The *whistle in the wind*! Just like Blade taught us. Pay attention to each other's whistles as we get closer, but only use it when needed. Once we're closer, I will whistle for us to meet up again to discuss a real plan of action, okay—"

"Okay," I replied. It dawned on me. This was the moment for all of Blade's training for wilderness survival to be put to test, and I felt far from ready. I felt afraid.

As we covered more ground, I wanted to turn back around and head home, but we were now a great way off from our homes and to leave Gershom was unimaginable. So, the thought was pushed out of mind as the journey took us to a meandering creek, and this made Gershom raise his left hand. He bent down and stumbled over to where I was to say, "Okay, I sense we're getting closer. I think we should go into eyes and ears formation. Okay!" Gershom whistled one low tune for all the hounds to come together as one. "Eyes and ears, everyone, eyes and ears," he commanded them, and off they went into two groups. Then he looked at me, and we both said, "Move!" Gershom and his hounds moved to the left, and I moved to the right with my own set of hounds, but we made sure to keep twenty feet of visual distance between each other at the moment.

We traveled a half a mile away from the gravesite before the peculiar sounds became a tad more audible, but it still remained indistinguishable. Fear and anxiety began to heighten my senses, to the point I felt I could see the wind and taste the air. This fear caused me to avoid touching any bush or plant in my path, until the moonlight forced me to seek cover behind a bush. The hounds, on the other hand, zig-zag in front of me, treading lightly through the calm of the night. I wondered what manner of thoughts ran through their minds as we proceeded closer to the unknown, but they only had smiles of on their faces. Maybe, this was how the hounds masked their fear, or maybe it was just me and I was overthinking things in my head as usual.

Gershom was a couple of feet away, covering the left side for anything unusual, while I covered the right. My mind kept me preoccupied with anxiety and reminders of what to do to stay alive.

Look beyond the horizon, Teraditus, my conscience said to me. Confounded by this, I decided to look. There, I saw a peculiar light—the sort of light that came from outdoor fires.

Wait . . . a typical fire cannot be seen this far, I argued silently with myself.

Correct, my inner voice replied. *The only kind of fires that can be seen this far are large sacrificial or ceremonial fires.* I was impressed by how spry and attentive my conscience mind was functioning tonight.

You may have a point, I said inwardly.

Before you proceed any further, inform Gershom of what you see, before you two become separated—or worse.

I knew exactly what my conscience was talking about, so I turned to sound the whistle to bring us everyone together—only to see that Gershom and the hounds were already converging to where I was.

"What the—" I began.

"Hey," Gershom said in a low voice. "I just saw the light beyond the horizon. The first thing that came to my mind was a fire—but it's no ordinary fire. It must be a ceremonial fire, or the kinds of fire people set up to praise their deity." Even in the midst of this danger, Gershom was still a know-it-all. "Why do you have that expression on your face, Teraditus? Are you listening to what I was saying?"

This was my moment to be the facetious one for once, and he had taken the opportunity from me yet again.

I sighed and said, "Yeah, that makes a lot of sense. What's the next move?" Gershom, who was now bent down next to me, had an incredulous look on his face. I assumed he was battling with his own thoughts, in his own way.

It should not have been a shock to me that Gershom's fears were similar to mine. Gershom knew this venture was something he didn't want to do, but he knew the greater risk if we turned around to head home.

"I wish we had our torches, it's becoming harder to see underneath the moonlight," Gershom whispered. "Let's split up this time so we can cover more ground from different points." The plan was simple and candid. I gave him a nod of agreement, and off he went, trying his best to stay low to the ground. He ran a couple of feet ahead but stopped for a while to observe anything unusual and check up on me.

I had this sense that every step I took was a step closer to the end of our chapter—or the start of a new one. Only time knew my fate—and Gershom's, as well. The anxiety was starting to subside within me now, since our ability to suppress our fears in order to focus on our tasks at hand could decide whether or not we would see another sunrise.

The wind continued to blow in the direction we were heading; it seemed even the wind was pushing us there. The moonlight cast an eerie light on the bushes and tall grass that shifted every time the wind blew, and the shadows from the verdant vegetation moved with us as we traveled. If felt as though we were all on the path to our doom. "*This wind will carry our scent to those around the fire before we reach them. This could change everything. The element of surprise would be in their favor, rather than yours.*" The information my conscious mind shared with me made sense, and I had to tell Gershom before his mind told him the same.

Gershom was still ahead of me, but to the left. Suddenly, he came to a stop as to circumspect his surroundings. This was my chance to step up, so I ran up to his left side. "Gershom, Gershom," I said with great urgency in my voice. Gershom peered into my eyes intuitively, but I could not read his stare. "Gershom, it occurred to me that we should redirect ourselves to the west, since the wind could carry our scent to them first. Who's to say they don't have hounds like us?" I said to him, yet he kept staring at me. "Gershom, did you hear what I said?" Gershom was acting stranger than he usually did—or so I thought.

The wind was blowing harder than before, and I became increasingly concerned with Gershom's peculiar behavior.

"Gershom, what's happening?" I asked in alarm.

All of sudden, the night winds blew more restless when Gershom opened his mouth and said in a ghostly manner, "Teraditus, run!" Those were the last two words I heard right before the wind ceased, and the next sounds I heard were the ferocious growls of the hounds which meant we were in danger. The moon above hid its face from us as if it saw the impending danger down below.

I turned around to run as Gershom instructed me when suddenly I heard.

"Watch out!" yelled Gershom frantically, while pushing me out of the way of a small, soaring arrow that slashed my right deltoid and struck Gershom in his left shoulder blade. Both Gershom and I dropped our spears, but only Gershom fell to the ground. I reached down for my spear, while Gershom still held his in his left shoulder.

"Defensive formation!" Gershom yelled to the hounds with intense zeal. I bent down to help Gershom back on his feet, but I sensed another presence skulking in the dark shadows. I whipped my head around in time see the silhouette of a massive hand reaching toward me, but Tut-Ra emerged unseeingly from the darkness with only his razor sharp, white teeth clutching around the hand intended to take hold of me and dragged that hand downward.

"Look out!" Gershom yelled again from the ground as a man appeared from another direction. My head snapped over to another closing in on us, but Akhen-Inu tackled the man to the ground. Both men cried out in agony, while Gershom stood to his feet. I watched him pull the dart out of his left shoulder blade and then he placed a small vial into his mouth, which I knew to be a charcoal concoction. We both assumed that the small arrow that pierced Gershom's left shoulder may have been poisonous.

"Quick, take some in case," said Gershom, handing me the small vial. I reached for the vial and that is when I noticed the cries of men in agony had ceased as the two male hounds staggered toward us over to Gershom and me, whimpering with the stains of blood smudge on their bottom jaws. With the return of the moon, cascading its silver light down, I vividly saw the two small darts jutting from their sides. I reached over pulled the two darts out of Akhen-Inu, and Tut-Ra was next.

Out of nowhere, another figure appeared out of the night, and in a single throw, three darts flew out his hand, and one struck me in the right hand holding Tut-Ra, while the two struck Tut-Ra again. Akhen-Inu ran instantly ran toward the man who was one with the night, and three more darts flew out his hands and down Akhen-Inu went before he could reach his target. It was the most impressive, deadly maneuver I had ever seen; I doubted if even Blade could do such a thing. "*Use your hidden daggers*," my conscience reminded me. I quickly removed the dart out of my right hand and reached to my left arm, slid out a knife, and took aim at the new and mysterious figure. At that very moment, he withdrew himself from our sight as the passing clouds hid the light from the moon. Suddenly a dart struck me between my fingers, knocking the knife from my hand and piercing into my right hand.

Quickly, I reached for the small dart and pulled it out of my right hand, while vehemently sucking air through my teeth to bear with the pain.

"Bend down," Gershom yelled from behind. Without any thinking, I bent down, and a fireball instantly flew over my head and burned the ground behind us. Soon more firebombs followed, wildly dispersing the flames at first, but I soon noticed the fire was encircling us and there was nowhere to run from the terror in the night. Through the light of the flames, Gershom and I saw the hounds held their guard stance by keeping these unknown assailants of the night away from us. The hounds constantly barked at them, forcing some of these men to maintain their distance, and others vanish into the distance. With the flames spreading wider with the help of the night winds, the air grew toxic and harder to breathe. That's when the coughing started, and soon my legs gave way. To the ground I fell, the palms of my hands and knees saved my fall, but not without suffering from any bruises. The coughing intensified.

"Here take this," said Gershom while he bent down to give me the same vial with charcoal in it. I looked at the small vial, and I saw four vials rotating in Gershom's left hand. I held onto my head with my right hand, when I felt Gershom place the small vial in my right hand.

"Hurry and drink, drink, before the poison takes effect," Gershom warned me, so I placed the vial to my mouth and drank the chalky, black solution. Before I could remove the vial from my head, Gershom reached down and struggled to pull me up, until I was standing on my feet. Gershom handed my staff over before he held me up, while he held me up by my left arm.

"We have to get out of here," Gershom whispered to me. But as I looked around, all I saw were the hounds barking at what appeared to

be a small militia of men standing and moving through the shadows of the night.

"Queen of the skies, help us, I pray," I whispered, looking at the ghastly danger ahead. There was no telling how many men were out there in the night, and I didn't want to know either. What mattered was finding a way out and warning our family about the strange things moving in the dark. A task that seemed almost impossible; behind us was the open flames, and in front us were men of the night. I glanced over to the open flames and back at the darkness where strange men awaited us.

"I'll take my chances with the fire," I said bitterly to Gershom.

"Me too," Gershom whispered back at me. "But can you run?"

"Yeah, I can run, but I never ran through the fire before," I replied to Gershom's question.

"I guess tonight is going to be *that* night." I glanced into Gershom's face, and he looked serious. A sigh fell from my chest as I removed Gershom's support from my left arm and said, "Let's move fast." Gershom gave me a nod of acceptance. Gershom turned to his left behind, and I turned to my right and took another look at the growing flames and felt we ought to reconsider the option of running through the fire. I redirected my focus back to Gershom in time to see a frantic expression written across his face, while he swung his staff upward, toward me. I held out my hands with my staff to defend myself when a massive hand grabbed Gershom's spear and snapped it with ease. I looked up and saw the eyes of a man whose head and face were covered with a black, linen cloth that had a bird's feather attached to the side of the headwrap. Without thought, I swung my staff to his abdomen, but his other hand grabbed my spear and proceeded to bend the wooden spear. However, I sensed what he was doing and pulled the spear out of his grip and pierced his right foot instead.

The man growled with anger before I looked into his eyes, which were fixed firmly on me and were white with rage, and I managed to see the tattoo under his left eye was the *all-seeing eye*. I could not believe it; he was from the land of Kemet. Quickly, I drew out my spear, while Gershom drew out a hand knife, and we both proceeded to stab this man. But he kicked Gershom right in the stomach, which propelled Gershom more than five feet into the ground and grabbed my spear with both hands and pulled me toward him, so he could knee me right in the abdomen which knocked the air out of me and elbowed me into the cold ground.

"Defense formation, defense formation," screamed Gershom tirelessly, while a massive man grabbed me by my head and carefully pulled me up from the ground. Still in pain and eyes barely opened. Somehow, I saw both Akhen-Inu and Tut-Ra were motionless on the ground, and I knew the poison from the darts were responsible. This was bad, but I wasn't going without a fight. Quickly, I pulled out a knife from the leather piece I made earlier in the evening hours and directed it toward his abdomen again. However, the mysterious man grabbed my feeble wrist with his massive left hand and twisted my wrist in the manner where my small knife slipped out my hand and straight into his right hand, and with my own blade he stabbed me in my abdomen. My entire body felt cold and numb. I knew deep down inside that this was it, so I stared into my killer's face to see his eyes—and I saw the white in his eyes as he looked at me with no sympathy or remorse.

"Tearditus, nooooo!" screamed Gershom.

CHAPTER 14

ANOTHER AFTERNOON WITH LOVED ONES (INTERLUDE)

[Mykonos Island / Aegean Sea, 29 AD]

Teraditus had reached a climactic point in his story, and he took a moment to reflect upon it.

"Please, let me guess," Ena said. "This was the first time you ever looked in the face of death?" She laughed quietly as she looked down at Diodotus, who lay comfortably in the warmth of her arms, deep in an afternoon nap.

Teraditus smiled at Ena and leaned over to Allidephi to say, "She's correct. I think Ena should tell the rest of the story, since she knows the full tale. Considering, she is known as the Goddess *Neith* to the ancient inhabitants of Libu or should I say *Lamia*."

"Oh!" Ena said in an astonished tone. "So, we're going there, huh? Bringing up the past."

"I'm confused," Allidephi said while glancing from side to side at Teraditus and Ena. "Are you saying that Ena is the Goddess Neith?"

"Well, let me just say, before the Athenians found favor and hope in their Goddess Athena, there were other men that worshipped Neith for similar reasons before she abandoned her first group of believers, changed her name, and built up a new nation. Even though, this same Goddess neglected her responsibilities to care for her first believers, I took up the responsibility to remind her of them," Teraditus explained with a smile.

"Wait a minute, are you the one responsible for sending me a stone craving of a ram's head with sapphire eyes every dark moon?" Ena questioned her elderly friend.

"What can I say, my Goddess, I want you to remember your people of the past, the same way you remember my many tales of the past," Teraditus replied with a juvenile smirk.

Ena knew what Teraditus was trying to do, so she decided to play along. "You know what, I will continue the story and add some embarrassing details you failed to mention," she said maliciously. "Where did you last leave off? Oh yes, Teraditus fell to ground as he drew in his final breaths, still holding onto the little life he had left—"

"Who's ready to eat?"

Priscilla's question made every head turn in her direction.

The hungry men replied in unison, "*We are!*" Then they all got up, one after the other, leaving Teraditus with the women and children at the patio table.

"Everybody, since we are out here, why don't we have supper out on the patio—how does that sound?" Priscilla asked.

The women unanimously agreed to the suggestion, but the men looked at the women, and then each other. Knowing the obvious—that they were hungry—the ravenous men just agreed with the women in order to get to their food faster.

* * * *

The sound of family in fellowship filled Teraditus's outside patio. The sun was completely down, and the backyard shone bright with the

flames from Apollo's torches. Diodotus was wide awake and back in his mother's arms with his father beside them.

Afterward, with everyone still at the table, Seleni said, "Priscilla, the food is amazing, especially the fish. What is it? I've never had a fish like that."

Priscilla pointed to Teraditus, who answered, "Yeah, I have a good friend who travels to the far corners of the east and west. He was the one who introduced me to this foreign fish, which he found in the northwestern fresh waters. The last I saw him, he promised to bring me back a crate of this exotic fish and more—"

Ena cut Teraditus off by asking, "What is this *exotic* fish called?"

"My friend calls it *pink fish*, but he made a joke that it should be called *snakehead fish*."

Seleni got up from the table to help Priscilla clean up and looked in Teraditus's direction to say, "I like the *pink fish*."

"I see more of a salmon color—maybe it should be called *salmon* rather *pink fish*," Ena injected as she got up from the table to help the women clean up. Teraditus smiled and agreed with Ena with a simple nod, while the others on the table continued with their side conversation.

The night was still young, and Teraditus knew his stories would not suffice to the young audience. "Who's up for a swim?" Teraditus asked his family out of the blue.

Everyone stopped to consider the suggestion, but Ena's head was already nodding to the idea of a late-night swim.

"I'll get the cart together," Teraditus said as he left the patio table. Seleni and Priscilla finished clearing the table, while the others got their necessary items for the swim and made their way to the cart. Teraditus got the cart together for their travel to the family's favorite spot for cliff diving.

On their journey there, Teraditus's mind drifted off. He had flashbacks of moments with his wife and children, who had all jumped off the cliff with closed minds and come up from the waters open-minded. The jump had a strange effect that way. Teraditus remembered the times his baby girl was afraid to jump off the cliff and her mother often stayed with her at the top, while everybody else dove off the cliff. His wife held her baby girl for a full year every time they visited the cliff, comforting and building her confidence, so, one day, Cassiani would be able to jump off. That day came when Cassiani took both her parents by their hands, and together all three jumped off. This was the most memorable moment for Teraditus at this cliff.

The reminiscing came to an end when Apollos announced their arrival. Telus and Apollos jumped out of the moving cart and raced to the cliff, with Rellos sprinting behind them. Ena laughed because she knew what the race was intended to prove who was faster. Ena hopped out after them and managed to pass them both before jumping in herself. The others remaining inside the cart jumped out of the moving cart and ran after the other four, once they saw how much fun they were having, racing to the edge of the cliff and vanishing below. Teraditus got off the cart and made his way to the cliff to see his family. When he heard a galloping horse, he turned around and saw his wife riding on the horse. She was beautiful as her long, white locks bounced valiantly behind her back. The moment the horse stopped, the young, white hair woman hopped off the horse and rushed over to Teraditus.

"Please tell me you're here to take a break," Teraditus questioned Priscilla, who was now in his arms.

She looked up at him with the moonlight on her face and said, "Yes!" Priscilla freed herself from Teraditus's arms and sprinted off the cliff. The sound of the young woman screaming and breaking the water's surface filled the evening air. The men and Ena cheered for Priscilla because they were all so glad to see her taking a break; she deserved it.

"Teraditus, it's your turn to jump," Ena yelled from the bottom. Ena's request motivated everyone in the water to request the same thing.

The repeated words "jump, jump, jump" were chanted from the base of the cliff, and even the horses joined in with the chanting.

Teraditus looked at the horses and said, "You know where to go, right?" Then he turned and ran to the edge of the cliff and jumped legs-first into the Aegean Sea. The young people extolled Teraditus, and the laughter filled the air. Some of them splashed each other, while others like Telus and Apollos raced each other in the water, and Rellos tossed the women in the air. The sound of laughter and happiness in the open sea reminded Teraditus of how much he missed these moments when his entire family came to visit. He was eternally grateful for these joyous times, especially at his old age. Teraditus never knew when the next time like this would be—or even if he would be fortunate to see a next time. Only a man who has lost so much knows the true value of time spent with those he loves.

An hour and twenty minutes had passed since everyone began frolicking in the water. Teraditus grew concerned about the child and two women they had left behind, so he told everyone, "It may be time to head back home to the others—"

"Ahh, no, just a few more minutes!"

"Yeah, we're having so much fun," they replied to Teraditus's suggestion.

"This is fun—more fun than I've had a long time, but—"

"*Look out below!*" yelled someone as an unknown person crashed into the water with such intensity that the seawater blinded everyone.

When everyone recovered from the tumultuous splash, the unknown figure was nowhere to be found. "Who in Hades's names was that?" Ena said while wiping away the water from her face. Five minutes passed since the figure had jumped in, and this made everyone in the water worried.

"Oh my goodness, something touched my leg," Priscilla said frantically.

Priscilla reached out and grabbed Telus, saying, "Hold me, and don't let go."

Priscilla latched onto Telus's back and pressed her head against his head.

"Ena, Telus, go check it out," Teraditus said to the couple. Without anyone seeing, Ena's eyes began to glow before she dove into the deep waters, but she returned in less than a minute, resurfacing with a smile on her face. "You won't believe who it is," she said to Teraditus.

Before Teraditus could finish asking who, the figure burst from underwater and wrapped herself around the back of Teraditus. "Did you miss me?"

Teraditus turned to look over his right shoulder and saw the figure of his young wife. "Cassiani, is that you, my baby girl?" Teraditus's voice broke a little when he asked her the question.

"You didn't answer my question, Father. Did you miss me?"

Teraditus freed himself from Cassiani's grip and hugged his baby girl. Tears flowed down his face, but only Cassiani saw and felt them. "I didn't think you were coming . . ."

"And miss this opportunity, Father? I think not," Cassiani answered, following with another hug.

"Okay, Teraditus, it's our turn to greet her now," Ena said with eagerness in her voice. Cassiani swam around to greet everyone in the waters. Cassiani even greeted Telus with Priscilla still clutched onto his body; however, Priscilla had to let go of Telus to hug Cassiani. Teraditus allowed everyone to socialize and bond with one another for an extra half-hour before he persuaded them to head to the shore.

The swim to shore only took ten minutes, but the two siblings and Ena made a competition of swimming there first. When Priscilla and Teraditus ran up on the bank, the competitors were quarreling among themselves as to who was the winner. The contentious competitors even asked Seleni and Allidephi—who were surprisingly waiting at the shore with a campfire, along with the horses from clifftop—who the rightful

winner was. The two women were embroiled into this dispute, both unable to enunciate their thoughts and opinions.

Teraditus stopped the argument by walking up to the athletes and raising both his hands. "Come on, you three, we are too old for this bickering. Plus, tomorrow is another day with new challenges." The competitors looked amongst themselves and nodded their heads to show their acceptance to what Teraditus had said. Teraditus turned to Seleni, who was no stranger to this sibling rivalry and saw relief on her face.

"Much gratitude," Seleni said to Teraditus.

Everyone gathered around the fire, while Seleni and Allidephi passed around the blankets to dry off and warm up the wet swimmers. Diodotus was wide-awake and wrapped in swaddling cloth around Allidephi's stomach so both her arms could be free to help Seleni distribute the blankets.

Cassiani walked up to her father and leaned against him.

"Cassiani," Teraditus began, "I assume you just reached the island." He could feel his daughter nodding her head on his left arm.

"When I reached the house, Seleni informed me of your moonlight swim." Cassiani lifted her head from her father's arm and shouted at the others in a slightly overwrought manner, "The ladies and I took the other cart to come down here to meet up with everyone." Cassiani resumed her resting position on her father's left arm, but she quickly picked her head back up to say, "Not to mention, the fire was my idea, so you are all welcome."

Telus started counting to three, and then in unison, everyone said, "Thank you, Cassiani!"

We sat around the fire conversing amongst one another about old times and future decisions. The amity and bonding between the family made us lose track of time. Allidephi grew concerned about Diodotus staying up this late, so she shrugged at Rellos and showed him her tired son in her arms. "Diodotus is ready for bed—it's a sign for us to head back."

Everyone agreed and gathered their belongings. The journey home began with Priscilla and Cassiani sprinting off first, and everyone else in the cart followed behind them.

* * * *

When the sun rose the next day, Allidephi was determined to hear what had happened that night with Teraditus and Gershom. She got up from beside Rellos, who was still deep in slumber and checked on Diodotus—who was also deep in slumber like his father. Allidephi made a confused facial expression as she looked at both her son and husband. She shook her head as she left her sleeping men to their slumber, and set off to find the one man who had a tale to tell. "But where was he?" Allidephi asked herself softly, and at that moment it hit her when she heard the rooster's frustration. Allidephi made her way outside to see the rooster trotting away and Ena smiling with Teraditus. Teraditus turned to Allidephi.

"I guess it's time, huh?" Teraditus asked Allidephi. Allidephi smiled as they all made their way inside the house.

CHAPTER 15

SAW DEATH AND LIVED

[Cyrene/Libu - Ten Years Before the Battle of Thermopylae (480 BC)]

The man's hand held me up with my own blade still thrust inside me. I was trapped in death's grasp, and I didn't know what to do. I felt helpless as cold air brushed across my face, but it was almost hard to tell. The warmth inside of me was slipping, while I struggled to hold onto life. I was immersed in fear as life was slipping away. Gershom screamed my name, but I'm sure even he knew my fate was decided.

I felt the frigid blade from my own knife piercing my numb body. I looked one more time into the face of this man, this mysterious figure with these familiar markings on his face, and saw the look of death in his eyes. I closed my eyes and accepted my fate. My body and spirit were dispersing from each other, but I clung on to the two. An attempt seemed to be futile, because the knife was severing the bond that held the two as one as it moved deeper into my flesh. I became an innocuous lamb being slaughtered.

I opened my eyes, expecting to see my spirit leave my body. When, all of sudden, the sound of rapid, ferocious footsteps shook the ground, and I saw my assailant turn his face from mine to witness the jaws of a hound sprinting over to avenge me. I felt the blade leave my body as the man lost his hold on me. I stumbled back before I could see another hound jumping toward the neck of the man. He yelled out of fear as the hound took him down to the ground, viciously ripping at his arm he used to defend himself from. Fortunately, the attack was brief and still enough to leave him injured.

Once I hit the ground, Gershom ran to my side. "Queen of the Heavens, you're bleeding a lot, we need to put pressure on it," Gershom said while he took the shirt off his own back to place over my wound and tied the garment over the wound. One of the mother hounds came over to my side whimpering; I believe she was mine, but she sprinted off to defend us again.

"What of Akhen-Inu and Tut-Ra?" I asked faintly.

"They're not moving—at all. You have to get up while the pups buy us some time," Gershom explained. The pups were in their adolescent years, which meant they had the strength to take down—or even kill their prey. These pups were our last line of defense to make an escape. Little did these men know, but the pups were trained to survey the enemies to outflank them. And by the sounds of men yelling and shouting in agony, mixed with ferocious growls, I knew the flanking had begun, which meant these men were encountering surprise attacks from all angles. The pups were smart enough to know they didn't even have to attack, all they had to do was entice fear into these men by sounding like they were about to be attacked, and since it was dark, the pups had the advantage and they knew this.

Gershom helped me to my feet and told me to hold onto my wound. He drew out the concealed knife from his right arm and threw it toward a man, who just fell dead on the ground. I couldn't believe it, Gershom just killed a man, as if it was nothing new to him. Gershom then reached for my spear, which was still whole, and held onto it. "Let's move," he said to me as I placed my left arm over his bare back and held my left

abdomen with my right hand where the wound was, and we were off. Hopping alongside the open flames, until we saw an opening safe enough to get around the fire. All the while, hoping not to be seen by the wrong eyes.

Still in pain, I managed to turn and see one of the pup's jaws latch onto the man's leg, pulling him away from the light of the wild flames and back into the darkness of the night. "Come on, Teraditus, you have to move," Gershom said, while struggling to move me faster and away from the mayhem. I knew Gershom meant no harm, but the pain was overbearing to move as fast as he wanted me to. Suddenly, we heard footsteps rushing toward us, which only meant one thing.

"Gershom, Gershom," I whispered viperously in his ear, but he responded not. Instead, he threw me onto the ground and spun in time to thrust the spear straight into the man's mouth. The man stood there, gasping for air with a spear through his mouth and out his neck. Then Gershom withdrew the spear and the assailant fell lifelessly to the ground. I became breathless by what I saw next.

Gershom raised the spear as high as he could, and then plunged it straight into the assailant's back. From where I sat on the ground, I could hear and feel the heavy thumps of the spear continuously breaking through the body of the victim. What little life he had left was undeniably gone now. Then Gershom twisted the spear and pulled it out of the enemy's back. I could not believe what my eyes were showing me. Gershom just killed another man, and the look on his face as he walked toward me was pure fury.

"Let's go," he said to me as he ran over to me and picked me up — the bloody spear in his other hand — and off we went. Away from it all, underneath the dark side of the moon, leaving the mayhem in the distance. Every new step I took, the pain started to subside, and I wasn't sure what to make of it. However, my focus was on Gershom. He was walking ahead of me, pulling me along and shivering, but his anger fueled his every move. This was not good because Gershom's anger could be intractable if he didn't calm down. I didn't know what to say. I could not find the right words.

"I'm worried about the hounds, I feel bad for leaving them behind, but I know they'll do their best to hold them back. Whoever those men are, I don't think that's the end of the story."

Gershom remained speechless, still holding me up and walking at a fast pace.

"What do you think, Gershom—what does all of this mean?"

Five minutes passed before Gershom could think of something sensible to say. "It means we will be seeing more of those men." The short-tempered response meant that I should leave him to his own thoughts so he could find a promising solution.

Suddenly, my wound seemed to be nonexistent. The pain seemed to have disappeared. I wasn't sure if the cold air had made me numb, or if my mind and body had moved to two opposite ends. Whatever be the reason, there was only one thing I knew in this moment: the sophomoric days of my life were coming to a drastic end. Life would not be the same. I wasn't sure why I was feeling this way, but I knew everything was about to change for both Gershom and me. I just didn't know if it would be a change for the best, or the worst.

CHAPTER 16

IT'S TIME

[Cyrene/Libu - Ten Years Before the Battle of Thermopylae (480 BC)]

The journey home seemed to take forever, but we got back in a timely manner. On the way, we were joined by the surviving pup hounds and the two mother hounds. They managed to catch up with us, even though some of the pups were limping, panting, and dripping with blood. We were all bruised and exhausted, but we made it to the house. Before we went inside, Gershom stopped me in front of the door and said, "Tonight—not over... it's not over." Those were the last words I heard from Gershom before he walked away with a group of hounds following him. I knew he was heading straight to Blade and Nephtali, and once they got word of our calamity, then everyone would know.

As I entered the house, my mother gasped as she laid eyes on my battered form. She sprinted over to the wall where her multi-purpose herbs and concoctions were on the shelves and pulled out all she needed. Then she guided me to a chair, so she could apply her necessary herbal remedies to all my wounds. She moved fast, without looking once at the vials to see if these were the right ones to mix. The way she moved was all-natural for her, but too surreal for me. As her hand moved here and there, I recalled how my mother entertained the three of us last night with an imaginable tale of her past life as a *black dove* in the great city of Babylonia. At a young age, my mother was a high priestess, often referred to as a **black dove**, which traveled to distant Kingdoms to carry out the temple duties. For my mother to be tasked with such heavy responsibilities in her early and mid-teens, meant she was beyond gifted—a child of promise which only walked the Earth once every fourth generation.

I watched her pour and mix all manner substances, which filled the air with earthly smells. It was evident her time at the feet of the master teachers inside the sacred temples, learning the herbal remedies to heal and improve the health of the human body with plants and alchemy was far from a waste. My mother turned to me and took out what looked to be a wet linen cloth from a small container and covered the stab wound of my left abdomen. This was a new embalming technique my mother she applied to the living. She applied five more and followed up by using a balm on the rest of the other wounds.

Suddenly, she handed me a cup of her famous black tonic. A hot brew comprised of strong herbs and thick oils. I was reluctant at first due to its emetic taste and smell, but my mother would not have such resistance. Carefully, she forced me to drink all the black tonic by holding the cup to my mouth, until the dregs only remained on the bottom of the cup. After the drink, she carried me to my bed and tucked me inside. Once she was done with me, she frantically ran out of the room, and started whispering something to my father. My father, on the other hand, took care of the remaining hounds that managed to follow us home. After such, he left us in the house after giving my mother instructions not to open the door for anyone until his return.

The nightmare was over for me, but it was just getting started for my parents. My father's footsteps leaving the house were the last sound I

heard before I blacked out. I knew not where he was going exactly, but I knew it was going to involve Gershom's father and Blade.

That same night, I dreamt about a series of women, all facing me with their eyes covered with linen clothes of four distinguishable colors: black, yellow gold, green, and red. As I walked through the sea of women, I heard my name being called in strange tongues; tongues I never heard before, but I kept on moving until I heard familiar voices calling my name. That's when I saw Nephtali, Gershom's mother, and lastly my own mother with their eyes uncovered. They were calling out to me, while fading away like the smoke from a fire pit, no longer lit. I ran to them and ran, but that very second with our hands reaching toward each other. The three women vanished, and I was alone with the rest of these women I knew not.

Woman after woman passed me, some caused me to feel highs, and others I felt low frequencies. However, in this vast sea of women around me, I felt nothing. As if they were only there to take up time and space, but in the end. Every one of them kept calling my name, while their eyes remained covered with a linen cloth of the four distinguishable colors. Suddenly, I stopped and there stood three in front of me. One to my left had a black linen cloth covering her eyes, the one to my right had a red linen cloth, and the third one in the center had green linen cloth. However, the one standing in the center was the one who said not a word. Instantly, I was immensely drawn to her, I could not explain it, but she was—the *one*!

"Who are you?" I questioned her. She smiled and removed her green linen cloth from over her eyes, and her beauty shone through her long, white locks, light caramel skin tone, and harvest gold eyes.

"It's not time to know who I am yet," she whispered to me. "But it's time to wake up because your mother is coming inside your room."

"Mom..."

"Teraditus, honey, are you awake? How are you feeling?" my mother asked me, while she embraced me with a hug and a kiss.

167

"Mom, I'm fine—you know us men heal overnight," I said, emulating the way my father spoke to my mother whenever he was sick or injured. As expected, my mother made a face. "Mom, today's Thursday, aren't you supposed to be running the shop with JuJu? Why are you here?" My mother owned a shop where she sold jewelry she had learned to make while growing up in Kemet. On Tuesdays and Thursdays, I typically helped her run the shop, unless the fishing crew needed more men on deck. However, today was different, because of what took place last night. It felt like everyone was on edge.

My mother calmly looked into my eyes and caressed my face. "You didn't see the way you came home last night. Something happened out there, and you are going to tell me every detail about what happened last night, okay?" I could hear the sternness in my mother's voice, even though she had a pleasant expression on my face. Those lovely, light brown eyes peered into my young soul and stole the truth buried within me. My mother had an impassive and yet calm way of influencing me to avow the truth. Therefore, I told my mother everything—well, almost everything. I didn't want to mention what Gershom had done by killing those men last night. I just felt obligated to protect his image. I knew he would have done the same for me without any hesitation.

"This is bad, really bad," my mother said, shaking her head from side to side. "Come on, we have to head over to your uncle's house." My mother stood up and gathered her footwear as well as mine. Then we made our way to Gershom's house with our hounds by our side. The moment we stepped out, we were greeted by wagging tails and eager smiles. There were more hounds than usual surrounding us. I quickly sensed these were other hounds from local farms near and far. They must have received word about what transpired last night and came out to support the pack.

"Akhen-Inu, is that you?" I asked in a confused tone, while the wounded hound made his way over. I could not believe it. Akhen-Inu

was back on his four feet, walking among the other hounds, but in a slower pace.

"Hey, boy, what are you doing here?" I asked the wounded alpha male, while I bent down to pet him on his head.

"Last night, your father, along with Blade and your uncle, journeyed some distance into the open field to search out this threat in the night. In their search, they heard the whimpers of the pups in the drifting winds, and that's how they found Akhen-Inu and Tum-Ra motionless with a couple of wounded pups whimpering beside them. If it were not for those pups' whimpering cries, I strongly believe Akhen-Inu and Tum-Ra would have passed away into the afterlife. They're fortunate to be alive since there were other pups that were not so fortunate and brought their bodies back home for a proper burial. Nevertheless, Blade and your father treated the hounds' wounds and gave them the rest of my black tonic, and now I have to make more. Come on now, the faster we move, the faster we can pick up the items I need from my brother to make more of the tonic."

"Wait, wait," I said to my mother, who was already taken five steps away from me. "So, they only found the remaining hounds out there? Nothing else?"

"Your father informed me about the wounded hounds. Was there something else they should have seen out there too?"

I wanted to answer my mother's question right away, but it would require revealing Gershom's sins. Therefore, I held my tongue and figured that the men in the night also carried away their dead for proper burial, too.

"Nothing else to be said," I replied to my mother's question before I walked ahead of her. The walk to Gershom's house was laden with heavy thoughts. When I had woken up this two hours after sunrise, I was briefly oblivious to everything that had taken place the night before; it had completely slipped my mind that we had found a mysterious creature, fought, and killed a few men on our expedition. It was far from a normal night. So… I wasn't sure how my mind had temporarily overlooked this memory, but it had, and now my brain was a tumultuous mixture of old and new thoughts. Every step I took was a new thought, a new question, and no answers.

We drew near Gershom's house and my anxiety level was waist-high. It was only a matter of time before my nerves were pushed over the edge of sanity. My aunt ran out to greet us. Apparently, she had seen us approaching her house and assumed we were coming there to find out if there had been any progress in this strange and new development. I was staggering a couple of feet behind my mother, but I could hear the two mothers discussing the recovery of Gershom and me.

My mother pointed to the swathed wound on my abdomen, and my aunt scurried in front of me. "You poor child, does it hurt still?" she asked.

I was confused for a moment, because I wanted to say, "I'm fine, Mom," but she knew I was being sarcastic and she gave me the displeased look all mothers gave their children quite often.

"I'm fine—we Kemet men heal overnight, remember?" I said this as assertively as I could, and this made my aunt smile, while my mother shook her head, since she knew what I had said was pure drivel. My aunt embraced me.

As we walked to the main entrance of my aunt's house, we saw Gershom standing at the main doorway to his house. He was leaning against the doorpost, and he had an ineffable look on his face. This look meant something—but I was unsure of what it meant or what to say. My mother questioned Gershom on his well-being before walking inside with my aunt.

"What did you say to her?" Gershom interrogated me when we were alone. He walked away from me with his arms folded and his head pointed downward. I quickly noticed the distrust in his voice.

"I didn't mention anything about your executions, so don't worry about that," I said defensively. Then I followed Gershom by lowering

my head and saying, "Other than that, I told her everything else." I was dismayed by the fact that Gershom had little trust in me, but I could not blame him at the same time. Gershom could personally attest to my truthful ways when it came to confessing to my mother.

"It's good to see Akhen-Inu is moving around . . ."

"Yeah, I take it Tum-Ra is moving the same way," I replied to Gershom assumingly. Tum-Ra came from the side of the house and he was properly greeted by my set of hounds. The way the hounds greeted one another—with yelps of joy—made me wonder if they had already forgotten about the killings from the night before; or maybe such things just did not faze them. The hounds just seemed to be happy that their fellow comrades were alive and well. This relaxed behavior from the hounds was a lesson to admire and consider during the hard days to come.

Two hours passed since the sun was at the highest point in the sky. The women were discussing upcoming matters that needed their attention this coming weekend. Our conversations, on the other hand, were stuck on the events of last night, as well as our next move. We spoke about how our mothers had looked after us so lovingly, and with great concern. Gershom told me about how his mother could not sleep because she stayed up to watch him sleep and make sure nothing else would happen to him. I wondered if that was the case with my mother, too, since both women had similar maternal qualities. Gershom also told me about how his mother used a special herbal potion to help mollify the pain. When he told me the ingredients of his mother's antiseptic solution, I was surprised to learn the similarity in the ingredients to my mother's antiseptic solution. Gershom proposed that our mothers were actual sisters switched at birth. We laughed at the idea, because this was the same idea I had in mind, too. Then we stopped laughing because maybe there *was* a slim chance that our mothers were related without them knowing.

Gershom and I talked about how we were banned from our day and night expeditions. We both knew that we would not sit well with this new penalty, so we contemplated on new ways to liberate ourselves. The afternoon was closing in, and we heard the sound of men on carts pulling near Gershom's house. The sight of our fathers with Blade and Nephtali made me wonder what questions they had in store for us.

"How are you men feeling?" my father asked us.

"We're alright," we replied together.

Nephtali came off from the cart and hugged us both. She had the pleasant aroma of cooked seafood on her body—she smelled *and* looked good. *What a woman*, I thought to myself as she continued embracing us.

"I hope you explorers know that your expeditions are suspended," Nephtali said, making a slight vertical slant with her lips. "Maybe banned," she added, nodding her head confidently. Gershom and I sighed because we knew Nephtali was right.

The men and Nephtali sat us down inside Gershom's house, while we told them a tale that was like none other. Blade left the table and readied his weapons, but he was not the only one. Both fathers gathered their spears, and thus began their preparations to journey back into unknown grounds where they could find those men responsible for attacking us last night.

* * * *

The sun was about to hide its face, which meant it was time for the moon to rule night skies. I was inside my own house, watching my father assemble the necessary tools for their journey. My mother was cynical about the men going into the pasture when the sun was down, and she despised the idea of Gershom and I tagging along. I was certain that Gershom was facing the same disapproval to go back into the pasture from his mother.

However, I heard footsteps and the barking of hounds in fellowship. "They're all here. Time to head out," my father shouted for both of us to hear.

I turned to see the overwhelming look of concern in my mother's eyes, but she knew how narrow-minded men could be toward a woman's intuition. "Please, be very careful," she said as she watched her men depart. I could only imagine what kind of thoughts and fears plagued her mind.

The moment came for us to find out answers and set aside this sense of discomfort, but with a larger pack of hounds by our sides. My uncle wanted to address some ground rules before we commenced our journey. The rules were simple; the formation we would use was similar to that we'd used with the hounds the previous night, while the objective was candid. My uncle informed us only to make sure two hounds were always by our sides at all times. My father took Akhen-Inu and the eldest male pup; this was the same pair my uncle decided to take with him, too.

The orange sun was already descending over the western hemisphere, so Blade recommended that we move fast. The intense jogging through the path that was so familiar but felt strange, pumped blood through my body at a rapid pace. Whenever we stopped for a quick break, I could feel my heartbeat vibrating the staff in my right hand. I wasn't sure if this was due to the running alone, or if my thoughts were what's weighing down on my mind. My anxiety levels were elevating with every step we took deeper into the approaching night. The not-knowing what we would encounter or find was killing me. I understood why the men wanted to go back, but something wasn't right. This feeling of great concern was beginning to spring up quite often in my mind and body, and I wasn't sure how to respond to it.

The sun was no more, only the drifting rays of amber light were left behind, and now the sea breeze pressed against our backs. I wondered if I was the only one affected by the chill of the sea breeze—I doubt it. I shook my head and smiled, because I knew no one would ever admit to being cold.

"There is it," Gershom said as he pointed at the bones of the mysterious creature, we had rediscovered last night. All heads turned to look.

"What is it?" my father asked Gershom curiously.

Gershom opened his mouth to respond to my father's question, but I cut Gershom off eagerly to say, "It's the mysterious creature we found last night. Remember we told you guys about the creature we assumed was from the underworld?"

All three men individually gave us a nod of assurance.

"Wait—something is missing! Where's the head?" Gershom and I looked at each other because the skull of the creature was actually gone.

Blade stooped down near the abdomen of the creature to get a closer look for a better understanding of what lay before him. Gershom and I could tell Blade was a bit astounded and baffled about the identity of the dead creature. Blade shook his head as though he was disagreeing with himself, and then he turned to say, "I don't know what kind of fowl this could be. It is definitely not the size of any bird I have ever seen."

"I could second that," my father said with his head still fixed on the mysterious creature. The rest of us just agreed with my father, just nodding our heads to his comment.

"Well, it was here at this site we began our journey to explore the strange sound. Then a mile or less later, we ran into those men—and you know the rest," Gershom said sternly as he pointed in the direction we had traveled last night. All heads turned again in the direction Gershom was pointing in order to see for themselves. I turned to see the reaction of all three men, and what I saw made me feel concerned for them. The men looked worried about the answers that would find them that night. The sun's last rays were diminishing and the time came for us to use our torches, so we all ignited them before we continued our quest.

Gershom despised when we tarried in a place for too long, especially when there was much more ground to cover. So, when he told us, "We should keep moving," I wasn't surprised. However, my uncle and my father shook their heads in disagreement and said, "Nope, you boys head back home—okay?"

"I think you guys dealt with your fair share from last night, so return home, boys," my uncle said with certainty, while my father and Blade agreed with their nods of acceptance.

I was surprised and yet somewhat *not* surprised by what they had required of us to do. But Gershom, on the other hand, was shocked by his father's words.

"We know the way better than you guys! If anything, you guys could end up lost or off-track," Gershom said while gesturing with his hands and torch. The fathers stood by their request and forbid Gershom and I from continuing this journey. We all saw the disappointment on Gershom's face. Gershom sighed and said insipidly, "Fine." Gershom spun around and vanished into the night with two hounds trailing, I glanced at my father and he gave me a nod of assurance, so I returned a nod back to him and departed from them.

The three men and the new pack of hounds continued their search into mysteries of the night, while we followed our orders to return back home. Gershom walking swiftly ahead of me which only meant one thing. I was in for a mouthful as we journey back home. Gershom's mind was laden with thoughts that he would randomly blurt out, sometimes as a word or a phrase. Either way, I was always confused, because the next words he said never matched with what he had said last.

"We're almost home," I said to Gershom, who was oblivious to his whereabouts.

Gershom picked his focus up from off the ground and said sarcastically, "Come on, Teraditus, I know we're home. You really think that I wouldn't recognize our own grounds?" Gershom had a point, of course, but his words were harsh and insulting.

"Yeah, sorry about that," I admitted with defeat. It was futile to go back and forth with Gershom; his misery wanted company.

The rest of the walk back was quiet and swift, but the bothersome part was how Gershom held the torch exceptionally close to his face. The sight of the light illuminating on the side of Gershom's face gave me flashbacks to a time my mother was teaching me about the power of our ebony skin. She said, "Our skin was spiritually designed to be one with the power of the sun, so Teraditus, make sure you embrace the Ra's star before it rises from one realm and before it sets in another realm. Even the fire draws its strength from the star of Ra, so that means even we can draw strength from the fire too. The star of Ra is the source of true power, Teraditus, and we need that power every day."

Gershom was drawing so much spiritual energy from the flame that he could not be burned, but his anger blinded him from observing spiritual observation. "How unfortunate," I whispered to myself.

We walked in front of my yard and received a warm welcome from the remaining hounds left behind. The wagging tails and giddy smiles of the hounds managed to put a smile on Gershom's face, which was a common effect the hounds had on him.

"Hey, they're back!" The sound of Nephtali's voice shift ed our heads toward her. Two of the hounds ran to greet the young woman, but she quickly gave them her back since she despised it when they ran toward her, jumping excitedly.

"Stop, stop," she screamed at them, but the two hounds continued to jump on her, playfully. Gershom laughed hysterically at his sister's distress, but not me. I ran over to her and shooed the hounds away from her. Nephtali said a few vile words before her nerves calmed down.

"Hey, Nephtali, what brings you here?" I asked her while approaching the entrance of my house, where she just came out from.

"I was checking up on your mother, getting counsel, the normal girl talk," she said to me calmly before her focus shifted over to her brother. "Is Gershom upset about being sent back home early?"

"Upset, disappointed, insulted . . . you know how he gets when things don't go his way," I replied quietly.

Nephtali gave me tensed a smile and nodded her head because she knew exactly what I was saying.

"Well, I guess it's going to be a long night for him. Anyways, I will take my leave with Gershom," Nephtali said before she bent down to kiss me on the forehead.

"I guess no story tonight from my mother," I said to Nephtali.

"Not tonight, I am still exhausted from that Tuesday night when your mother told us great deal about Blade's life when she journeyed Babylon for her priestess's duties," she responded to statement. I watched her walk over to her brother to say something of comfort to him before she held her brother close to her side and dispersed from my presence.

"Teraditus, did you men find out anything new?" my mother asked me the minute I stepped inside. I shook my head in dismay, so she walked over to me. She took my head and pressed it against her soft stomach. I looked at my mother's stomach oddly and then into her warm eyes. She laughed while affectionately rubbing my face. "You felt her moving, huh?" she asked me. I gave my mother a childish grin and a nod. I laid my head again on her tender stomach. All the while, my mother rubbed her hands through my soft hair. Whoever was inside my mother's stomach, she sure was moving around a lot, and I did not know why.

"I think she knows her big brother is near her—this is why she is moving so much," I said to my mother.

She laughed as she held my smooth face and said, "Yes, my love. Hey, how long do you think your father will be out there?" My mother's question was one of the many questions that ran across my mind when Gershom and I were walking home. I wasn't sure how to respond, so I just shrugged my shoulders. "Yeah, I can't imagine you would know that sort of information," she said.

My mother took my hand, guided me inside, after which she double checked to make sure the entrance was properly shut and locked. Once the door was secure to her liking, she sojourned to her chambers and I sojourned to mine own. As I lay on my cot, I thought of the men and the hounds wandering into the strange night, searching for answers, answers they would not find, but more questions than answers. I sighed and felt the heaviness on my eyes, so I closed them and allowed the slumber to take me to another realm.

In this realm men called a *dream*, I soared through from the celestial skies, flying through the blue and green clouds like a shooting star, until I stood on solid ground. Darkness surrounded me, no matter where my head turned, darkness was there. Suddenly, I smelled the rich aroma of mixed fragrances from behind me, so I turned around and saw a door in the midst of darkness. Strange as it was, I soared toward the door and opened it, and there she was pacing back forth, gathering vials and trinkets to bring to her shrine to the Queen of the Heavens, Auset.

My mother knelt at the shrine in her priestess attire and lit three sticks of incense by rubbing her fingers at the tips of the sticks. She then applied her makeup by drawing the *eye of Ra* on her right eye and the third eye in the center of her forehead. Then she tied her braided hair upward before reaching for her head piece that had the head of a silver serpent extending outward. She placed the head piece that resembled the crowns of the Queen pharaohs of Kemet on top of her head with the serpent covering the drawing of the third eye. Once the head piece was on her head, she began to pray while mixing and crushing the herbs and the solutions inside the marble mortar with the pestle. All the while, constantly whispering her prayer of enchantment. Suddenly, a whispering whiff of smoke emerged of out of the mortar and the eyes of Auset on the shrine and the eyes of the serpent on her head wear lit up like a white light, and flames of turquoise color emerged out of the marble bowl.

A gasp fell from my from chest at the sight of it all. Then I realized my mother, who had her eyes closed, had stopped praying, while the serpent on the crown of her head slithered down to her neck and revolved around her neck four times, each time changing into four different colors: onyx black, gold, emerald green, and red ruby. Before slithering down her right shoulder onto her right arm into her right hand and straight to the bowl of fire. Suddenly, the fire changed from turquoise to silver-white flames, and my mother's eyes burst open and glowed white like the shrine and the open flames.

Horrified by this display of power, I covered my mouth and wondered about the depths of my mother's abilities. It felt strange looking at this woman I knew my whole life, it was as though I didn't know the true her. All of a sudden, she placed her right hand inside the bowl of fire and pulled out a fist of turquoise flames. My heart sank at such a sight, so I moved closer. In time to see her open the fist of fire and there it was. A white glowing stone with a glassy appearance.

"What is it?" I asked my mother, but instead of a response. I heard the cries of the whimpering hounds, so my focus shifted to the main entrance door and I proceeded closer to open the door. Everywhere I look, there were dark shadows of men everywhere, surrounding my home, while the barking of the unseen hounds continued. I wondered to myself as I look to my right and left, if these dark shadows of men were those that attack us out in the wilderness the previous night, and what were they doing here? However, I knew these were questions without direct answers, but my ignorance got the best of me.

"Why are all of you here?" I shouted my question to them, but instead of response. The shadows of men started to move closer toward me, ominously. I quickly took a step back and watched them make their way closer to me from all angles.

"No! *Stop!*" I yelled while covering my face, and sure enough they stopped. However, it was not of my own accord as I saw the rays of white light emitting from behind me.

"Step aside, child," said a voice from behind me, so I turned around and I beheld the sight of the Queen of the Heaven, Auset herself. She proceeded out and raised her hands up to the skies and every dark figured bowed down. I couldn't believe it, my mother was Auset, but how?

"Child," she said with the power of the white light surging through her eyes, "*it's time.*"

Suddenly, I opened my eyes and I was back on my cot and sat up, and that's when I heard footsteps approaching my chambers. I knew it was my mother, of course. It was normal for her to walk around the house, making sure everything was safe and secure, especially when my father wasn't home. However, my mother was troubled, more than normal, and somehow, I was able to sense it as she stood behind the doorway of my chambers. Nevertheless, I could not blame her for being this concerned. Then I heard the low growls of the hounds outside and my heart sank with fear.

I snuck a peek out of the window-hole inside my room and saw the shadows of men approaching my yard. All this made me feel concerned for my mother's safety, so I ran to find my door of chambers, and to my surprise. There my mother stood, dressed in her priestess attire, even the head wear with the serpent was on her head.

"Auset … you were praying to her for our deliverance," I said to my mother.

"I was praying to her, for your safety, but how did you know?" my mother asked me with a sense of amazement. I stepped out walked toward her shrine where three incense sticks were still smoking, and the aroma of rich spices filled my nostrils.

"I know because she told me— *it was time,*" I said to mother, while pointing at the shrine. Suddenly, our focus shifted when the hounds started barking aggressively, which we both knew something wasn't right outside. My mother grabbed my right hand; it was beginning to sink in my head how serious this situation was. My mother took me to

the pantry that had an escape door leading to the hen house, which was near the road and a quicker way to the Gershom's house.

"Listen to me closely, Teraditus, Mommy needs you to be a big boy and warn everyone else of the approaching danger," she said quickly. The sound of a bark quickly shifted into the sounds of aggression mixed with whimpering cries. We both turned our heads to the sound, and then back to each other. I felt the heartbeat of three people, and the fear in my mother's teary eyes. "Baby, I need you to be strong, okay?" she said to me, trying not to break down into tears.

"Mom, please come with me," I said with actual tears in my eyes. "We can make it out together—"

"*No*," she said fiercely, while holding onto my arms. This was the first time my mother struck new fear in me. "Teraditus, focus, please!" she said, trying her hardest to compose herself. "You need to go and do as I say," she admonished me as she stared into my eyes. "I need to buy you and our family some time to run away, because only the gods know what happened to your father."

I knew she was right, so I said. "Okay, I will go and warn them."

"Take this too," she said painfully placing a glassy, onyx stone in the palm of my hand. The stone was very warm, which meant Auset in my dream was right—*it was time*—time to go. My mother wiped the tears away from my cheeks, and then hugged and kissed me the way someone would do if they knew this was the last time they'd ever see each other— in this lifetime, of course.

Such final farewells were, and forever will be, the worst experience for any human being to endure. It could take the stoniest heart and make it flesh again.

CHAPTER 17

THE LAST PRAYER

[Cyrene/Libu - Ten Years Before the Battle of Thermopylae (480 BC)]

I watched as my mother closed the trap door. The moment she did, a small light could be seen flickering through the cracks while I was submerged into chilling depths of darkness. The woeful cries of men being viciously attacked by the hounds for inveigling their space filled my ears and head with vile thoughts. However, I kept moving till I got to the hen house. When I smelled the foul scent of the birds, I knew I was near. I took my time to open the next trap door on the outside of the hen house. It was unwise to make any unnecessary sounds to agitate the hens, because their skittish behaviors could alert the intruders to my whereabouts. I took my time opening the door, making only a slight crack, but it was pointless. The hens were already in a frenzy, but it was not due to any of my movements. The hens were startled by a hound tackling an intruder near to the hen's house. The hound fought intrepidly, but the heroic act was short- lived. The next sounds I heard were the whimpering cries of a defeated hound and the footsteps of a man fleeing the scene.

Carefully, I emerged from my hiding place and made my way to the edge of the hen's house, where I saw the lifeless hound on the ground. In the distance, I also saw the shadows of men walking into my home. My heart was still as I saw them enter by the numbers. My mother was in trouble, and all I could tell myself was, *Run to Gershom's house. Run to Gershom's house.* But how could I be so weak? My mother needed my help, and here I was cowering beside the hen house. Suddenly, I felt the growing heat in the palm of my fist, and I opened my hand to see the stone in it. I remembered the dream of Auset, and I knew the goddess was with her. So, around I turned and sprinted toward Gershom's house.

With the winds rushing into my face, I ran and ran, without even a single breath of air. The light of the moon guided my path, while my slender body managed to cut through the cold winds. On the horizon, the house could easily be seen, but it felt as though I was getting nowhere. I also could not help but notice the night was awfully quiet considering that men were unexpectedly moving in the shadows; not even the belligerent attacks of the hounds defending our grounds were heard in the distance. I was five feet away from entering the yard when a whistling arrow grazed my left shoulder. But I felt no pain, so I kept on moving for the sake of my mother's last request.

"Gershom, Gershom. We're under attack, we're under attack," I screamed out, panic carrying my words louder than I thought possible.

"Teraditus!" I turned to see Blade coming around the corner of the house with the Swords of Ra burning with blue flames. "Gershom and his mother have made their escape down the road. Hurry up and catch up with them." Blade said to me without even stopping once. I turned to watch him wield the swords to some approaching arrows, and the blue flames extended like a rope and burned the arrows into ashes.

"Whoa," I muttered in surprise. "The tales are— But, that would mean Blade is a descendant of— Wait, hold on… If Blade is here, then where's my father and uncle?"

"Teraditus, run!" Nephtali screamed from on top of the roof. I looked up to see her with a bow in her hands. I had never known she was skilled with a bow and arrow, but then again, she was in a relationship with Blade—so it made sense.

"Run, love, run," Nephtali said as she released several more arrows into the air.

"Save my mother, she's in danger!" I cried.

"We will, we will! Go *now, go!*" Nephtali looked down at me to give me the assurance I needed before I disappeared into the night.

I turned to run in the direction Blade had instructed me to run, and off I went as fast as possible to catch up with Gershom and his mother. Each step I took, away from the mayhem, I heard shouts of men in travail and Gershom's hounds brutally attacking all those that did not belong. There was so much going on with no time to process it all. Starting with the whereabouts of Gershom's father and mines. All manner of strange thoughts ran through my mind as I pick up speed on the path leading to the docks.

I ran and I ran. All the while, remaining true to the path as the traveling clouds above hid me in their passing. The more ground I covered, the feel of the sea breeze started to increase, which meant I was running in the right direction. However, I was still a good way off, and still no sign of Gershom and his mother. Suddenly, I heard the whistling in the air and an arrow struck the ground, five feet in front of me, but I kept on running. The sight of this arrow caused me to glance behind me, and I saw no one who was responsible for the arrow nearly striking me. This troubled me greatly, so I began to move faster since nothing was making sense. Hopefully, before this path comes to an end, one of many questions running through in my head will find an answer.

I ran a great way in under a few minutes, and the results proved to be promising. In the distance, two figures could be seen moving northbound. I knew it was Gershom and his mother. A feeling of relief came over me at the sight of them. The two were a good distance ahead of me, but we were all nearing the open seas. The wind intensified with every step I took and the roar of the unsettling waves filled the air. That which was uncertain about this night seemed clear to nature; it was as though it knew what was to come, but failed to have informed any of us about the dangers on the horizon.

I knew I had to get their attention, but the winds forbade me from doing so. "Gershom… Gershom… Gershom!" I shouted his name aloud, but my attempts proved to be difficult due to the winds. The seed of hatred for the wind was beginning to sprout within me.

Observe, Teraditus, the winds have their gaps, my conscience said to me.

"Yes, the winds gaps," I responded to myself. "I will shout Gershom's name when the wind dies down for a while." I just had to time my words accordingly, but the winds were unmerciful. It was as if they knew my intentions and saw to make my task difficult by blowing harder than usual. This was strange, but I waited until I felt every gap in the wind. In which, I yelled, "Gershom…Gershom …Gershom!" Unfortunately, the distance was still a factor in my attempts to get their attention. So, I tried to increase my speed when I could, but the sea winds did not approve.

Patiently, I waited for the wind to give me the chance to yell out their names, but they stayed true its strength. The potent gusts pushed and shoved me backward each time I took three steps forward. It was almost impossible to walk, let alone stand upright. I had to close my eyes and use my outstretched hands as eyes to guide my path. I threw my entire body weight into the winds and yet the winds held me up, while my legs struggled to move forward. Soon the struggled to move forward ceased, and I just stood there while the wind bruised my body with heavy blows and filled my ears with a sinister roar. The wind was too much, and I was losing my composure, and at this rate. Gershom and his mother were long gone; this was bad… very bad.

"No, no, no—*Gershom!*" I yelled at the winds and the winds suddenly stopped, and to the ground, I crashed. Knees first and hands right after to finish breaking the fall. With my head bent down, a cloud of condensation fell from my mouth. I was exhausted from the fight with these winds, and now I needed a moment to regain all that lost energy. A lingering draft passed by and embraced me with its frigid touch, and that's when I heard a slight whistle. I turned to my left and saw two arrows submerged into the ground.

"No!" I whispered secretly to myself. "Ger—!" I shouted but a hand covered my mouth.

"Hush my child, get up and *run!*" said Gershom's mother with a terrified look in her eyes. To my feet, I stood and off we ran, until Gershom was visible in my eyesight. "Run boys, just run," she repeated constantly, while the air whistled unexpectedly from the arrows soaring in the air.

"I think they're shooting arrows at us," Gershom said aloud.

"Yes, they already shot three at me," I explained to Gershom. "If only I could see the archer."

"Don't look back, Teraditus," Gershom's mother whispered harshly at me.

"Yes, mom," I replied without thinking of my word choice.

"Keep your eyes in front… so your legs know where to go."

"She's not your mother," Gershom unkindly reminded me.

"I know Gershom," I snapped at Gershom, "she just reminds me of my mother."

Gershom did not respond right away, but when he did. He said, "You're right… they are very similar—apologies!"

"Apology accepted—Whoa! Did you see the arrow? It almost hit me," I said as I held onto the left side of my head. "That's it, I'm running faster now." And off I went, running ahead of Gershom.

"I'm right behind you," replied Gershom to me.

"Good, let's get out of here,"

"Mom, you have to move faster—Mom!" Gershom yelled back at his mother but he received no immediate response. "*Mom*, did you hear me, you have to run—*faster*." Gershom's voice began chillingly silent, which caused me to stop and look back.

"Mom?" Gershom called out into the darkness, but no response came from her.

"She was … right behind us. Doesn't make sense." I tried to make sense of the unexpected.

"Mom… mom… *mom!*" He repeatedly called out to her before he took off into the darkness.

"Gershom, wait," I called out to him, but he was gone, and I stood there alone. "*Shit!*" I whispered to myself, and off I went in pursuit of Gershom.

Fortunately, the run was not long. Since I saw someone standing in the midst of the path. So, I stopped running because I knew that it was Gershom. As I got closer, Gershom fell to his knees where his mother lay motionless on the ground. At that moment, time seemed to stop as we gazed down at her lifeless body. It was simply too much to take in mentally and emotionally, so I stood there while he knelt on the ground. Gershom leaned over his mother, who had two arrows through her back, and said not a word. I knew Gershom was emotionally distraught. There were no words of comfort to give him, so I shared none. Even the winds ceased from its blowing, while we tried to fathom the moment of this untimely demise.

"Gershom, get out of the way!" I screamed, while pulling him toward the left. We slammed into the damp ground and looked up to see a group of men emerging out from the darkness with their faces covered in black linen by the number.

"We found their sons," said one of the men in the group.

"Good to hear," said a man making himself visible with a bow armed with an arrow. "Our orders are to bring in the criminal and kill everyone else. That includes the women—and children, too." He peered straight

into our eyes with the look of no remorse. As if to say, his orders were his orders, and he would see them through. That's when he took aim at Gershom and me and pulled back on the serving point of the string and closed his left eye.

Suddenly, a hand from the ground ascended and grabbed the bow and arrow, while the other hand plunged a hidden dagger through the archer's neck.

"You're not harming none of my boys while I'm still alive," Gershom's mother said callously, while the archer was gasping for air. She then threw the lifeless body on the ground as she stood in a staggered manner over his body, emitting a sense of unexplainable fear to all around her. Then she awkwardly turned her neck around toward us on the ground and only said one word, "*Run!*"

Gershom's mother turned back around with two arrows still inside her back to face the men that emerged from the dark and let out a shrilling scream. That sent a surge of fear to all far and near, even the men stepped back, but I saw the window of opportunity she was giving to us. To my feet I stood and pulled up Gershom to his feet.

"We have to run," I said to him

"But she's alive," he replied not wanting to leave, while his mother, who continued to scream. One of the men stepped up and swung his sword at her, but she dogged the attack and plunged another hidden blade through his neck. The men were shocked by this again, but I wasn't. She had more hidden daggers on her; but if only Blade could see Gershom's mother in action. He would be proud. All that she learned while training with Blade was about to manifest in the sight of all these men, which was all to buy us time to make our escape.

The men started moving in closer to her, but she showed no fear. The numbers of unknown men started to become more visible with each attempt to restrain Gershom's mother. A task that was not easy as she tottered around to maintain her stance, while dodging and throwing daggers at those foolish enough to get closer to her. However, her moment of strength ceased when a man grabbed her by the right hand and thrust a small sword through her abdomen.

"Mom, no," Gershom cried, while I constrained him. She stepped back and looked at the small sword through her abdomen, and then looked at the same man while she drew the sword and slashed his throat. The man stumbled back, while holding his open throat before falling backward to die suffocating on his own blood. Gershom's mother fell on knees and looked at us with tears of blood streaming down her face and said, "Run, please!" Deep inside, she knew this was it, her killing spree was over, and now it was her time to go and she accepted her fate, intrepidly. Another man grabbed by her head, pulled her up to her feet, and a massive sword burst through her chest and pulled it out before she fell to the ground slowly breathing.

Gershom broke out of my grasp and ran to his mother and held her onto her, while he cried with such pain I've never witnessed before. His mother struggled to get her arms around her son one last time, but she did and together they said one of the many prayers of *Ma'at* for the last time. A prayer of preparation for the next life, but his mother never finished the prayer. Instead, she closed her eyes and listen to her son as her soul slowly drifted into the other realm. The men stood still, out of respect for a son's loss by their hands, but Gershom took advantage of their sympathy by quickly reaching for the small sword his mother just had and swung it at the man responsible for the final assault to his mother. Gershom was mad, however, the man reacted quick by knocking the small sword out of Gershom's hand with his sword and raised his sword up to kill Gershom.

"Gershom, watch out," I yelled before a long spear soared through the air and struck the man with the sword. The spear went straight through his chest, instantly killing Gershom's assailant. Everyone turned their focus in the direction from whence the spear came from, and out of the darkness of the night. Men adorned in cloaks of midnight gray soared majestically under the light of the moon. I could not believe

it was them. The Grecian soldiers we had seen yesterday at the docks—the "*Spartans!*" My father referred to them. These men exploded out of the darkness with a roar of ten thousand men ready for war, taking down two to three men in under a minute. These soldiers moved swift like the winds, they looked solid like a rock, and they struck men down like lightning.

The presence of the Spartans was an overpowering force that pushed these men of the night back, while leaving some running for their lives. However, those that stayed to fight these Grecian soldiers had a challenging time getting around their massive shields, the *aspis*, which seemed to be more of a weapon than a shield. There was one Spartan with a symbol of a bull on his shield, and he used his shield to slam into the heads of all those that oppose him, rendering all of them unconscious. Another soldier threw his massive shield, with a symbol of a hound with three heads, on his back, and started howling like a hound, while wielding two swords at a time. The rest had shields with symbols of a six-headed sea serpent revolving clockwise; strikingly similar to Mu's tattoo.

The Spartans fought as though they were bred for war from the time of birth. They seemed to enjoy the killing; as if it was something joyful for them. I could not see their faces under their bronze helmets, but I could hear their laughter with each successful kill. The killing must have been like a game to them—a sport, or a means to relieve stress and have fun. It was simply sadistic and unnatural how much pleasure killing another man brought these Grecian soldiers. However, I was still grateful for the service of their sword and shield.

When the fight dwindled down and the men from Sparta had subdued all that opposed them, I saw one of the Grecian soldiers with red horsehair strands sticking out of his helmet in a crested shape started speaking to Gershom, who was still holding onto his mother dearly. I quickly drew nigh and saw the lambda symbol engraved on his helmet, but to my surprise, this Grecian spoke fluently in the tongues of my mother.

"It's best we leave before they return with more," the Grecian soldier explained to Gershom, but Gershom was unresponsive as he held on to the body of his mother. Another soldier approached the one speaking to Gershom and said something in a harsh tone. I sensed he wanted to get out of here too, but Gershom was beyond devasted. So, I approached Gershom and rested my left hand on his right shoulders, while I steered at my beloved aunt finally resting.

"How did you know we were here?" I asked

"My father Myaneus sent us," the Grecian answered me.

"Myaneus, you say? That would mean you are Mu's grandson."

"Yes, I am. My name is Dimitrios," he said to me. I was about to ask another question when a Spartan ran over and said something frantically to Dimitrios, which changed his mood.

"We have to go, in case they returned with more men." Dimitrios whispered sternly to Gershom, but Gershom was still unresponsiveness. However, the Grecians had no time to be empathic for Gershom's loss, so Dimitrios told the same soldier that warned him to pick me up and Mu's grandson picked up Gershom.

"Wait, no, I can't leave her. Please, I can't leave her!" Gershom cried hysterically in Dimitrios's arms. The pain in Gershom's voice and words broke me down emotionally. This was the first time I'd ever seen and heard Gershom in such agony. Dimitrios called to the Spartan with the symbol of the bull on his shield and told him to take the body of Gershom's mother. The Spartan detached his midnight gray cloak from his bronze *cuirass* and wrapped the body of Gershom's mother. Dimitrios even had his cloak detached as well, with the help of another Spartan, to double wrap the body. Once his mother was securely wrapped, the Spartan placed his massive shield behind his back and carefully picked up the body of the lifeless woman. Then, we were off with the men of Sparta into this strange night.

PART IV:

DISCOVERING

DESTINY

CHAPTER 18

THE FEAST AT SUNRISE (INTERLUDE)

[Mykonos Island / Aegean Sea, 29 AD]

Hey, time to eat out there," Cassiani said joyfully. The sun was four hours away from reaching the highest point in the sky, and Cassiani's message could not have come at a better time. Teraditus's stomach rumbled, while Allidephi followed right after with the same sound.

"It would seem your stomachs are in a competition," Ena said to them while making her way back to the house.

Teraditus looked into Allidephi's eyes and said charmingly, "If this is so, I believe I would win."

Allidephi gave Teraditus a childlike giggle and started making her way to the house for the feast at sunrise.

Teraditus watched as the two women entered the house, and his mind reflected on the past and smiled before making his way inside. The table was crowded with fresh picked fruits, loaves of bread, and oinochoe pitchers filled the passion fruit juice and a splash of something nice. It's almost impossible to find the eating utensils, but everyone else seemed to have managed. Cassiani was sitting in my chair, the master chair, and she had her legs resting on the table. The image displeased me, but I was still grateful that everyone was there. I was grateful that she did not have her feet near anybody to cause discomfort.

Cassiani took a bite into a white peach and said, "Father, this chair is *very comfortable.* I am not sure how long it will take me to rise from it, so I won't. You don't mind, right?" Then she casually took another bite into the peach. It was as though Teraditus was staring at his wife all over again. This put a smile on his face, but it made Telus and Apollos quite irritated. Teraditus knew his special treatment to his only daughter made his sons envious of Cassiani, but in Teraditus's eyes, his sons failed to understand what it meant to have an only daughter.

Teraditus gave his sons a slight grin because he knew what he was going to do next would send them over the wall. Teraditus sat in the chair closest to his daughter.

"You don't let me sit at the head of the table," Telus muttered.

"Yeah, why is that, Father?" Apollos added.

Teraditus was about to respond to his sons when his daughter aggressively responded to them instead. "Jealous much, you two?" She asked before she bit into the peach again. "If you want the chair, fight me for it," Cassiani said to her brothers as she banged the table with her right hand.

Teraditus shook his head in dismay since he knew what the challenge and the banging on the table signified in this house. "*Sibling rivalry*" was something both Teraditus and his wife tried to discourage among their children. The parents, with time, realized that their disapproval would only encourage this kind of behavior among their own children. Teraditus's wife spent the most time with Cassiani to make sure she was the least competitive among the children. This ended up being an impossible mission for Teraditus's wife, because Cassiani was surrounded by male figures and their hunger for competition could never be filled. The brothers did not help to prevent Cassiani's

competitive side by taunting her and calling her all manner of names. This only motivated her to prove to her older brothers that they were wrong about her not being a threat since she was a girl.

Cassiani was far by the fiercest female competitor Teraditus had ever encountered in his lifetimes. She was a natural Spartan woman, and she did not even know it. However, that Spartan Spirit came out whenever she participated in the Olympic games, which was overbearing for the female participants and eventually the males as well. She was a gifted archer, second-best archer only after her mother, who taught Cassiani everything she needed to know. In a matter of time, she started beating her own siblings at archery games, and this made the boys highly upset.

However, Cassiani's choices always had her at odds with her mother. Her mother was quick to condemn Cassiani for indulging in man-like activities, and refusing to embrace the role of a modern woman. Cassiani was more of a rebel towards her mother, refusing to walk the path her mother wanted, but quite often. Teraditus knew how to persuade his daughter to consider why her mother was so hard on her. There were many conversations where Teraditus would remind Cassiani how fortunate she was to have her mother around, considering how early in his life he lost his mother at a young age, so she would never forget to not take advantage of the precious and fleeting time parents have with their child. It was conversations like these that painted a different perspective for his daughter to cogitate on, it gave her the opportunity to appreciate the time she had with the people who loved her the most— such as her mother, who always kept a special eye on Cassiani because she did not want her daughter to make the same mistakes she made at Cassiani's age.

Teraditus's sons never saw Cassiani through the eyes of their parents, so they never understood why their parents treated her the way they did. All they saw was an out-of-line female competitor who had what it took to beat them in various obstacles. This reality greatly troubled their masculinity and egos. At the table now, Teraditus watched—along with the women and child—as his children threw verbal abuse at each other about each others' lack of performance in sporting competitions in their more youthful days.

Eventually, the siblings were done with the verbal attacks and it was time to put their words into action. They stood and watched each other vehemently; even Diodotus could see the fire in their eyes. Allidephi was amazed to see how Cassiani was able to take on her two brothers, who were massive compared to her.

Teraditus sighed and said, "Can I safely assume this sibling rivalry will always be the case when you guys gather together as a family?

"*Yes!*" the siblings answered in unison, while maintaining their aggressive stare at one another.

"Well, let's get things set up because I want to be in this competition, too," Ena interjected while standing to her feet with a smile of determination. Teraditus knew this air of competition was quite enticing, so he turned to Rellos, who was about to spit out his desire to be a candidate in these games.

"I—" Rellos began.

"Hey, ladies, count me in. I long for a good challenge," Priscilla said with a smile after cutting off Rellos. This stunned everyone, except for Cassiani and Teraditus, since Priscilla was the apprentice of Cassiani.

"You boys better pick Rellos to make this fair for you guys. I wouldn't want any excuses now," Cassiani said to her brothers.

"Come on, boy, it's time to put these women in their proper places so they can resume their kitchen duties," Apollos said confidently.

"Oh, really?" Seleni responded in an offended manner.

"Hold up, Seleni, it's just a part of the spirit of competition—"

"Okay then, in the spirit of competition, count me in for some of these games. I think these men need to be put in their places, which is below us," Seleni said. The women laughed and high-fived each other because they now stood four strong and fired up to see victory till the end.

"Well, let's set up, so we can commence these games," Cassiani said fervently. Everyone agreed and left the table to make their way outside.

Priscilla turned to Teraditus, and he shooed her away, because he knew what Priscilla's look meant. "Well, Allidephi, it's just you and me—"

"Don't forget Diodotus," Allidephi responded to Teraditus, while holding up the baby so he could bounce on his stubby legs.

Teraditus and Allidephi helped clear the table, while the others set up their obstacles for the games. "I take it that you were not much the competitive type of girl," Teraditus said.

"Well, not in the sport manner, but in other fields of interest, I can be a very worthy competitor," Allidephi said to Teraditus while arranging the table with Athena's vase in the center. Allidephi had to multitask with her son wrapped around her, helping Teraditus with the table, and speaking to him as well.

"A mother's job is never-ending; it demands more and gives less," Teraditus observed.

"True, but once a mother holds her child in her arms for the first time . . ." Allidephi and Diodotus both rubbed their noses together. Then Allidephi looked up at Teraditus and said, "You just know you want to be there for every step they take."

Teraditus smiled at the young mother playing with her son. "It is good to see Diodotus playing with you instead of Ena for a change," Teraditus said to Allidephi, who looked at Teraditus when he made this comment. She thought about what Teraditus had said, but Diodotus drew her attention back to him.

"Ena seems like an amazing woman," Allidephi said to Teraditus, who was putting the serving bowls away.

"Ahh, Ena's alright—"

"No," Allidephi said, rejecting Teraditus's coy description of Ena. "No, Ena is not just alright—there's something special about her. There's something special about all the women in your life. From

Cassiani to Priscilla, these women are peculiar in a special way, it makes me wonder about one thing." Allidephi turned to Teraditus, who was now facing her. "What happened to your wife?"

Teraditus's countenance dropped, and Allidephi saw it. "I knew this question would come up eventually, but I didn't think it would come up now. I assumed you would be more curious about Ena than my wife," Teraditus said.

"Oh no, I am still curious about Ena, but your wife . . . She seems like someone I need to meet," Allidephi said to Teraditus as he made his way back to the table to have a seat. "Please, Allidephi, sit. I want to finish my story in the correct order, because every little detail leads up to the moment of how I met my wife."

CHAPTER 19

BLOODY SPARTANS: A NIGHT OF BLOOD (PART ONE)

[Cyrene/Libu - Ten Years Before the Battle of Thermopylae (480 BC)]

E very step the Spartans took, we sank deeper into darkness. Meanwhile, the life Gershom and I knew was fading away, thus leaving us to a reality we had no choice but to accept. *Was this our fate now?* I asked myself. I began to see memories of my past life slipping away as we ran underneath the drifting clouds, which hid us from time to time from the light of the moon. It was all happening too fast: the changes and the fear of the unknown journeys that lay ahead. I wanted none of this new life which fate had in store for us. I shook my head and said to my conscience, *Is this what Auset meant when she said—It's time?*

These were just some of the thoughts that plagued my mind, and now I was lost in a boundless sea of my troubled thoughts. At times, I knew my mind was not the place where I could make sense of it all, but at a time like this one. There was nowhere else to go. The thoughts just kept coming; running through my mind, demanding solutions. I was drowning in my own head, so I closed my eyes to block out all thoughts of concern and allowed the sway of the Grecian soldiers to rock my troubled soul away.

The truculence winds ceased for the moment while we furtively hurried away from such despair. A thought suddenly dawned on me as my eyes were still closed. How was it possible for these soldiers to run this fast with all that body armor made of bronze? Briefly, I opened my eyes and counted twenty-five men, then thought to myself how exhausted they must be running with all that weight on them, but still, I was grateful they had the strength to carry us and the weight of their armor, too. However, the soothing feeling of being swayed in the Grecian's arms gave me a sense of ease, so again, I closed my eyes and that opened my ears to the incisive sounds of the night. The sounds of men breathing harder and harder with each step more laden than the last. I also heard the occasional rubbing of their massive bronze shields on their breastplates, which was also made of bronze and very cold for my warm body to be pressed against.

In the moment of thought, I suddenly heard something whistling sound in the wind, and I knew as fast as we were running. These Grecian soldiers did not have one ounce of foot speed like these men of Canaan.

"*Arrow!*" I yelled with my right hand pointing upwards. I startled the Grecian which held me in his arm and all those running, too. However, before anyone could look up to see what I was pointing at, an arrow struck one of the Grecians in the back of his head and knocked him flat onto the ground. His bronze helmet slid from his head and rolled away from him. Everyone stopped and looked back at the man on the ground, wondering whether he was dead or not. By the gods of my mother, I thought he was dead, but little did I know the way these Grecians knew. One arrow was never enough to take out any Spartan soldier. The soldier I thought to be dead slowly emerged from the dark grounds with his massive shield still attached to his left arm and piercing

white eyes filled with fiendish fury for vengeance. He turned around and sprinted off toward the small militia of men that had returned to finish us off, while yelling furiously at them with his battle cry.

Another soldier bent down and picked up the helmet from the ground and said in the Grecian tongue, "He forgot his helmet." The remaining Spartans laughed amongst themselves. Dimitrios gave an order and a group of nine men ran after that one soldier struck down by the unexpected arrow, while the rest held their shields over their heads as we continued away from the fight. We ran and ran until the robust smell of the ocean filled my lungs and the slight roar of the ocean was heard faintly in the air. All this meant, we were nearing the docks, which felt good after all that had transpired thus far in the night. Dimitrios led the remaining group of Spartans to the docks. They moved quietly as they ran in and out of dark spots that hid their existence, trying their best not to alert anyone of their presence. It was impressive how they slipped in and out of dark spots with ease. Not even the sulking cat in the dark or the occasional drunks were aware of our comings and goings.

Dimitrios led the men down alleyway after alleyway, trying his best to avoid taking any streets, which had more lights and night owls that were preoccupied with the affairs of their personal shop. Dimitrios made a left on a street way where the lighting was scarce, and nobody could be seen anywhere, not even an alleyway could be spotted in case of an emergency escape route. It was down this same street way; the scent of the sea grew stronger with each step closer to the harbor. A scent I was all too familiar with, but the only difference was the crowd was unfamiliar. In just one night, the world I knew was fading away as we drew nearer to the docks. "*How was this even possible*?" I kept wondering to myself, it just made no sense. Did someone in our family anger the gods of my mother? Or was it just my mother alone who abandoned her position to be the next high priestess to Auset herself for love?

"Arrow!" screamed Gershom, but Dimitrios was quick by placing his massive shield in front of him. The arrow slammed straight into Dimtrios's shield, which made a loud bang for all to hear. Suddenly, men sprinted toward us wielding swords and double-sided axes, while yelling belligerently like men amid battle. The calm of night instantly changed into an atmosphere of war, and Gershom and I were right in the middle of it all. Dimitrios yelled out a command at his regiment and the men assembled themselves into a straight line with their shields side to side and their spears ready for the attack. Gershom and I were placed together, with the body of Gershom's mother behind three wooden barrels nearby a vendor stall. Dimitrios firmly instructed us to stay out of sight before he joined his men, shield to shield.

The men approaching the wall of Spartans hammered into them with immense force, but Spartans moved not. Instead, the Grecian soldiers pushed the men back and thrust their long spears as they marched forward, leaving dead bodies behind them on the ground. Their strategy was working since no one could get pass that wall of defense. However, that all changed when one man jumped over the wall, then another followed, and another. Soon there were seven men behind the Spartan wall, which forced Dimitrios to yell another command and the men shifted into a circle. Five faced north and five faced south, and the remaining five stayed in the middle with the spears facing upward with slant in case anyone decides to jump in the middle.

Their new defense stance was solid, but no one dare approach the wall of Spartans. Meanwhile, more of these men filled the street way with lit torches and archers with their bows ready to find the right spot. There was no escape for the Spartans; it looked hopeless for us all. With all these lit torches, the darkness fled from this street way and everything appeared visible, especially all these men ready to oppose the Spartans. What seemed to be a horde of soldiers were just mere men that were all adorned in different garments with little to no armor whatsoever. One thing that was certain for sure, these men were nothing in comparison to the organization of the Spartans.

One by one, the five archers shot their arrows hoping to make contact through the spacing of the ring wall, but no luck. Then came a man of great stature and towering over all the men, including the Spartans. He had a thick, bushy black beard, a scale breastplate that glistened even in the nighttime, a bronze helmet with a pointy tip in the center, and a blue linen cloth wrapped swimmingly around the forehead of his helmet. He pushed his way through the crowd with his wooden oval-shaped shield and a heavy battle hammer with a peculiar design. His garments were gaudy with embroidery designs of colors of purple and blue. However, what stood out to me was the symbol of the man's head on the body of a lion. The symbol of a man's head on the lion's body was painted over his massive wooden shield three times. It resembled nothing like the sphinx in Giza, but I could see where this man found his inspiration on the monuments and walls of Kemet.

Moreover, the giant yelled something to the Spartans in their tongues, surprisingly, but the Spartans replied not. So again, he yelled, and the response remained quiescent. The giant of a man turned around and walked away with his head hung low to his chest. Suddenly, the giant took off running toward the Spartans with his heavy battle hammer lit with fire at the head of the hammer, and jumped high into the air and slammed his hammer on top of the Spartan soldier in the middle of the Spartan ring facing north bound. The impact sent an explosion of fire everywhere and shook the ground. Gershom covered his face from the explosion of fire and light, but not I. It had no effect on me. Plus, I did not want to miss a second of the mayhem.

The shield of the Spartan who was struck by the heavy blow from the giant was dented, while the Spartan soldier was unconscious on the ground. However, the Spartan ring remained audacious as they pulled their unconscious comrade into the middle with a dented shield on top of him and closed the ring. The giant laughed, while some of his own men frantically put out flames that disperse onto them. Again, he walked away, but further this time and yelled at the Spartans in their tongues. Still, no response came from the men in the ring of shields, so the giant spun his battle hammer with flames burning brighter than before and sprinted toward the Spartans men with a speed to a make deadly impact. Then, he took off into the air and yelled in a truculent manner as he came down with a torrid swing of his hammer, but his hammer never made contact with the shields of the Spartans. Instead, a long spear soared through the air and pierced the giant through his right shoulder.

The giant man dropped his battle hammer and placed his shield right in front of him just as another spear tries to penetrate his shield. Out of nowhere came the remaining ten Spartans, bursting into the scene with an odious spirit to kill all that stood in their path. They entered the street from the south end, and their unforeseen presence swept in like raging winds before the approaching of a storm. It was absolutely soul-shattering to witness first-hand such a militaristic company of men. I knew not much but what my father had informed me about these Spartans, but they were certainly leaving an unforgettable moment in my mind.

The giant stepped back and yelled at the remaining men to attack the Spartans while he turned around to make his departure. However, as he turned to run away, a muscular Spartan with a black and gold tips on his crested, horsehair helmet and a pitch-black cloak with gold Greek strands on the edge, was soaring in the air with a long spear. He thrust his long spear through the giant's chest, and down they fell with the Spartan standing on top of a dead man. He pulled out the spear from the lifeless body of the giant man and yelled his battle cried in the tongues of the Grecian. "*For the lambda!*" That's when a wave of Spartan soldiers roared into the battle scene from the north end of the street way.

The men of Sparta were ready for a fight. Particularly, these four Spartans, who also shared similar helmets and cloaks to the one Spartan that slew the giant, were the first company to arrive from the north side,

soaring in the air with their long spears in front of them and their cloaks sailing behind them. The four Spartans landed with their spears thrust through four separate bodies, which they picked up with their spears and threw the lifeless bodies behind them. The expressions on some of these men's faces when they saw how the four Spartans killed those four men was enough to know some of these men wanted to run for their lives. But there was nowhere to run. Considering, how the other Spartans from the north with their long spears and massive shields were charging relentlessly toward them with the roar of a new battle cry. I assumed these were the remaining Spartans on the naval fleet who came just in time to lend their swords, shields, and remarkably long and strong spears.

The four Spartans joined with the one muscular Spartan that slew the giant, and together they fought their way over to the Spartan ring where Dimitrios and the other fourteen Spartans were still huddled together. There was something exceptionally special about these five Spartans, as they penetrated through the crowd of men with no trouble at all. Their fighting style was dynamic and meticulous; it was as though they had eyes behind their heads, while taking down two to three men in less than a minute. They were an army of five all by themselves. No one stood a chance each time they thrust their long spears and swung their swords, especially that one Spartan with the silver dory. He was beyond skillful, each time he spun his silver spear all around him, a body or two fell. His silver spear helped to clear a path for the other four to reach the Spartan ring. Suddenly, fifteen became twenty and together all the Spartans fought these men from the north, south, and the middle. It was the perfect strategy. The battle was now in hands of the Spartans, and nothing was going to change that.

Blood was everywhere, even sprinkled across my face, while the faces of the Spartans were drenched in it. Their white teeth gleamed with visibility to the naked eye, while their armor and weapons wore the blood of their enemies. The long spear, my father referred to as their *dory*, was a weapon of utmost demise, especially since the spear gave the Spartans the upper hand in battle by causing harm to any more than seven feet away from their person. The Spartan with the silver dory thrusted his long spear through three men, threw his shield on his back, and pulled out a sword, the *kopis*, from his left side and fought two men on opposite sides of himself. All the while, still holding onto the long, silver spear thrust through the three men groaning in agony of the pain. Another Spartan kicked a man so hard in his chest that he just lay on the ground coughing out blood until he had no strength to cough any longer. I saw another Spartan throw his long spear at a man and the spear pinned his head to a wooden door.

The sight of this battle was horrendous as the street ran red with the blood of fallen men. Every direction I turned, someone was dying or about to die; and these Spartans were the one's carrying out the death sentences. Whoever these men were that stood toe to toe with these Spartans were no match for them. One man slashed a Spartan diagonally across his cuirass and his sword broke off his hilt and the blade fell onto the ground. Needless to say, the man's fate was like his broken sword as he lay headless on the ground. The severed limbs and heads were beginning to pile up as the Spartans bathed their swords and spears in the blood of men. Truthfully, these mysterious men of the night did not have a chance against the militant Spartan soldiers. The Spartans were slaughtering these men that oppose them by a landslide. I almost felt remorseful for these men, whoever they were, but they all deserved to die by the hands of Spartans. Considering, how they attack us and killed our family. However, a few managed to slip through the Spartans' massacre by pretending to be dead, but the minute they saw freedom. They rose from the ground and ran for their lives, leaving their comrades to be slaughtered mercilessly.

There was something beyond normal about these men of Sparta. It seemed like killing was a form of art for these men—an art where their weapons were their utensils to create and the deaths of their foes were

their masterpiece. This was probably the reason why they had smiles on their faces—they simply enjoyed their artwork, especially the Spartan with silver dory. He was the true master, artist on the battlefield. Each time he swung his silver spear around about him, more than two men fell to the ground holding onto their necks.

Gershom and I watched the Spartan with his silver dory fought three men at the same time and slew all three with ease. After those three, the same Spartan proceeded to cut a man in half and beheaded before the body split in half on the ground. He then moved on and killed two more men unknowingly as they fought other Spartan soldiers. Basically, stealing kills from his fellow Spartan soldiers, which infuriated the Spartans he stole from. However, he kept on moving and stealing more kills from one Spartan to the next. His skills were unparalleled to anyone else. He moved with a style so sleek and unpredictable, it was impossible to get close to him with his long silver dory. This Spartan just knew where everybody was before they knew he knew. I was convinced wholeheartedly he had eyes behind his head, or he was simply that talented. He was a nightmare with a silver spear.

"Come on, you two," Dimitrios said to us anxiously. "We have to get out of here." He reached down and grabbed both of us, while another picked up the lifeless body of Gershom's mother and together, we all ran north bound where he was accompanied by two other Spartan soldiers. However, as we ran away from the battlegrounds. I saw that some of the Spartans were practically jeering at the demise of enemies; it brought them unspeakable joy. The death of a man brought amusement to their souls, and it was the most chilling sight I had ever seen.

The Spartans fought as though they were soldiers of death sent to gather souls for the underworld. No matter where I set eyes on this battle scene, it was all for me to digest what I was seeing. "*What manner of men are these*?" This was a question that constantly replayed in my head, while Dimitrios zealously meandered through the battlegrounds with us securely in his arms. The street way was a gory sight of overflowing streams of blood and dismembered corpses, but Dimitrios ran through it all with ease. As if he was immune to all this brutality and bloodshed, but not me. All of this was a nightmare I could not wake from, nor find rest. This was an actual nightmare—a nightmare of endless bloodshed to which I saw no end.

CHAPTER 20

BLOODY SPARTANS: CHILD FORGE IN BLOOD (PART TWO)

[Cyrene/Libu - Ten Years Before the Battle of Thermopylae (480 BC)]

I n a matter of eight minutes, we ran onto the docks and over to where their ship was stationed. The cold winds hugged me with a chilling grip as we ran onto the main deck. That's when I felt the cold drip of something wet cascade down my leg. Once Dimitrios set us down, I took a good look at myself and saw that I was drench in blood, and so was Gershom. It must be the blood that seeped off Dimitrios's cuirass onto our garments, he had blood all over him, especially on his hands. Wet garments and open sea winds equals shivering, and both Gershom and I were shivering more than we usually did when we went out on our night expeditions.

Dimitrios called someone to give a command, and in less than five minutes a spry, elderly man came toward us with two blankets and helped to cover us up with them. The elderly man gave Gershom and I a warm smile before attending to other matters such as getting the naval fleet together for departure. I wondered briefly if the elderly man was a helot my father spoke of yesterday morning, while groups of the Spartan soldiers made their way onto the main deck, also soaked in blood. One Spartan wiped the blood from off his body armor, threw off his helmet, and proceeded to draw a line streaming down the left side of his face and did the same on the right side as well.

I quickly noticed the red symbol on his face was like the lambda symbol on some of the shields of the Spartans. Then he stuck out his tongue and yelled triumphantly, which captured the attention of his fellow comrades—motivating them to join in his moment of celebration. That's when the other Spartans began to wipe the blood off from wherever the blood could be found. The Spartans wiped the blood off their shields, swords, helmets—even their greaves they wiped off the blood and drew the lambda symbol onto their faces. Then came the rejoicing from the soldiers who just returned from satisfying victory as they recited the same words repeatedly.

"*We bleed for the lambda, we bleed for the lambda, we bleed for the lambda—For the lambda we bleed!*"

Gershom and I looked up and saw Mu's son, Myaneus, as he translated what the Spartans were chanting repeatedly. "All that blood," he continued, which redirected our focus back to the Spartans. "They should be called *bloody Spartans!*" He was right, there was so much blood streaming down from everywhere, including their beards. "Dimitrios told me what transpired out there—my sincere apologies for all your losses." Myaneus continued to speak, but my focus shifted to Gershom who was sulking beside me. The reality was too much and had not fully set in for me, but Gershom. Gershom was somewhere else; I could see it in his eyes. He was battling his thoughts in his head, and his thoughts were winning. Suddenly, out of nowhere, Mu loutishly rushed over to us and bent down to embrace us with a hug. A hug that brought Gershom to tears. Little did we know, Mu had just come from viewing

the body of Gershom's mother before he received word we were on board, and now here we were in each other's embrace. The last of our crew and the last of our family.

Myaneus shouted at the men to get ready to push out to sea, while more Spartans continued to make their way onto the main deck. Spartans like the *army of five* ran onto the main deck, with that one muscular Spartan holding the head of the giant by its beard. The head instantly drew the attention of others, including Myaneus, who groaned at the sight of it. "Why does he have a head?" asked Myaneus in a bewildered manner, but a sigh fell from his chest. "I should expect nothing less from the Spartiates, the elites of the royal guard for the king—and I've been blessed to have five on my fleet."

The muscular Spartiate walked over to Myaneus to have a few words with him, while still holding the head of the giant man he slew. He removed his helmet, thus revealing the light caramel skin complexion of his bald head. His beard and facial hair were neatly shaved thin, as if Blade shaped him up himself. However, there was something that stood out about him compared to the Grecians, who also removed their helmets and had their hair flowing down to their shoulders.

As the two men spoke, eight Spartans rushed onto the main deck, yelling out something of concern to the other Grecian soldiers. Dimitrios ran to the edge of the sea fleet facing the docks and quickly turned around to shout a command in the Grecian tongues. "Shields to wall, shields to walls—now, now!" Before he could properly finish what he was yelling, arrows started to rain down from the night skies. Everyone on the main deck went into a frenzy, immediately reaching for their shields and helmets while the arrows continued their tyranny. Myaneus reached for his shield behind his back and covered all three of us, while the muscular Spartiate made his way over to the edge of the fleet where Dimitrios was still yelling out commands left and right.

"Get the dories, get the flying dories on deck—dories on deck, dories on deck!" yelled Dimitrios in a truculent manner.

I could not see much, but I could feel and hear the footsteps of men running about as the occasional arrows continued to thump against the wooden hull. Suddenly, we smelled smoke, and that only meant one thing. "Fire!"

"Helots to the oars, helots to the oars—get this fleet out of here!" Myaneus yelled while banging pugnaciously on the deck.

"Captain, wait!" yelled a soldier unexpectedly. "There are five men still missing—"

"If we stay here, we'll burn—get us out of here now!" replied Myaneus, while he banged again on the deck. After he shouted his command, the sea fleet started rocking and shifting from side to side, while individuals below the deck were shouting commands and moving things to ready our push-back from the docks. I could only assume the helots below were preparing and the oars into the rightful positions.

"Wait, wait, here they come," shouted a Spartan with certainty. That's when we heard the footsteps of men rushing on board. A sudden urge came over me to just glance at who these Spartans were that were almost left behind, so I did just that to see only three men rather than five. Also, one of the three Spartans had a body over his right shoulder. The three were screaming at others on board. I assumed the three were just informed about the captain's orders to leave them behind, which was troubling since the other two were still missing. I extended myself for a better look, but Mu felt my unnecessary extension and drew me back in his grasp underneath Myaneus' shield.

"Captain, captain," said one of the three Spartans who rushed over to our position with his shield over his head. "We cannot leave yet; we were gathering intel about this militia we are fighting; so we kidnapped two of their men. Unfortunately, only have one now, but we still have two of our men still out there, doing some more reconnaissance. Captain, I begged you, we cannot leave them yet." A heavy sigh fell from Myaneus. I did not know what this Spartan was saying, but his words seem to have Myaneus cogitating his commands to leave the docks.

However, the moment of thinking things over was interrupted by a glass bottle exploded on the shield of the young Spartan. Gershom and I jumped in fear from the unknowing, but the three men were unmoved as his shield was set ablaze. We looked up at his shield and Myaneus sighed again, while shaking his head from side to side.

"Helots that are archers, take your positions—

"They're already in position," Dimitrios replied his father's command.

"Captain, the catapult is ready for launch!" yelled another Spartan standing near what was clearly an engine of war.

"Fire away, fire away!" Myaneus yelled back and the catapult tossed something into the air. In a less than a minute, the fireball exploded on the docks, which sent men running and yelling agony. A few Spartans started to cheer, but that was short-lived. While more glass bottles exploded liquid fire onto the floor of deck. Myaneus stood up and carefully guided us to the bow of the sea fleet, where we saw an extensive line of Spartan soldiers lined up on the edge with their shields line adjoin together to form a wall.

"Get this sea vessel to the top of the bay—"

"But captain, the other two have not returned," replied the young Spartan whose shield was still on fire.

"Young man, we will wait for them at the bay, but we cannot stay any longer or else the special coating on the sea fleet will not be able to resist the flames of the fire for much long—You men down below, get this ship out of here. Let's go, let's go, let's go!" Myaneus started shouting fiercely, while he stomped harder and harder on the deck. "Those men have fifteen minutes to swim out to the bay and from there we will pick them up. You have my word, son." Myaneus explained to the young Spartan to ease his troubled mind for his fellow comrades. The two men gave each other a simple nod of acceptance, and the two went their separate ways.

I could feel the motion of the sea vessel departing from the docks. Carefully, to my feet, I stood, and set my eyes to the docks I knew all too well, with a longing to return home, but as I looked toward the docks. It was no longer felt like our home anymore. *Who are all these men? Where did they come from? Why are they here?* I asked myself as I looked out and saw all these strange faces just standing there at the docks, no longer shooting arrows or throw throwing these explosive devices.

"It seems to be an invasion of some sort," Gershom whispered behind me.

"It may be so," I whispered back to Gershom, while the sea fleet drifted off with speed.

"I just wished we knew ahead of time—that way my mother would be alive." As I contemplated what Gershom just said I knew he was wrong.

"How could any of us in the family have known how serious this invasion was going to turn out? We don't even know who these men are, or where they came from, or why they're here?" I questioned Gershom.

"Let's find out—"

"Gershom, Gershom, where are you going?" I questioned him, while he walked away from my sight. Mu signaled for me to help him, so we could follow him. The wall of Spartans remained strong, while the speed of the sea fleet began to increase. Nevertheless, busy bodies ran up and down throughout the deck, putting out small fires here and there, while others swept off the glass shards into the sea. All the while, Gershom was still missing. Suddenly, a Spartan shouted out something as he pointed downward at the waters below. It was the same young Spartan who just spoke to Myaneus. He rushed over to the main mast of the naval fleet to pick up a rope already attached to the mast and ran over to the edge where the wall of Spartans slowly dispersed out of his way. Word was sent below for the helots to cease from their strenuous rowing, but the trireme kept gliding on the open waters with ease. The young Spartan threw the rope down into the dark waters and in three minutes two

Spartans climbed up on board. The Spartans threw their helmets on the deck and squeezed the water out their silky hair, while Myaneus spoke to the two Spartans about their intel.

With the two rescued Spartans now on board, the trireme bolted out the mouth of the bay. Both Mu and I turned around once more to see it one last time. A place we knew to be home was gone. This was good-bye, so I opened my mouth and said, "*Good-bye.*" Mu nodded in acceptance. We both knew this was it: our life of simplicity, from family to the sea, was all gone in just one night. It was in that moment under the moonlight and steering at the docks of Cyrene fading away in distance. I recalled the wisdom of my mother: *What takes years to build, can be destroyed in a day.* It was not until tonight, I finally understood what her words of counsel finally meant.

I closed my eyes to fight back the tears because this was a life lesson. A lesson I was not ready to learn. Mu nudged me with his bony elbow to get my attention. I glanced at the elderly man and he pointed in the direction where I only saw Spartans congregating. The deck was now teeming with more Spartans soldiers than I could count. Some of the men were laughing, others were having private discussions, while the majority belabored about their moves on the battlefield by showing how they used a combination of their shield and long spear. However, Gershom was still nowhere to be found.

Mu, on the other hand, kept pointing in the direction where another group of Spartans gathered. "What's over there?" I questioned Mu knowing well he could not respond. Mu tugged me to walk, so I did just that to please him. However, as we both drew nearer to this group, the men started cheering ebulliently, while others from neighboring groups ran over to have a look for themselves. That's when I saw the dark skin complexion and juvenile figure of Gershom leaping into the air with his left fist propelling into the prisoner's face. The aerial attack excited the men around about him. Gershom's attack caused the man to fall backward, but he managed to hold his footing by hanging on to his fetters.

Nevertheless, the attack was strong enough to bring this prisoner to one of his knees. The prisoner looked up at his attacker and saw the malevolent eyes of a young boy emerged in emotional turmoil. A turmoil fueled by great loss. Gershom held the prisoner by his wooden breastplate and struck him again with his left fist, which was followed by an elbow attack to the side of his head. The usage of the elbow was a fighting style Blade started teaching us some months ago. The prisoner's head shifted to the right, but he turned back around started laughing at Gershom. That laugh infuriated Gershom to kick the prisoner right in his groin. The man bound to his fetters dropped to the ground in excruciating pain, with his hands tucked between his legs.

The Spartans laughed hysterically at the prisoner in pain, while Gershom walked over to a Spartan holding a long, rusty fetters and took it out his hands without asking. A quick hush came cross the Grecians eagerly watching as Gershom wrapped his left fist with the iron fetters. Gershom bent down and turned the man facing upward. Left to right and right to left, Gershom swung his two fists repeatedly on the face of the prisoner. It was brutal to watch, but the Spartans enjoyed every moment of the assault. They extolled Gershom on with every strike to the head and face. It brought them a sense of new joy to their hearts.

Gershom ended his sequence of attacks by holding the man by his breastplate with his right hand, and with his left fist. He unmercifully rained down his indignation. Blood splattered across the deck and covered the face of the prisoner. Gershom dropped the head of the prisoner into a small pool of his own blood, while he stood up to take a short breath of air. His left fist, with the fetters still wrapped around it, was soaked in blood to the point that it cascaded off his hand.

I could not believe all that my eyes just showed me tonight. *Was this really happening?* I wondered while Gershom stood over a bleeding man. Even Mu had a horrified expression written on his face at the sight

of Gershom's unexpected assault on this man. This was not the Gershom we knew, or maybe it was. Maybe, this was who Gershom was all along; but unfortunately, it just took unfortunate circumstances that occurred tonight to bring out this transformation inside of him. A transformation where a young boy puts away his childish ways, so he can become a man. Tonight, Gershom was a man, and a man always sees through glass more clearly when justice is not served.

Gershom bent back down and picked up the man by his breastplate once again, but this time he asked, "Who are you people and why did your people attack us?" Instead of a response, the man spat blood straight into Gershom's face and smile, before he started laughing again. Gershom dropped the man back onto the blood stain deck and wiped the blood from off his eyes with his right forearm. He turned around to a nearby Spartan and quickly reached for the hilt of his short sword referred to as *xiphos*. After such, Gershom picked up the bleeding man with his right hand again and thrust the sword through. However, the short sword made no contact with the bleeding prisoner. The muscular Spartiate held back Gershom's left arm and said perfectly in the Kemetic tongue.

"Patience, child forged in blood,"

"Why?" asked Gershom with anger in his voice.

"We still need information from him first—after such, I will personally give you my blade to kill him yourself. You have my word young one."

Gershom returned his focus to the bleeding man and the bloody prisoner laughed again. Gershom dropped the man back on the deck and handed the muscular Spartan the short sword before he walked away from the sight of bloodstain men. The prisoner lay on the deck laughing and laughing until he started coughing on his own blood.

"Long live the King," said the prisoner in the Kemetic tongue, "The King of Persia!"

"Long live the King," he said, but this time in the Grecian tongue, "The King of Persia!"

All the Spartans looked at the prisoner as he over stressed these words repeatedly five more times, while laughing and coughing out his own blood onto the deck. All that stood there, listening to this man bound in fetters of blood, knew that tonight was simply just the beginning of something bigger to come, and we were all involved. One way or the other. Whether we wanted to be involved or not, we all had our part to play in what was to follow next base on all that occurred tonight. I knew this to be true, just by the expressions carved on the faces of all the Spartans soldiers surrounding this dead man talking. The Spartans understood all that took place tonight was indeed far from over—this was war.

Long live the King—The King of Persia!

CHAPTER 21

FROM CRETE TO SPARTA

[Crete - Ten Years Before the Battle of Thermopylae (480 BC)]

The next day I woke up and found myself covered with an old sheet. It smelled like home, so I rubbed my eyes to have a better look at my surroundings. Gershom was sitting next to me with his back against the bulkhead of the sea vessel with his legs outstretched and apart from each other.

"Mu told me that we will have to help out with fishing," Gershom said tirelessly, without even looking into my face once. I sat up and looked at the tattered sheet to notice that this belonged to Mu. He must have placed it on us when we were sleeping, but I still felt cold, like this kind gesture was more damaging than helpful since I needed to grow a tougher skin.

I stood up to see the open, blue sea all around us. The soothing air blew against my slender body and the sunlight reflected from my mahogany skin. The day was beautiful and the waves were calm; it was as though nature wanted to provide us a remedy for last night. Even the Spartans seemed to have transformed back into their true forms of mere men. The brightness of day was simply a mask that hid the true events of yesterday's night events and the uncertainties of our future.

Gershom stood up as well and looked around at the splendor of the open sea. "The way this day is looking, one would never have assumed that the spirit of death paid us a visit last night." It was good to see that Gershom and I were starting to think on the same level. This kind of mental unison and open communication with each other would always keep us looking out for each other's back, and most of all, help us stay alive. The journey ahead was unknown, but we knew we were not going to let each other do it alone. Gershom was not aware of it then, but that day—underneath the light of the sun—he became my blood brother. I no longer considered merely a cousin. He turned to me for a couple seconds, and then he returned his focus to the open sea. "You're the only family—blood family that I have left in this dark world." Then he sighed and walked up to the edge of the fleet.

Gershom tried to fight back the tears, but the weight of losing his mother in his arms made it impossible. He placed his hands on the edge of the hull, but his arms remained outstretched. I watched scrupulously as the tears fell from his eyes. Gershom hid his face from the eyes of the Spartans. He did not want them to see him in his moment of grief and sorrow. The sun may have transformed these soldiers into normal men, but we knew their true form when the sun went down. The sight of tears seemed to be forbidden among the Spartans, such display of emotions felt like something these men would shun on board this naval fleet. Thoughts such as these kept even me from placing my hand on Gershom's back to comfort him. Gershom started to wipe his tears across his left deltoid muscle.

"Everyone is gone, Teraditus," Gershom said weepily.

"Explain?" I asked.

"Blade made it back to our house, and he told us about the invasion," Gershom said. "He told us that our fathers instructed him to go home and warn the rest of us to flee to the docks. He said our fathers, along

with the hounds, stayed back to hold off the invaders in order for us to make our escape."

Gershom shook his head with tears falling from his eyes. I knew why the tears fell; it was the same reason tears were falling down my face. Our fathers were dead, and I choked because the thought of my father had barely crossed my mind. It was inconsiderate of me to not wonder what had occurred to my father, and to Gershom's father, as well.

"Only the Queen of the Heavens knows what happened to your mother—I pray she did not suffer from the hands of death as mines did," Gershom continued brokenhearted.

"The last I saw of my mother was—when the men, who may or may not be from Persia, entering my house by the numbers. However, I too wonder if she did suffer at the hands of death," I replied with a strong voice, but teary eyes. The thoughts of loss were overwhelming us, because the outcome of it all seemed so hopeless. Our spirits were in great distress and off balance, which was something my mother cautioned me about in great detail, some moons ago. Mother always said, *An unbalance spirit is a soul lost at sea, with no oars or a map to make their journey to a destination of purpose. Therefore, that soul is left to the will of the sea to take them anywhere at any time.* I looked to the open sea and realized I had no oar, nor a map, which meant I too was a lost soul at sea. However, the will of sea was not taking us anywhere. No, our destination was to the land that produce these men of war. "Sparta" was what they called this land—a Greek city-state the Spartans referred to as home. Still, I preferred to go to Kemet, but I doubt that option was on the table.

Then it hit me. "Hey," I said as I wiped away any tears left on my face and eyes, "when I ran to your home, I saw Blade and Nephtali."

Gershom looked at me with waterlogged eyes. "So, do you think they are still alive?"

Uncertainty was the only way to answer Gershom's question. "The last time I saw those two, they were fighting those Persian invaders—"

"Were they now?" Gershom asked, turning his head again to wipe off his tears.

"Oh, yeah!" I slapped Gershom's right shoulders. He turned his head to a certain degree, which cryptically revealed that his right eye was staring at me. "I saw the Swords of Ra in action!" This drew his attention away from the thought of love ones.

"What did you just say?"

"You heard me, Gershom," I said excitedly. I saw the swords in action."

Gershom removed his hands from the edge of the ship's rail and stood tall.

"Explain?"

"Blade burst out of the house wielding these two fiery swords. Well, Blade may have kicked the door down, but the swords were burning with blue flames." Gershom made a face, and I knew why. "Hey, I was wondering why they were blue too, but the fire from the duel swords turned the arrows of the Persians into ashes." Gershom's eyes grew with interest

"So, the swords do have the power to spray out fire . . ."

"Yeah!" I responded.

"Wow, so Blade was actually right about the power of the swords after all."

"Wait!" I said in amazement. "You didn't believe his stories?"

Gershom shook his head from side to side. "You knew how I felt about those tales. I always assumed it was one of those stories where adults tell children to keep children's imaginations alive before they went bed to dream at night. Let me guess, Teraditus—you actually believed the tales to be true?"

I wanted to respond quick with a yes, but I fear of being derided by Gershom. Instead, I shook my head from to side to side, but he did not accept and called me out on my lie.

"Wait!" I said in rebuke. "I believed in this tale, and this tale turned out to be true after all. So, in your face!" Gershom took his focus off me and stared into emptiness as he was mulling over my words. I laughed to myself at the sight of Gershom deep in thought by my words; it rare, but always appreciated. Gershom looked at me and gave me a slick grin.

"Okay, smartass; what about Nephtali?"

"Oh, yeah! She was on the roof shooting arrows at the Persian invaders, but I did not stay to see what happened next. Nephtali kept yelling at me to leave, so I ran to meet up with you and your mother." Gershom started fidgeting with his fingers and mumbled something under his breath.

"What did you say?"

"I wonder about them, Nephtali and Blade. I wonder if they're alive—"

"Men!" Gershom and I turned around to see the affable son of Myaneus with loaves of bread in a basket and a wine skin around his right shoulder. We made our way over to where the Dimitrios had set up wooden crates where we could sit and eat. Dimitrios placed the bread and wine in front of us. He probably assumed we had not consumed much with all that took place last night, and he was right as he watched us scoffed down our bread and drank the wine with ease. Dimitrios laughed at us since he was impressed to see us drink wine the way we did. This was the first time we ever tasted wine, and it had a burning aftereffect when it flowed down our esophagi.

"How are you two holding up?" Dimitrios son asked. I knew Gershom would not answer the question, so I did.

"We're hanging in there," I said sadly.

"You speak the language of my people well for a Grecian?" Gershom shared his observation.

"I'm no stranger to the Egyptian tongue. When I was noticeably young, my family was fortunate to have one the Venuses from Delphi in Corinth residing with us at our home. This Black Dove was born and raised Egypt, so she spoke the common tongue of her people. She taught me the common tongue of her people and culture, but her real mission was to provide our family and others with spiritual guidance."

Both Gershom and I looked at each other and said, "*Egyptian*?" This was the first time we ever had heard the word "Egypt" used to describe our native homeland.

"Can I assume the Greeks refer to Kemet as Egypt?" Gershom asked Dimitrios, in a somewhat irritated tone.

However, Dimitrios showed no sign of remorse for offending our home country. Instead, he quaffed more wine down his throat and said, "Yes, we do."

* * * *

Dimitrios entertained us for the remainder of the afternoon, until sunset. I was quite intrigued by the tales Dimitrios told us, but he was more determined to learn about us. Therefore, I informed Dimitrios about our family, our fishing boat business, and all the lessons we've learned from Blade. Dimitrios was quite impressed to hear about Blade to the point that he wished he could have met him just to spar with him. These Spartans were madmen, and they were highly skilled, but I knew Blade's skills would have given them a worthy fight. I told Dimitrios that I was convinced that the fight would have ended in a draw. Dimitrios broke into an arrogant laugh and convinced me that the training the Spartans experienced would make it impossible for any fight the Spartans were involved in to end in a draw. I was not exactly sure what he meant by the training, and after what I had seen yesterday. I wasn't going to question it, either.

Our conversation even drew the attention of other Spartans who were able to speak a bit of the Kemet dialect. The Spartans amused Gershom and I with their graphic tales on the battlefield or on their adventurous campaigns. They were the first and best actors I'd ever seen, because they emulated every battle form and every dying man's

facial expression as though they were there right now. The thought of massacring men was horrible, but these Spartans sure found a way to make it seem quite comical.

The moon was out, and the trireme glided a lengthy distance underneath the white glow of the moon. The temperature dropped drastically, while the wind blew mercilessly. This cold temperature had no effect on the Spartans whatsoever, and just watching them parading through the ship unbothered and half-naked made Gershom and I feel colder. Gershom and I huddled up together to increase the warmth underneath the old cloth Mu had given us. The night was bitterly cold because of the robust winds that increased the ship's velocity. It was just too cold for Gershom and me to fall asleep, especially when our bodies were tirelessly shaking like cattle bells. We required rest for fishing tomorrow at dawn; these winds were quite punitive, prohibiting us from our rest.

I guess we're not getting much sleeping tonight, huh Teraditus? I mused. Instead of responding to my own thoughts, Gershom nudged my right side to direct my focus to the sight of Spartans with their lyres, wooden flutes, and panpipes. The men started a count off, and then the melody of music danced across the fleet's deck. The music facilitated the unruly sea winds by serenading them with songs of the Grecians. I had never heard music such as this before, and it eased my frustration and calmed my troubled mind. The last thing I heard was the voices of Spartans singing in unison before I fell into a deep slumber.

* * * *

I don't know what happened, but as soon I closed my eyes I had to open them again after what seemed to be a couple of minutes. Mu came over to where we were sleeping and shook us out of our slumber and gave us the look to get ready to fish. The sun was low on the edge of the horizon, and so was our energy that morning. Dimitrios and the rest of the Spartans were all awake. Dimitrios and four other Spartans who had sat with us yesterday evening to converse with us helped us with the massive net.

"Let's do some fishing before we set foot on land, okay, men?" Dimitrios said to Gershom and me. We both turned around and saw land to the southeast of us. It was a small fraction of an island called *Gavdos*, I was told.

I looked at Gershom and said, "I have mixed feeling about this . . ."

"Yeah, I can relate to that," he responded.

As far as I could tell, we did not have any chum or bait to attract the hungry fish, but maybe I was wrong. "Mu," I asked, "do we have any chum?"

Mu looked at me and shook his head from side to side. "We don't need that here ... all we need is Persian blood." All the Spartans broke into laughter. Gershom and I even cracked a smile to ourselves— without letting the Grecians see us, of course.

The Spartans all started dipping their long spears, the *dories*, into the sea to soak off the blood. Others threw their cuirasses, helmets, swords, and shields into the sea around about the naval fleet. As Gershom and I stood near the edge, we could see the sea stained from the blood of men. *That's a lot of blood*, I thought while two helots also threw out something from their buckets on opposite sides of the fleet. Fifteen minutes pass and to our surprise, the fishes came, which made me wonder how appealing Persian blood was after all. The fish came steadily, and they came for a variety of reasons. Some came to nibble on the whatever was in the buckets, while others came in hopes of finding smaller fishes they could consume. Nevertheless, the fishes came, and the Spartans hastily prepared their nets. These nets were attached to the main mast, which made it easy for the Spartans to securely tossed the nets into sea from the opposite sides of the fleet and pulled the nets comprise of fish onboard.

As we were pulling the net out of the water, Gershom and I spotted two swordfish approaching the fleet, and they drew the attention of

everyone. One Spartan screamed out to another Spartan as he threw his helmet with the crested shaped horsehair off his head and jumped overboard with only his leather wrist bracers and greaves from his entire body armor. Gershom and I ran to the edge where this crazy Spartan jumped off, and my eyes could not believe it. Down below, this Spartan had hold of the two swordfishes by their sword-like noses, while the fishes tussled with him for their liberation. Soon after, two other Spartans, in full armor, took the opportunity to jump into the water with their *xiphoses* to lend their swords. However, one of the swordfish broke free from the Spartan's left hand and swam off, leaving the other to meet its demise. Once the Spartans on board saw the liberated swordfish submerged under water, they became hysterically frantic running here and there while shouting throughout the naval fleet. It was beyond odd, but the way these Spartans were behaving. It would seem these Spartans had bad blood with these marine creatures in past, and they were ready to settle differences once and for all.

The Spartans on board quickly armed themselves with dories and fishing spears as they search out the open sea for the liberated swordfish. "There, there, I see it," Gershom said with enthusiasm, while pointing at the other swordfish swimming around the naval fleet. One by one, the dories and fishing spears pierced the sea, but not the intended target. Two more Spartans jumped into the water with their full armor and massive shields, the *aspides*, to create a shield wall to protect the three other Spartans that already stabbed the other swordfish to death. All five Spartans in the water swam to the hull of the trireme where three more shields dropped into the water for more protection, just in case the swordfish tried to attack them, which it did. We all saw the alarming speed of the sword as it glided through the surface of the blue sea, but that did not stop the other Spartans from tossing their dories and missing each time. The swordfish swam straight into the Spartans' shield wall, which absolutely did no damage to the shield. However, that impact left the swordfish a bit dazed, as if it was suffering from a slight concussion. That's when silver dory pierced straight through the eye of the swordfish. Instantly, killing the marine creature, and leaving the lifeless body floating on the surface of the water. Everyone looked up and saw the one Spartiate skilled with the silver dory with his helmet off, which revealed his low-cut, thick black hair and his neatly trimmed, goatee black beard. The celebration followed right after, but the Spartiate made his exist, unknown to those around him. Thus, leaving the rest of us to help the others to make their way back onboard.

I looked over my shoulders and I did not see the Spartiate who just killed the second swordfish. I could not put my finger on it, but these Spartiates were in category of their own, separate from the other Spartans. The Spartiates were a different classification of soldiers, and exceptional and gifted class of men. Nevertheless, this was a memorable fishing experience, never had I witnessed a militaristic approach applied to fishing. Somehow, these men had found ways to incorporate battle techniques into all areas of life. In less than an hour, we had caught a small school of tunas and two swordfishes of three meters long. This was remarkable.

"The old crew couldn't do what these men just did," Gershom admitted to me with a whisper.

"Oh, I know," I replied. Gershom was right, there was no comparison. Our old crew, the *Wonders*, was a group of creative, artistic, and strategic men. These Grecians were simply peculiar men of war that used their military skills in fishing, and fortunate for them it worked. The Spartans brought the two deceased swordfishes onboard and continued their fair share of admirations.

Gershom and I both watched these men in amazement. The Spartans, knowing we had been fisher men back home, turned to us with their blue and hazel eyes to give us a thumbs-up. I returned their gesture for approval with my own thumbs up, while Gershom gave them nods of approval. When I looked at the two marine animals with their mouths still open, a sense of sympathy came over me because I knew the second

swordfish wanted to save the first. Something I would have done if it was Gershom. However, the attempt to rescue was all a tragic fail, and unfortunately, resulted in both of their demises. The thought of the swordfishes' death was too much to dwell on, so I turned to help Gershom finish securing our catch of the day. Meanwhile, the fleet made its way around the massive island to find the right docks to anchor this naval fleet.

When the fleet pulled into the docks, we saw a few more Spartans waiting for us to pull in. Dimitrios turned to us and said, "Welcome to Knossos, the greatest city in all of Crete. From the women to the entertainment, this city has never failed to surprise me." It felt good to be on land again, and most of all with the Spartans. The sun was out, and the sea winds were pleasant with their touch. To my left of the docks, the local sea birds sang their warmly greetings, while the occasional shadows from above provided us brief moments of shade. The life on the docks brought back memories of home on Cyrene. A home that no longer existed, which left me a sojourner in this world that had no place for me. At a moment notice, I could feel my thoughts slipping into a dark place with each step-down memory lane, but Gershom grabbed my right shoulder just in time and brought me back to the present.

As I glanced around, I noticed the docks were teeming with all manner of faces from different regions of the world, but those that stood out were the merchants, of course. My father taught me to always recognize merchants by their head wraps and the sashes that held daggers and swords close to their waist. He also showed me how to wrap the linen around my own head. For this was a common practice among many merchant companies of low and great status. With practice, I learned, and now I had the eye to distinguish them among the crowds. My father also taught me how to observe the merchants carrying daggers visibly in front of their person or concealed. The revealing of the dagger had multiple meanings about the merchant's status or the company he was associated with. Listening to the tales about my father's encounters with these merchant companies, especially the merchant companies from Tyre and Zidon, were some my favorite tales to hear from my father. His tales were endless adventures, but he was still careful with how much he shared with me. Something I now regret since he was no longer in the realm of the living.

Gershom grabbed me by the arm and pulled me in the direction of the Spartans already on the move. We stayed near Dimitrios and his grandfather while surrounded by a unit of Spartans. Our unit was responsible for selling the catch of day to the vendors in the marketplace. Everyone in the unit carried something. People were everywhere on the inner region of the docks, attending to a variety of duties.

"I wish we had our daggers with us," Gershom said underneath his breath.

"Daggers," Dimitrios said irately. He drew his *xiphos* and handed it to Gershom, who nearly dropped it due to the alarming weight of the sword. "It is time you men grew up and realized that this is a man's world, and quite honestly, you men are a couple of years behind."

Mu touched his grandson on the shoulder and gave him the look to give us mercy.

"I know," Dimitrios said to Mu, "but they're going to need to learn, especially if they are going to survive the life in Sparta." Mu dropped his head in dismay, which made me a bit concerned.

As the unit made their way deeper into this Greek town, the number of people around us became overwhelming. The marketplace was overcrowded with everyone you could possibly imagine: people buying and selling, people socializing with peers and associates, and there were even people on the rooftops of these white, stone buildings. We sold our catch to various vendors, and to townspeople as well. Gershom and I received our fair share of payment each, and it was more viable than I expected.

"I never knew fishing on a Saturday could be so rewarding," I mentioned to Gershom while admiring the sack that held the silver coins we had earned. Gershom nodded in agreement to what I said, while maintaining a candid demeanor with the *xiphos* firmly set in his left hand.

The sight-seeing on this island was different, but I still saw the similarities between this island and the city of Memphis, especially with the columns and palm trees. Everywhere I looked, there were sculptures of naked men posing for us in every way possible. Gershom shook his head in disapproval each time I physically forced him to look for himself, but he pushed me off him every time. A smile appeared on Gershom's face, something I have not seen in a while, which made me feel good. Nevertheless, I appreciated how the sculptors managed to capture the beauty of humanity in these sculptures. Once we reached a small marketplace where they sold figurines of snake goddesses, paintings of people always drinking out of what Dimitrios referred to as the *kantharos* and the *kylix*, and more sculptures of naked men. The Grecians embraced the human image, while we, the Egyptians—as Dimitrios would call us—captured not only the essence of the human image, but the essence of the connection between humanity and the supernatural universe.

No matter where I turned, this island was full of life and new sights to explore with each step. People just seemed to be hustling and bustling with own activities for the day, but they did everything with a smile on their faces. A sense of serenity one wakes up to each sun rise ready to take on the day's duties without complain, nor concern. People on this island was genuinely happy, from the eldest to the youngest, and from the locals to the foreigners, such as the Spartans and me. It was rejuvenating to be around lively people again. The energy from this island was electric, which makes sense to why the Spartans overflowed with childlike excitement to get their destination more in-land.

Nevertheless, as the journey continued, the ground changed from everyday dirt to light gray bricks that sparkled with the touch of the sunlight. The combine scent of the different foods was riveting. All I could smell was the rich aroma of smoked meats and the warm smell of freshly baked cinnamon bread. The temptation to spend our silver to buy a roll of bread and seasoned ham was irresistible and distracting, but Gershom saw my wandering focus and cleared his throat to re-direct focus now and then. I sighed and returned focus back to the small unit of Spartans. However, my attention span was shirt-lived, considering all the activities of people around me. The faces of men and women were a sea of diversity. It was hard to distinguish between the foreigners and the locals, but the people came in all shapes and colors. Nevertheless, the one observation I was able to distinguish for certain was, there was an abundant of women of in this city in comparison to men.

At that very moment, a group of young women rushed past Gershom and I to greet Dimitrios and couple of other Spartans. The eyes of these Grecian women were beautiful, with colors more exquisite than the Mediterranean Sea. A young girl with green eyes was the first out of the seven women who caught my attention. I had never seen anyone with green eyes, and they matched with her blonde, curly hair. There was one woman with pitch-black hair and light blue eyes who was nice enough to smile at us and ask who we were in the Grecian tongue. Dimitrios, of course, informed her about our sad tale, which led to her giving us her condolences in our original language. Surprised, she knew how to speak out in our tongues. She told us her name was "Elysia," and in return we shared our names with her and her only. However, the white-haired woman with the deep Mediterranean-blue and a hint of green in her eyes was the most intriguing out of the seven. This was the first time Gershom and I had seen a young woman with such silky, white hair. Elderly men and women were typically the individuals we were accustomed to seeing with such white hair, but she was the exception.

Looking past this unique aspect about her, she wore the look of mischief on her face, which was quite a rush for a young boy. In addition, she seemed particularly affectionate toward Mu. Gershom turned to me to give me a confounded look. I knew he was thinking the same thing I was thinking. We never took Mu to be a lady's man, but the women seemed to be very fond him. They greeted Mu with extensive hugs and kisses and friendly words to fill his ears.

The day was progressing into the early afternoon hours. The group of women escorted us out of the market to a massive establishment with huge ionic columns and multiple rooms. Inside, we saw colossal sculptures of more than twelve winged humans pouring water out from their vases. Elysia said something to Gershom and me, but we didn't understand her, since she said it in Grecian tongue. I assumed it was something along the lines of, "Isn't it beautiful?" I was all beautiful, from the designs on the walls to the people inside this establishment, it was breath-taking. Suddenly, we walked into an area where people were lounging in an enormous pool, and in the middle of the pool stood a monumental sculpture of a giant man made of green beryl stone and marble. My mouth and eyes opened wide at such grandeur. In his right hand, the giant man held a golden pitchfork in his right, while on his head was gold crown with five huge spikes and seven smaller spikes.

"He must be some type of god to the Grecians," Gershom said to me.

"He's *Poseidon*, the god of the seven seas—and Atlantis before it sank," Elysia explained to Gershom and me in our Kemet tongue.

"We've heard of Atlantis, which existed before the days of the first rulers of Mesopotamia—"

"Yes, King Nimrod was one of the many great Kushite Kings to walk the Earth and ruled the regions of Mesopotamia. That was part of the story my mother told us Tuesday's evening when she was telling us all the tales of Blade's secret life and his experiences, while he lived in Babylonia during the latter days of King Cyrus of Persia's reign," I continued right after Gershom's statement. Elysia smiled at us, while leading us up a flight of stairs to the second floor. On the second floor, Elysia and the green eye, blonde hair girl stopped Gershom and me in front of a chamber with a see-through, white veil, while other Spartans continued walking on the same floor. However, before we departed, Dimitrios assured us that we were in good hands and to enjoy our time—and then he gave us a wink.

Elysia and the young woman with the green eyes guided Gershom and I through the white veil and into a room where men were fully nude and cleaning themselves with water running out of an elongated bronze tip.

"Look Teraditus, they have the same thing in Kemet, Gershom pointed out to me.

The two girls looked to what Gershom was pointing at.

"Oh!" said Elysia still holding onto us. "It is called a 'pipe,' and it pours out water for the men and women to drink and clean themselves," Elysia said to us, while the other young woman played with her blonde hair.

Both Gershom and I were amazed at how advanced this island was in comparison Kemet. Well, it would be foolish to compare this island to such a powerful nation such as Kemet, so I pushed the thought out of my mind and entertained it no more.

"Wait," I said to the Elysia. "What women?" She pointed behind us to our right. Low and behold, Gershom and I were fortunate enough to see actual women—that were naked. The girl with the white hair and blue eyes said something to us in her native Greek tongue, which was pointless since we did not understand the Grecian tongue.

"Try not to stare too long, or you might lose your eyes," Elysia said to us before the two broke out in giggles. I, of course, blushed in embarrassment and apologized.

However, Gershom flung his *xiphos* onto his left shoulders and said, "This is nothing new to me."

Elysia stopped laughing and made an expression of disbelief on her face, and translated to her friend what Gershom had said, and she too replicated the same expression of disbelief before breaking into a smile.

"Okay, enough of the talk. It's time for us to clean you guys up." Elysia's words caught me off guard to the point that I could feel my heart jumping out of my chest.

"What do you mean?" The two young women could hear the fear in my voice so together the two giggled and walked behind us to guide us to the elevated pipes coming out of the marble walls. Both Gershom and I looked at each other with so many questions on our faces. Before we were placed in the area where the water fell out of the bronze pipe, Elysia stripped me naked so quickly it was as though my tattered clothes wanted to leave my frail body. I looked over to where Gershom was with the green-eyed girl, and he was already naked with the *xiphos* covering his manhood. She laughed at Gershom and tried her hardest to take the *xiphos* away from him, but Gershom resisted her attempts to liberate the small sword from his hands.

I, on the other hand, had nothing to cover myself with. This was the first time I was fully naked in front of an actual woman, other than my mother. I looked cowardly in front of Elysia as I tried to cover myself up, but she laughed hysterically at me. Then she turned me around to watch the other woman, with the white hair, successfully cleaning Gershom's face with a washcloth, after lathering the rest of his body with soap. It appeared Gershom had just given up on resisting the young woman, because she had turned him around to rest the back of his head on her chest and whisper something into his ear.

"What's her name, Elysia?" I asked, trying to draw attention away from my nudity, while Elysia lathered me with her soapy washcloth.

"Who Bethania?" she questioned loudly enough for the young woman with the white hair to look over at us, which resulted Bethania pointing at me and laughing. I dropped my head in humiliation.

The two women guided us into the area where the water was flowing out of the two separate pipes. The icy water shocked my body into a state of numbness. Elysia felt my shoulders tense up and said, "It's all in your mind, sweetheart." Her words of comfort brought me back to thoughts of my own mother, which was enough to bring warmth to my unresponsive state. Elysia turned my back around to see my boyish face. I turned to see five beautiful girls standing there with crates in the arms. One of the girls began pointing downward and laughing, and the rest joined in too.

The laughter of multiple women drew the attention of others who wanted to know what was so hysterical, and in this case, it was us, unfortunately. I felt instantly mortified. This was my first time around strange and beautiful women, and I was embarrassed to the highest degree.

"It's the cold water, it tenses up everything," Gershom said distastefully. However, the girls laughed harder after Gershom's comment. All Gershom and I could do was cover up some more to save ourselves from further humiliation. This made them laugh even harder, because the two girls washing us tried removing our hands from where they were.

"What's the point, boys? We already saw it all." said Bethania in the Kemet tongue. Our mouths dropped as she continued what she was saying. "You boys better enjoy our company while it lasts, because of where you're going next." She shook her head from side to side, while the other women around her started emulating her head movements. "There's going to be a serious case of abstinence." Bethania continued to speak, but the word she said caused a flashback. Considering, I've heard that word before—abstinence—when my mother had questioned Gershom's mother about Nephtali being abstinent with Blade. I never heard the answer, since they kicked me out house to play with Gershom and the hounds to finish their gossiping privately. My mother had

robbed from an opportunity to learn a new word—one that would have been important in this moment.

The two women allowed us to rinse underneath the pipes for a few minutes before taking us into another room on the ground floor, where Poseidon towered in the center of the pool. This was the very moment when things went from down to up. The women told us to get into the pool, which we did. However, in a matter of minutes, only two of the five young women joined us in the pool after disrobing themselves. I finally understood why Dimitrios had said this was "the greatest city in all of Crete."

The other three women began taking things out of their crates and used them to clean and groom us. They flung white and blue petals from the lotus flower into the pool and poured exotic perfumes into the water before they left all of us there. This was very exhilarating for me, but I wasn't sure about Gershom. He was still fighting the two girls from taking away his small sword, which he grabbed back after getting laughed at. However, the two girls had erotic strategies for obtaining Gershom's full cooperation. They all attacked him with kisses and bites to his neck. Gershom's grip on the hilt of the sword loosened up before the white-haired woman with blue eyes took the short sword again. "So, are you going to keep giving us trouble?" she asked Gershom with the voice of a fully mature woman.

Gershom looked straight into Bethania's blue eyes and said, "That's the plan." I shook my head in dismay and watched as they attacked him again.

The feeling of abashment quickly changed into one of tranquility as the women tended to our bodies. The women rubbed our backs and chests with soapy washcloths and their hands. They massaged our heads, backs, and toes. Their sentimental touch was sweeter than honey and warmer than the kiss of a new sunrise. The young women sensually ran their hands over our bodies, holding onto us so tightly that we were practically secured in their succulent bosoms.

This was the first time I experienced this level of intimacy with a woman—or in this case, women. There was no escaping such an embrace such as this; we were trapped, and it was quite fine. This experience was too good to be true; it took our minds off the tragedy that had occurred two days ago. I began to wonder if this was Dimitrios's plan all along. If so, then the objective was well accomplished, because by the look on Gershom's face, one would never be able to tell that he had recently lost so much in a matter of minutes and hours. I felt Elysia reach behind her and begin shaving the hair off my head.

"Hey, why are you cutting my hair off?"

"Trust me, it's for the best," Elysia whispered tenderly into my ears while caressing my face.

Meanwhile, Gershom was on the other side, resisting his haircut. Gershom had one arm wrapped around Bethania's waist and the other holding the shaving blade away from his body. Bethania carefully tried to pull Gershom's off the hand that held the shaving blade, but he was adamant about not getting his hair cut.

"I demand an explanation as to why you're doing this," Gershom said distastefully.

Bethania leaned close to Gershom's face and said loud enough that even I heard her say, "You're going to Sparta. Please understand your world is about to change in a way you can't even imagine." Then she turned to me and said, "You both must prove yourself, or else you both will be lower than the helots." Her focus returned to Gershom, while he liberated her hand that held the shaving blade.

Our heads were shaved clean. This reminded me of how Mother despised this style of haircut for men. I recalled the time we had journeyed into Kemet to see my great grandmother before she died. I had cousins whom I've never seen before with their heads shaved clean with a single lock of dangling from the left side of their heads. My mother grew to hate this hairstyle for men, and she forbade both my father and me from shaving our heads again. She claimed that the

shaving of a man's head took away his strength and attractiveness. Therefore, the shaving of my head now was causing me to wonder if I was going lose these valuable aspects of my manhood, which I was just newly discovering.

Elysia kissed the top of my tender head and whispered in my right ear, just like Mother always did when she needed me to feel her words. "I believe you two have what it takes to make it through to the end. Just make sure to look out for one another—promise me that you will look out for your brother." Elysia's words caught me off my guard. She had acknowledged that we were brothers, even though we barely looked alike. Or maybe she knew that we needed to have each other's backs more than ever, especially when Sparta was our next stop.

It wasn't before long that the other three young women returned to the pool with gray clothes and pairs of strapped shoes in their hands. We all left the pool together to dry ourselves off before putting on our gray garments. The cloth of our new apparels wrapped around our right shoulders and reached as far down to our knees. The leather sandals were as black as Elysia's hair.

Ten minutes after we had left the pool and dressed ourselves, we heard a new voice. "Nisis, Nisis, Nisis!" A servant humbly came into the pool area, calling for this person. That's when the white-haired young woman approached the servant girl with her hair dripping with each step to discuss a pressing matter. I turned to Gershom, who also turned to me, and we both said *"Nisis!"* The white-haired woman turned around to us to give a bewildered steer when she heard us say her name the way we did before she resumed her original focus on the servant.

Nisis signaled to all of us to follow her outside the room, while the servant girl held out her hand, escorting us out with a smile on her pale face. The center was crowded with men separated into different factions, discussions pressing matters concerning Pericles and the Athenians' involvement in the Persian War, but Nisis kept moving till we were all outside and staring at the low rays of the sun.

"You men had an exciting time?" Dimitrios asked us.

"Of course, they did," Nisis replied to Dimitrios before we could even move our lips. "We aim to please," Nisis said sternly to Dimitrios before giving Gershom and I a scolding look.

"Excellent. Men, say your farewells, because your journey starts now."

Elysia turned me around to hug me and kiss me on the forehead. "I wish you two all the best, and please make sure to look out for one another." Elysia's words were as comforting as my own mother's. All the women gave us a farewell hug and kiss—even Nisis did so with additional words of encouragement.

"I thought your name was Bethania?" asked Gershom

"Nisis is my business name, only close friends called me Bethania—until another time you two." Nisis explained to us before she walked away from us.

The walk back to the fleet was filled with questions and concerns running through my head. Each step we took was a bit closer to our new life. I turned to Gershom and said, "Why don't they just leave us here? I like it here, don't you?" Gershom moved his head up and down.

"This place is amazing, I must agree, but it's not reality," Dimitrios said to us. "Sparta, on the other hand, will be your new reality, so please start by preparing your minds for a transformation like none other. Crete was a moment under the sun, but Sparta will shape you men for many more moments under the sun." After a pause he spoke again. "Sparta awaits you two."

CHAPTER 22

TRIUMPHANT MEN (INTERLUDE)

[Mykonos Island / Aegean Sea, 29 AD]

C rete sounds amazing!" Allidephi said with a smile as she sat with a sleeping Diodotus in her arms. Teraditus was about to open his mouth when the sound of men cheering and Cassiani screaming "no" drew his attention away.

"I wonder what's going on out there?" He paused and shook his head, "However, not to get sidetracked, but an hour passed since we left the port of Knossos, and now we were deep in the Mediterranean Sea. Myaneus came to spot where Gershom and I resided on the ship, and he wasn't alone. Mu and Dimitrios accompanied him. The three men sat down next to us and explained to us that we had to join the Sparta military school."

Teraditus shook his head and laughed. He looked up at Allidephi and smiled at her.

"What's so funny?" Allidephi asked the smiling Teraditus.

"All I remember was how I took a deep breath in, and then let it out. Gershom gave me this confused looked and said to Myaneus that we were too young to join the military—and to a certain degree, he was right. Nevertheless, Myaneus shook his head and told us that every Spartan boy joins the military school at age seven, and we were three years late since we enrolled at the ages of ten. He also told us the next best option was to become slaves. Gershom and I looked at each other, and then back at the three generations of Spartans who sat in front of us."

"What an ultimatum to be faced with at such an early age . . ."

"Oh yes, and we chose wisely." Teraditus leaned back on his chair with his hands cuffed together to hold his hairless head. "Gershom, of course, knew best in situations such as this, so he asked Myaneus to explain the challenges and obstacles we were likely to encounter. Myaneus looked at us and told us without blinking that the school involved a lot of fighting. 'A whole *lot* of fighting,' Dimitrios said to us in a way that added more emphasis to what his father had just said. Myaneus also informed us that all odds were against us, and this was true, but he promised that he and Dimitrios would do everything in their power to prepare us as best as possible for what was to come. However, he reminded us that we had to make sure we held our weight and prove to Sparta that we were fit to be Spartans, no matter what our origins were; especially when we had a common enemy."

Teraditus looked down at his hands and fidgeted with them.

"What was your experience like living in Sparta?" Allidephi asked quietly.

Teraditus, still focused on his hands, opened his mouth and said, "It was a nightmare!"

"I'm sorry . . ."

"No, please. If it weren't for Sparta, I would not be who I am today. That *nightmare* molded me for many more moments under the sun. I guess Dimitrios was right after all." Allidephi turned her focus to Diodotus, who began squirming in her arms. The infant was fussing, and soon it was feeding time for the whaling babe. Teraditus got up and left the kitchen so the mother could be alone to breast-feed her son.

Ten minutes passed, and Allidephi brought the cheerful baby outside where she saw the competition was in full swing. Teraditus was outside already, watching the intense competition amongst siblings. He also started gnawing on his fingernails with his teeth. Allidephi could tell that the father was nervous about his daughter playing rough.

"What games are they playing now?" Allidephi's question was ignored since Teraditus did not hear one word. "Teraditus," she said in her motherly voice, but only Diodotus responded. Allidephi walked closer to where Teraditus was standing and watching attentively.

Teraditus looked to his left and saw the mother with her child in her arms, and wondered aloud,

"When did you get here?"

"A while ago, and I asked you a question, but you were very focused on the activities in front of you."

Teraditus returned his gaze to the activities in front of him, "Apologizes, Allidephi, I just don't like this sport—"

"Pankration," Allidephi said. Teraditus nodded his head in agreement, "I heard Spartans were banned from competitions that involved this style of fighting in many of the Greek city-states." Teraditus gave Allidephi another nod and started laughing.

"There was a time when Gershom snuck into the Olympian games in Olympia, identifying as an Egyptian with Grecian citizenship, but with no mention of being a fully pledge Spartan. I was terribly afraid of getting caught because we had a mission to carry out, but it turned out that Gershom's involvement in these games gave our unit the perfect distraction we needed to execute the mission properly. His performance throughout the games gave us five days of proper distraction. We were practically finished with our mission ahead of schedule and were fortunate to watch some of the games ourselves."

Allidephi took her eyes off Teraditus and focused it on Telus and Cassiani wrestling on the verdant ground, "Are you sure your daughter is not a Spartan in disguise?"

Teraditus laughed and said, "Cassiani has entered Olympian games, and she was victorious in the running disc-throwing competitions."

Allidephi's eyes grew wide as she looked at Teraditus and said, "Wow, that's impressive." Teraditus began to nod his head, while the mother made her way to one of the chairs on the patio. "It is good to see that Cassiani is keeping the legacy of Olympian women alive," she added.

Teraditus turned to the mother with a surprised look on his face and said, "Yes, she is. Wait—I assume you've heard of the first woman who entered into the competitions and won?"

Allidephi started nodding her head while making adorable baby sounds that made Diodotus happy. "Kyniska of Sparta was the first female Olympian," Allidephi said without even picking up her head. "Therefore, it all adds up—Cassiani is a daughter of a Spartan, so it makes sense why she is this way. Cassiani has Spartan blood running through her, just like Kyniska, which means Cassiani has what it takes to win these competitions in the Olympics."

Teraditus smiled while nodding at the knowledge Allidephi displayed. A loud *thud* on the ground was heard, followed by a female groan. The thud was enough to alarm Teraditus and Allidephi, and the groan made them even more concerned. Teraditus quickly turned to see Rellos on the ground, moaning in agony. Rellos's left arm was out of the socket.

"Oh no," Allidephi said with teary eyes. The sight of her lover with a grotesque limb was too indelible for her to bear. Allidephi handed Diodotus to Teraditus and ran to help her husband inside.

Allidephi was more of an intellect than a competitor, so to see her husband in this much pain was hurting her more than him. Teraditus watched from a distance as the frantic wife asked several questions as she held her husband's head close to her bosom. Cassiani was explaining as much as possible that she was responsible for his injuries. This made Allidephi examine Rellos's body, and she found scrapes and scratch marks on his arms and neck. She gave Cassiani a furious look for hurting her husband.

Ena got down on her knees and wiggled her fingers over Rellos's grotesque arm. Ena looked at Telus and he grabbed Rellos's mouth. She wrapped her right arm around his left arm and elevated it vertically, while her left hand remained firm on Rellos's left shoulder. Every movement Ena made with Rellos's arm made him moan in excruciating pain, but Allidephi's cries were louder. Then Ena applied gentle force with her right arm to guide the arm back into its proper place. A *pop* sound traveled as far back to where Teraditus was standing with the curious baby. Rellos's agitated body became still, and then he started moving the injured arm as though it had never been injured. Telus removed his hand from Rellos's mouth and Rellos looked at Ena to say, "There's no pain, there's no pain! Gratitude, Ena, gratitude." Rellos stood to his feet, pushing his wife out of the way up to hug and repeatedly thank Ena for fixing the problem. Allidephi felt irrelevant as she warily watched her husband embrace the woman who was an actual solution to his problem.

Rellos freed Ena from his embrace and raised both of his arms in the air, and the men yelled out in triumphant for his speedy recovery. The games were back on. Allidephi made her way back to the patio, but Ena had noticed and sensed Allidephi's hurt. So, she called Rellos and told him what she had seen with Allidephi and how to fix it. Rellos sprinted to Allidephi and scooped her up in his arms so he could spin her around and kiss her passionately, thanking her for her motherly care and concerns. Before he placed his wife down and wrapped one arm around her waist while the other hand tenderly caressed her face. He gave her a kiss before leaving to return to the games. Rellos's intimate gesture left Allidephi rosy and smiling. She managed to meet Ena's eyes when she was turning back around in the direction of the patio. Ena gave Allidephi a wink before she returned to the heat of the competition.

"It's good to see that Rellos will be okay," Teraditus said to the mother walking up the stairs to the patio.

"There's just something about Ena. I can't put my finger on it, but she—"

"It's truly something special," Teraditus finished.

Allidephi navigated her eyes to look straight into those of Teraditus. She had a perplexed look on her face, and she shook her head from side to side, because she knew he was right. "You have to tell me her story, Teraditus."

Teraditus sat down with the giddy baby. "We'll get there, but let's finish up first . . ."

"Okay, please continue, Teraditus."

"Oh yes, so Myaneus was giving us an ultimatum and we were terrified about the options. Myaneus told us that military academy was the best way to go, and then he told us we had to start preparing ourselves now." Allidephi's left eyebrow rose up. "Oh yes! We had to fight the Spartans on the naval fleet, and they didn't hold back." Teraditus looked at the mother from across the table.

"So, it's true—Sparta really placed their young boys in such harsh and rigorous militant programs."

Teraditus could hear the compunction in Allidephi's tone, but he did not allow his emotions of these difficult memories to get the best of him.

"The same day we left the island of Crete, in the middle of the night on the open sea. Myaneus told Gershom and I to remain conscious for only five minutes in a brawl with four Spartans on the open deck," Teraditus sighed and shook his head. "Those five minutes were brutal.

The first two minutes we applied the fighting techniques of the *Montu* which Blade had taught us, by using our shorter heights to our advantage, but the armored men caught on to it. Then we suffered from a series of blows to head, stomach, and back . . ."

"Oh, my goodness!" Allidephi said before covering her open mouth.

"Please," Teraditus said while using one hand to brush away Allidephi's concern.

"Those five minutes were a breeze in comparison to the entire Spartan experience. Myaneus gave us two-minute rest before the next brawl, but he gave us the option of fighting the Spartans with their armor on or off. Foolishly, we choose the option for no armor, which resulted in the Spartans soldiers moving faster and hitting harder. I was knocked into a state of unconsciousness in less than a minute." Teraditus smiled at the thought of the Spartan who had knocked him out in his second round of the brawl. Allidephi kept her hands near her mouth in a horrified manner. "Oh, I failed to mention that Dimitrios was the one who knocked me out—"

"Really?" said Allidephi, with her hands still covering her mouth.

"Oh yeah," said Teraditus with a hysterical tone in his voice. "Dimitrios was our first and most influential Spartan mentor, so he held nothing back from us. He always reminded us that life wouldn't go easy on us, so why should he?"

"Five minutes passed since my blackout, but I awoke to the sound of Gershom's coughing. I saw Gershom coughing out copious amounts of blood on the deck. Gershom picked his head up from between his arms and looked at the Spartans for them to see that he wasn't giving up as long he was breathing. One of the Spartans said something to Myaneus and Dimitrios, which led to Dimitrios walking over to Gershom to say, 'There's a potential Spartan in you after all, but I can't say that about Teraditus. However, you two can work together, and you men will see it through the end. Keep in mind, we do have two days at sea to start building you men up before we reach the shores leading up to Sparta, because we are entering into the lion's den and the only way to survive is to fight in Sparta. So, please take these two days seriously.' In time, I started to see that Dimitrios's words were a compromise of truth and hope.

"I got up with a new mindset and painfully made my way over to where Gershom was standing weakly. I looked at Gershom, and he said to me, 'Don't worry, I had your back. We're in this together.' I gave him a nod of gratitude, and then we braced ourselves for the next round . . .'"

"No—there was another round?" Allidephi said aloud; even Diodotus looked at her with concern in his eyes.

"There was a total of five rounds that night with only five hours of sleep before sunrise, which also included doing some more fishing before the sun was completely up."

Allidephi raised her index finger toward Teraditus to suspend the conversation, and then she walked over to have a better look of Ena outrunning Apollos. "This woman . . . is there anything she cannot do, Teraditus?"

Teraditus picked up the child, who now had heavy eyes, and walked over to Allidephi to say, "Come on, let's put Diodotus down for a brief nap, and we will prepare a victory feast for our Olympians. This will also give you more time to hear about our journey to Sparta." Teraditus cautiously cradled the baby's head in his arm to look at Allidephi and say, "Trust me, you don't want you to miss this part."

Allidephi looked at the sagacious grandfather and replied, "Okay."

CHAPTER 23

OUR NEW HOME

[Sparta - Ten Years Before the Battle of Thermopylae (480 BC)]

Gershom and I found ourselves waking up early before the sun could ascend from the depths of the eastern horizon. We woke up with little to no strength inside of us. The only motivation to keep on going was for the sake of each other. I felt solely accountable for him suffering more than I did, considering how I had blacked out early in the second session of the brawl. Even though Gershom refused to show any form of intense bodily injury, every movement had some form of muscle and bone ache. Mu woke us up with a sad look on his face. I knew he did not want us to have anything to do with the Spartan heritage, but what choice did we have? What other option was there?

Two days at sea since we left the Isle of Crete and our time on this fleet continued to grow unbearable. Mu stood alongside Dimitrios, who was alarmingly too lively in the mornings. Mu's grandson held a fishing net in his hands and wore a devious smile on his face. This was the second time Gershom and I saw Dimitrios without a crested helmet. Dimitrios had dirty-blond hair somewhat similar to his father's hair, which flowed down to his shoulders. He kept his armor off while he helped us fish. We threw the net down into the open water and patiently waited. A Spartan walked up to Dimitrios to give him the signal that it was time for something to occur. Gershom and I saw this gesture, and we became concerned. Dimitrios turned to us and said, "Do what I do." Dimitrios started running in place, so we started running in place. Then he started jumping with his arms and legs extending far out, so we did the same.

Our physical activities drew the attention of other Spartans. Myaneus came outside to watch us replicating everything Dimitrios did. Dimitrios held his hands in front of him and pretended to sit on a chair. I didn't think much of what I was doing, but after two minutes, my legs—and Gershom's too—were violently shaking. The Spartans got a good laugh out of this. They were practically yelling and jeering at us in their Grecian tongue, as though we understood a word they said. However, I assume they were telling us to hold the position we were in for a few minutes because the Grecian soldiers began to add weight by resting their hands on our shoulders to add more weight.

These Spartans were the ideal description of madmen because they started giving us different weaponry to hold in this position, they referred to as the *resting squat*. What followed next was the short sword, *xiphos*, and afterward were two fishing spears. I turned to look at Dimitrios, who was as still as the monuments in Knossos, but Gershom on the other hand. Let's just say his legs shook so badly that his right leg shook faster than the other. From the side of my eye, Gershom had invented a new dance. Gershom's legs shook so fast that his entire body vibrated uncontrollably. The Spartans laughed hysterically, but they didn't stop there. They placed their five-pound bronze helmets on our tiny, bald heads and gave us each a twenty-pound *dory* to hold as well. The Spartans were on the floor rolling with laughter at Gershom—even Myaneus was laughing while maintaining a stern face.

However, now I could not see Gershom from the side of my eye, since the helmet blocked my side view. I really wished I could see his latest dance, because judging by the way the soldiers were laughing and carrying on, I was missing the performance of a lifetime.

Get it together, son, I thought. *Gershom needs your words of encouragement. Remember how Elysia informed you that you two would need to have each other's back.* My conscience was right, of course, so I took a deep breath in and then irritably let it out.

I remember the time Blade taught us the concept of "mind over body" when Gershom accidentally stabbed his left leg with a four-inch dagger. The dagger pierced him horizontally above his knee, and it stuck out of his outer thigh. Both Blade and I were horrified at the sight, but it was too much for Gershom. His eyes rolled to the back of his head, and then it was lights out for Gershom. Blade grabbed a piece of cloth to apply slight pressure to the wound before attempting to slide the dagger out. Blade's attempt somehow revived Gershom, and he began screaming madly. Gershom's cry of terror startled both Blade and I, but Blade covered Gershom's mouth, suppressing his cry of agony before it drew the attention of his parents. "Mind over body, Gershom, mind over body!" Blade whispered angrily to the wailing Gershom. "Teraditus, go get my special honey," Blade said to me, while Gershom shook his head in fear. I ran and recovered what Blade had requested me to bring to him, and then he told me to cover Gershom's mouth. "Mind over body," Blade told Gershom, and then he pulled the dagger out. I never forgot how Gershom compressed the muscles in his face, and how hard his body shook before he became still. Blade hurriedly smeared the honey antiseptic on the open wound before he wrapped up the wounded leg. I removed my hands from Gershom's mouth, and Gershom said feebly, "Mind over body!"

Of course, I didn't fully understand the concept of *mind over body,* at that point in my life, until I felt the weight of the *dory* in my hands and the helmet resting on my fragile head. The concept was clear as daylight. "Gershom, mind over body, mind over body! Can you hear me? Mind over body!" I yelled out to him. I didn't hear him respond, but what I heard were the grunts of a fighter. The laughing ceased temporarily, and I saw nods of approval. This sight gave me the additional strength I needed to maintain my position and hold the weight.

Myaneus saw that we were learning to apply the concept of mind over body, so he decided to challenge it. Myaneus spoke in his loud voice, and the next thing I knew was that the *dory* was removed from my hands and replaced with a massive *aspis*. I instantly felt my strength drop from ten to zero. The Spartans kept yelling at us to not let their shields touch the deck in their Grecian tongue, we didn't understand, but we figured that's what they cautioned us not to do, of course.

Sadly, Gershom dropped the shield first, which pulled him straight onto the deck. The very moment I heard the crash of someone falling to the deck, I grew very worried about Gershom, so I stood up and allowed the shield to rest on my bony feet. I turned my body to the left where Gershom was supposed to be standing near me and saw him on the deck. Gershom looked defeated and I felt responsible, so my conscience told me to help him up. However, I saw one Spartan bend down and pick up the *aspis* rather than aid Gershom to his feet. This made me slightly furious, so I threw both the *aspis* and the helmet to the ground to help Gershom to his feet. The Spartans gasped in surprise at what I had just done; some of them even covered their mouth. I didn't care, because I needed to help my brother to his feet.

Myaneus walked up to us and spoke in his native Greek tongue, and the Spartans all yelled, "*Yeah!*" Meanwhile, some of the faces of the Spartans grew grim; even while those who were pulling the catch of the day onboard stopped to observe our disgraceful behavior. Mu stood was beside Dimitrios, who was still enduring the resting squat exercise, which Gershom and I failed to maintain. Both men shook their heads in

dismay. Gershom was panting hard when he said, "I think we're in more trouble than ever . . ."

"You men have no idea," Dimitrios responded to Gershom's comment while still shaking his head and maintaining his stance with his shield and helmet.

Both Gershom and I, stationed at a post on the ship, were severely flogged with paddles by the Spartans who had given us their shields to hold. By the third lash, I was on my knees in pain and light-headed, but that did not stop the abuse. The fourth lash shocked my crippled body, while the fifth desensitized me. I didn't feel the sixth or seventh lash. The next thing I remembered was darkness all around me. I was convinced that the darkness and I were really destined for each other.

The salty seawater was dumped on my face, and I was back in the land of the living. Waking up a second time in the day was not my style, especially during the weekends. The heat of the sunlight was beating down on my face, and the sea breeze filled my congested lungs. As I opened my eyes, I saw Gershom fighting his body to push himself up from the ground.

"Come on, Teraditus. Join me!" Gershom's words were all I needed to make it to my feet and walk over to where he was on the deck's floor, and then we started doing push-ups.

Dimitrios walked by and gave us pieces of wheat bread. "You men have potential, and this is what I will say for now, so listen." Dimitrios pointed to a group of Spartans holding their *aspides* on the backs and left arms. "Men, weaponry is the number one reason we are here today—it's the reason you two are alive right now, and most of all, it's the reason why we will continue to see many days in this lifetime. Therefore, we never disrespect our shields." Dimitrios looked into our eyes and finished off his words of advice by stating, "Please remember this vital information." He then fixed his gaze upon the open deck and said, "Consider this the first lesson, men, okay?"

Gershom and I both nodded at Dimitrios and said, "Okay!"

The sun was making its way to the west and taking with it the ship's main source of light. For the remainder of the day, Gershom and I kept ourselves busy by exercising, building our strength, stamina, and working on our wrestling techniques—in particular, a fighting style Dimitrios called "pankration." As the sun finally set, Dimitrios mentored us about the *dos* and *don'ts* when we entered Sparta. A young Spartan brought us a couple of old scrolls where Dimitrios showed us the symbols of the five major and ten minor units inside the military program.

However, Dimitrios directed our focus to the five major symbols, due to their significance in Sparta's military system. The first image that caught my attention was a symbol of what seemed to be the side view of a Spartan helmet with the crescent-horsehair and two swords crossing each other on the bottom of the helmet. Dimitrios told us this emblem represented the unit called *Ares Brotherhood*. The next unit was known as the *Wild Bulls* and their symbol was the head of a bull. A hound with three heads was the next symbol and this unit was referred to as *Cerberus*, but the unit was also known as the *Pack*. The symbol of the six-headed sea serpent was a symbol of familiarity. A symbol that represented the *Hydra* unit, and the unit Gershom and I were assigned to join—according to Dimitrios, of course. The last symbol was the *Nemean Lion*. Dimitrios told us that this symbol represented the unit called the *Descendants of Hercules*, and the royal family of Sparta. A royal family who were direct descendants of a militaristic nomadic tribe that resided in the southern region of the Peloponnesus peninsula, referred to as the Laconia region, while these nomadic inhabitants became known as the *Lacedemonians*.

THE FIVE MAJOR UNITS OF THE SPARTAN
MILITARY PROGRAM

He also demonstrated the proper way of greeting the elders of Sparta, and even the royal family. Dimitrios looked at us and said, "The language barrier will be the most difficult obstacle for you two, so it is a good thing you're young. Learn fast." Dimitrios pointed to various objects on the ship and began translating them in his native tongue. The first thing we learned to properly say in Grecian tongues was the Greek alphabet. Dimitrios made us say the Greek alphabet while we worked out. There were times he would make us start over our entire routine if we missed a letter in the alphabet. I must say, it was pure evil, but it was effective.

Minutes turned to hours, and sunlight, at last, turned into the night and cold winds. Gershom and I tried to wrap ourselves underneath the old, tattered sheets Mu had given us, but it was insufficient. The frigid winds were forcing their way into our nest of warmth with each synchronized row of oars.

"Cursed by the gods, it gets colder every night on this ship. We were not made for this nightlife on the sea," I said to Gershom, who was lost in his mind, but like always he heard every word.

"Shh!" Gershom said to me, slightly shifting his head in my direction. "You know these men have supernatural hearing—you want them to find some way to challenge us in this cold?" Gershom's chastising words did make sense; the Spartans' hearing abilities were unbelievably good, and Dimitrios was our prime example.

"Besides, we're here—"

"*What?*" I astonishingly asked Gershom, while I moved my head to the side to get a good view of him. "How do you know we've arrived at Sparta?" I questioned Gershom again. I mean . . . I know he's gifted and whatnot, but you can't be that good," I assured myself.

"Someone's coming," Gershom cautioned me in a whisper. It was a Spartan who was often referred to as "the βόδι ," which was the Greek translation for "ox." The βόδι called some other Spartans over to the edge of the ship, and they all started smiling while patting each other on

the backs and shoulders. The βόδι turned to us to say in our native tongue, "We're finally back in the Peloponnesus region." He took his helmet off and ran his fingers through his brown hair. "And in a matter of time, we will be making our way to Sparta."

After ten to fifteen minutes, we pulled into the docks of Gytheion. Gershom and I got up from our current location to help the soldiers unload the necessary cargo off the trireme. The feeling of gratitude that came over me when I finally placed my feet on solid ground again was enough to make me kiss it; however, the flow of men and soldiers unloading cargo would make this attempt impossible. The sea breeze was colder than ever since we came out from under the Mu's covers. We carried a couple of crates off the fleet. I examined the quiet but active docks to see if there was anything we could relate to and saw nothing that reminded me of home.

Dimitrios commanded us to carry what we had to one of the many wagons that were lined up in the direction facing north. I loaded the wagon with the crate I had in my hand and Gershom followed right behind me. His face was laden with the thoughts and concerns that were running through his mind. The last couple of days with the Spartans had served as a bit of a distraction for us, but the wounds of our losses were too fresh for us to be completely distracted from our twist of fate—our new reality. I wondered if the death of his mother was replaying in his mind—or he had not yet come to terms with the idea that his mother was no more. I didn't know for sure because Gershom would never tell—especially not around men such as these. Only the gods knew how these men would deride and torture him mercilessly for being weak and emotional. Gershom had to be strong for his sake and mine, as well.

Mu tottered over to where we were standing near the cart, and we helped him onto the back of the cart. He grabbed us by our shoulders, and then he held us by our faces before he drew us together. This was the first time I ever saw Mu this affectionate, and it hurt. I knew why he held us this close, and out of sight from the other Spartans. All three of us were in tears, especially Gershom. I knew this was perhaps our last chance for tenderness and emotional honesty. Therefore, I wisely took advantage of this moment and allowed myself to outwardly express my pain and indignation.

"Come on, men, it's time to go your new home," Dimitrios said to us before he could see any us wipe away any of our tears. We journeyed up with a caravan that had traveled down from Sparta to help the Spartans carry their various goods, but never to carry them nor any components of their personal armory. The journey to Sparta was long, hot, and exhausting; however, I preferred this to being on the boat for another night.

The caravan traveled fifty kilometers underneath the sunlight, and soon the sunset was nearing the western horizon. Dimitrios pointed out some well-known landmarks as we traveled, even the Taygetus Mountain, which we were able to see from where we were on the road.

We finally arrived at the city known as Sparta. Dimitrios opened his arms wide and yelled aloud, "*καλ ς ηρθατε στην σττάρτη*," which meant "Welcome to Sparta." Soon all the Spartans were bellowing, "*Hu, ru, ha, ru, ha, ru*!" This ignited excitement among the citizens of Sparta retiring from a day of labor, and us as well. The citizens came out of their homes to show the naval militia their appreciation and gratitude for the military service by shouting motivating cheers or joining in on the Spartans' battle cry.

Myaneus was at the head of caravan, riding on his black stallion. He rode strong into the moonlight with his head held high. A young Spartan ran up to Myaneus to properly greet and inform him about pressing matters that required his attention; this young man also had his *aspis* secured on his left arm with his *dory* on the other. The two men led the caravan of proud Spartans into the military campgrounds, which was more spacious than I imagined. As we pulled inward into the infamous militant grounds where young boys are built into the Spartan warriors, we saw young Greek men of all ages indulged in all manner of activities. It was as though their day had begun in the early hours of the morning.

A mixture of feelings and thoughts ran through my head, causing my stomach to turn in distress. There was so much occurring within these grounds, especially for this time of the late evening hours. Pieces of the puzzle were finally coming together. By just seeing these young Grecian boys with little to no clothes on, and somehow this spry in the cold of the night. It made sense why the Spartans who had rescued Gershom and I were immune to the cold nights on the open sea. Every foundational aspect that builds a person into a full Spartan was rooted into them from their youth, or maybe deeper. Who knew! However, one thing was for certain, this militant lifestyle was designed to shape and groom these young minds in the direction Sparta's society required them to take in order for them to earn the appellation "Spartan!"

The cart that carried Mu pulled up next to an establishment with an open, verdant courtyard full of tall, slender Cypress trees, which were planted adjacent to the path leading up to this white-stone establishment. The caravan of Spartans, unknowingly broken off into sections of their own and ventured into their various locations. I assumed those Spartans went to their respective homes to see their families. "*Must be a good feeling to see your family once again after a lengthy journey*," I thought to myself. There was no response from my conscious mind; it must have been since my comment was unfair. Who knew that silence could be deserved!

The large caravan from docks of Gytheion now consisted of a family only. I helped Mu out of the cart, while Mu pointed at Gershom to gather items from out of the cart. Mu guided us into one of the quarters inside the establishment, as if he never left this place. Once Mu found a chair to rest his foot on temporarily, we joined Dimitrios outside to help him bring the other items in from the cart. The second we stepped outside, two shirtless boys walked to the eastern region of the courtyard where a wooden post held a flag of the rotating six-headed sea serpent at the top. The two boys shouted something in their Grecian tongue and hugged the post to braced themselves to which was a sight that sent chills down my spine.

"Oh, man!" Dimitrios said casually with a smile on his face. "You men could not have come at a better time. Dimitrios explained how these two young men just avowed to their crime of stealing and getting caught. Observe how we deal with our lawbreakers in the military, you two." Gershom and I looked to the far right of the courtyard and saw these younger Spartans walking toward the two adolescent boys, hugging the post. The two Spartans stood directly behind the adolescent on the left side of the post. Dimitrios shouted a command and the two Spartans sprinted toward the adolescents and jumped at a certain point before they spun themselves diagonally with a black strap spinning with them in mid-air. As soon as the Spartans' right feet touched the ground, the black straps elongated itself and landed straight on the young man's naked backs.

The sound of the leather contacting human flesh bounced off the walls of the courtyard repeatedly; it was the sound of stinging echoes. My body instantly froze with the first lash. The body of the young adolescent jerked and tensed up as though he had just been struck by lightning. Horrifically, another lashing quickly followed the first, then another, and another. The two lashes at the same time just kept on coming and coming without mercy, but the young man held on tighter. One of the Spartans stepped back and waited until he saw his window to swing his whip, and soon the lashes came right after the other. Each strike to the back of this young man tightened up my own muscles as though I was being hit. But not once did I close my eyes or looked the other way, my eyes stayed fixed to every lash that made contact with his skin.

Suddenly, the two Spartans swung the whips above their helmets and crossed their hands before landing the two whips in a crisscross configuration across the back of the teenage boy. Both Gershom and I

swallowed air through our teeth at how far the Spartans would go just to discipline their own, which was borderline abuse.

"Is this really what Sparta is about?"

"It seems so," replied Gershom.

That's when Dimitrios shouted another command and they stopped. I assumed the teen on the right was next, but the two Spartans left the courtyard altogether with their whips dripping with blood. The teens held onto the post a little while longer, speaking to each other. Dimitrios yelled something impetuous at the two teens, and two adolescent boys unlatched themselves from the post and walked away with their heads held high to wherever the night would take them. The teen's facial expression showed they were already masters of the concept "mind over body.

"Well, I hope you two enjoyed the show," Dimitrios said, which led to an uncertain facial expression. "Even though they went easy on the boys . . ."

"What?" Gershom asked in surprise.

"Oh, yeah." Dimitrios could not sound more certain of anything in the entire world, which terrified me. "Listen to me when I say that they went easy on them, especially since they only used two whips."

"*What?*" Gershom and I said simultaneously.

"Don't tell me that you, you . . . guys can use more than two whips at the same time," I said.

Dimitrios laughed hysterically at the terror in the way I had asked my question.

The chills ran down my back again. "Some Spartans can and have used up to four whips at a time, which was amazing in my opinion," Dimitrios added.

I could not see Gershom's face, since it was facing in the direction of Dimitrios, but I could only imagine it was one of shock.

"However," Dimitrios continued, "only skilled or ostentatious Spartans use more than one whip, but only a few Spartans possess that skill. You two should be more concerned with proving yourselves worthy to be accepted into our '*agoge*' program." We both knew what the term was referring to; Myaneus mentioned to us about such a program, it was Sparta's military institution where young boys trained to be Spartans. "Men, what you two just witnessed was an example of the years of training and growth one needs to undergo if they want to survive nights like Thursday's and the hits that those two boys just did in an ineffable way," Dimitrios pointed to the two posts. "Experiences such as those are inevitable for those who desire to wear this armor. You know what," Dimitrios said, nodding his head, "come and touch it, come feel your future, you two, because you have not accepted your reality."

Gershom extended his left arm to touch the bronze cuirass that protected Dimitrios's midsection. I emulated what Gershom did, and I felt the muscled indents of the bronze cuirass and the many scratch marks made in battle. "You feel those scratch marks?" Dimitrios asked us. We both nodded our heads. "The time will come when you two will feel the scratch marks on your cuirass and recall this very moment. Maybe then the reality of life will become all so real for you two. You men may not see it now, but we are at war. You two heard what that Persian said on the deck in a pool of his own blood. There will be a response from the King of Persia, and you two have as much reason to fight in this war as us. And when the opportunity comes to fight, you men will avenge all those who were lost and taken away from you unjustly. So, what do you two say—are you in or out?"

As Gershom's mouth opened to answer Dimitrios's question, I said, "We're in, Dimitrios." Gershom turned his head to face me and started nodding.

"Good," he said with a stern face and tone. "Let's finish unloading this cart and settle in for tonight, because the sunrise will signify a new day with new challenges to bring you men closer to your destinies." Gershom and I grabbed a couple of items from off the cart and followed

Dimitrios inside. "Men, welcome to my home, but a temporary stay for you two. When things proceed as planned, you two will be sleeping in a different location on these grounds, but for now, get some rest, and that's an order!"

Gershom and I answered Dimitrios's command with a *"Yes, sir."* Dimitrios's words were the last we heard before settling in for the night.

CHAPTER 24

WELCOME TO *AGOGE*

[Sparta – Ten Years Before the Battle of Thermopylae (480 BC)]

All I could think about as I lay on the cot beside Gershom was how fast time flew by since that Thursday night when we lost it all. From my cot, I patiently watched the light from the sun creep its way into our chamber as the sun made its ascension from the other realm into ours. As I continued to lie on my cot, I could feel the establishment come to life with the footsteps of busybodies walking from one end to another, attending to household matters long before the first light on the eastern horizon. Gershom and I were wide awake long before sunrise, fully rested and ready for the unexpected, hopefully. Well, I hope we were ready. Ever since that Thursday night, good rest was hard to come by. The minute I placed my head down and closed my eyes for the night's rest, I was out. The very next minute, it seemed, someone was yelling or shaking me to wake up. I was already certain that this Spartan society did not believe in a good night's rest. Sleep was seen as a privilege to the Spartans and not a right. I sighed, because I knew this could be a problem for me personally. "I love sleep," I said to myself.

"Who in their right mind doesn't?" Gershom asked, which stupefied me.

"Oh, my goodness, you can hear my thoughts?"

Gershom turned his face toward me and gave me a ridiculous look by raising his left eyebrow. "Only when you say them loud enough for me to hear."

How afflicted at mind must I be to be speaking out my internal thoughts? Or maybe Gershom was better at reading my mind than he thought, because I knew for certain no sounds left my mouth. However, by the time I had wiped away the eye discharge that makes everything blurry in the morning. Mu was entering the chambers where we've lain for the night, already fully clothed in the typical Greek apparel referred to as the *toga*. This was the first time I'd ever seen Mu actually look like a Greek.

"I must say, this look fits him well," Gershom said to me, while I examined Mu in his heather gray toga. Mu nodded his head, but he still wore the stress of concern on his face. He knew what was to come inside the Spartan culture, and he truly did not want us to be a part of it.

"You men ready?" boomed Dimitrios's voice. I jumped to my feet and stood right beside Gershom, who had also jumped to his feet. We spent two days at sea since we left the Isle of Crete on a Saturday night, and arrived at Sparta's sea docks, Gytheion, on Tuesday morning. During that time at sea, all we did on board was vigorously train before the sun rose and kept on training past the sunset. I knew the answer to Dimitrios's question this early Wednesday morning, which was *no*, we are not ready. But I knew he would not like such a response.

"You two should thank my grandfather for persuading me to permit you guys to sleep till the sun came up. Trust me," Dimitrios's face became hard as a rock, "it will not be happening again. Let's move, men." We both looked at Mu's concerned face to see him pointing at his

grandson. This was an indication for us to follow Dimitrios. We turned to see Dimitrios's red cloak visibly moving away from the front of our chambers.

We dashed out of the chambers and followed right behind Dimitrios. More faces started to appear with every step we took following Dimitrios inside this establishment. None of the faces were familiar until we reached the main entrance and saw other Spartans that were on the naval fleet as us. This was the first time we saw Dimitrios and the other Spartans with their crimson, red cloaks attached to their battered cuirasses. As the group of soldiers spoke briefly on a pressing matter, I wondered why Dimitrios and the Spartans on the ship did not have their dark red cloaks from the moment we first saw them.

"Where was this red cloak the moment we first saw you?" Gershom asked Dimitrios suddenly.

"Really?" I said, incredulous.

Gershom looked at me with startled eyes and asked, "What?"

I just shook my head at Gershom, because he was doing it again, and like always he never had a clue of saying things that were also on my mind.

Dimitrios stopped speaking to give Gershom an austere glance before he walked outside. His fellow soldiers followed him, and we did the same. The moment we stepped outside, we saw their faces and they saw ours. Young, Grecian boys around our age and height, but mentally and physically conditioned.

"You two have been exercising since we left Crete, and I need you men to maintain that flow of exercise." Dimitrios then pointed to the unit of nine boys who were already glistening with sweat from their jog from their early hours before sunrise. "This is your Hydra unit number thirty-six—they were ordered to stop by for your sake, while you two had extra hours of rest." One of the boys in the unit shouted a command at the other boys and they were off after Dimitrios's candid introduction. I assumed this boy was the one in charge of the unit by the way he led the unit out of the courtyard. Dimitrios did not need to say anything more, because we knew what Dimitrios wanted us to do next.

We dashed off to join the unit of boys while Dimitrios yelled somethings to the unit. The boys ran out from the courtyard and throughout the military grounds. Inside these grounds, young boys of all ages were already active in the manner of physical activities. To my left, I saw a regiment of young men practicing their stance with the shield and dory combination. And to my right, I saw the faces of small boys in formation performing the marching drills with their superiors shouting the commands. Everything I was seeing on the military grounds was too much to wrap my head around, but the jog continued in silence.

Fifteen minutes into the jog, all eyes were on Gershom and I as we ran behind this unit of boys. If the eyes of all those staring at us could kill, both Gershom and I would have been dead before we could return to the courtyard. The Grecian boy leading the unit said something in their language while pointing to the back of the unit with his left thumb and the other boys laughed. Disgust was written all over Gershom's face since we interpret a word of insult, but I knew he was no match for the malicious glares of the young boys. Using quick thinking, I drew him to my speed and whispered, "You need to relax. I know that seemed disrespectful, but you need to remember we are new here. So, you must expect the hostility until we've earned their respect. Plus, I think the one in front of the unit is the leader, so let us not get on his bad side." Gershom gave me a nod of acceptance and we kept on moving.

The same Grecian boy leading the unit led the unit out of the military grounds, and the view was tranquil. The horizon was lush with the golden harvest and green vegetation. Sparta was a new beauty to behold, especially this time of the year. The temperature was exactly right for this kind of jogging. The summer breeze was against my back, the light from the sun was warm, and the company of young soldiers jogging with me in unison—this was the kind of motivation needed for

a gratifying jog. The countryside of Sparta was vast with viridescent colors and peppy creatures to decorate the view of nature. In every direction my head turned were countless sights waiting for Gershom and I to explore.

I made sure I stayed close to Gershom as the unit was led deeper into the countryside of Sparta. The unit ran uphills, downhills, around trees, through vineyards and open pastures, and we even cut through villager's front yards and around animal dens in the countryside. One similarity Sparta shared with our own homeland was the lack of shade from the trees, which explained why some of the Grecians were darker than others. However, the complexion of most Grecians was not as dark as ours.

There were houses built up and down the hills with bountiful acres of farmland. Some little boys and girls burst out of their homes to join us in our jog through the pasture; well, that was just before their mothers would order them back inside. The sight of their mother's concern took me back into my memories. I sighed, shook my head, and stayed focused on the current journey.

As our jog took us into hectic parts of the main city, every Spartan citizen, male and female, young and old, all had their eyes on Gershom and me. Some even pointed at us, while others ceased whatever activities that occupied their attention to get a look at us.

"Wow, look at the way they stare at us," Gershom said to me while maintaining his breathing.

"Yeah, I see them," I quickly replied to Gershom's observation. "It's as though they are watching descendants from the underworld running behind their future Spartans . . ."

"No, it's more like they've never seen two asses running behind these boys before."

I looked at some of the eyes that were fixed us on, and there it was. The bizarre stares of men and women who were looking at things they could not understand or explain. I saw exactly what Gershom meant by comparing us to two assess. I kept my head straightforward and focused on the unit's movements, and I advised Gershom to do the same. My advice to Gershom could not have come at a better time, because the unit came to a brief stop. Myaneus ordered the unit to make their way over to where he was standing, and he wasn't alone. The unit jogged over to where Myaneus was standing in the company of four dignified men dressed in togas made of fine linen. Out of the four, three wore imperial gray togas, which meant they were from the senate, and the fourth one wore a strong black toga. The minute the unit reached in front of Myaneus and the other four men, they greeted first Myaneus before properly greeting the other men in a manner you greet the members of the royal family. Gershom and I emulated the unit as best possible in the proper greeting styles, but our greeting was noticeably late, even though we knew how to do it since Dimitrios had shown us how.

The men next to Myaneus walked in our direction, while Myaneus spoke to the young boy leading the unit in our jog. I could sense Gershom's rapid heartbeat; it was actually in sync with mine.

"Do you two know who I am?" asked one in the black toga. To our surprise, he knew how to speak in our native language. Gershom and I turned our heads to face each other with wide eyes, and I saw that he knew who this man was. "*The King, the King,*" Gershom whispered, and I gave him a simple nod. We faced forward and evaded all eye contact as best possible and said exactly what Dimitrios taught us on board the naval fleet.

"Βασιλιά Κλεο ενης — or King Cleomenes!"

A slight smirk appeared on the face of the Spartan King. Gershom and I kept our heads up after acknowledging and greeting King Cleomenes in the proper manner, which was a right fist to the left chest. The eyes of the Greek boys in our unit were filled with rage and dislike, but we did not intend to fawn over the Spartan King. I was curious to know how Gershom figured out this man was the Spartan King. So, I

snuck a glance at the King's left shoulder and saw the symbol of *Nemean Lion* on his golden pendant that held his elegant black toga. Suddenly, I recalled the moments Dimitrios showed Gershom and I the symbols of the five major units and ten minor units that make up the entire Spartan military system. Out of the five major units, the symbol of the *Nemean Lion* stood out in my memory because it was a symbol that represented the unit referred to as the *Descendants of Hercules*, and this unit, according to Dimitrios, contained the majority of the royal family which included the King of Sparta.

"My deepest condolences for your loss," King Cleomenes said to both of us while holding us by our shoulders. "I was informed about Myaneus's rescue mission due to the unexpected Persian attack." The Spartan King sighed and removed his heavy hands from our scrawny shoulders to say, "It appears that this Persian Empire is growing at an alarming rate and becoming more of a problem than I could ever have imagined."

He ran his hands down his long, black hair and said, "You know, there was a time when my half-brother, Dorieus, had a garrison established in the west of your home country of Libu." King Cleomenes stroked his light gray beard as he held onto his black toga. "Unfortunately, the colony failed to grow because we were viewed as unwelcome guests by the neighboring inhabitants of Carthage."

A strange expression appeared on his face as he contemplated the last word from the King of Sparta.

"Carthage? Do you mean *Kart-hadasht*, because we know of a place called *Kart-hadasht* since we have family residing in *Kart-hadasht* from Teraditus's father's side of the family."

I looked at Gershom and nodded before I looked at King Cleomenes.

"This is true, my father has . . ." I stopped, to correct myself. ". . . my father had two brothers and a few cousins who have set up a trade business many years ago at the place you referred to as Carthage, which we know as *Kart-hadasht*. But to be honest, the Isle of Tyre is more famous as a merchant center for many Zidonians and Tyrians to do trade business, it is often referred to as the market of the nations."

"I see," said the King, nodding his head. "I mean, I am more than aware of the booming trade businesses which take place on and off the Isle of Tyre, since many merchants pass through Sparta and Athens with their formidable ships of Tarshish. However, I did not know you two had family ties with Zidon and Tyre. Quick, tell me something." The King gestured his hand toward us. "Would you two know how to read and compose the calligraphy of the Zidonians?"

Gershom struck me on the same shoulder again, and I gave him a nod of approval. The King started nodding his head and smiled at me. "Great, this will be a useful skill to improve the communication of trade relationships with the merchants of Tyre and Zidon. Now that I am speaking to the two of you, I am glad I sent Myaneus to check up on matters in Egypt. This placed him near your homeland in Libu, just in time for the invasion, and now you two are here. Extra hands and skills will be needed for this uprising war with the Persians, which is on the horizon. I guess one could say fate led you both here." I could feel my conscience nodding inside my head. "And if that's the case, you guys are more than welcome to train and fight with us in stopping this mad kingdom," the King said this with his right fist clenched near his face, "once the Senate has sanctioned your enrollment into our military program."

The Spartan King walked away from us, but not before dismissing us so we could rejoin our jogging unit. The King said something to the unit, but it was in the language of the Greeks. Then he turned to us personally and said, "This journey will not be easy; it will test you in ways you never thought you could be tested. However, I guarantee that you two will enter as boys, and we will do all in our power to make sure that you two not only come out as men but as Spartans—*ha, ru, ha, ru, ha, ru!*"

The King's words were heartfelt and motivating. Myaneus said something to the unit leader, and we were off to our next adventure. The young leader said something to the unit in a lengthy manner, and this troubled me since Gershom and I did not understand what he was saying. I assumed he was saying which path we were going to take rather than taking the usual route, but my spirit sensed something was not right.

The unit jogged for a while until they were out of sight from the five men. Then all mayhem broke loose. The leader began sprinting, and the unit did the same. Gershom and I noticed the unit's attempt to get rid of us, but little did they know about our background. We were natural-born runners! The unit ran into the marketplace and split up, in hopes of *really* trying to get us lost, but sadly, these Greek boys did not know we were no beginners when it came to running through busy marketplaces. Sparta's marketplace was not as crowded as what we were accustomed to back home, which made this attempt of theirs more fun. We jumped over livestock, spun around people, and ran across walls. We even did a little flipping—well, Gershom did most of the flipping, while most of my flipping consisted of summersaults to avoid injury. Gershom and I laughed at their attempts to lose us because there was nothing in the market that could slow us down. To be honest, their attempts backfired on them since we outran some of the Greek boys in the unit.

Gershom kept a sharp eye on the leader, and I kept a sharper eye on him. The other boys tried their hardest to mislead our direction by taking random turns down a different path, throwing things in our path to make us fall, and bumping into us as well. Baskets of barely wheat were sailing through the air, while fruits were rolling in every direction on the ground. Every step we took, some humble vendor became a victim to our animalistic stampede. The unit, along with Gershom and myself, drew unwanted attention from the citizens of Sparta. It was utter chaos in the marketplace. The leader noticed the citizens' vexation due to our considerable disruption in the marketplace. I too noticed the distress of the people, just by the way they stared and yelled at all of us, and I knew Gershom and I were going to pay for it as the day progressed.

The leader led the resembled unit out of the market square and back on track. He then led us through people's front and back yards. That leader of ours made us run through mud mixed with animal dung by leading us into a pigsty. This made me highly upset because these were brand-new shoes given to us by the beautiful women of Knossos. Now they were ruined because of this foolish Greek boy who was leading this unit back to the military campgrounds.

All manner of thoughts ran up and down my mind. Evil and vengeful thoughts were all I could feel toward these Grecian boys, but I stopped to re-consider and realized these hateful thoughts had nothing to do with these boys. It mainly stemmed from the Persians, who were solely responsible for all the changes in our lives, which we were now mandated to see it through to the end. Lost in my own thoughts, I still maintained a good view of Gershom's movements—including a good view of a small fist striking Gershom in the face. I could not believe that one of the Grecian boys in our unit had done this.

"*Hey!*" I screamed out indignantly as though anyone understood. I sprinted even faster to defend Gershom. Another boy with blonde hair and green eyes came out from around a corner and tried to jump on top of me from my right side. Sadly, again, these Greek boys underestimated my speed. I spun around in time to use my right arm to throw this boy off me. He fell and rolled to his feet, and then looked fiercely into my eyes. "Oh, no," I said.

Time stopped, and I saw everything clearer than I'd ever seen before. My head turned in the direction where Gershom was last seen on the ground to see him now on his feet with four boys on the verge of striking him. I looked behind me and saw four boys quickly approaching me, while the other one I had thrown to the ground was on his feet with more determination than before. Five boys on their way to kill me, and

four attempting to kill Gershom. I was beginning to see what Dimitrios meant when he said that we were entering into the lion's den and we would have to fight to survive in Sparta. How foolish of me for taking his words of counsel lightly. I thought to myself, while analyzing the circumstances we were now facing. There was only one outcome in a situation such as this one. "Fight!"

"Gershom," I cried out in anxiety, while he threw one of the four boys onto the ground. I vigorously made my way over to him and tackled all three Greek boys at the same time. Gershom reached down and picked me up from the stacked bodies I had pushed into the ground. "Gershom, watch out," I cried. A fist was flying straight into Gershom's head, and I could not let that happen. I pulled Gershom's right shoulder out of the way and used my left hand to block the strike intended for Gershom's head. Then I struck the Greek boy's nose in the same way Blade had shown us by using the palm of my right hand, and he stumbled backward, holding his nose. The strike to the nose proved effective, and now it was time to take out the rest.

A strange feeling overwhelmed me when I saw the other four boys approaching me. I finally saw the battlefield for what it really was, and I wasn't going to accept it. No, I refused to accept this fate without a fight—a fight to death, to be more precise, and by the looks of things. We had already lost too much, and now the cost of losing what I had left was enough for me to kill to live.

I could feel my muscles tensing up, and a rush of energy flowed all over me. "Ahh!" I screamed as I charged into one of the four. We clashed arm to arm. I knew this could be a problem, so I mustered up all my strength and swung him to my left. The boy held on for dear life till his feet were securely planted on the ground. He then pulled me closer to him and kneed me straight in the stomach, which shocked my body in a downward position, and then he elbowed me in the head. I crashed straight into the ground, but I could not stay down. This rush that was surging throughout my body propelled me back onto my feet in time to stop another attack, but it was too late for me. The remaining three boys rained down a series of punches and kicks on my brittle body, while the other boy who I had struck in the nose had recovered and was ten times more upset than before.

The Greek boys were stronger than we ever could have imagined. There was no way we could take on these boys by ourselves. For starters, we were outnumbered and untrained. These Greek boys had two years of training under the Sparta military system. These boys had a sturdy foundation comprised of learning military tactics, physical discipline, fighting styles, and a mixture of endless physical workouts all hammered into them for months. Gershom and I stood no chance against one of them, let alone nine. We were as good as dead. Our hits must have felt like branches against their granite bodies. These boys were trained to absorb and become one with physical attacks and pain. The concept of "mind over body" seemed like the core of their training, and they were two years ahead of us in building off this core concept—a concept we were now just starting to learn.

My life flashed before my eyes again, and in the flash, I thought about leaving Gershom alone in this godforsaken land. I couldn't let that happened, so I prayed to the gods of my mother and father to bestow power upon us in such a time of need. A dark fire emitted inside of me like I had never felt before, and I emerged out of my cocoon of weakness with such strength that it pushed all five Greeks backward. The Grecian boys quickly recovered their stance, and I clashed into one of them in hopes of picking him off his feet and thrashing him into the ground. The Grecian boy caught me in a headlock and laid a series of heavy thumps across my bareback. Instantly, I became debilitated by the series of hits. When he was through with me, he pushed me backward into the care of another boy, who spun me around to give me a good punch in the face. I spun straight into the arms of another to receive a knee once again in the chest, and the sequence of the ring assault went on for however long. By the fourth punch to the face, I completely blacked out with no knowledge of whether Gershom was alive, or whether I was finally dead. There seems to be no hope for us. Everywhere we turned, the next stage of misery was waiting for us, giving us no time to rest or heal from the unwanted pain.

* * * *

"Gershom, I . . . I failed!" I said aloud. "Gershom, please . . . forgive me!" A wet cloth was applied on my head, and another on my right shoulder. The stinging feeling of antiseptic was running through my sore body, while I heard someone that sounded like my mother. I was unable to explain it, but this was all too strange for me, and what did it mean? What was happening? Once again, I found myself struggling to open my eyes. "Gershom," I said with a soft tone.

"It's okay, my child," someone replied to me. Then I heard it again, my mother's voice. My mother was a three-day journey away from this place, and she was dead, I think? My mind was playing cruel tricks on me. Gershom was the only family I knew who was still alive—and could not allow that to change.

"No, Gershom, where are you?" I screamed out, while trying to look around with my slightly opened right eye. Suddenly, an awful pain emerged from my left eye, which felt like a pounding inside my head. I tried to open my left eye, but it refused to open. That's when my heart began to race as I touched my left eye and felt that it was mildly swollen. I shook my head and sighed in defeat.

"My child, my child, please relax," a beautiful, aged woman said to me in the tongues of my mother. Then another figure came on the opposite side of me and continued to apply the antiseptic cloth across my head.

"Who are you people, and where's Gershom?"

The sun-kissed woman placed her hand on my bare chest and the other on my shoulder. The weight of her hand and the hand of this faceless figure on the other side of me gave me a feeling of ease.

"Who are you people, and where is Gershom? I demand to know, please!" I said to the woman and faceless figure.

"Listen, child of Kemet, we rescued you and your brother, so please hold still and let us tend to your wounds—"

"Wait, how do you know I'm from Kemet? Are you from Kemet, too?"

The woman stared at me and pulled out a black amulet that had a gold symbol of life and rebirth, *ankh*. I saw the symbol of my mother's gods, but my mind remained determined to know Gershom's whereabouts. "Where is Gershom?" The woman slightly turned her head in the direction behind me. I tried to follow her head movements, but I knew my body would not allow me to turn as far as she had looked. Instead, I kept screaming Gershom's name. "Gershom, Gershom, Gershom!"

The woman did not like my shouting very much, so she covered my mouth and said, "Relax, my child."

"Yeah, Teraditus, relax yourself," a stern, raspy voice said to me from the back.

"Gershom, is that you?"

"Who else would it be answering you so fluently in the tongues of our mothers?" I felt my conscience nodding inside my head, "*Yeah, that's Gershom!*" I sighed in relief, and at the same time it dawned upon me that I had not realized this woman was speaking the Kemetic tongue the whole time. The beating must have done a number on me to the point that I was still in recovery. Moreover, I was grateful Gershom was alive, and so were his sarcastic ways. I reclined on my cot and allowed these people to tend to my wounds.

"What happened to us?"

"You mean, how did you get here?" the faceless figure asked me in a voice of a man. This had to be the woman's husband, I could only assume.

"Yes," I replied to the man. "And why is it so dark in here, and are you from Kemet too?" I felt the man's presence dwindle away from our own presences, while the woman answered my question.

"He was born there—"

"What?" both Gershom and I said together.

"We are both from the Land of Ra, my child," the woman calmly explained.

"What happened?"

"What happened is, if it wasn't for Theo finding you two in the alley near the marketplace, you two might still be there, unconscious and dying!" I could hear the assurance in the woman's voice. Gershom sucked his teeth in a repulsive way. The woman chuckled and said, "The road to becoming a Spartan warrior is a road where many have traveled, and only the strong survive." Her words were similar to Dimitrios's, which only added to the spirit of fear that continues to grow silently inside of me.

"*Wait,*" I thought to myself. "*How—*"

"Wait, how did you know we have an association with the Spartan military program?" Gershom cut me off to ask the woman.

I felt my anger boiling up inside of me, so I elevated myself from the cot to say, "Ger . . . *sss!*" I sucked in the pain through my teeth. The woman guided me back down to my cot and told me to relax again, but I could not. Gershom stole the words right out of my mouth, and now I had to relax. I was more than convinced that Gershom did this on purpose because he knew it infuriated me when he cut me off from saying what I wanted to say. Especially, when it was a moment to make me look astute. Nevertheless, my body was in too much pain to allow me to properly retaliate or respond to Gershom in the manner I wanted to.

"Child, we've been here longer than you two," said Theo in the distance. "Greek boys—such as the ones who nearly killed you two— always stand out. No matter where you are in Sparta, every citizen can identify a Spartan trainee, so when I saw you two running alongside with these trainees in the marketplace, I grew concerned, and that concern convinced me to keep an eye on that unusual scene." I heard footsteps returning to where I was on my cot.

"That makes sense," I said with both eyes closed.

"What makes sense?" Theo knelt next to me. "The fact that children were running through the market creating havoc, or that two Kemite boys were running with Greek boys through the marketplace?" Theo asked while holding my head upward to sip water from a copper cup. Once the cup was removed from my face, I raised two fingers in front of my face indicating that the second point was more logical, of course. The man grunted and said, "Does this look like a society comprised of people that look like you and your brother?"

The question had a point, so it made no sense to respond to it. I took a deep breath in and let it out. "I'm sorry, we are trying our best," the woman said, "but we're not supposed to aid trainees in Sparta. The Sparta's citizens see it as inhibiting the trainees' growth in survival for the real campaigns. Any citizen caught helping a trainee can result in severe consequences for both the helper and the trainee, as well. Therefore, we have little to no light in the room, because we don't know who may be looking for you two, or who may have seen Theo bring you two in here."

"Well," Gershom said in the back, "we're not actually trainees." Gershom went silent as he made his comment. "By the looks of things, we may not even be allowed to join this training program . . ."

"You mean the *agoge* program," said Theo.

"Yes, the *agoge* program," Gershom said with disappointment. "The way those boys attacked us; I could only assume all the disappointing things they're telling Dimitrios. I feel defeated."

"If this is the case, Gershom, we need to get back to the military base and tell Dimitrios the truth," I said without a doubt. "Plus, I'm not sure

what time it is, but we need to make our way back." My words seemed to be sinking into Gershom's mind since he did not respond right away.

"I don't think you're in any condition to be heading out yet. Get some more rest, it will do you both some good," the woman said.

I shook my head and said, "No, we should go—"

"No! You need more rest, trust me," the woman responded to me with certainty. This was something my own mother would have said when she knew her way was in the best interests of those involved. And still, no word or comment from Gershom at this point; his mind must have been full of all kinds of thoughts. Gershom's silence suggested that we should stay a few more minutes to rest ourselves.

I sighed and said, "Fine, we will stay a while and rest up."

The woman smiled at me and said, "Good! In the meantime, I will assemble something to eat."

The woman removed herself from my presence to assemble our meals to restore our strength. Theo returned to my side with some hot brew he had just given Gershom. I could smell the aroma of the concoction that Theo had brewed for us. One whiff of this brew and I was deep in my memories again of my mother's black tonic. I did not want to make assumptions, so I tasted the concoction, and it was atrociously bitter. "Blah, this is awful . . ."

"It has a bit of honey in it, as well," Theo replied with laughter in his voice. "It also has some coriander and hemp seeds in there. Try and get some to chew on." I did just that. The chewing helped me relax and guided me into a noonday rest.

* * * *

In my sleep, the skies were dreary with the colors of purple and dry crimson. Then I shifted my head to the ground below my feet. I was in a mountain pass, and the ground was trailed with blood, and gore was dripping from the blade tips of fallen soldiers. The sound of bronze hitting bones and the terrifying shrieks of dead men ran through my soul with a petrifying force. Every hair follicle on my body stood up with attention, while all six of my human senses became vigilant with every direction my head turned. I was clearly in the midst of warfare, but what did it mean? The torn and ripped red cloaks were everywhere, but they covered the grounds where I stood, with their lambda sign on *aspides* attached to their arms. These were undoubtedly Spartan soldiers. I shook my head from side to side, and then it struck me like an unseen arrow; the pain of loss, a feeling I was growing accustomed to, pressed down on my heart yet again.

A part of me was dying, and I did not know why, so I looked around the corpses in hopes of finding a solution. A sense of familiarity darted through me as I continued my investigation. Then someone called my name; it was the voice of a dying man, and it gave me the chills.

"I knew this voice," I told to myself. I turned to see a dying man in the distance, lying on the floor next to the corpses of Spartans. He waved his bloody hand in the air to give me a better view of his current location. I scampered through the field of dead Spartans to reach the dying man before death claimed his soul entirely. As I ran, something like a wreath was seen on the head of one of the deceased Spartans. I wasn't sure what a wreath signified, but somehow, I knew in this dream that it was customary for wreaths to be worn by important figureheads in society. However, I kept running and running with hope on my mind—the hope that I would make it to this Spartan, the hope I would make it in this life. I could not explain why I needed to make it to his side, but I just had to.

Therefore, I kept moving and moving. As I ran, my eyes caught the reflection of a red cloak following me, the crested-shaped horsehair bouncing on my head with every move I made, a heavy shield in my left hand, and a long spear in my right.

"Am I a Spartan?" I asked myself. I shook my head and blew this ridiculous idea out of my mind and stayed true to my objective. I kept moving with a shield and spear clutched in my hands until I saw the man with the bloody hand had a missing finger and a right diagonal

slash across his helmet. I cast the spear and shield to the red ground, which created a loud, chilling vibration throughout the pass. I threw myself to my knees and grabbed the man's right hand with my left.

He spoke to me in the language of the Greeks, and I understood. "The road . . . the road ahead is unknown," the dying Spartan said faintly. I did not know what he meant, but his words were hard to deny—for the journey thus far is unknown.

The man looked at me with blood streaming down from his head, which made it difficult to distinguish his identity. His eyes had a sense of familiarity—he was someone close to home, someone who was influential in my life. "Who was this person, and what does this dream mean?" I wondered. There was only one way to answer that question. I had to remove the helmet, so I leaned in and pressed my warm finger against the Spartan's helmet. Instantly, my finger became as cold as the midnight air. I began pulling off the helmet, but I realized it required more strength than I had on my knees, so I stood to my feet to obtain a better grip on the helmet. The minute I stood to my feet, I discovered something was horribly wrong as I pulled off the helmet. The helmet was empty, while the body remained visible. "What the—"

* * * *

"Teraditus?" I opened my eyes and saw a look filled with daggers piercing my soul. "Get up," Gershom said with anger in my voice. "The time has come for us to return to the military base." I sighed and sat up without any pain whatsoever.

"Wow, that concoction worked. The pain has subsided, even my eyes feel . . ."

"Don't forget to give credit to your afternoon rest, but that's good to hear," the woman said to me while handing Gershom and I wooden plates with whole wheat bread and with pieces of seasoned smoked ham. Gershom and I had nothing to eat at all in the morning, so the moment the plate touched our hands, the food was gone in two minutes, max.

"Oh my goodness," the woman said, holding her mouth, "Did you two inhale the food?" Our mouths were too full to respond, so we just nodded.

A second plate was assembled for both Gershom and I before we made our departure. We weren't full, but the meals were enough to carry us for the remaining day. Theo surveyed the front and back entrance of their home before we left. Theo's face was still a mystery to us. He had his face covered the whole time as though he was one of the many merchants who had traveled through the marketplace in Crete. Theo left first and waited at a certain point for us to guide us back to the military base. The back entrance was our way out; however, I had to know this woman's name before a proper departure.

"Wait," I said before I left through the door. The woman looked at me with interest. "What is your name?"

She turned and glanced at us for a while. "My name isn't important, child," she said while removing her head wrap and a cloth garment off her shoulders.

"Queen of the heavens, Auset," I whispered in utter astonishment when I saw the image of a woman with colorful wings sprouting from her arms, which were lifted above her head. Gershom and I took to our hands and knees to say a prayer to the Queen Goddess. "Apologizes, high priestess, we had no idea, but we are grateful for your kind acts to us," I said with my face still to the ground.

"Stand to your feet, you two," the high priestess said to us calmly, "it's time for you two to return to the hands of the Spartans." Up we stood and we humbly walked out the doorway. "When you have time, search for me at the temple where the daughters of Venus reside, especially you, Teraditus. Plus, Auset would want you to have this," the high priestess said to me while placing a glassy, onyx stone in my hand. I glanced at the high priestess and handed the stone back to her.

"I sense this will be better in your care … I just hope with time, you can explain why the stone was given to me by Auset in the first place?"

The high priestess smiled and gave me a simple nod of acceptance before we walked away from her and her home.

Gershom led me through the backyard into another backyard before we reached the active main street. We saw Theo from a distance on the other side of the roadway and followed him from our side. In a matter of twenty minutes of walking, one of the Spartans we had traveled with on the ship spotted us and instructed us to follow him back to the base. Without any hesitation, we listened to his command and began following him. Gershom and I turned around to have our last glimpse of Theo, but he had vanished without a trace.

The journey only took fifteen minutes before we were back where we had first begun on the military grounds. Dimitrios was one of the first who saw us entering the military grounds. He signaled for us to make our way over to where he was standing with a group of his fellow companions. "What happened?"

I knew Gershom's nerve was over the edge, so he did what he knew best. "Oh, where do we start—"

"Gershom," I interrupted.

"No, Teraditus. We left here on a jog with empty stomachs in the early hours of the day. We ran into the King and your father, and that went well. Thank you for teaching us the proper way of greeting men such as the King in this society, it was much appreciated, if I must say."

Gershom was losing his mind; I wondered if he had forgotten whom he was talking to, and where we were currently. The other Spartans ceased their conversation to tentatively listen to Gershom's temper tantrum.

"Gershom, please, relax," I pleaded with the madman. But it was futile, Gershom needed to say what was on his mind, and there was nothing I could say to disquiet his troubled mind.

"You know what was the best part of that jog? The surprise ambush attack by the unit we were running with, and I should mention that they nearly killed us."

Dimitrios laughed at Gershom's comment, and so did other Spartan soldiers who were near him. Gershom took a deep breath in and cautiously let it out. "I guess this is funny to you," Gershom said grimly.

Dimitrios moved his head up and down. He looked to his left and called out, "Magneus, come here." The young leader of the unit walked over to where we were all located and looked at us with a malevolent smile.

"*You!*" both Gershom and I said together. I shook my head in aggravation, while Gershom clenched his fist.

"Gershom and Teraditus, I want you to meet Magneus. The son of Myaneus, and my youngest brother."

Dimitrios's words sunk in for a moment before Gershom pointed out the obvious. "The way he treated us was unjust and uncalled for," Gershom said while pointing his finger at Magneus.

Magneus shrugged his shoulders and said with no remorse, "Welcome to Sparta!"

Dimitrios nodded his head at both of us. "Start getting used to this lifestyle. Every day you will get a new taste of what '*Sparta*' is about, and what will be required of you to survive. So, stop whining like little piglets and man up, because we don't train Athenian men here. You two know what we are all about, you two have seen us in action, which was an opportunity most boys in agoge will not see until they are eighteen years of age and campaigning as fully pledged Spartans. The jog was a test, and the fact that you two made it back on your feet with your heads held high and battle scars say more than you could imagine." Magneus was nodding his head to the last comment made by his older brother.

"By the way, you two look as though your wounds were treated." My heart jumped in fear, but I made sure to avoid any suspicious movements, and Gershom did the same.

"What makes you say that?"

"Well, Teraditus, we sent some of our guys to check for you two, and no one was there to be found." After hearing those words leave

Dimitrios's mouth, it hit me that Theo was right after all. There were eyes lurking out and about.

"We didn't think it was safe or wise to remain in our current location in the condition we were left in by the hands of our new unit."

I could hear the indignation in Gershom's voice. I didn't need to look at Gershom to know he was staring vehemently at Magneus. Gershom was not alone with his venomous look, because Magneus returned a fearless stare back to Gershom.

"Okay, you two, save it for training," Dimitrios said to discontinue the hostile staring between the two boys. "Moreover, men, get something to eat, because your day isn't over. We are going to do some physical training, since you two missed the academic part of the day. You can make it up by building up your muscle tone in the evening."

I sighed internally because I knew this meant we were going to exercise with the boys that attacked us earlier today, but I was glad the topic involving Theo was over. I didn't want these men linking anything to Theo and the high priestess, especially for their kind service. The gods knew we would need these people's help, and their kindness should not result in punishment from the Spartan warriors.

"Many may not have faith in you two, but I always will. Don't let me down, and most all, don't let each other down!" Dimitrios's words were always heavy on the mind and the body, so we turned to leave the men of Sparta with our thoughts all over the place.

Suddenly, Magneus dramatically walked closer toward Gershom and I with his arms behind his back like a true soldier and said brazenly.

"This is just the beginning, so quitting is still on the table. This is the time to consider it!" Gershom and I glanced at each other for a moment and gave each other a nod of acceptance.

"We're not going anywhere, so when do we begin this program?" asked Gershom Dimitrios

"You men begin now!" Dimitrios said with a confidant smile.

"WELCOME TO AGOGE!"

.... TO BE CONTINUED

GHOST CHAPTER:

THE NAME BLADE

[Cyrene/Libu – Two days before the Thursday night invasion (480 BC)]

As I looked up into the purple and crimson skies, I saw the amber sun just sitting on the western horizon, refusing to set for the moon to rule the night. Meanwhile, the tails of the hounds refused to fan off the pesky field flies. All nineteen hounds, including the new pup, just lay on the coarse ground trying to soak up what little warmth the sun had to offer before it traveled to the other realm. However, the sun just seemed to be lingering in the afternoon skies, which was strange. Was mother right about the sun gets tired from its daily routine?

"Yup, it's another lazy Tuesday's afternoon," I said in an exhausted manner.

"It sucks!" admitted Gershom, while he sucked air through his teeth. "I hate Tuesdays and Thursdays in the summertime."

"Agreed!" I said

"I'm just glad tomorrow, we're going finishing for tunas. I think my dad's chum is going to beat your dad's record time ten minutes and eighteen seconds," Gershom said confidently.

"I doubt it!" I replied without hesitation, which caused Gershom to have a derisive expression on his face.

"We will see tomorrow! Anyways, I'm going to watch Blade practice his shadow dance, you want to come?" I glanced over to Gershom and thought about his mission to spy on a man who had more mysteries than all the oceans combine.

"Would it not be wiser to wait until the sun is set—completely?" Gershom thought about my words for a few seconds before he responded.

"You're right—but I'm so bored," Gershom said with his shoulders slouching. He was right, it was boring. I gave Gershom a nod and we made our departure from in front of Gershom's house to search for the location where Blade was practicing his shadow dance this evening. He always practiced in locations far from our homes, especially where the winds blew the hardest. This meant Blade's shadow dance often took place near the sea; so, this afternoon, our journey was to explore the coastal lines of the Mediterranean Sea. Gershom and I ran to my house, so I could grab all the items needed for this expedition.

The moment Gershom and I reached near my home, we started tiptoeing to see if we could hear where exactly my mother was in the house to know if she was tending to household matters or not. However, in our sneaking around in the back of the house, where my mother was often found in the kitchen area, we heard laughing from a woman in the inner regions of the house, which was a good thing since it meant my mother was distracted at the moment. Gershom gave me a thumbs up and I returned one to him.

Carefully, I positioned myself to open the door to the back of the house, because it often creaked when it opened casually. Unless, I used

my special technique I developed with time, which factored in speed and strength.

"What are you two up to?" asked Nephtali unexpectedly. Both Gershom and I let out an unmanly scream.

"Yeah, what mischief are you two up?" asked a more mature woman.

Gershom and I looked up to see my mother opening the back door to our house. The expression on her face said it all. "Both Nephtali and I sensed the presence of two you the moment you tiptoed into the yard." My mother continued with her spiritual insightfulness. "Teraditus, you know better than that—get inside both of you." She commanded while stepping aside for all three of us to enter inside before she closed the back door and locked it. We all took seats at the family table, where the all the eating utensils, plates, and cups, which were all made of copper. In the middle of the table was a statue of the Queen of the Heavens, Auset, with her arms outstretched with wings array in colors of the rainbow. Gershom and I sat across the table from my mother and Nephtali.

"I'll be brief, I just want my stuff for our nighttime expedition, and we'll be on our way," I said candidly, while getting up from my chair. Unfortunately, the scolding stare from my mother caused me to reconsider, so I sat right back down without her having to say one word about that.

"And yet you were sneaking around because you figured if I found out, I would object to your nighttime ventures," my mother explained.

"That is correct," I replied boldly.

"Why can't you boys explore when the sun is up, and you have light?"

"It's not the same—there's something about the night that brings more life to our surroundings—a sense of thrill and adventure." Gershom's dramatic comment left both Nephtali and my mother nodding in agreement to what he said.

"Where exactly are you two going to be exploring?" asked my mother curiously, which caused Gershom and I stare at each other hoping one of us had a reasonable response. Gershom turned around to face my mother, so he could say something clever and acceptable. But Nephtali beat him to it by saying, "That's a lie!" We all faced Nephtali, while she had a devious expression composed on her face. Suffice to say, Nephtali was right. Whatever Gershom had to say was going to be a lie, no doubt about it, but the expression on Nephtali's face indicated she knew more. She knew the truth!

"You two are going exploring to find Blade?" Nephtali said calmly.

"Wait a second," Gershom said with his words hissing through his teeth like a fiery serpent. "How do you know that? Are you spying on us?" Gershom questioned his sister.

"When the moment is needed," Nephtali responded with a hint of attitude.

"How beneath you—spying on young boys. I must say this is a new low for you," Gershom said with contempt.

"Gershom enough," my mother quickly snapped at him

"No, it's fine. He has point," Nephtali admitted with no shame. "You two found Blade the last time he disappeared to practice his shadow dance, so I know two will find him again today."

"Wait?" Gershom said in a bewildered manner. "You just said the last time—the last time we found Blade practicing his shadow dance was the last first quarter moon. You've been spying on us that long ago?"

"That is correct—and yet I have no shame," Nephtali said with no remorse.

"You should be ashamed—shame, shame, shame—"

"Enough!" my mother said firmly to Gershom. "That's your older sister, show her some respect."

"She deserves *no* respect—"

"Little boy, not another word from you," my mother said with more authority. Gershom humbled down when he heard seriousness in my mother's tone.

"You three need to leave Blade alone when he practices his shadow dance, it's a spiritual custom that was passed down to him by forces that no longer dwell in this realm." My mother got up from the table to retrieve the pitcher of a fresh-squeezed passion fruit juice and started to pour juice for Gershom first before she moved to me, and Nephtali followed right after me.

"What more do you know about Blade?"

"What do you mean, my child?" my mother responded to Nephtali's question.

"You cautioned us to stay away from Blade when he is performing his shadow dance since it is a spiritual custom passed down to him. It seems like … you might know more than you want to say." Nephtali had a point, it did seem like my mother knew more than she wanted to say. "I overheard my parents saying things behind closed doors; so I know they know secret things about Blade, which they don't want to acknowledge or share with me. I am about to make this big decision to spend my life with Blade, and at times I feel as though I am with a man who has more mysteries than the deepest sea. I also sense he is trying to run away past. Whenever I ask, he always tells me to be patient or in time I will come to know all. Help me so I can help him and be the right kind of woman for him." I could hear the pain in Nephtali's voice, and so did my mother as she drank the entire cup of juice with a throwback to the head.

"Boys, you can leave—"

"*NO!*" both Gershom and I immediately responded to my mother. Both women jumped in fear, while steering at us in a horrified manner.

"You're not the only one curious to know the secrets of Blade. We all have our questions that need answers, we're staying in for tonight." Gershom said brazenly.

"It's all up to your sister," explained my mother.

"Boys, you can go," said Nephtali, while steering vehemently at Gershom.

"Think again," Gershom replied, "you spied on us, so you owe us this moment."

"Fine!" replied his sister still upset at Gershom. "They can stay." Gershom stuck out his tongue and Nephtali stuck out hers in response. I laughed at their sibling squabble, while my mother smiled at them before carefully grabbing the young woman's hand tenderly to re-direct his focus.

"What do you want to know my child?" Nephtali looked at her hand in the embrace of my mother and pondered over the question.

"What is his real name?" Her question caught me off guard. It was not a question that ever crossed my mind. I mean, I have wondered about it at one time in my life, but it would not be the first question I would ask.

"The name Blade!" my mother said carefully. "It's a title he earned while he lived in Babylonia in the latter days of King Cyrus of Persia's reign. This title, *Blade*, is only given to master swordsmen trained to be assassins for an ancient organization, which ruled great Kingdoms, far and near, but from the shadows.

"What's the name of this organization?" Nephtali questioned my mother with fear in her voice.

"The Order of Re-Birth!" said my mother. The name sent a chilling feeling down my spine, while hairs on my arm stood up. My spirit within was uneasy, as if it knew this organization was bad news from some unusual past encounter.

"How dangerous is this organization? Nephtali continued to ask her questions

"Very dangerous, my child!" my mother replied quickly. This Order existed in the days of the first Babylonia after the death of the first Kushite King, the Great Nimrod. Nimrod's wife, the Queen, created the

Order with the sole purpose to prepare for her husband's return to the realm of the living, but as time progressed. The Order's purpose changed, their duties became corrupt with a thirst for power and control, and their works are done in the shadows of the day and the night. This was part of the reason I had to flee our homeland in Kemet." Once I heard the last words from my mother, my curiosity intensified, because I always wanted to know the real reasons why my mother had to flee out Kemet the way she did. Whenever I asked her to share her story, she told me I was too young to hear such tales, but Nephtali was now the window of opportunity to finally know why she fled the way she did.

"Wait, stop, stop … stop!" Gershom said with his hands waving dramatically. "We are not going to just … keep on talking as if the elephant is not in the room."

"What do you mean?" asked my mother in a confused tone.

"If *Blade* is a title … what's his real name?" Gershom asked my mother. We all watched as the countenance of my mother changed, while she shifted her focus toward Nephtali, looking for her approval. I watched as Nephtali took two slow breaths in and out before she gave my mother her approval with two simple nods of acceptance. My mother opened her mouth, but no words came out. Instead, she rubbed Nephtali's hand tenderly again, while searching for the right words. At that moment, none of us knew the afternoon sun made its descension, leaving the moon to rule the skies with the stars by its side. Gershom and I forgot about our quest to find Blade, nor did we consider our normal nighttime expedition. We wanted to hear, we wanted to know the tales our parents hid from us in the name of secrecy and protection, starting with his name. The real name!

"You two," my mother said specifically to Gershom and me. "What I say is for Nephtali only and not for you two," she explained sternly to us before she turned to face Nephtali and said. "What you do with this information, is all up to you. I just pray you do wisely with it, my child."

Nephtali nodded her head in acceptance to what my mother said to her. "With that being said, you two have to promise me not to repeat what is said at this table to anyone—"

"We promise!" Gershom and I said right away, without hesitation.

"Good," my mother replied to us, while she poured herself a drink of the fruit juice and drank out of her copper cup. "The name *Blade*—is not his real name ... it's a title," she started to say as if she was second-guessing herself or choosing her words carefully. My mother squeezed her cup and looked Nephtali straight in the eyes and said.

"His real name is ..."

.... TO BE CONTINUED

WRITER'S REMARKS

You want to find out Blade's real name and his connection to an ancient organization?

Pick up a copy of the Spartan Chronicles in the latest comic editions where you can the find the rest of Blade's story and so much more excitement.

"The relaunch of volume one was necessary to remedy the many setbacks from the first edition, and start rebuilding in a direction more fitting to the author's eye for creative adventures and a company ready to see new horizons. With that being said, these chronicles will cover a variety of backstories for characters" These Chronicles will cover a variety of backstories for characters, while explaining scenes more a detail for a more vivid understanding. The Spartan Chronicles are sure to take readers through a rich journey through a time where men believed in their swords and shields to answer the call of injustice, while others preferred the intervention of gods and spirits. Nevertheless, let's see where the story will take the children next in the remaining three volumes of Book One as the two nations draw closer to the unforgettable battle at Thermopylae. Also keep in mind, whenever there is a ghost chapter inside the main story line, you are sure to find the rest of the story and more inside the Spartan Chronicles, which can be obtained on The LP Production website. Thank you again for joining us on the adventures of the Children of Sparta, and stay intrigued for more works from the *Author's Collection* and even more works from my dreams which I fashioned into a reality called the *"Dreams of my Reality"*.

www.ingramcontent.com/pod-product-compliance
Lightning Source LLC
Chambersburg PA
CBHW081327090726
47907CB00010B/2398